48 stitches
16 sides

A CURSE WORSE THAN DEATH

Zargal and King Laza had arrived at the top room of the castle. There in the center of the floor stood a bed hung with dark velvet, wherein reposed Princess Bellora.

She was unconscious. Her skin had taken on a dreadful grayish tinge, and her entire figure seemed to have shriveled. She looked as if her muscles were loosening, her flesh losing its tautness, her very bones starting to shift. She might almost have begun to decay, though she was yet alive.

"She's dying!" There was no doubt in Zargal's shocked mind. "She is dying!"

"No," King Laza said sadly. "She will live. But she will not recover. She is doomed—by the Curse of the Varingians!"

P9-BWK-954

D0980571

The Curse Of The Witch-Queen

Paula Volsky

A Del Rey Book

BALLANTINE BOOKS • NEW YORK

WEE BOOK INN
10310 - 82 AVENUE 432-7230
8101 - 118 AVENUE 474-7888
10423 JASPER AVENUE 423-1434
15103A STONY PLAIN RD. 489-0747

A Del Rey Book
Published by Ballantine Books

Copyright © 1982 by Paula Volsky

All rights reserved under International and Pan-American
Copyright Conventions. Published in the United States by
Ballantine Books, a division of Random House, Inc., New
York, and simultaneously in Canada by Random House of
Canada, Limited, Toronto, Canada.

Library of Congress Catalog Card Number: 82-90449

ISBN 0-345-29520-X

Printed in Canada

First Edition: December 1982

Cover art by Darrell K. Sweet

CHAPTER I

It was well past ten o'clock when the strange traveler
appeared at the door of the Peacock, an old inn situated
on the road to Szar, the fortified city of Duke Jalonzal.
Master Krawmis, owner of the Peacock, was puzzled for
a variety of reasons. Travelers arriving so late were rare,
though not unheard of. But this one would have seemed
odd at any time of the day or night.

Although it was only early autumn and the weather was
still mild, the gentleman was swathed from throat to ankle
in a great purple cloak, embroidered in gold and trimmed
with sable, which camouflaged his entire figure. Upon his
head he wore a high-crowned hat with a sweeping brim;
and in the uncertain moonlight, the shadow of that brim
lay black upon his face.

The man was seated in an open sedan chair, borne by two
lackeys—great hulking fellows, well-liveried, but of a de-
cidedly foreign appearance. A third lackey held a flaming
torch. And well behind them all, a fourth carried a large
bundle under one arm. In his free hand he held the end of
a leash, to which was attached an animal of some kind. It
was all extremely peculiar. But something told Master
Krawmis that it might not be a good idea to ask too many

questions, at least not right away. Krawmis was curious by nature, but for the moment he contented himself with staring.

"I require lodging for tonight for myself and my servants," the stranger announced. "Refreshment, dinner, and some information as well. Are you prepared to accommodate me?"

His voice was as singular as the rest of him, both resonant and halting, with a kind of gurgle, as if he were trying to speak through a mouthful of hot potatoes. Nevertheless, he exuded authority.

The man was odd, distinctly odd; downright suspicious, Master Krawmis decided. He stood gawking stupidly for a time.

"Are you prepared to accommodate me, fellow?" the stranger repeated sharply.

"Er—yes. Of course, sir. I bid you welcome to the Peacock."

"Excellent. And if I am welcome, then perhaps you will be so good as to prove it by standing aside and letting me in?"

"Oh, begging your pardon, sir. Of course." Master Krawmis admitted his visitors and found that they were even more unusual than he had thought.

The servant with the torch led the way in. Then came the next two, bearing the sedan chair in which their master was seated. Krawmis could get a better look now and noted with misgiving that the splendid purple cloak seemed to mask a twisted, misshapen body. One shoulder was certainly higher than the other, and several misplaced lumps were imperfectly concealed. The man's face, however, was still shaded by his wide hat. The entrance of the fourth lackey was heralded by a devilish hissing sound, as of molten lava hitting cold water. This noise issued from the throat of the creature that the lackey held on leash—a silvery-scaled, long-clawed lizard. Its leash was made of strong steel chain, Krawmis noted, but he did not relish its presence in the common room of his beloved Peacock. "Ah—I'm sorry, gentlemen," he objected, "but we don't allow pets in here. Rules of the house, you know."

As if it had understood his remark, the animal uttered a terrible roar, wrenched its leash out of the grasp of the servant, and launched itself straight at Master Krawmis' throat. Things might have gone badly for poor Krawmis, had the man in the purple cloak not given a whistle which stopped the creature, practically in midair.

"Down! Down, I say!" he commanded, and the beast dropped to the floor, puffing and hissing. "Bibka is no pet," he explained mildly. "She is a full-grown slatku—the so-called little dragon of the swamp. She is a huntress, and the mother of hunters, an eater of all flesh—*all* flesh, you understand me?—and most assuredly no man's pet. We have a mutual understanding. Take care what you say in her presence, for she is very sensitive."

"Very sensitive," Krawmis echoed.

"I strongly suggest that you allow her to remain."

"To be sure," the innkeeper agreed with alacrity.

"Excellent."

One of the lackeys stepped forward and assembled the contraption he had been carrying. It proved to be a small chair, upholstered in sapphire velvet. But instead of resting on four legs, this chair sat atop four wheels. The servants gently lifted their master from the sedan chair to the wheeled seat. Someone placed the end of Bibka's leash in the gentleman's hand, and the silver lizard drew chair and man across the room to a comfortable place near the fire. The lackeys seated themselves at a table.

"Innkeeper!" the stranger called out, pleasantly but rather imperiously. "Approach me, if you please."

With an uneasy glance at Bibka, who was watching him steadily, Krawmis obeyed.

"What is your name?"

"Krawmis, if it please your Honor. I'm Krawmis, master of the Peacock! And you are—?"

Bibka uttered an indignant hiss, but the stranger answered calmly, "I am—incognito. You may address me as 'milord.' That will suffice."

"Yes, milord. And you're a stranger in these parts, you say—?"

At this, the listening slatku snarled and half rose to her feet. "I would be entirely willing," milord said kindly, "to overlook your impertinence and answer all your questions. Unfortunately, my sensitive Bibka cannot endure these inquiries. In order to avoid upsetting her any further, I suggest that you dispense with them. You understand that *I* have no objections, none whatever, but, alas, Bibka is delicate—"

"Oh, quite, milord! Quite so! No sense in stirring her up." Krawmis took a step backward and then another.

"Stay where you are. I have not dismissed you. Now, then, perhaps you can tell me how far distant lies the city of Szar?"

"A good three hours upon the road tomorrow morning will bring you to the gates."

"Excellent. Now, as for dinner—what is your best dish?"

"Roast peacock, milord! There's none better to be had for miles about!"

"Very well, then. Prepare some for my servants. As for me, my digestion is not good, so I will have a goblet of white wine and a dish of forest frolloberries. And see to it that they are fresh."

Milord leaned forward a little in his chair, and the firelight fell across the lower portion of his face, leaving the rest in shadow. Krawmis caught a fleeting glimpse of a horridly scarred and pockmarked complexion and a pair of twisted, strangely immobile lips. Then the stranger leaned back again, and all his features were once more obscured.

Master Krawmis did his best to carry out milord's orders, and his preparations took some time. It was getting on for midnight before the peacock was done. Krawmis would normally have been fast asleep by that hour, but this night he did not even feel drowsy. As he arranged the bird's tail feathers into a lifelike fan, thousands of questions were flitting through his brain. But he did not quite dare to ask any of them.

Just around midnight, the peaceful atmosphere of the Peacock was violently disrupted. From some distance away came the sound of a loud hallooing. Then there was the thud of horses' hoofs approaching, yelling and wild whoops of laughter, footsteps, and finally, a heavy pounding upon the door of the inn.

"Innkeeper!"

"Come forth, Master Krawmis!"

"Krawmis!"

"C'mon out, Krawmis!"

"Let us in, or we'll burn the place down!"

"Oh, no!" the beleaguered innkeeper groaned. "Not this! Not again! Not tonight!"

"Who's there?" milord inquired.

"Those young demons!" Krawmis responded.

"Oh?"

"It's—" Krawmis' explanation was interrupted by more pounding. Somebody outside had started to play a lively tune on a flute, and somebody else was thumping viciously on the door in time to the music.

"Better let them in," milord suggested, and Krawmis quickly complied.

Instantly the room was filled with a gang of young people. There were perhaps half a dozen youths, highborn, by the look of them, and a couple of wenches—lowborn, by the look of them.

"Well, you certainly took your time about it!"

"Do you dare to trifle with us, sir?"

"You must beg our pardon, Krawmis!"

"Yes, or else be tossed in a blanket!"

The innkeeper held up his hands placatingly. "Gentlemen, and—ladies—I beg your pardon most humbly. How may I serve your lordships?"

"Wine! Lots of wine! Right away!"

"Some food, and be quick about it!"

"But first, lots of wine!"

It appeared to Krawmis that they had all had quite enough wine already, but he did as he was told. No sooner had the wine been supplied, however, than a member of the gang climbed up on the table, proposed a bawdy toast, and ceremoniously flung his glass into the fireplace. All the others followed suit. More wine and glasses were called for; these glasses, also, were smashed; whereupon Krawmis asserted that all his goblets were gone and started giving them pewter tankards instead. After that, the revel grew wilder. When they got tired of singing and dancing, they amused themselves with amateur fisticuffs, smashing bottles, and tossing each other in one of the largest curtains torn down from the front window of the Peacock.

Throughout all of this, milord sat by the fireplace, watching quietly. Once a weedy youth approached, shouting. But Bibka, with a bloodcurdling growl, lashed her long tail like a whip and sent the young fellow flying through the air to land in a heap in the corner, where he lay for some time. After that, nobody but the innkeeper came near milord. "Who are these people?" he inquired of Krawmis.

"Oh, they're a gang of idle young scoundrels, milord. The sons of our greatest nobility, some of them—but useless and lazy, with no honest work to keep 'em occupied, so they're into mischief all the time."

"What sort of mischief?"

"Every sort! They drink and dance and swear, as you can see. They fight and brawl in the streets of the city, and then burn hay-ricks in the country. It's said that they're not above a bit of robbery on the open road. Anyone who gets in their way has his head cracked open. And they're worse when young Zargal's with them—showing off for him, you might say. And he—well, he's not too bad when he comes here sometimes by himself. But with them egging him on, he's the leader in every form of deviltry. He should be setting them a good example, being who he is, but—"

"Who is this Zargal?" milord interrupted.

"That's him! That's the one!" Krawmis indicated one of the revelers—the instigator of the glass-smashing episode. The young man was now sprawled out in a chair, with a girl in his lap and a tankard in his hand. His face was flushed with wine, his eyes bright, and his dark hair falling in careless strands across his damp forehead. "It's a sad day for Szar when he takes over!"

"What do you mean, inkeeper—when he takes over?"

"Why, that Zargal—he's Duke Jalonzal's only son. And he'll be Duke of Szar himself one day, may fortune protect us all!"

"*That* is Duke Jalonzal's son? That reprobate? That wastrel? Poor Jalonzal!"

"Yes, sir."

The actions of the revelers were growing wilder and more destructive as time wore on. Some of them were merely dancing on the tabletops and causing no real trouble. But most were grouped around the great fireplace. Zargal had somehow managed to obtain a magician's bottle of colored powder. Each time he sprinkled some of the powder onto the fire, the flames shot up as if alive, divided, and were transformed into a pair of golden cockerels that

lamb; spinach puree; braised kohlrabies; a dish of stewed pears; buttered noodles; almond broth; and a large apple tart. Zargal ate it all, and Krawmis' wonder slowly turned to awe.

When the Duke's son had devoured everything before him, he patted his stomach, which remained as flat as if he'd been fasting for a month. "I must think about returning to Szar now," he remarked. "Saddle my horse."

"Your horse is gone, my lord," Krawmis had the pleasure of informing the overbearing guest. "It must have galloped off last night, when all your friends got chased away."

"Then I must use one of yours, I suppose. I hope you have a decent one for me, Krawmis."

"*I*, my lord? I have none. It isn't for the likes of me to ride a horse like a gentleman, is it?" In point of fact, Krawmis had two perfectly good horses tethered in back of his inn, but he didn't choose to admit this to Zargal.

"What? You mean I shall have to walk all the way home?"

"It can happen to the best of us, my lord."

"Damn! Well, if I must, I must. But first—get me something to eat."

"You can't still be hungry! It's not possible!"

"It *is* a bit unusual, isn't it? But don't stand there gawking, man—fetch me some food."

"Well, I can't do that, you see," Krawmis objected, amazed to discover that young Zargal had grown as insatiable as he was insufferable.

"Why not? Worried about the price?" Zargal carelessly tossed a fistful of coins onto the table. "There. That should cover all damages done to your inn, too. Now hurry and bring me some food."

Krawmis pocketed the coins without mentioning that the stranger of last night had already paid for the damages. "I don't have anything left," he announced plaintively. "You've eaten all I've got."

"There must be something!" There was a note of alarm in Zargal's voice. He bounded to his feet, flung open the cupboard doors, and rummaged through the contents. But Master Krawmis had spoken truly; there was very little to be found. Zargal unearthed a shriveled apple, a tinder-dry crust of bread, and an elderly hunk of cheese, pocked with spots of green mold. All of these things he crammed into his mouth and bolted, without even bothering to scrape the mold off the cheese. But after that, there was really nothing left.

"I must start back to Szar at once," Zargal said, "if I'm to arrive in time for dinner." He strode quickly out of the kitchen and through the common room, pausing once to pick a bone off the floor—a remnant of last night's roast peacock—and suck it absently. Then he continued on out into the courtyard while Master Krawmis stood in the doorway to watch him go. Once outside, Zargal hesitated, then turned back to address the innkeeper.

"The man last night," he said with some difficulty. "That mad stranger who cursed me—"

"What about him, my lord?"

"Do you suppose it's possible—could there be a chance —do you believe that he was really King Laza of Obran?"

Krawmis smiled. "Yes," he replied, and slammed the door.

CHAPTER III

It was a beautiful, soft autumn day, and the weather was perfect for hiking. The road to Szar wound through stretches of farmland, open countryside, and one small village. Zargal was walking along quickly, and he paid scant heed to his surroundings, since they were very familiar to him. His mind was still fixed on the events of the previous night, insofar as he was able to recall them. Given the choice, Zargal would have preferred to remember the incident clearly or else forget it altogether. But the choice was not his, and the imperfect recollections that stirred in his brain simultaneously frustrated and frightened him. Soon, however, disquieting thoughts fled from his mind as he noticed that he was walking past a patch of autumn melons, protected by a hedge of daggerthorns and a sign that threatened: TRESPASSERS WILL BE PROSE-CUTED TO THE FULLEST EXTENT OF THE LAW. Zargal snapped his fingers at the sign and took a flying leap over the thorny hedge, which was higher than he had supposed. He did not quite succeed in clearing it; he arrived on the other side with torn clothing and bleeding from a dozen scratches. His annoyance at this accident vanished as he started to eat the melons, which were delicious. The short stay he had intended lengthened imperceptibly into hours, and it was only when he realized that he had finished off every melon in the garden that he was able to tear himself away. His return leap over the daggerthorns was none too successful.

"These peasant farmers are an inhospitable lot," Zargal said aloud, and his stomach rumbled emptily in reply. It was a relief when he traveled a short distance farther down the road and came upon a field of squashes unprotected by fence or hedge. There was, to be sure, a sign; but it only suggested mildly: TRESPASSING INADVISABLE.

Zargal usually ate his squashes cooked, but this time he was willing to make an exception. He cast a quick glance over his shoulder. No one was watching. Road and field were both deserted. With no more hesitation, he ducked into the field and found himself in the middle of a collection of gourds and squashes as colorful as a flower bouquet. There were more varieties of squash than he had ever seen in his life, squashes of every size, shape, and description. Some were narrow and long, some round and squat, and others were weirdly formed with long, crooked necks and lumps that looked like swollen glands. They ranged in color from dark green to orange, and one very prevalent species was a deep, glowing crimson.

Zargal did not pause to admire. Grabbing the nearest squash, he yanked it off its vine and sank his teeth deep into the golden flesh. He hardly noticed the rustling and shuddering that ran along the network of vines, from the ones close beside him on out to the farthest corners of the field. Completely absorbed in his meal, he did not heed the faint vibration of the leaves, nor the shrinking movement of the nearby tendrils, as if they sought to escape his greedy hands. His attention was focused exclusively on the pleasant task of eating.

The squashes were extraordinarily good ones—their meat the tenderest, the most delicate, he had ever tasted. One kind only he did not care for. The dark crimson squashes were hard to pull from the vine and resisted his efforts with strange tenacity. Their flesh was tough, and the seeds were jet-black and bitter. After eating two or three of them, Zargal decided that they weren't worth troubling about and picked no more.

His first intimation of peril came when he felt a slow, powerful pull on his lower leg. Zargal looked down and perceived that one of the crimson squash plants had sent out a couple of tendrils, which had quietly wound themselves around his calves and were now exerting a pressure strong enough to throw him off balance.

Formerly he'd been standing in a small clear patch in the midst of all the plants. Now he noticed that a number of creepers, all of the same species of red squash, had invaded the area and were littering the ground at his feet. With an exclamation half of surprise and half of impatience, Zargal bent down to dislodge the clinging vines. They were stronger than he had thought, and it was only with great difficulty that he succeeded in tearing his right leg free. The creeper in his grasp pulsed like a beating heart, and Zargal attempted to throw it away, but it had already managed to wind itself around his hand and wrist. In the meantime, another green shoot went snaking around his right ankle. The one already clinging to his left leg was gently working its way upward, as if he were a trellis.

Zargal cast a wild glance around and saw that all the green leaves on every crimson squash vine in the field were turned in his direction, as if his face were the source of their sunlight. The vines were aware and watching. The Duke's son was no coward, and he did not panic now. In his heart of hearts he vowed never again to eat another squash, and then turned all his thoughts toward escape. The vines, he saw, were strong but slow. If only they hadn't caught him unaware, he would have had every chance to get away. If he could free himself now, there would still be plenty of time to flee.

Zargal managed to wrench the entangling vine from his right wrist and leg, swept his sword from its scabbard, and hacked violently at the surrounding creepers. The blade flashed up and down in the sun, biting deep into scores of vines. Sap spurted and ran in viscous streams from hundreds of vegetable wounds. Flurries of broken leaves floated to earth to wither and die, while the ground became strewn with severed tendrils that continued to writhe and jerk as long as any vestige of life remained in them.

Across the length and breadth of the field, unnatural stillness and silence reigned. Not a leaf rustled, not a twig stirred; but the atmosphere was alive with tension. Stems that normally drooped in languid arcs now stood bolt upright, distended with intense turgor. Beads of moisture stood out on every crimson squash, although the morning dew had long since vanished from the ground. It was as if the plants were straining with every fiber to concentrate on the struggle.

Zargal employed his blade with desperate abandon, chopping squashes, shredding leaves, and dicing tendrils. Mounds of wilted salad were beginning to pile up all around him, the mute testimony to his zeal. But the sun was high in the sky, sweat was running down his face, and Zargal was growing very weary. His foes continued to advance with unhurried undulation of vine and branch. With so many united against him, it was inevitable that they would succeed in breaking through his guard. And thus, as the Duke's son dealt a slashing blow at one tendril closing in on his left ankle, another assaulted his right, obtained a good hold, and pulled. Zargal, startled, shifted his defense to the threatened area, whereupon a third vine, attacking from the rear, coiled itself around his left knee. A thin, tough shoot curled around his elbow with the grasp of a sergeant-at-arms. Zargal hit the ground with great force. His sword was knocked from his hand and went flying through the air to land upright, its point sunk in the earth. For a few moments he struggled to rise, but it was a useless effort—the vines had him pinned fast.

Now that he could no longer defend himself, more and more of the tendrils were creeping near and twining around his arms and legs to bind him to the earth. All over the field leaves were starting to sway and quiver, as if the spell that held them motionless had broken. On all sides, twigs tapped sharply against each other, and vines slapped themselves against the ground. It sounded much like applause.

Zargal lay upon his back and wondered what would happen next. He suspected that his vegetable foes intended to strangle him; all it would take would be one strong vine looped around his throat to do the job. He could not really blame them; he had to admit that they had ample cause. And yet it was a terrible thing to die so young, with so much before him, and such brilliant prospects. To die so ignobly—the life choked out of him in a vegetable garden!

In his darkest imaginings, the Duke's son had never dreamed that this was the way things would end.

But the vines made no move toward his exposed throat. A red squash, approaching from the left, rolled itself carefully to Zargal's side, then up onto his chest, where it sat quietly above his heart. Zargal raised his head and peered at the motionless vegetable, but all he could see was his own anxious face, reflected in its curving, polished sides. He allowed his head to fall back again. Another squash rolled up onto his chest and deposited itself beside the first. Another came, and then another—four cool and motionless weights upon his chest.

Now red squashes from every part of the field advanced purposefully on Zargal. Singly or in pairs, they reached his supine form and rolled themselves up onto his body, where a pile was growing. The weight of the vegetables heaped on his chest and stomach was becoming oppressive. It was then that Zargal understood. They were going to pile themselves on top of him until their combined weight prevented him from drawing his breath and he smothered to death beneath them. Zargal lifted his voice in a series of frantic calls for help.

No one came.

The attack of the squashes was as prolonged as it was relentless. The vegetables moved with placid lack of haste, but eventually he could not breathe deeply enough to cry out. Zargal lay still and helplessly watched them coming upon him from all sides, until he could bear the sight no longer and shut his eyes. The breath was rasping in his throat. Behind his closed lids, yellow lights seemed to explode. A pain was growing in his chest, a fiery pain that told him his exhausted lungs were on the point of failing.

He was nearly unconscious when he became aware that the weight on his chest was easing. For a few seconds he thought the relief was imaginary and that death was drawing nigh. But this was no dream. The pressure decreased, he was able to draw in oxygen without pain, and soon his blurred vision cleared, allowing him to take stock of his surroundings. He beheld a short, stout, elderly gentleman with crinkly gray hair, busily removing squashes from the pile and laying them aside.

"Well," the man said genially, "I knew the plants were

behaving oddly. There had to be an explanation, and here we have it—an intruder."

Zargal did not yet attempt to answer. The vegetables were no longer crushing him, but the vines still held him down.

"Investigation into the facts will always provide the solution to any problem," the man announced, his voice laden with immense self-satisfaction. A smile curved his plump little mouth. "That is the basis of the scientific method. Investigation is the rule. Investigation! Needless to say that training, technique, and extraordinary intelligence are required as well. Young man, what are you doing in my garden?"

"Squashes," Zargal gasped painfully. "Those squashes—"

"Magnificent, are they not? I raised them myself. The world has never seen such squashes before!"

"I—believe—that."

"Thank you. That shows you to be a young man of rare discernment, but it doesn't explain why you are trespassing in my garden."

"I was hungry." Zargal was finding it easier to speak. "I only wanted to eat a squash or two. Surely you wouldn't begrudge me that?"

"A squash or two," the man repeated, and ran a thoughtful eye over the heaps of maimed plants that lay on all sides, drying in the sun. "I see. But you seem to have taken a little more than that."

"Well, what choice had I? Those things attacked me. I believe they might have killed me."

"Indeed they would, young man. Make no mistake about it—if I hadn't come along, you would most assuredly have suffocated. It would have been a unique form of death, though. Not many men experience the paradox of a vegetative demise." He chuckled in appreciation of his own wit.

"You've trained them to kill people?" Zargal exclaimed. "I suspect that's illegal. But let me up immediately, and we'll say no more about it."

"Softly, young man. It doesn't seem to me that you're really in any position to issue orders. Who are you, anyway?"

"I am Zargal, son of Jalonzal, Duke of Szar."

"The Duke's son—well! I've heard of you. And I," he

announced, "am Professor Horm, late of the University of Szar. Professor emeritus," he added with indescribable complacency. "Foremost member of the Department of Botany, pioneer researcher in the field of vegetable vitality. I specialized in plants. Perhaps you've read my book *A Search for Intelligence Among the Complex Fungi?*"

"I seem to have missed that one," Zargal confessed.

"A pity. What about *Auditory Reflexes in Squashes and Melons: A Comparative Study?*"

"No."

"No? Not very well-educated, are you? But I'm sure you must have seen that rather sentimental little popular piece of mine—*Devotion: The Heart of an Artichoke?*"

"I'm afraid not. Now, Professor, will you kindly call off your squashes and let me go?"

"Not so fast. You are a bit hasty, young man, and your manners are atrocious. It will do you no harm to stay where you are for a little while. Besides, I so rarely have the chance to talk to anyone about my work since I left the University."

"Then why did you leave?" Zargal asked resignedly.

"A good question. A very good question. Perhaps you are not aware of it, but I was an extremely important man there, a man to be reckoned with. A man, I might even say, to be feared. Need I add that there were many who were jealous of me, and many who resented me? And thus, there were plots."

"Indeed?" Zargal asked skeptically.

"Yes indeed! My theories were revolutionary, my research wholly original and of the greatest importance. My intelligence is of such scope that I was as a giant among dwarves, and they couldn't help but know it! It is an odd thing to be a giant among dwarves," he mused. "You inspire terror, but derision as well. Those around you fear, and yet they laugh. However," he told Zargal, "I doubt that you'll ever know what I'm talking about."

"But what was this remarkable research of yours?" Zargal asked, in an effort to get the wandering Professor back on the track.

"I told you, young man," Horm said, "that I specialized in plants. And I discovered something that no one before me was ever able to prove—that they have minds. They possess consciousness, and they have intellect, although not of a very high order. Between you and me," he added confidentially, "they are really not very bright. And yet they can be trained to perform simple tasks. Everyone knows, of course, that vines can be trained to climb over fences and walls, or that bushes can be trained to grow in certain shapes. But that is only a beginning! They can be taught to work, to toil, to serve mankind in numberless ways. You can see, can't you, that it was a great and wonderful work I was engaged in? You understand the tremendous significance of it?"

"It is—interesting," Zargal said.

"It was magnificent. A work of true genius. The other professors were jealous, of course, and who can blame them? How trifling and petty their projects were, compared with mine! They plotted night and day to rid themselves of me, and when an opportunity arose, they took advantage of it. I was betrayed," the Professor pronounced darkly.

"How so? And when are you going to let me go?"

"When I feel like it. Don't be so impatient. Surely you want to learn of my great discovery?"

"Oh, all right."

"I enjoy addressing an interested audience. However, as to my discovery—I found that plants vary in intelligence, as humans do. On the whole, the cultivated plants tend to be cleverer than the wild ones—or at least more receptive to instruction. By far the brightest of these happens to be the squash."

"That's good to know, and I'm glad you've told me. Will you let me go now?"

"No. As I was saying, I found that the squash surpasses all other plants, as man surpasses all other animals. I decided then to breed a supersquash, a genius among its kind. A veritable Horm of the vegetable kingdom. I struggled and worked until, after many failures, at last I triumphed. I created the most intelligent plant in all the world—the *Cucurbita Hormiensis*. That, young man, is the red squash now holding you prisoner. A squash with a mind of its own. Is it not a supreme accomplishment?"

"Perhaps," Zargal admitted. "Although those are not exactly the words I would have chosen to describe it."

"And yet how strange life can be! For it was this very squash which caused my downfall and led to my expulsion from the University."

"Why?"

"Because it is not perfect, that's why! Because its great intelligence is accompanied by a minor flaw in character. *Cucurbita Hormiensis* is—a little willful. A little hot-tempered. And very unpredictable. Thus, when its territory is invaded, it tends to react with violence."

"Really?" Zargal asked grimly.

"Alas, yes. There have been—certain embarrassing incidents."

"I don't wonder. Are you going to release me or not?"

"I'll think about it. In any case, an overly inquisitive student of mine let himself into the greenhouse one day, and my little red beauties finished him off. My enemies seized that opportunity to attack me and my research. Think of it! One small mistake, and they claimed that the entire project was a failure. In the end, I was dismissed from the University. I, their most brilliant member! It was their loss, not mine. They could send me away, but they could not stop me! They destroyed my squashes that day, but they didn't know that I preserved a packet of seeds. I came to this place—and *Cucurbita Hormiensis* has risen anew! Pure science will always prevail!"

Zargal was beginning to learn the merits of diplomacy. "That is magnificent, Professor," he approved. "I congratulate you. But I wonder if the effort of holding me here isn't exhausting your squashes. Perhaps it would be a kindness to the plants to let me go."

"Oh, I don't think so," Horm returned cheerfully. "It's no strain on them at all. They could hold you here forever and never get tired."

"What do you want of me?" Zargal shouted.

"Only what's owed to me," the Professor replied amiably. He gazed speculatively at the young prisoner, noting the richness of his clothes, the jeweled buttons on his coat, the silken cravat, and the red leather boots which were worth a small fortune. "I once wrote to your father the Duke, requesting him to grant me a modest allowance so that I might continue my research," Horm remarked. "However, he refused me."

"What of it? You seem to have continued with your research anyway," Zargal pointed out.

"That is completely irrelevant. What is important here is that Duke Jalonzal will provide me with the gold after all —albeit indirectly. Young man, how much money are you carrying?"

"How should I know?" Zargal never bothered much about money.

"Well, we shall investigate." Professor Horm bent down, adroitly removed the purse from Zargal's pocket, and opened it. It was filled with gold coins. "Seventy-two grinlings," the Professor counted. "Very good; that should do nicely." He put the coins in his own pocket and returned the empty purse.

"You're stealing all my money?" Zargal cried.

"Oh, no. You are merely paying for the plants you've destroyed."

"You're a thief!"

"May I remind you that you are the one who has trespassed on my property and slaughtered and devoured hundreds of my squashes? *You* are the thief."

"I won't stand for this!" the Duke's son seethed from his place on the ground.

"We shall see." Professor Horm's eye fell upon Zargal's sword, which stood upright in the ground a short distance away, its ruby-studded hilt winking in the sun. "Now, then. You have, in your own objectionable way, requested my aid in freeing yourself of the vines. Are you willing to pay for it?"

"You mean with my sword?" Zargal asked, following the Professor's gaze. "You go hang yourself!"

"Oh, you wouldn't want me to do that, young man. If I did, there'd be no one to help you out of your unpleasant situation, would there?"

"You're not getting my sword, you extortionist!"

"Well, please yourself. I don't intend to argue with you." Professor Horm turned and started to walk away. As soon as he did so, two of the crimson squashes began to roll toward Zargal.

"Wait!" Zargal cried. "Where are you going?"

"Back to work, of course. You've rejected my offer, so I don't see that we have anything more to discuss."

"But what will happen to me?"

"That's a matter entirely between you and my *Cucurbita*," the Professor explained significantly.

Zargal regarded the homicidal squashes in silence for a moment and then gave in. "All right," he conceded sullenly. "You can take the sword."

Professor Horm immediately did so, plucking the weapon from the ground and thrusting it through his belt. Only then did he turn his attention to the vines. "Now you'll see for yourself," he declared triumphantly, "how marvelous a creation *Cucurbita Hormiensis* really is. Watch carefully, young man. You'll enjoy this." The Professor addressed his squashes. "Release the stranger at once," he bade them. "Your creator commands it."

Nothing happened. The tendrils wrapped around Zargal's arms and legs remained motionless, but he could sense their tension.

"Didn't you hear me? Release him instantly!" Horm insisted. *Cucurbita*'s leaves quivered slightly at this, and the vines took firmer hold on their prey.

"Can't you even control your own plants?" Zargal asked.

"Of course I can! They're just a little slow, that's all. It's only because their intelligence is of such a low order. But they'll obey me." Horm said, "Let go of him!" The vines tightened around Zargal until it hurt. "Do as I say, confound you! Release him!"

The vines clung doggedly, and Zargal began to worry again.

"You must obey me!" Horm cried. "I created you! You owe me your loyalty. Don't you understand that?" *Cucurbita* rattled its twigs, and Zargal could have sworn that he detected a note of mockery in the sound.

"Don't think you'll get away with this!" Horm threatened, now thoroughly annoyed. "I know how to deal with you! Don't think for one instant that I've forgotten how to use my pruning shears!"

This was the first remark he'd made so far that had any effect. The tendrils relaxed their grip, ever so slightly. Seeing this, the Professor bent down, roughly dragged one of them away from Zargal's leg, and threw it aside. The plants reacted violently to this unaccustomed treatment. Leaves rustled, and myriads of twigs tapped and rattled. The chastised vine, vibrating with rage, snaked over the ground toward the Professor, paused at his feet, and then—very hesitantly, very experimentally—coiled itself around his ankle.

Horm angrily detached it and kicked it aside. He then dragged several more vines off the prisoner, despite their resistance. "The rest of you," he addressed them, "will let go of him this instant. I'll prune five years of growth off you if you don't do as you're told."

And at last, he was obeyed. Slowly and reluctantly, the twisted mass of creepers loosened their grip until Zargal was able to rise from the ground. Bruised and exhausted, he nonetheless managed to take several shaky steps away from his resting place—enough to put him safely out of reach of *Cucurbita Hormiensis*.

"You see, I haven't entirely succeeded in perfecting the species," Professor Horm explained a little apologetically. "There are one or two minor problems still remaining."

"Minor problems!" Zargal echoed. He regarded the restless, angry vegetation. "You've created a monster, can't you see that? They're a danger even to you."

"Come, come, young man. This bitterness of yours is most unbecoming." Horm said, jingling the gold in his pockets.

"Then, Professor, I will leave you and your creation to each other. There are two things that I hope the both of you may someday share." Zargal checked to make sure he was well out of reach of the *Cucurbita*. "One is blight. The other is mildew. Good day."

As Zargal walked away, he could hear Horm's fat chuckles arising like gas-filled balloons. He turned and looked back briefly. The Professor was standing in the midst of his squash plants, laughing.

CHAPTER IV

It was late afternoon. Zargal walked along quickly, determined to put as much distance as possible between himself and *Cucurbita Hormiensis*. He was scowling, and his mind was filled with unpleasant fancies, as it had been for most of the day. The loss of the gold did not much trouble him, but the humiliation and the loss of the sword did. Moreover, there was the matter of the stranger's curse. He certainly didn't believe in it; but on the other hand, he couldn't quite seem to forget about it. "Nonsense," Zargal tried to persuade himself. "It was coincidence, and nothing more."

There was a slight breeze blowing toward him, and an odor carried on that breeze reminded him of food. He realized then that he was very hungry indeed. Zargal tried to identify the smoky aroma and failed. It was not until he rounded a bend in the road and came upon a small group of people sitting around a campfire that his curiosity was satisfied.

It was a band of Turos—instantly recognizable by the boat-shaped caravans in which they traveled. Nobody but the Turos owned caravans built to resemble ships on wheels, complete with pointed prows and figureheads. According to Turo belief, the shape of the wagon was a perpetual reminder of the fact that they had originally been a seafaring folk. Whether that legend was true or not no one could say, but one thing was certain; the Turos had not been sailors within human memory. For generation upon generation, their scattered clans had roamed the countryside, the towns, and the cities, never invited to stay, for they brought mischief with them. Despite their dishonest ways, however, Turos were never to be found in any prison cell or castle dungeon. Practice and limitless experience had made of them the greatest escape artists in the world. There was no trap from which they could not easily free themselves, and certainly no prison had ever been built that could hold a Turo. So refined were their abilities that they had given rise to the popular, albeit mistaken, belief that Turos could render themselves invisible. They were a mysterious people and much distrusted, but one of their inventions was immensely admired—the famous stew Blue Rosshinska, a mixture of rice, the white meat of chicken, the white flesh of three or four varieties of fresh-water shellfish, ground almonds, and a heavy lacing of the blue spice tavril, which accounted for the pungent flavor and distinctive coloring. It was the scent of a potful of Blue Rosshinska that was now driving young Zargal mad with longing.

There were perhaps two dozen Turos seated around the fire, and they regarded the Duke's son with interest as they ate. Zargal's impulse was to plunge his hands wrist-deep into the simmering stew. But he restrained himself and made a graceful bow; he could exhibit the manners of a courtier when he chose. "Good afternoon," he said courteously. "Permit me to introduce myself. I am Lord Zargal of Szar. I have been traveling on this road all day and I am weary and famished. I ask leave to avail myself of your hospitality."

An ancient Turo turned to one of his companions, a dark-featured young man. "What does he say, Barnak?" he asked, in the quavering tones of extreme old age. "What does he want?"

"Victuals," the other answered laconically.

"The young lord wants our Rosshinska?"

"Aye," Barnak returned.

"What did the young lord say his name was?"

"He says—"

"I am Lord Zargal of Szar," Zargal interrupted. "And you are Turos, are you not?"

"That we are, sir—poor, wandering Turos, outcast and despised. And oppressed," the old man quavered. "Very downtrodden and oppressed. I am Ninko." He indicated his companions with a feeble gesture. "These are my people—my four sons, their unhappy wives, their under-privileged children."

"May all roads be open to you," Zargal replied, hoping that this might be the sort of thing that Turos would like to hear.

"Did ye hear that?" Ninko inquired of Barnak. "Did ye hear that, now? The young lord honors us. Isn't that kind, now?"

"Aye," Barnak replied.

"The young lord does us too much honor," Ninko maundered. "We're not used to such kindness from the gentry, indeed we are not. Blows and curses are our portion, young lord, blows and curses!"

"I am sorry to hear it," Zargal sympathized politely. "The world is full of black injustice. Now, about that stew—"

"Black injustice! You say truly!" Ninko broke in. "And we a poor, harmless band of wanderers, as never did any man harm! Black injustice it surely is!"

"Peace, old one," Barnak suggested.

"You mustn't mind him," a young Turo woman told Zargal discreetly. "He is very ancient—and he has suffered so! As have we all, of course."

"I quite understand," Zargal reassured her. "There's no need to apologize."

"Oh, thank you, sir!"

"Perhaps, madam, you might allow me a taste of that very appetizing stew—"

"What does the kind young lord say, Chersa?" Ninko demanded fretfully. "What does he wish?"

"Food, grandfather."

"Oh, young lord," Ninko cried mournfully, "we know how you feel! All Turos know what it is to be hungry—so hungry that it feels as if an iron hand was a-clutching at your belly! So hungry that you wrap your belt twice around your waist! We know!"

Zargal looked at the Turos. They were filthy and unkempt, but appeared well-fed and healthy. He did not feel, however, that it would be wise to point this out. "I know your life is hard," he agreed.

"Hard indeed, young lord! We starve, we suffer, we roam from land to land, never having peace or rest! The farmers and peasants hate us; they set the dogs on us when we come! And you want to know why, young lord?"

"Why?" Zargal asked resignedly.

"Because they're guilty! Because they took all we had and don't like to be reminded of it!"

That wasn't quite the story that Zargal had always heard. "Things will be better someday," he soothed.

"Oh, aye—someday we Turos will come into our own again," Ninko declared. "But in the meantime, we wander like beasts, and we starve!"

Zargal surveyed the cauldron, nearly overflowing with its spicy mixture of chicken, rice, and shellfish. Nearby stood an entire keg of ale. The young woman Chersa was busy cutting up and distributing a dozen loaves of dark bread to accompany the evening meal. "You do not go hungry tonight," he pointed out. "In fact, you have so much that I wonder if perhaps you could not spare a—"

Ninko uttered a wispy sort of laugh. "Ha—a fine jest!" he piped up. "But you cannot fool us. We all know that a grand, young, wealthy lord like you would never take the food of hungry, unfortunate Turos without giving anything back for it! We've been cheated and robbed by everyone, but I know that you'll deal fairly with the poor Turos!"

"Yes, I know he will!" Chersa put in warmly.

"Aye," Barnak said. The others all nodded in trusting agreement.

Zargal was somewhat taken aback. "Well—I can't pay you anything for the stew, if that's what you mean," he informed them. "I don't have any money."

"What's that? What does the fine young lord say?" Ninko wheezed.

"No money," Barnak said.

The laughter ceased. Ninko, Barnak, and Chersa conferred rapidly in the Turo tongue while Zargal stood contemplating the Blue Rosshinska. At last Chersa spoke. "My grandfather wishes to know," she said pleasantly, "how it is possible that a lord of Szar could be traveling without money. It would be best if you humored him, my lord—he is so old, and his life has been filled with such hardship!"

"I was robbed," Zargal explained, truthfully enough. "All my money is gone."

Many of the Turos were nodding in grave sympathy. "We know what it is to be robbed," old Ninko declared. "We Turos were robbed long ago of our lands, our goods, our money."

"What lands?" Zargal inquired. "I thought you were supposed to have been seafarers."

"Before we became seafarers," Ninko insisted testily. "Now, young lord, as to the Blue Rosshinska—it would give us joy to share, for we are a generous, free-spirited people. But," he added as Zargal took an eager step toward the pot, "as it is, we are poor and starving, and can spare nothing."

"Nothing," Barnak said.

Zargal was becoming desperate. "You don't understand," he argued with great intensity. "I must have that stew. I'll pay you later. I'll put it in writing."

"We do not accept promissory notes," Ninko said regretfully.

"I'll give you anything—anything I have!" Zargal cried. "But you must let me eat some of that stew. Don't you understand—I *must* have it!" The Duke's son was bitterly ashamed of this exhibition, but he couldn't seem to help himself.

All the Turos were staring as if a treasure chest had suddenly materialized in their midst. "Is that the way of it?" Ninko asked slowly. "Is that the way of it, now?"

"I tell you, I'm starving!"

"Ah, but there's never any need for a young lord to starve," old Ninko observed, "when he's wearing a grand coat with jeweled buttons! Oh, but that coat of yours is so fine, it brings to my mind the lost riches of the Turos!"

Zargal stripped off his coat, which was decorated with eight ruby buttons. "Take it and welcome," he said. Ninko seized the coat and cradled it in his arms. Presently he produced a magnifying glass and began to inspect the buttons.

While he was thus engaged, the woman Chersa addressed Zargal in a low voice. "Oh, thank you, sir, for humoring my poor, unhappy grandfather. His mind has been weakened by the sorrow and misery of the life we all lead—the good old man! We would be honored, my lord, if you would consent to share our humble meal." She ladled him out a not ungenerous bowlful of stew. He also received a hunk of bread and a mug of the ale.

It seemed to Zargal that he had never before tasted anything quite as good as an authentic Blue Rosshinska, cooked by a Turo woman and eaten out of doors beside a campfire. He ate with a will, and soon he was mopping up the last bit of sky-blue sauce and holding out his empty bowl for a second helping.

Old Ninko raised his head. "Something troubling you, young lord?" he inquired. "Something amiss with our Rosshinska?"

"Not at all," Zargal assured him. "In fact, I liked it so well that I could eat some more."

"It fair rips my heart," Ninko mourned, "to have to refuse you. It's a shame to us all." A tear slid down his furrowed cheek. "But we are a poor, hungry band of wanderers, my family and I, and our Rosshinska is all we have."

"Not quite all," Zargal reminded him acidly. "You have the ruby buttons on my coat as well."

"That's true," Ninko admitted. "And if we had that handsomely embroidered pair of gloves of yours—"

"That's outrageous!" Zargal cried. "You want my coat *and* my gloves in return for one meal?"

"Your coat and your gloves—oh, young lord, that's so little compared to what's been taken from us by the gentry! What are a coat and gloves compared to the loss of our lands? Compared to our sufferings? What are a coat and gloves compared—"

"Take them!" Zargal interrupted quickly. "Very well, take them!" Ninko complied, and the Duke's son received another bowl of food, which he wolfed down with voracity. He had intended, upon finishing the meal, to continue on his way. But somehow he was unable to tear himself away from the Blue Rosshinska. While the Turos watched in fascination, he purchased another helping, and then another and another—losing his plumed hat, belt, empty scabbard, empty leather purse, and handsome red boots.

Finally Zargal had nothing left but his shirt and breeches. So hungry was he that he would undoubtedly have tried to barter even these for another taste of the Rosshinska. But this was not possible, for all the stew was gone. The cauldron was empty, and the fire beneath it had died. Zargal, still ragingly hungry, got to his feet. His tongue and lips were stained a vivid blue. "None left?" he asked.

"Gone," Ninko replied. "The pot is empty, young lord —as empty and barren as the lives of the wretched Turos! Now my poor family must go hungry again, for you have eaten all we had. It is ever thus."

"But we don't begrudge you your meal, no matter what it cost us!" Chersa declared generously. "We only hope that you enjoyed it!"

Zargal did not answer. Silently he turned and began to trudge down the road. He heard the gabble of the Turo language behind him, and the sound of unrestrained laughter.

Darkness had fallen when Zargal finally arrived at the little village of Cornaszar, which lay just outside the walls of Szar. He had walked for miles over the stony road since his encounter with the Turos. He was very tired, and his feet were bleeding from several cuts. The air had turned cold with the approach of evening, and Zagral was keenly aware of the loss of the coat. All these discomforts, however, dwindled into insignificance in comparison with the terrible hunger that had tormented him ever since his last meal.

The streets were deserted, but there were lights in most of the cottage windows, for the townsfolk were at dinner. Zargal fervently wished that he could say the same. Then, as he neared one of the vine-covered little houses, he paused. The window was open, despite the chilly weather. From within came the sound of voices and the smell of cabbage soup. Zargal lingered to sniff and yearn. His presence there at that hour, together with his shoelessness, evidently marked him as a tramp in the eyes of the cottager's dogs. A couple of great brindled mastiffs came racing around the angle of the house, baying furiously. Zargal instantly fled up the main street of Cornaszar, with the dogs in close pursuit. Doors were opening, and villagers were emerging from their cottages to see what was happening. Zargal lowered his head and ran on. Once he stumbled and slipped to his knees. One of the dogs seized the opportunity to tear a large swatch of linen from his shirt. He rose once more and continued his flight, heading blindly in the direction of the city gates. The dogs remained with him, snapping and snarling upon his trail, until he had actually passed beneath the great portcullis and entered Szar itself.

Zargal stood within the familiar walls of his native city. He need only return to his father's palace and the day's misfortunes could be forgotten.

But he was still hungry—more so than ever before. None of the troubles which had come to him during the course of the day had been enough to divert his mind from that obsessive topic for long, nor had the massive quantities of food that he'd already consumed succeeded in killing, or even satisfying, his appetite.

But now, as he walked through the city toward the palace of his father, the idea that had hovered all day around the edges of his consciousness was finally able to claim his attention. This vast hunger had to be the result of the stranger's curse—the recollection of which was hazy. By no stretch of the most active imagination could this appetite be considered natural. It was a sickness of some kind, and its author was the stranger he had so recklessly offended last night. Unlike most other illnesses, this one would not go away. He might remain in the same condition for the rest of his days.

Zargal tried to envision an entire lifetime of desperate gluttony. He considered the prospect of the years stretching out before him, wasted in an endless quest for food. He pictured a dreary succession of days, each of them similar to the one he had just gone through, with himself the helpless slave of appetite—forever. The idea turned him sick with panic.

Zargal had no idea how to deal with adversity, for he had never before encountered it. His position as heir to the

Dukedom of Szar had always stood between him and any ill the world might offer; in all his life he had never been crossed, much less threatened. He had little to do with his parents; his mother had died years before, and the great Duke Jalonzal, being much absorbed in affairs of state, had left his son's upbringing to the care of a squadron of servants and tutors. The servants, through fear or ignorance, had indulged the boy disastrously. Zargal had been born clever, and it had become apparent to him at a very early age that, with a little bit of determination, he could always have his own way; he always had had it. Thus, while not at all bad-natured, he had grown up headstrong and haughty. His arrogance had never received a check, because there had been nobody who cared to become an enemy of the heir of Szar—until now.

"It doesn't matter," the young man tried to persuade himself. "I'll just exercise some self-control, that's all. I won't give in to this, and it's bound to go away in time. I'll eat normal meals and nothing more. Willpower is the answer." Indeed, willpower had always been the answer for him, and whatever he set his heart on, he'd always achieved. It was impossible to avoid wondering, however, how useful willpower might prove in opposing the magic of ghastly-faced strangers with trained lizards and flashing rings. "Willpower," Zargal repeated, as if it were a charm. "Willpower." A battered apple was lying in the gutter, close at hand. It had probably slipped from someone's market basket earlier in the day. Zargal's eye lighted on the fruit and he made an automatic move to pick it up, then stopped himself. "I will eat no more today," he declared aloud. With a tremendous effort, he averted his eyes from the apple and kept on walking. "Willpower," he reminded himself.

Zargal was now approaching his father's great palace, which stood in the middle of the city, surrounded by a high wall. He did not venture near the iron-barred, guarded gates that stood before the building; there was usually a crowd of people assembled there for one reason or another, and he did not wish to be seen. Instead he proceeded along a darkened alleyway that led him to an inconspicuous side door in the palace wall. The door was always kept locked.

But for several years now, the Duke's son had found that it suited his convenience to be able to enter and leave the grounds without attracting attention, and he possessed a key. It hung on a thin gold chain around his neck, and had fortunately escaped the notice of the Turos. Zargal let himself in and locked the door behind him.

He stood in the privy gardens. Before him rose the imposing palace—massive, formal, and blazing from within with the light of a thousand candles. Zargal made his way toward the building without wasting a glance on the marble statues and fountains that loomed up as pale as a congregation of ghosts. It was a splendid spectacle, but he had seen it too often. He did not even pause to appreciate his father's wonderful collection of plants and flowers—rare plants that had been brought back to Szar from a hundred foreign lands. Zargal did not bother to look, but then, neither did his father very often; the remarkable collection was but one more manifestation of Duke Jalonzal's desire to make his palace the most magnificent, the most stupendous, that the world had ever seen. If he inhabited the world's finest palace, Jalonzal had always reasoned, then people were bound to realize that he must be the world's finest Duke.

The Duke's son entered the palace through a small back door and made his way toward his own suite of chambers. He deliberately chose a roundabout route through the building in order to avoid meeting any courtiers, servants, or guards. This time, luck held with him. The corridors and galleries that he traversed were deserted. The candles burning in the sconces on the walls illuminated endless empty vistas of gilded carvings and columns, giant mirrors in golden frames, crystal chandeliers without number, paintings, statuary, and inlaid marble floors. Everything here was built on the grand scale—huge, ornate, and lifelessly formal. Zargal caught a glimpse of himself in one of the mirrors and was almost amused at the sight of his bedraggled and filthy figure, clad only in breeches and shirt, in the midst of all the grandeur.

He made it back to his own apartment without meeting a soul. His valet was nowhere in evidence, and the fire had burned low in the grate. Zargal prepared himself for sleep without a servant's assistance, for once. Then he climbed into bed and pulled the brocaded curtains completely shut around him, as if for protection. Despite his fatigue, his mind was so full of anxiety and hunger that it was a long time before he was able to fall asleep. From time to time he mumbled, with a note of unconscious pathos, "Will-power. Willpower . . ."

CHAPTER V

When Zargal awoke the next morning, his first thought was of breakfast. He felt as if he hadn't eaten in weeks. "I'm entitled to breakfast," he assured himself. "Breakfast is healthy, and I'll eat a large one. Very large." He pulled back the curtains and then, without arising, yanked the tapestried bell pull which hung beside the bed.

An instant later, his valet, the mysterious Flimm, entered the room and advanced on noiseless feet. Flimm was very tall and of skeletal build. His skin was white, his lips bloodless, and his hair and eyes were black. He was dressed in unrelieved black, and all his movements were fluid and soundless. But if the man resembled an escapee from a cemetery, his nature belied his looks. His thoughts were certainly not fixed on the world beyond; there was not a soul in the palace more acutely aware of the happenings in the world of here and now.

"Good morning, my lord," Flimm said. "I trust you spent a restful night. While you were asleep, I took the liberty of disposing of your shirt and breeches, both of which were spoiled. The trousers were marked with blue stains, identifiable by their odor as tavril—probably present in a large quantity of Blue Rosshinska, if I am to judge by

the grains of rice I found in the pockets. I gather you met
with a band of Turos, my lord, which would also account
for the absence of your money and the rest of your attire.
I noted, too, a quantity of viscous matter, resembling vegetable sap, which I would judge came from some variety of
squash plant, but not one with which I am familiar. Your
shirt, my lord, was torn and bloody. The muddy paw prints
on it were obviously those of dogs of a breed indigenous to
Cornaszar. The only possible explanation is that the villagers were offended. I presume your lordship's day was
eventful." These remarks were delivered in a toneless voice,
with no change of expression.

"Yes, quite eventful," Zargal answered. "Have some
breakfast sent in to me, and lay out my clothes. I shall be
going out this morning."

"I've already laid out your clothes, my lord. But I regret
to inform you, sir, that you will not be going abroad this
morning. His Grace your father will shortly be sending a
messenger with the request that you present yourself at the
levee."

"Oh, not again!" Zargal exclaimed impatiently. The
levee was the ceremony performed in the morning, as
Duke Jalonzal arose from bed. It was attended by the
highest dignitaries in the palace, who took turns serving
the Duke his morning meal and helping him to dress. The
ritual usually included a concert and a recitation cele-
brating the origins and deeds of the noble ducal house of
Szar. Zargal hated it with all his heart. "The fourth time in
a week! Where did you hear that I'm to be summoned?"

"His Grace's valet informed the Chief Chamberlain, who
confided in an underchamberlain who will, for a trifling
consideration, pass on such information to me, my lord.
The report was confirmed by one of the cleaning maids,
who overheard the Duke issuing orders to his scribe and
told me about it."

"I see," Zargal murmured. He was always fascinated to
hear of Flimm's network of spies. "There's only one thing
to do, then—I'll get dressed and out of here before my
father's messenger arrives." He glanced at Flimm to see
whether or not the man approved; but as usual, the valet's
face was impassive. Zargal could never tell what Flimm
was thinking. Neither could anyone else, for that matter,

but nobody ever considered dismissing him—he knew too much.

"In that case, my lord, I suggest you make haste. The messenger is approaching your chamber and has by this time probably reached the Silver Gallery."

"You're right, I'd better—" As Zargal spoke, he tossed the heavy bed coverings from him, leaped to his feet, and stopped. Something was wrong—so very wrong that instinct warned him of calamity before he'd had a chance to realize what had changed. The room looked peculiar. Flimm was staring *up* at him with an expression of unwonted amazement in his black eyes; but Flimm was normally half a head taller than Zargal. The Duke's son gasped. "Flimm!" he accused. "You have shrunk!"

"No, my lord, not I. I doubt that the Duke would permit it."

"Then why am I now at least six inches taller than you? What's the meaning of this?"

"What indeed, my lord?"

"You're quite sure you haven't shrunk? That's to say, you are really certain?"

"Completely certain, my lord. There is one inescapable conclusion."

Zargal was forced to agree. As he glanced around his room, he understood why it had looked so odd a moment before; he was now observing things from a considerably higher vantage point. In fact, he was over a foot taller than he had been before he went to sleep. Since he had been rather tall to begin with, his height was now outlandish. Zargal raced over to the mirror to get a better look at himself. The pale face that stared back at him from the depths of the glass was unchanged. He was unchanged, he saw, in feature, proportion, or coloring—but he had become enormously, ridiculously, tall.

"It isn't real. It isn't happening. I'm still asleep."

"I beg to differ, your lordship," Flimm contradicted in his monotone voice. He wore the guarded look of one who reserves judgment until he has acquired more information.

"I couldn't have grown a foot taller since I fell asleep!"

"Perhaps not, my lord. It is always possible that a portion of the growth took place before you went to sleep, and you did not notice it at the time."

"Flimm, you are not helping matters!"

"I beg your pardon, my lord. What, then, does your lordship require of me?"

"I don't know! What shall I do about this?"

"That depends entirely, my lord, on what caused it," Flimm said judiciously. "Do you know the cause?"

Zargal allowed himself to sink into a chair, but kept his eyes fixed on his image in the long pier glass. "There can only be one cause," he muttered. "That man in the tavern. He did this to me. I wish I'd had the presence of mind to kill him."

"To whom do you refer, my lord?"

"He claimed—" Zargal unconsciously lowered his voice. "He claimed to be King Laza of Obran."

"If it is indeed King Laza who has caused your misfortune," the valet observed, "then it is just as well that you did not attempt to kill him, my lord, as he would undoubtedly have inflicted a most severe punishment."

"He's done that already!"

"It would be much worse if you had seriously insulted him, my lord. But he is not quick to take offense. The only cause of true annoyance to him seems to be any reference to his unfortunate appearance. You did not, by any chance—?"

"I did. I asked him if he'd put his face on inside out. I said that they ought to put him on exhibit in a cage and charge admission. It's all coming back to me now. I believe I called him a gargoyle."

"A gargoyle, my lord?"

"A gargoyle."

Flimm winced. "I see. That was perhaps rash."

"Yes. Yes. However, I did it! The question is, what shall I do now? How do I get out of this tangle?"

"I think it would be best, my lord, if you—"

At that moment there came a knock upon the chamber door. "Who is there?" Flimm asked blandly.

"A message," a voice on the other side of the door answered. "A message for Lord Zargal from his Grace the Duke."

"His lordship is seriously indisposed," Flimm responded without hesitation. "You may give the message to me, and I will see that he receives it."

"His Grace ordered me to speak directly to Lord Zargal. Admit me."

"His lordship is ill. He is feverish. I suspect that the malady may be contagious."

"The Duke ordered me to deliver a message to Lord Zargal," the voice insisted stubbornly. "Do you want me to tell him that you wouldn't let me follow my orders?"

Zargal and Flimm looked at each other for a moment, and Zargal shrugged. "Let him in." He dived back into bed, pulled the covers up to his chin, and shut his eyes. Flimm opened the door. A huge lackey stood on the threshold, clad in the red and gold livery of Duke Jalonzal's household servants. He entered the room and advanced cautiously toward the bed. As he drew near, he took a handkerchief from his pocket and applied it protectively across his nose and mouth.

"How fares your Lordship?" the lackey inquired.

"Water," Zargal croaked piteously. Under other circumstances, he might have been enjoying himself. "Water!"

"No more water, my lord," Flimm answered. "You have drunk too much already; 'twill cause the boils to swell."

"Boils? Lord Zargal has boils?" the lackey asked, edging away from the bed.

"Only a few," Flimm assured him. "Small ones. There is no cause for alarm."

"Buboes!" The lackey recoiled as if confronted with an evil spirit. "He has the plague!"

"Perhaps—or perhaps not," Flimm said. "It is still too early to tell. I believe you have a message for his lordship?"

"Yes! Yes! His Grace Duke Jalonzal commands the attendance of Lord Zargal at the levee this morning. His lordship is to present himself before the duke in a quarter of an hour. No excuses are to be accepted." The man chattered out his announcement as quickly as he could, retreating a step closer to the door with each word. Zargal moaned and tossed restlessly beneath the covers.

"He cannot hear you," Flimm explained. "He is delirious. You will inform his Grace of the situation."

"He'll accept no excuses," the lackey said. "Not this time. Not for any reason."

"Not even," Flimm asked gravely, "if his son is dying?"

"Don't let me die!" Zargal pleaded. He opened his

eyes and focused upon the lackey. "You—come closer," he commanded. "Come near me; whisper your message in my ear. Sickness cannot touch you if you are pure in heart."

The servant manifestly distrusted this theory. "I've given you the Duke's message!" he cried. "If anyone asks, you tell them! I followed my orders!" With that he was gone, slamming the door behind him. For a few seconds they could hear the sound of running footsteps in the corridor, then silence.

"This will explain your lordship's absence at the levee," Flimm remarked.

"But it's only a temporary respite. I don't know what I'm going to do. I can't be seen in this condition."

"We will make every effort to locate some magician or savant who can counteract the spell," Flimm suggested.

"Is there any magician or savant who will dare to cross King Laza of Obran?"

"Since you press me—no."

"Well, then?"

"My lord," Flimm mused, "it is possible that all is not lost, even if you must remain as you are. You've grown unnaturally tall. But remember—great stature always commands respect and admiration. There is such a thing as making a virtue of necessity. In this case, that means telling people that you've done it on purpose."

"On purpose? Grown a foot taller overnight on purpose?"

"Indeed. You are the future Duke of Szar. As your birth has set you above other men, so must your stature set you above them as well."

"That's very neat, Flimm. My father would like it. But nobody would believe that tale."

"You are still young, my lord. In time, you will perceive that people will believe anything. You will then be ready to rule."

"I must give you credit; the idea's ingenious," the Duke's son conceded. "But I don't want to explain my height. I want to find some way of reducing it!"

"Of course, my lord. I spoke only of what might be considered if all else fails. Perhaps you should journey to Obran and throw yourself upon the mercy of King Laza."

"Do you think I'd go crawling to him? The thought disgusts me. I'd prefer to remain as I am."

"Well, if that's what you'd prefer, my lord."

"No, we must think of something else. Between the two of us, I don't doubt that we can get the better of King Laza." He paused, awaiting Flimm's confirmation, but the valet was silent. "But I can't think before I've eaten," Zargal continued uncomfortably. His great hunger had not abated in the least. "Go bring me back some breakfast, Flimm—the larger the better. Do you think you can manage to avoid being seen?"

The valet came as close as he ever came to smiling. "I think I might manage it," he replied, and was gone.

In the absence of his servant, Zargal attempted to dress himself, but it was not a very successful effort. His loose-fitting shirt and breeches presented little problem—although the breeches were far too short, and the full linen sleeves stopped considerably short of his protruding wrists. His stockings and shoes, however, were far too small; he couldn't get them on at all. And when he tried to don his jacket, the garment split across the back and shoulders and had to be discarded.

In due course Flimm returned, bearing a platter of cold roasted meats and some fruit. "The levee is still in progress," the valet reported, "but it is nearly finished. I have it on good authority that his Grace is in a very bad temper. The musicians played off-key, and the odes were not well-received. In fact, I gather that the poet is to be banished to a small island in the middle of the Sea of Ice."

"Never mind about that," Zargal said as he ate. "We can always spare a poet or two. Now, Flimm, do you have any idea at all where I may find someone who will restore me to my normal size?"

Master and servant had little time to discuss the question before an authoritative rapping shook the chamber door. "Admit me immediately," commanded an angry voice recognizable as that of the Duke of Szar.

Zargal jumped to his feet and glanced around him as if seeking escape from a trap. "He can't see me like this! He'd never forgive me!"

"Lord Zargal is ill, your Grace," Flimm proclaimed calmly. "You risk infection if you enter this room."

"It is useless to try to shield him. I have ordered you to open this door. Do you defy me?"

"Never, your Grace." Having little choice, Flimm unlocked and opened the door—but not before Zargal had once more hidden himself beneath his bed coverings.

Duke Jalonzal stalked into the room. The Duke was a firm believer in the idea that the personal life of a ruler must reflect the power and dignity of his office. Thus it followed that a great leader must live in an immense palace, maintain a magnificent and formal court, and demonstrate, with every word and gesture, that he existed as the personification of the glory of a mighty city-state. The Duke's entire life was bound by his regard for public appearance and governed by a passion for form rather than substance. Zargal understood all this instinctively and hated the life of the Court. But he was young enough so that he had never stopped to think why he hated it. As for the Duke, he was bitterly disappointed in his unpromising heir.

Jalonzal advanced to the side of the bed, then paused and stood there, a perfect vision of ducal splendor from the top of his great, curling periwig down to the high green heels of his shoes, designed to elevate an already imposing figure. His face wore its usual expression of hauteur, but now the thin lips were curled in an additional grimace of anger and impatience.

"As your Grace can see," Flimm said, "Lord Zargal is bedridden—"

"Leave the room," the Duke commanded, without removing his eyes from his son. "And do not presume to address me again without leave. You forget yourself." Flimm bowed wordlessly and retired. "Your valet is impertinent," the Duke informed Zargal. "I will not tolerate laxity among the servants. Why did you not present yourself at the levee this morning?"

"I deeply regret," Zargal answered, in the formal style he always used when addressing his father, "that sudden illness deprived me of the privilege of attending your Grace."

"Indeed. And what illness troubles you, pray?" The Duke's cold voice took on a sarcastic note. "A sickness born of overindulgence in wine? Did you take a chill while you were out roistering all night in the taverns? Perhaps you've contracted some disease from your lowbred companions. I'd prefer not to hazard a guess as to what it might be."

"I am unable to satisfy your Grace's curiosity," Zargal replied, his face wooden. "But I do assure you, I am not myself."

"I am not interested in your excuses, sir. If you have an aching head or a queasy stomach, you've brought it on yourself, and that is your affair. But I will not permit you to allow such trifles to interfere with the fulfillment of your public obligations—which would reflect poorly on me. Do I make myself clear?"

"Perfectly, your Grace."

"Your absence at the levee was noted and remarked upon. Such behavior undermines my authority." The Duke paused, but Zargal did not speak. "Well—have you nothing to say?"

"I hardly think, your Grace, that I was in any fit condition to appear. My presence would have done you little credit."

"That is true at all times, sir," Jalonzal returned cruelly. "But it does not signify. You are my son, and your attendance at official functions is required. It is trial enough for me that my son must needs be a dissolute, spendthrift wastrel. Must I also endure his attempts to humiliate me before my people?"

"I have made no attempt to humiliate your Grace," Zargal answered, "on this occasion or any other." He was white with anger, but his courtesy did not falter.

"It would set my mind at rest, were I able to take you at your word. But how can I believe you, when your behavior is a public scandal and a disgrace to your father? Your life is shameful, and your every action proclaims to the world that you will never be fit to rule this city. What am I to think but that you engage in a deliberate campaign to discredit me?"

"What reason could I have for doing so?" Zargal inquired, in tones as icy as the Duke's.

"What reason would you need, sir, beyond sheer perversity? You neglect official functions; you ignore all rules of decorum; you never bother to spare a thought for the dignified and regal bearing that ought to be the outward symbol of your rank. In short, you have demonstrated complete contempt for your own birthright. What is all this, if not evidence of your determination to flout me at every turn?"

"You mistake me, your Grace. I would not willingly fail in the duty that I owe you, both as my parent and as my Duke."

"I am past believing you, sir," the Duke sneered. "Formerly I've attributed your misconduct to youth and folly. Now I begin to realize that it must be due to deliberate malice."

"I give you my word—"

"Don't trouble yourself. Even now you refuse to arise from your bed to pay your respects to me."

"There are sound reasons for that, your Grace."

"There are no reasons, other than stubbornness and insolence. But I'll not endure them any longer. Get out of that bed, sir! You will stand up in the presence of the Duke!"

"I am ill, your Grace," Zargal argued desperately. "I cannot arise. Do not ask it of me!"

"I do not *ask* it of you. I insist. Get up! You will obey me, or be prepared to face the consequences."

"I implore your Grace, permit me to stay where I am!"

"It is time that you learned who's master here," Jalonzal declared menacingly. "Will you obey me, or must I call in the guards to drag you from your bed by force?"

Zargal searched his father's face and saw no sign of softening there. Argument was useless. Slowly, he pushed the covers from him and then, very reluctantly, rose to his full height.

For a few seconds the room was silent, as the Duke's eyes traveled slowly up Zargal's gigantic figure, from the floor clear on up to the face that now towered above him. Jalonzal's own face was frozen with shock. Zargal waited in dutiful silence, and at last his father addressed him. "What—have—you—done—to—yourself?"

"I have done nothing to myself, your Grace. You might better ask what has been done to me."

The Duke shook his head, as if he could not believe his eyes. "Is there no limit," he asked slowly, "to the lengths to which you will go to make me appear ridiculous?"

"I'd say that I am the one who appears ridiculous here, your Grace."

"Yes." The Duke nodded. "I am well aware that you would do almost anything to spite me. But I must confess I never dreamed you'd go this far!"

"Surely you don't believe that I'd do such a thing to myself out of spite? You're not serious?"

"I do not know what to think. I only know that your entire life has been expended in efforts to annoy and embarrass me. And if that is your goal, you could not have hit upon a more certain means of achieving it than this. If you are seen in public in this condition, I shall be laughed out of Szar. Is that what you wanted, sir?"

This was more than Zargal could take. "I have not inflicted this misfortune on myself out of any desire to annoy you," he snapped. "In the first place, I don't have the power. If I did, then this is not the way I would use it. And I will be the one laughed out of Szar if I am seen, your Grace—not you."

"Beware of adding disrespect to the list of your failings," the Duke warned. "You have so often offended me in the past that I am forced to suspect you. But I must consider all this at my leisure. I must ponder the problem. In the meantime, it is of the greatest importance that you remain concealed from public view. If anyone should catch sight of you, I should be at a loss to explain your bizarre condition. Therefore, you will not set foot outside this room until further notice. Under no circumstances must you be seen—I would be mortified." Duke Jalonzal turned deliberately and moved toward the door. Before he walked out, he turned back and announced, "There is one thing that I wish to make quite clear to you. I am displeased, sir. Highly displeased."

Zargal, drained and dejected by the encounter, flung himself down again upon the bed, which creaked and groaned beneath his increased weight. He was still hungry.

CHAPTER VI

The days that followed were a nightmare for Zargal. Despite the Duke's desire that no one learn of his son's condition, he was obliged to confide in his personal physician, Dr. Getros. The Doctor, a vague and amiable specialist in exorcisms, was sworn to complete secrecy, conducted to Zargal's rooms, and commanded to cure the sufferer. Upon beholding Zargal, the Doctor, his eyes bulging, voiced his opinion that the case was a hopeless one; whereupon it was explained to him tactfully that it was upon Zargal's restored good health that his own continued good health depended. Getros was not happy, but he rose manfully to the challenge and commenced his experimentation, making use of every medical technique he knew.

The experiments were not altogether pleasant for Zargal. Dr. Getros began with the ancient and honorable treatment of bloodletting. He produced several specimens of large, healthy-looking leeches, a couple dozen mosquitoes, and one tame vampire bat; he applied the assorted creatures to Zargal's arms and legs and permitted them to feast undisturbed. Zargal writhed and twitched under these ministrations, but he could not shake his tormentors off, for the

Doctor had taken the precaution of strapping him down to the bed.

In due course of time, the leeches swelled to monstrous proportions, released their hold, and dropped off. The mosquitoes hummed away out the chamber windows, completely sated. And finally the bat, which had crouched upon his breast, allowed itself to roll off his body and onto the floor. It landed upon its back and lay there, its belly protruding, and a look of great peace upon its hideous little face. Zargal, however, remained as tall as ever. As a result of the treatment, he was now covered with itching bites and hives.

The Doctor next fed his patient a series of potions designed to cleanse and purge the body of all illness. The potions were all revolting. They did not succeed in purging Zargal's body of illness, but they did purge him of all the food he'd consumed within the past twenty-four hours.

Following these attempts, Dr. Getros settled down to serious business and prepared himself and his patient for an exorcism. It was the Doctor's strong opinion that any illness which could not be conquered by means of bleeding or medicines must be the work of demons. Demons inhabiting a human body could always be driven forth if their resting place were rendered sufficiently uncomfortable, and this Dr. Getros proceeded to do. The unfortunate youth was suspended from the ceiling by his wrists while the doctor drew a pentagram on the floor, several feet below him, and built a fire within it. Onto the fire Getros tossed a variety of powders and oils, and soon a thick, nauseating vapor arose, completely enveloping Zargal's hanging figure. The Doctor paced around the pentagram, chanting in an ancient tongue and calling out periodic commands for the demons to show themselves. All that happened, however, was that the fumes cut off Zargal's oxygen supply; he began to choke and eventually fainted. The Doctor was obliged to take him down from the ceiling and put him to bed for a few hours.

The Doctor took advantage of his patient's unconsciousness to perform yet other experiments. He smeared Zargal's face and hands with unction and recited certain incantations. He placed various talismans at points of power around the room. He immersed Zargal in a bath of warm oil, honey, and sheep's blood, in the hope that the healthy properties of the fluids could draw the evil humors from the youth's system. He performed ritual gestures with a cat-o'-nine-tails in an effort to terrify the demons. He even placed a network of silver and copper wires over Zargal's body, in the hopes of harnassing the magnetic currents in the air and using their power to purify his patient's blood.

None of these methods worked, and Dr. Getros was at last forced to admit defeat. The Duke was willing to forgive him his failure, but felt that the physician possessed dangerous knowledge. In order to prevent that knowledge from spreading, Jalonzal ordered the Doctor locked up in the deepest dungeon beneath the palace and personally dropped the key into the garden fish pond.

In the meantime, Zargal continued to eat and continued to grow. With each passing day, his appetite became more and more uncontrollable, until it strained the resources of even the great palace kitchens to keep him fed. At first he tried to fight his appetite, but that was a task far beyond his powers, and he soon had to give up the struggle. He could no more banish hunger than he could have ordered his own heart to stop beating. He had no choice but to surrender to his cravings.

The Duke gave out word that his son was deathly ill. He shut off the corridors leading to Zargal's rooms and posted guards to make certain that none of the courtiers ventured into the forbidden territory. He caused falsified reports of Zargal's condition to be posted in the galleries and banqueting halls; and as far as anyone knew, the heir of Szar lay in bed, burning with a mysterious fever.

The only inhabitants of the palace who noted anything really peculiar in the situation were the cooks, the kitchen staff, and a couple of lackeys. Each morning the cooks were ordered to prepare two or three roasted oxen, a couple of sheep, a brace of wild boar, assorted roasted fowls, fifty or sixty loaves of bread, half a dozen crates of vegetables, and a dozen baskets of fruit. The lackeys were given special permission to wheel this food on silver carts to Zargal's suite. They left it upon his threshold, knocked on the door, and retired.

Only once one of them lingered in the hall, concealed behind a statue, to see what would happen. He saw the door open; Flimm came forth and started passing the pro-

visions to someone within. Then an immense hand appeared
from inside the chamber, took hold of a wild boar, and
disappeared again. The servant rushed screaming along the
hall and down to the kitchens to tell his fellows what he had
seen. They did not believe him. For several days he told his
tale to all who would listen. Then he vanished and was not
heard from again.

Imprisoned within his room, Zargal ate ceaselessly and
increased in size from hour to hour. He grew too large for
all his clothes and was forced to contrive garments from
sheets and blankets. When he grew too long for his bed,
he slept stretched out on the floor. But these discomforts
soon appeared as trifles when he started to grow too large
for the room itself. One day his head was tapping against
the lofty ceiling. The next, he could not stand upright and
was forced to pace the chamber with bowed head and
hunched shoulders. Later on, he could not stand at all and
was reduced to crawling around on hands and knees.

Zargal's misery and desperation increased along with his
stature. As his situation worsened, he was subject to fits of
gloom and terror; at times he became almost frantic. His
feelings were confided to Flimm alone, for the valet was
the only human being he ever saw. Duke Jalonzal had
been in the habit of calling upon Zargal every other day
to check his son's progress—or rather, his deterioration.
Soon, however, the Duke decided that these visits were
distressing, whereupon he discontinued them.

And thus, about six weeks after the incident at the Peacock tavern, Zargal and his valet sat together in the bed-
chamber which had become a jail.

"Flimm," Zargal said, "I can't stand much more of this."
He was sitting on the floor, with his back against one wall
and his legs extending all the way across the room. It was
the most comfortable position he could find. "If I stay
cooped up in this room any longer, I believe I'll go mad."

"Your lordship would do well to cultivate the virtue of
patience," Flimm answered impassively.

"My patience ran out a long time ago. I've been shut up
here for six weeks! How long is it going to go on?"

"Beyond a doubt, your lordship is in need of diversion.
Shall I bring you some books?"

"I'm sick to death of books. I've read hundreds of them

since I've been here. I never thought I'd live to become so well-educated. Is there anything left in the library that I haven't read?"

"Very little, my lord," the valet admitted. "One or two scientific works, I believe. Might I interest your lordship in *A Search for Intelligence Among the Complex Fungi?*"

"Definitely not."

"As your lordship wishes. Perhaps you might enjoy a game of chess?"

"Well—all right, I suppose so. Set up the board, then." The valet complied, swiftly arranging the little figures on their green and white alabaster board. When Zargal attempted to play, he discovered that his fingers had grown so huge that he was unable to pick up any piece without knocking over several of the others. "It's no good, Flimm," Zargal observed despondently. "I can't do it. You might as well put them away."

"Would your lordship favor a game of cards?"

"Not particularly," Zargal snapped, then added more politely, "But what did you have in mind?"

"Ombre?" Flimm suggested. "Piquet? Gleek? Patience?"

Zargal darted a sharp glance at him, but Flimm's expression was unreadable, as always. "I don't think so. I want you to tell me," he commanded suddenly, "what efforts my father is making to find someone who will cure me."

"His Grace does not take me into his confidence."

"I am sure of that. And I am equally sure that you can give me the information I want, if you will." Flimm's black eyes glazed, and his thin white lips all but disappeared, as if he were inwardly debating whether or not he ought to admit what he knew. "I've a right to be told," Zargal insisted.

"His Grace," Flimm explained carefully "believes that his public reputation might suffer, were it to become generally known that his heir is afflicted with giantism. He fears that the situation might result in a certain unrest among the populace and that his enemies would seize the opportunity of maligning him. Above all, he dreads the loss of dignity."

"Certainly," Zargal replied. "And all that gives him more reason than ever to find someone who will cure me, as quickly as possible."

"No doubt, my lord. And yet—"

"And yet—what? What could hold him back?"

"That is what I am trying to make clear to your lordship. In order to find help for you, the Duke must obviously confide in somebody. And this his Grace has not been willing to do. Ever since the failure of Dr. Getros, the Duke has not been able to bring himself to place his trust in another. The secret remains locked within his heart."

"And I remain locked within my room."

"Quite so, my lord."

"Do you mean to tell me that my father has not even tried to find anyone to help? I have been sitting in this room for weeks on end—nearly sick of boredom and loneliness —growing more monstrous with each passing day. And all this time, he has not even been trying?" Zargal made a move to leap to his feet, but subsided when his head knocked against the ceiling.

"Perhaps he hoped that the matter would resolve itself, if given time."

"It's certainly not going to resolve itself. He'd better do something! How long does he think I'm going to stay here? I'm not prepared to sit here for the rest of my life!"

"Your lordship will recall that his Grace has expressly ordered you to remain in this chamber."

"I'm not interested in his orders." Zargal's eyes were blazing with indignation—enormous eyes, in a gigantic young face. "I've had all of this that I can endure. In any case, there's no point in trying to keep my condition a secret. It can't be concealed forever. Doesn't he realize that?"

"Apparently he thinks that it's worth a good effort, my lord."

"Well, he can think again, then. It won't work. People are bound to talk. The courtiers must already be wondering what has become of me."

"There are many rumors, your lordship."

"Indeed?" Zargal looked slightly pleased.

"Yes." Flimm was on familiar ground here. "It has come to me from various sources that you are generally believed to be seriously ill. But there is little agreement upon the nature of your illness. Some believe it to be a wasting fever. There is a faction which favors the theory that you have run mad and are locked up for your own protection. Some believe that an excess of wine and night adventures have brought you low. There is a story that you quarreled in a tavern and were hit over the head with a bottle of ale. Some say that a local baker cracked your skull with an oaken rolling pin. There are those who swear that you were seen dueling six weeks ago in the Vischka Gardens and that you were felled by your enemy's sword. Still others assert that you are not present in the palace at all—that you incurred your father's wrath and he has banished you. And some," Flimm concluded, "are certain that you are already dead, my lord."

"Dead?"

"Yes, and buried in secret."

"I suspect that I may hope for no assistance from them. But I tell you, Flimm, I'm not willing to stay in this room much longer. Whether my father likes it or no, he must find the solution to this problem—or I'll go out and find it myself. You can tell him that when you next see him."

"I have seen him very little of late, my lord."

Flimm's voice might have belonged to a speaking automaton, but Zargal knew him well enough to prick up his ears at that. "Why not?" he asked uneasily.

"He has been much occupied, my lord."

"With what?"

"His intentions have not been revealed. In fact, I believe that he would prefer to avoid attracting attention to his projects. His helpers have been sworn to secrecy. Nonetheless, the sister of the wife of the page of the backstairs succeeded in unearthing some information. She confided in one of the guards, who passed it on to me."

"Well—what is the Duke up to?" Zargal wasn't entirely certain that he really wanted to know.

"His Grace," Flimm answered, after a long pause, "has secretly commissioned a series of very large underground excavations beneath the palace. No one knows what his purpose may be."

Flimm and Zargal sat very still for a time and stared at each other without saying a word. There was nothing very encouraging to be said. Zargal wound his disconnected bell pull around one finger a couple of times. "So—you no longer see the Duke very often," he mused absently. "Perhaps I should send him a letter."

A group of courtiers was standing in the Silver Gallery, discussing many things. They spoke of the weather, the taxes, the latest fashions. They argued the relative merit of a number of fine wines. And they spoke of Lord Zargal.

"I say he's dead," announced a gray-bearded count of imposing girth. " 'Tis most certain. That lad was possessed of a devil, and if we do not see him or hear of him, there can be but one answer. He's dead and gone."

"Nonsense, my lord!" one of the ladies broke in. "Utter nonsense! He is alive and well. He has, however, repented of his former wildness and become a holy recluse, living by himself in the depths of the Twisting Forest. I have this on excellent authority."

"Indeed, madam! And what authority is that, pray?"

"My chambermaid. She has had a dream, a vision—"

"Od's life, madam!" a foppish young earl exclaimed. "Believe in a serving wench's dreams! I'd as soon believe in her honesty!"

"You may laugh if you please, sir! But I'll take my oath that Lord Zargal is a blessed hermit now—"

"A blessed highwayman, more likely," a skeptical marquis interjected, "if he's living in the woods!"

"He's not in the forest," one of the ladies-in-waiting announced with complete assurance. "I have heard that he has fled over the border to Strell. He was caught selling state secrets—he needed the money to pay off his gambling debts—and now he is banished forever!"

A sensation greeted this disclosure. But a baron now remarked quietly, "It's my belief that he's here in the palace, and has been all the time."

"Explain, my lord."

"His Grace the Duke has shut off the passages leading to his son's apartment," the baron continued, "and Lord Zargal is seen no more. Is it not reasonable to assume that he must be within?"

"Come, come, sir! What could the Duke hope to gain by imprisoning his son?"

"I have no idea," the baron confessed. "The Duke is secretive—now more so than ever before. His actions are difficult to understand. What, for example, is the purpose of the workmen who labor beneath the palace every day? Has it anything to do with Lord Zargal's disappearance? I fear we shall never know."

"Od's fish, sir!" the earl exclaimed. "His Grace may be closemouthed, but I'll wager the workmen are not! They're certain to tell us everything they know, if we but ask them. The rogues would hardly presume to defy persons of quality, surely?"

"Why not put it to the test?" the baron suggested. "Here come a couple of them now."

A pair of laborers were advancing down the gallery. They carried shovels, pickaxes, and crowbars. Their hands and faces were smeared with dirt. The courtiers made a few murmuring noises of protest at the sight of so filthy an apparition in the splendid halls of the ducal palace. Their disapproval did not, however, prevent them from questioning the workmen.

"A moment, fellow," the earl addressed one of them with pleasant condescension. "We wish to question you."

The workmen exchanged dark glances. "We was just going out, milord."

"You may leave presently. In the meantime, you will answer all questions put to you."

"Will we—my lord?" one of the men asked, with an ill-favored smile. Both of the laborers were, in fact, of distinctly disquieting appearance—short and muscular, with broad cheeks, jaws, and noses, narrow eyes and lips, and stony expressions. The workmen's bearing expressed a definite mockery.

"What sort of project are you engaged in?" the marquis demanded.

"Digging."

"Digging what?"

"Digging dirt—if it please your lordship."

"Don't try our patience, fellow," the marquis advised. "Remember your place. Now answer the question."

"No." The workmen shook their heads. "No," one of them repeated coolly.

"This is intolerable!" the count blustered. "Do you know who we are?"

"That don't matter. It don't matter who you are," one

laborer replied, with unmistakable satisfaction. "We're not to answer any questions."

"We're just not feeling very talkative today," the other added.

"You impertinent peasants," the count fumed. "I'll have you whipped for this. I'll have you kicked!"

"Better think again, milord," a workman advised. "The Duke wouldn't like it."

"The Duke! But what of the Duke?"

"He's given us orders not to tell no one about our work. You wouldn't want us to disobey the Duke, would you— milord?" The peasant smiled a sinister smile.

The count could think of nothing to say to this, but the quiet baron could. "We wouldn't want you to disobey your instructions," he remarked, "and you needn't tell us what you're doing—but perhaps you could give us some idea of how it looks down there, where you are working." He handed the men a number of gold coins, which they accepted as if they were doing him a favor.

"It's a big hole," one of the men admitted. "Very big. You might say it's turning into a kind of cave."

"It's pitch-dark down there," the other added. "We have torches burning all the time."

"Very damp—"

"And deadly cold."

"There's a great iron door across the entrance, with a heavy bar and three padlocks."

"And there's a pallet on the ground—like a man's pallet to sleep on, only a lot bigger."

"And a water bucket the size of a cistern."

The courtiers were listening uncomprehendingly. "What else?" the baron demanded.

"Nothing else. That's all there is."

"Do you know what it's for?"

"No." Both workmen now looked shifty and sly. "It's better not to know, my lord. Sometimes it's much better not to know." The two of them hurried away, leaving the courtiers more mystified than ever.

Quite suddenly one night, Zargal decided that he'd waited long enough. He had been entirely alone in his room all day. Even Flimm had been absent, for a banquet was being held that evening in honor of the Ambassador of Strell, and the valet's services had been needed elsewhere. Moreover, Zargal had not eaten all day, and pangs of raging hunger had nearly unhinged his mind.

Now he sat staring out his chamber window. Across a wide courtyard he could see the lighted windows of the banqueting hall. All the courtiers were assembled there. The lords and ladies, decked out in their brocades and velvets, their furs and jewels, were seated at the long table, chatting, laughing, enjoying the music, and filling themselves full of food and superb wines. Whereas he, Zargal, the legitimate heir to it all, sat alone in his room, an outcast, starving to death. The comparison was more than he could stand.

"I've waited for weeks, and his Grace has done nothing," he said aloud, as if justifying himself to an invisible critic. "I'll wait no longer. I will tell him so." After a long pause, he added, "I'll also inquire about those excavations."

The door was barred from the outside, but Zargal's strength had increased with his size. He placed his shoulder against the wood and pushed. For a little while it held. Then he could hear the sound of splitting timbers, a series of loud, cracking noises as the three bars burst, one after another. Suddenly the door gave way, and Zargal toppled out into the empty corridor. It was the first time in over two months that he had set foot out of his room.

The hall was completely deserted. Even the household guards customarily stationed nearby were off in another wing of the palace, attending the festivities. The chandeliers were unlit, and many of the wax tapers in the sconces had burned out. It was dim and gloomy. The chill of early winter sharpened the air, and Zargal shivered. He was wearing a couple of blankets, but his arms and legs were exposed and quickly became covered with goose pimples the size of raindrops. For a moment he wavered in his resolve and considered going back into his room and staying there, where no one could see him. He realized, however, that if he went back now it would probably be forever. Taking a deep breath—which stirred the prisms on the nearest chandelier—he started off in the direction of the banqueting hall.

The ceilings of Duke Jalonzal's palace were imperially

lofty. But the Duke's son had grown so tremendous that he could only proceed on hands and knees, his head bent down low between his shoulders. It was a painful progress. Worst of all was when he had to pass through doorways. For that, he had to flatten himself, stomach to floor, force his head and shoulders into the opening, and wriggle on through as best he could. Once he inadvertently tore the pediment from its place above a door as he passed. When he came to a staircase, the only way he could get down was to slide. His descent was so rapid that he was obliged to grab at the banister to control his speed, and the entire balustrade came away in his huge hand.

Despite all the noise he was making, Zargal attracted no attention. He met no one, saw no one. But as he neared the banqueting hall, the sound of music grew louder. The gay strains of a country dance came floating down the corridor. The hum of human conversation and laughter became audible. Glasses clinked and cutlery clicked.

Zargal finally reached his destination. For a time he rested there beside the closed door, simply listening. Once more he thought of returning to his own apartment, leaving the merrymakers undisturbed. It would be like returning to the grave. Hesitating no longer, he threw wide the door and thrust himself into the room beyond.

The banqueting hall was a blaze of light and color. Assembled there was a gathering of the greatest nobles of the realm, each attempting to outdo all others in magnificence. The display of plumes, gold lace, and embroideries was remarkable, the display of heirloom jewelry even more so. The long table was laden with a king's ransom in sculptured gold plate and ruby-studded crystal. The wine in the glasses was both redder and more valuable than the rubies.

At the head of the table sat Jalonzal, resplendent in copper brocade, with black lace at his throat and wrists. On his right-hand side sat the Ambassador of Strell, an exotic figure in his white robes, his face covered with the lilac tattoos which were, in his own country, indicative of his rank. In one corner, the musicians were playing. A professional trainer and his group of dancing Ebboes were performing for the guests. A bright flock of the little winged creatures was dipping and wheeling through the air in elaborate patterns and formations. But nobody deigned to pay much attention to them.

At the entrance of Zargal, the music abruptly ceased. A fiddler broke his bow, a flautist choked, and the others simply stopped short. The guests instinctively turned toward the door. For a moment no one spoke or moved. Then a woman screamed, and others echoed her. Many of the guests leaped to their feet, overturning glasses and chairs as they did so. Some of them headed for the exits, making their escape in the direction of the palace kitchens. The Ambassador was firing rapid commands in Strellian to the members of his entourage. The Ebboes went mad with fear and started swooping around the room in great, hysterical curves, whistling and shrieking as they went. Some became enmeshed in the crystal ropes of the chandeliers. Others, in their terror, flew violently at the mirrors on the walls, knocking themselves unconscious as they collided with the glass. The behavior of the Ebboes was matched by that of a number of the guests, who cowered, screaming, against the walls, or else sought refuge beneath the table.

Zargal remained in the doorway, staring wordlessly at his father. Duke Jalonzal sat rigidly and upright in his chair, hands clenched before him on the table. With eyes narrowed and nostrils slightly distended, he stared back at his son. The expression on his face was terrible.

"Will you not help me, father?" Zargal asked quietly.

The Duke took a long time to answer. He seemed to be struggling to collect himself. At last he spoke. "How dare you? How dare you come here?"

"I've come because I can no longer stand the life I've been leading. I've come because I need the help that you've refused me and because I'm no longer willing to continue living in prison."

The Duke's thin lips twisted. "You are becoming maudlin, sir," he observed. "Have you so little sense of dignity that you are willing to be seen in this condition? Is there none of me in you?"

"Enough of you in me, your Grace, that I refuse to spend the rest of my life hidden away in my chambers."

"You refuse!" The Duke's voice sounded like a steel trap snapping shut. "You will spend the rest of your life as I choose to command. But this is not the time or place to discuss the matter. You will return to your apartment immediately."

"Not until I've obtained your promise, your Grace, that you will have my condition investigated." Zargal spoke clearly and steadily enough, but in reality his thoughts were in a turmoil and he was burning with embarrassment. Everybody in the room was now watching him in fascination. Even the Ebboes had grown quiet.

"You dictate terms to me!" Jalonzal exclaimed. "To me! I have ordered you back to your room. You are dismissed, sir. Go."

"So eager to dismiss me, your Grace? It was only a short time ago you complained that I neglect official functions —and so I am here."

"Ah, you grow openly insolent," Duke Jalonzal answered contemptuously, "when you discover that your feeble bid for public sympathy has failed."

"Sympathy, your Grace, is not what I seek."

"In that case, why do you parade your deformities before the eyes of my guests in this disgusting manner? You are determined, no doubt, that the world shall know that the son of Duke Jalonzal is a pathetic grotesque."

"All I desire is a cure, nothing more. A cure—a normal life, freedom, air, and light. Surely, father, that's not too much to ask?"

The Duke cast an uneasy glance around him. "Let us not indulge in sentiment," he advised in a lower voice. "You have humiliated me enough as it is. I almost wonder if I shall be able to find it in my heart to forgive this outrage. You have disrupted a state banquet." Jalonzal deliberately unclenched his hands. "You have forced your way in here and exhibited yourself to the Court in an effort to embarrass and discredit me. Such calculated action against your Duke almost verges on treason. I am ashamed to call you my son, sir!"

Zargal looked down and for a moment regarded his enormous figure, clad only in blankets. "I can well believe it," he conceded dryly. "Nonetheless, your Grace, I *am* your son—and your only heir."

"Are you?" Jalonzal asked softly. "Are you?"

"If not for my sake, then for the sake of your city, you would do well to search for a cure for me."

Jaonzal slowly rose to his feet. "It is hardly your place," he pointed out frigidly, "to remind me of *my* duty to the city, when you have spent a lifetime evading your own. Nonetheless, there is something in what you say. I owe it to Szar to see to it that this question is settled once and for all. Therefore, I shall devote my attention to your plight— you may be certain of that. In the meantime, you will have the decency to remove yourself from our sight."

Zargal inclined his head and withdrew from the banqueting hall. As he went, he could hear his father apologizing to the Ambassador of Strell for the interruption.

Zargal made his way back to his own suite as quickly as he could and shut himself in again. For hours he sat alone, thinking about the unpleasant encounter and wondering what would happen next.

Around midnight, Flimm returned. The valet did not waste words. "You must flee the palace at once, my lord," he said. "I have just learned that the Duke plans to lock you up in the hole beneath the palace—for the rest of your life."

Zargal's face did not alter. It was almost as expressionless as Flimm's. "That comes as no surprise to either one of us, does it?" he asked. "How soon does he intend to do it?"

"The guards will come for you tonight, my lord," the valet replied.

"Guards. And what if I defend myself?"

"Then they will use force. Need I point out, my lord, that you would be hard put to fight back?" Flimm's eyes ran significantly around the chamber. "There is not enough room in here."

"In any case," Zargal observed, "they'd have no need to overpower me by force if I were determined to resist. They would find it easy to starve me into submission, would they not?"

"Only too easy, my lord."

"And then what? After my loving father has imprisoned me underground, what does he plan to tell people?"

"That your illness has caused you to run mad, and you are being restrained for your own protection."

"What about the succession of Szar? Am I not his only son?"

"He will adopt one of his nephews as his heir."

"Yes." Zargal nodded cynically. "No doubt he's thought of everything. He's always efficient."

"My lord, there is no time to waste. You must be away."

"Away?" Zargal laughed briefly. "I'm not sure I wouldn't rather stay. I'm probably strong enough now to pull the palace down around his ears."

"If you will permit me to say so, your lordship does not have the time to indulge in theatrics."

"If I succeed in escaping the palace, what's to prevent the Duke from having me pursued?"

"I believe," Flimm answered judiciously, "that you mistake him, my lord. His Grace your father is perhaps somewhat unfeeling, but not malicious. In this case, his only desire is to suppress the entire affair. If you leave, then it is doubtful that he will take any further action."

"And where do you suggest that I go?"

"As to that, is there actually any question in your lordship's mind?"

"I know. You think I should make my way to Obran and beg King Laza to remove his curse. It's not a pleasant prospect."

"Nor, I think, is it a pleasant prospect to spend the rest of your life in your present condition, imprisoned in a subterranean vault. But I am possibly hasty in assuming that your lordship will remain as you are indefinitely. It is far more probable that you will continue to grow."

"Oh, excellent, Flimm. You're most encouraging. What," Zargal asked, "if I go to the King and he refuses to help?"

"Then your situation will be no worse than it is now. And you will not," the valet added, "be languishing underground. But do not be too swift in judging King Laza—he is far from predictable."

"It seems that I have very little choice," Zargal decided. "I must go to Obran and confront this barbarous King. If all goes well, then he'll undo the harm he has done me. But if he will not—if he will not, then I shall find a way of striking back. I'll have that satisfaction, come what may." His face was somber and determined.

Flimm turned his anthracitic stare upon his expanded master. "I would counsel you to proceed with extreme caution," he advised. "In the land of my youth, there is a say-

ing amongst the peasants. 'True vengeance is a bargain.
False vengeance sells dearly.' Consider it, my lord."

"That's very colorful. What are they trying to say?"

"In the opinion of my countrymen, the successful re-
venger achieves his aim at no cost to himself. If he wreaks
vengeance, but loses his own life or freedom in the process,
then he has failed. My people are connoisseurs of vengeance."

"Really, Flimm? Who are your people? Where do you
come from, anyway?"

The valet bowed. "I choose," he answered gracefully, "to
regard myself as a citizen of the world. To be quite blunt,
your lordship," he continued, "it would be most unwise of
you to attempt any attack upon King Laza of Obran."

"I hope I won't need to." Zargal held up his hand, forestalling any reply that Flimm might have been about to
make. "You've told me I haven't much time. Very well
—take a sack and gather together whatever you think I
ought to bring with me."

Flimm obeyed. In the meantime, Zargal stripped all the
remaining covers off his bed and wrapped himself up in
them as best he could, seeking some protection from the
cold outdoor air, which he hadn't breathed in such a long
time.

Soon the sketchy preparations were completed. Zargal,
festooned with quilts and multicolored coverlets, resembled
some enormous scarecrow. Taking the sack that Flimm
handed him, he fastened it at his waist with a length of
cord and then he was ready to leave. "Is there a safe way
out?" he inquired.

"The guests are still in the banqueting hall," Flimm assured him. "Your lordship may proceed without fear." Together, they made their way through the quiet corridors
until at last they reached the nearest exit that led out into
the gardens in back of the palace. There Zargal paused.

"If your lordship will proceed in an easterly direction,
you will soon find yourself upon the open highway," Flimm
told him. "A journey of several days should bring you to
the borders of Obran. Upon reaching the border, you would
do well to take every possible precaution to ensure your
safety. I am informed that the region is inhospitable. It is
inhabited by ghosts, or winged reptiles, or tribes of krorks,

or possibly all three—reports vary. Once your lordship is past the borderlands, however, your journey should prove uneventful."

"I see." Zargal cast an unwilling glance off into the darkness and drew the quilts closer around himself. "Well—well, I suppose I'd best get started."

"The sooner the better, my lord."

"There's no way out of it, is there?"

"None, my lord."

"No. Well—good-bye, then, Flimm. I don't know if I'll ever be back again."

"Farewell. I wish your lordship good fortune."

Zargal bent very low to squeeze himself through the door. He departed from his ancestral home on his stomach.

CHAPTER VII

The banqueting hall was still lighted, and the music was still playing. The Duke's son paused to take a last look at the palace. It looked remote and foreign; already it was becoming difficult for him to believe that he had spent most of his life there. With a shrug, he turned away, and did not look back again. As quickly as possible, he made his way through the deserted gardens. When he came to the gate, he hesitated, automatically fumbling for the familiar key that once had hung around his neck. But now it was no longer there. After a moment's thought, he realized that it was a perfectly simple matter for him to leap over the palace wall. He did so, and found himself in one of the back alleys of Cornaszar.

The sleeping village spread out before him, but he was observing it from a new vantage. He now towered far above the thatched roofs of the cottages; only the steeple of the village church could come close to matching his height. Not a light was burning, and there were no signs of human activity. The moon, as white as a skull, and the bright stars in the clear sky were the only sources of illumination. Over the roofs of the houses, beyond the silent village, he could see the highway stretching out across the open fields, off into the darkness, toward the eastern mountains and Obran.

A sharp breeze knifed through the streets and stirred Zargal's quilts. The longer he stood still, he realized, the colder he would become. Reluctantly, he advanced through Cornaszar, making his way with exaggerated caution in order to avoid rousing the villagers. For the most part he was successful, and there were only a few minor mishaps. Once he inadvertently set his foot down on a rail fence that ran alongside the road and smashed the wood to kindling. Another time, a restless dog caught his scent and rushed out of its kennel, barking furiously, Zargal, fearing a repetition of his former humiliation, quickened his pace. But his fears were unnecessary, for the dog, when it beheld him, whimpered and slunk away, its tail between its legs.

Zargal breathed easier once he had left Cornaszar behind him. The road had taken him out of the village, and he was hurrying past meadows and rolling fields, now empty of their crops. His enormous strides ate up the distance, carrying him forward as swiftly as his favorite horse had done in the days before his transformation. He had traveled a long way when the faint gray light on the horizon before him signaled that the night was ending.

It was essential that he avoid being seen, and he wondered where he could conceal himself during the coming day. The region through which he was traveling was not thickly wooded, but the ground was hilly and uneven. Zargal headed away from the highway as the sky grew brighter and kept going until he came upon a hollow amongst the hills, wherein he might rest hidden from the eyes of chance travelers. He lay down at full length upon the frosted grass and composed himself for slumber.

Zargal slept all through the day. The sun had already gone down again when he awoke, refreshed but intolerably hungry. During the past several weeks he had learned to endure his own unnatural appetite, and he was able to go for some hours without eating; but his present hunger was more than he could stand. His first hope was that Flimm might have packed something for him to eat, but such was not the case. There had been no food left in his room at the time of his departure. Zargal examined the contents of his sack. The valet had provided him with a mixed collection of odds and ends: twenty-eight grinlings, a coil of rope, a couple of hooks and pulleys, flint and steel, a large hunting knife, several jeweled buttons torn from various garments, a gold snuffbox filled with the strange powder that Zargal had been carrying the night he'd visited the Peacock, a few linen handkerchiefs, and an illustrated quarto volume—*Surviving the Wilderness: Memoirs of a Gentleman Voyager*. There was nothing of any immediate use to him.

Zargal resignedly made his way back to the road. The evening was chilly, and his makeshift coverings did not provide adequate protection. His bare feet were freezing and sore, for he had reached the beginning of the Eastling Wolds, and the terrain was growing rougher.

As he approached the highway, instinct prompted Zargal to stop and crouch behind a hillock. It was well that he did so. A moment later a coach, drawn by four horses and hung with many lanterns, appeared on the road ahead. It drew nigh and rattled on into the night, heading toward Szar. Zargal knew then that it was not possible for him to continue along the highway. Even at night, there was too great a risk that he might be spotted by passing travelers.

Zargal wandered unhappily away into the wild woldlands. He was unable to think about anything other than food. His worries and the discomforts of coldness and sore feet faded away to nothing. All that remained was an intense longing for a large meal. He endeavored to satisfy his cravings by devouring quantities of the feathery weeds that grew throughout the Wolds, but his efforts were not successful. Experiments with various species of moss, gorse, and woldwidd were equally disappointing.

The ache in his stomach had increased dreadfully, and Zargal was starting to grow desperate, when he finally had a stroke of luck. He came upon a whole field of greshunki, the hardy bush that bloomed in the autumn and developed its soft seed pods in early winter. The Outcottagers of the Wolds were wont to gather the pods, dry them, and use them throughout the year to impart a characteristic flavor and texture to their ragouts and fricassees. The greshunki were covered with seed pods now, but within minutes Zargal had devoured the entire crop. It did not banish his hunger, but it helped.

As he continued across the rolling, darkened land, Zargal sometimes met with other windfalls. There were more fields of greshunki; there were outbuildings in which woldcock and venison had been hung to age; there were barns wherein grain had been stored; there was the occasional bin of blifilnuts, set aside for winter use. Once, when he ventured near a particularly isolated home, he discovered that some unwary Outcottager's wife had left her clean bed-sheets hanging outdoors overnight, no doubt in the hope of freezing them dry. Zargal appropriated a couple, tore them into strips, and wrapped them around his feet before going on his way. His reluctance to steal was, he discovered, more than offset by his reluctance to starve or to suffer frostbite.

He sped swiftly across the face of the Eastling Wolds. His progress was silent, and the hard earth bore no imprint of his foot. There was nothing more than a succession of despoiled barns and fields to mark his passing.

In a room in the palace of Szar, Duke Jalonzal sat alone. The chamber was hung with golden tapestries, and a great blaze was roaring away in the fireplace. A stack of papers sat unnoticed on the desk before him. Jalonzal was staring out the window toward the east. A light snow was falling—the first snow of the winter. The Duke's eyes were hooded, his expression enigmatic. There was a knock upon the door, and he turned his head. "Enter," he commanded, without inflection.

The heavy door swung open. Flimm paused a moment upon the threshold, then slid soundlessly into the room. "Your Grace." He bowed.

It was some time before Jalonzal replied. "I am informed," he remarked quite mildly, "that Lord Zargal has been missing for the past week and a half. Affairs of state have prevented me from granting the incident the attention that it perhaps deserves. The interests of Szar take precedence over my own personal misfortunes." Flimm inclined his head silently. "Nonetheless, I have summoned you here today to tell me all that you know of the affair."

"As your Grace wills. No doubt you will recall that Lord Zargal put in an appearance at the Ambassador's banquet eleven days ago?"

The Duke's face congealed. "I remember well," he replied.

"Upon leaving the banquet, Lord Zargal returned to his own apartment, where he remained for several hours. Shortly after midnight, he gathered together certain belongings and took his leave. Within a quarter of an hour of his lordship's departure, a party of armed guards arrived at his door and found him gone. The guards presumably informed your Grace of their discovery."

"Have you any idea," the Duke demanded, "what prompted Lord Zargal to leave so suddenly—and contrary to my express commands?"

"No idea whatever, your Grace."

Jalonzal examined the valet moodily. "Any effort on your part to deceive me would be a grave error in judgment," he observed.

Flimm returned his master's regard. "I am incapable of deceiving your Grace," he replied.

"I believe otherwise," the Duke said, "but I will not stoop to argue the matter with you. I am a busy man, a tired man—" Jalonzal breathed the suspicion of a sigh "—and there are innumerable demands upon my time. The troubles of an entire Dukedom rest solely upon my shoulders. I am the repository of my subjects' ills, and at times the burden oppresses me. But that is the price of greatness. That is my fate."

Flimm's face was as still as waxworks. "Uneasy lies the head that wears a coronet."

"Yes. You express yourself well, and very truly." Again the valet bowed. Jalonzal seemed to be in an unusually communicative mood. "Regard these reports," he commanded, indicating the sheaf of papers which lay upon the desk. "They represent problems to which the people look to me, their ruler, for solution. Like helpless children, they confide their fears and griefs in me. Blinded by the glory of my position, do they not forget that I, too, am a man?"

"Bear with your children, your Grace. Sometimes it is easy to forget."

"The reports," the Duke continued meditatively, "are extremely varied. Here is one from the farmers of the Sulla region, who complain of a plague of carnivorous insects—I fear there is little that even I can do about that. They will have to keep their windows shut. In the Myrd, a two-headed baby has been born and is growing with frightful rapidity. And not two hours away from Szar itself, the dead body of an elderly man—a former professor of the University— was discovered in a squash field. No one can say how he died. As you see, not even the most trivial of happenings within my realm are beneath my notice."

Flimm waited for the Duke to go on.

"It is the reports from the Eastling Wolds in which I take the greatest interest. The Outcottagers complain that they are afflicted with a Graschak. According to their local legends, a Graschak is a type of malevolent spirit—a super-natural being of immense size, much given to various forms of mischief, most notably the kidnapping of young women of marriageable age, the destruction of crops, and goat stealing. The Outcottagers have observed recent signs of Graschak activity."

"The Outcottagers, then, are suffering a shortage of goats?"

"Not to my knowledge. Their supply of marriageable maidens remains undiminished as well. Unfortunately, the same cannot be said of their crops or their winter stores. They have reported pillaging on a massive scale. Entire fields of greshunki have vanished overnight. Whole barns have been despoiled within the space of minutes. Smoke-houses have been raided, storage bins ransacked. The Out-cottagers insist that no gang of thieves could operate so efficiently and in such secrecy. The work is far beyond the power of a single man. Hence they conclude that a Gras-chak roams the Wolds. How could they know that it is beyond the power of any single man—save one?"

"Your Grace?"

Jalonzal eyed the valet coldly. "Surely it is unnecessary for me to call your attention to the fact that these reports have arisen within a few days of Lord Zargal's flight? I trust you would not dare to suggest that the connection is coincidental?"

Flimm was silent. He would not dare to suggest it.

"Particularly in view," the Duke went on distastefully, "of Lord Zargal's abnormal and repulsive gluttony. There can be no doubt of it. He is in the Wolds now and heading eastward. Perhaps he seeks sanctuary in Obran."

"If your Grace will pardon my presumption, do you intend to intercept him?"

"What, and acquaint all the world with my shame? I shall make no move to hinder his flight, which eases my dilemma, if not his own. He will leave the realm of Szar with far more ease than he may hope to re-enter it." With a gesture, Jalonzal dismissed Flimm. The Duke shoved the reports before him to one side, took a clean sheet of paper, and began filling the page with his handwriting. He was drafting an ordinance that would grant him the new title of Archduke.

Outside, the snow continued to fall.

In the Eastling Wolds, the sun had just set, and streaks of lackluster red still stained the sky. A winter wind was on the loose, sweeping across the stark landscape, shaking the gorse and woldwidd, chilling the snowy hills and hollows, and clawing at the roof of a house that squatted in a valley formed by two steep bluffs. The house was a typical Outcottage—small, low, thatch-roofed with very thick walls of sod. The event taking place within was far from typical, however. A meeting was in progress—and such a meeting was almost unheard of, for the Outcottagers were among the most unsociable folk in the world and, in fact, regarded each other with distinct hostility. To a man, they prized solitude and privacy. It was only a situation that they looked upon as a serious danger to all that could have induced them to come together.

Inside the one-room house, some sixty or so men were gathered. Some sat on the floor, others were standing against the walls. They were keeping as widely separated as possible, but there was not much space, and they were crowded together in a way that outraged the sensibilities of each and every one of them. The lady of the house was walking to and fro, grudgingly handing out small portions of smetch—a kind of liquor distilled from fermented greshunk pods—which were just as grudgingly received. Firelight played red upon dozens of unsmiling faces. After a time, the owner of the cottage stepped to the hearth and began to speak. His choice of words revealed that he was unaccustomed to public speaking. His manner showed that he didn't enjoy it.

"Well," the tall Outcottager said without preamble, "a stony field is all in a bad day's plowing. Neighbors, I don't like this no better than you do. But least said, soonest done with."

"Then quit jawin', Wilpp, and get on with it," one of his guests muttered.

"You got any complaints, then you be welcome to get out o' my home. There's the door," Wilpp fired back promptly. "Neighbors, you all do know why we be here. We got to band together and decide what must be done, for we do have a Graschak upon the Wolds!"

" 'Ee don't know that, Wilpp," one of the rustics spoke up. " 'Ee always be running off half-cocked. 'Ee got to stop and consider things."

"Oh, aye, and if we did stop to consider things like 'ee do, Kreenly, we'd all be a-covered with moss by now!" Suppressed snickers greeted this sally, for all the men present were far too disgruntled to produce real laughter. "Everybody here do know that we have a Graschak!"

"Aye, that we do! There's hardly a man here who's not lost his greshunk crop. What we'll do for smetch this winter I do not know," an Outcottager named Deeth remarked.

"The way your woman brews smetch, that be a small loss," Kreenly answered.

"I've had all of this that I can stand," Deeth snarled. "I'm a-leavin'." He stalked to the door, flung it open, took deep breaths of the fresh air, and hurried away over the Wolds. The others regarded the open door with obvious longing, so Wilpp wisely shut it.

"We got business to decide before anyone else leaves," Wilpp insisted. "Now, do all agree that we do have a Graschak?"

But it was beyond the power of the Outcottagers to agree on anything so quickly, and a heated argument ensued, during the course of which several more men departed. The cautious Kreenly maintained his opinion that the existence of a marauding Graschak had not been proved, and a number of the others attempted to convince him.

Wilpp cast an eye of profound dislike upon his opponents and silently wished himself a thousand miles away. "If there be no Graschak, then who lifted the carcass of

venison out of my barn?" he demanded with an air of dole-
ful triumph.

"And what were the great shadow, like the figure of a
man, but bigger nor any man, that my woman saw a-passin'
over the Wolds, under the moon?"

"Your woman's got maggots in her brain. And so do
'ee."

" 'Ee be a fine one to talk—can't cure a decent side o'
bacon to save your soul!"

"It's got our crops. After that, 'twill be the goats. Then
the young maids."

"Dreams! Mullytwaddle!"

"The young girls next. 'Ee mark my words."

It was never an easy thing for the Outcottagers to endure
one another. One of them, a pleasant-faced lad in his teens,
sat near the fire and listened closely to the dispute. He said
nothing, but occasionally jotted down notes in a small
journal.

Wilpp held up his hand for attention, and he got it.
"Enough of this palaver, neighbors! Enough of words!" he
implored, expressing a sentiment with which they were all
in hearty agreement. " 'Tis action called for now! What's
to be done?"

For a moment there was silence, and the lad by the fire
looked around eagerly. Then one of the oldest of the Outcottagers, a white-bearded rustic named Stonn, spoke up.
He was bent and wrinkled, but alert and warlike yet.

"There ain't been a Graschak upon the Wolds in nigh on
seventy years," he announced, seeming to direct his gaze
straight through the cottage walls, toward scenes that nobody else could see. "They said then that it had come down
out o' the hills, from over Obran way, but no one could be
certain o' the truth o' that. Sure it was, though, that a
Graschak walked at night. And sure it was, too, that 'twas
a creature formed for mischief. No man's crops were safe.
And as for the goats—why, they did vanish like candied
berries off a plate at holiday time! All over the Wolds, the
Graschak left its pickin's—the hair and horns and hoofs of
our goats. Not a man of us dared to lift a finger, nor
wouldn't have, neither, had the creature not laid hands
upon our women. Aye—neighbor Woonly lost his youngest
girl, and Stroop's daughter vanished as well. So, too, did

Fleddan's girl, but she was found a-wanderin' upon Three Fingers Ridge a couple days later. She wasn't much good for anything after that, though." Stonn paused to take a good swig of smetch before continuing. The lad on the floor by the hearth was scribbling notes feverishly.

"Those among us with the hearts o' men," Stonn went on, "vowed vengeance upon the Graschak. We did gather together to hunt it down in the dead o' night, when we knew it was abroad. Those creatures o' the night, as you do know, cannot abide the sight o' fire—and so we judged that 'twas fire would do our business for us! On a cold winter's night—colder and darker nor this one be—we did venture forth over the Wolds in search o' the Graschak, armed wi' naught but torches. They were men in those days!"

The old Outcottager held his audience spellbound. He was displaying a flair for drama most unusual among his normally laconic people.

"We knew the creature to be somewhere out in the dark," Stonn continued, "so we spread out, a-keepin' each other in sight by the light o' the torches. Miles we did go afore we caught sight o' that hulking shape. Then we circled around it, a-comin' closer and closer with our fires! The Graschak tried to break through—a snarlin' and roarin', it tried to charge our line, but it did fear the light. Closer and closer we come, and the snarls grew more fearful, and the roars more dreadful, until we thought our ears would crack! When we were so close that the light was a-playin' full on its great eyes and sharp fangs—a horrible sight it was!— it gave a sort of a scream and leaped straight ahead, a-tryin' to break away. But 'twere too late. In a moment the creature was a-blazin' itself, for they do burn like dried faggots. It took but a few moments more afore the Graschak burned away to ashes—but during that time he danced, and twitched, and shrieked, so as I do recall it to this day, though I was but a lad at the time. Aye, in those days we were men! Can the lot of you say the same?"

Stonn had done a first-rate job of unifying the Outcottagers, whose differences were forgotten in the common rush of blood-lust that animated the entire group. Even cautious Kreenly was suffused with enthusiasm. "Neighbors, we must fight to protect our homes!" he cried out, leaping to his feet. "Now be the time to strike! Take torches, every man o' you! We'll hunt him down and burn him—that we will!"

For once, the Outcottagers were in agreement. Excited, aroused, and delighted to have settled upon a definite course of action, they crowded to the door. With wild shouts, they exploded from the house into the cold outer air.

For a moment the young note-taker remained where he was, journal and pen in hand. Though he was undoubtedly excited, the expression on his face indicated that his thoughts were far different from those of his neighbors. Still clutching his notes, he dashed out after the others.

CHAPTER VIII

⁓

Zargal sat alone in a field in the moonlight, quietly stripping the pods off every greshunk bush in sight, as he pondered the question of footprints. For the past couple of nights, the ground had been lightly covered with snow, and he had been leaving a trail of immense, blurred footprints across the Wolds. Zargal was uneasy, but could think of no solution to the problem. His depression grew yet deeper as he silently observed, for the thousandth time, how cold he was, how hungry, and how much he loathed greshunki.

The Duke's son raised his head and gazed toward the east, straining his eyes for some glimpse of the mountains of Obran. Obran's border was not far away, but the peaks were shrouded in mist and could not be distinguished. No horizon was visible in the east; sky, stars, and earth merged into the fog. Few citizens of Szar could say what lay beyond, for excursions to the neighboring land were rare. Obran did not extend a welcome to visitors, and the borderlands were noted, as Flimm had pointed out, for their inhospitality. Zargal glanced idly to his left, to his right, and down at the ground. He ate another few pods—hungry as he was, he didn't relish them—and looked up again. This time he caught his breath sharply and stared.

Far away—miles away, he judged—a line of tiny lights, like a procession of fireflies, glimmered through the dark. Zargal narrowed his eyes and leaned forward, trying to get a better look, but he could see the distant points of light and nothing more. There was no telling what they were, or what their source might be. He sat quite still for a while, watching the lights as they inched forward in formation over the hills and wondering what it meant. Zargal was not alarmed—there seemed to be no cause for that—but the sight of something so much out of the ordinary made him uncomfortable. He bolted the last of the greshunki and rose to his feet.

The coverlets in which he was so inadequately swathed no longer concealed his wrists or lower legs. He was, he noted grimly, still growing. The strips of bed linen that protected his feet were dank and frigid. A bristly stubble covered his chin, and his nose dripped in the cold.

Muttering a heartfelt curse upon the head of King Laza of Obran, he started off again in the direction of his enemy's domain. Periodically, he glanced across the Wolds at the moving line of lights. They seemed to be maintaining a course roughly parallel to his own.

As time went on, Zargal began to have the feeling that he was being followed. The string of lights which extended along the horizon on his left side was getting longer. But quite aside from that, there seemed to be something—or somebody—not far behind him. Once or twice he stopped suddenly and swung around in his tracks, but saw no one.

Distinctly nervous now, Zargal quickened his pace, hoping to win past the unfriendly region. He did not run, but his strides were so long and so rapid that a human being of normal size would have had to run to keep up with him. Then, very suddenly, he stopped and turned again. This time he thought he caught a glimpse of something moving; a swift shadow slipped across his field of vision for an instant, before disappearing amongst the hillocks. More of the orange lights had appeared upon the Wolds behind him, and they were drawing nearer, a line of them bending across the landscape in a great horseshoe shape. The sight was uncanny.

Zargal broke into a run, and soon the curving band of lights had receded until he was just barely able to see it.

He had easily outdistanced all possible pursuers. The ghostly sound of footsteps no longer troubled him. He was a little winded, and he sat down, back against a hillock. Zargal breathed deeply and regarded the footprints that blemished the snow behind him. A frown marked his forehead with creases the size of small gullies. There was no help for it. If someone were indeed following him, then his trail was impossible to disguise.

Perhaps, he decided, his imagination had been playing tricks on him. After all, if his father had commanded his capture, then surely his pursuers would have consisted of at least a brigade of cavalry, well-armed, and easily recognizable by their uniforms, insignia, and regimental colors. It would not be Jalonzal's way to send forth some shadowy spy to carry out the mission. Zargal passed on to a detailed analysis of his father's actions, habits, and character, while his expression grew blacker than ever.

What finally roused him from his unpleasant reverie was a persistent sound. He listened intently. From somewhere nearby, he could just detect a faint scratching noise. The sound came from behind a clump of bushes. Zargal stood up, took two or three swift steps forward, and yanked the bushes apart, exposing his pursuer to view.

Behind the bushes crouched a youth with mouth agape and wide open light eyes. A snub nose and round cheeks gave him an agreeable, boyish countenance. It was hard to tell by moonlight, but his mussy hair might have been red. His simple costume was that of an Outcottager. An open journal lay on the ground beside him, with ink from an overturned bottle spilling across its pages. The boy still grasped a quill in his slender, long-fingered hand as he sat there, frozen, staring at Zargal. The scratching noise which had alerted the Duke's son had evidently been nothing more than the sound of pen on paper.

"Who are you?" Zargal snapped, startled at the harshness of his voice. It had been days since he'd spoken aloud at all. "What are you doing here? Who sent you?"

The boy made a couple of unsuccessful attempts to answer, and finally managed to whisper, " 'Ee can speak!" He was trembling in fear, and yet his eyes glowed with a strange exultation. " 'Ee can speak, just like a mortal man."

"I asked you who you are. Answer me!"

" 'Ee look like a man, too, only great and huge. They be wrong, then—there be no fangs, nor red eyes like fire, nor yet a tail. They all be wrong. Old Stonn be woolly-headed!"

"What are you babbling about? Tail? Fangs? Who set you upon my trail, boy?" Zargal demanded menacingly. "Speak up, or you'll regret it."

"Nay, I regret nothing," the boy returned with a certain air of exalted zeal. " 'Tis worth my death to behold the Graschak, to see for myself what it be."

Zargal was beginning to believe that the strange boy was not quite right in the head, perhaps a wandering maniac. But the lad looked like any other normal, healthy young Outcottager. "Who are you?" Zargal repeated more gently.

"Rothadd be my name," the lad answered. "Rothadd, Rotha's son."

"Your father, I presume, is one of the local farmers?"

"Nay, not just a farmer," Rothadd returned with pride, "but an Outcottager, a true Outcottager o' the Wolds! He looks to himself, he does, and sees no man from one end o' the year to t'other!"

"Well, Rothadd, did your father tell you to follow me?"

"Him? Oh, nay! What do 'ee do," Rothadd inquired unexpectedly, "with the young maids when 'ee do steal 'em away?"

"Why, I've never carried off a wench who wasn't willing—" Zargal broke off, recollecting himself. "Who told you about that?"

"Do 'ee eat 'em, like the goats?" Rothadd persisted. "Or do 'ee kill 'em because 'ee do hate 'em?"

"Kill them? You must be a loony, boy!" Zargal exclaimed. "What do you take me for?"

"I know 'ee for the Graschak! The Graschak right enough, but more like a man nor anyone ever reckoned. Oh, if only they could know!"

"What—a Graschak? Is that the word?"

"Aye, for certain. Why, do 'ee have another name for yourself? What is it?"

"What is a Graschak?" Zargal demanded, beginning to lose his temper again. "Explain yourself!"

"Graschak be the Outcottager name for creatures such as 'ee be," Rothadd replied obligingly. "Evil spirits, huge and tall, that do roam the Wolds, a-killin' the crops and a-carryin' off the young maids and the goats. And now I've seen with my own eyes!"

"That is what you and your people believe me to be?"

" 'Tis proved, now that I've laid eyes on 'ee! Good as dead I be, for 'tis certain 'ee must kill me—but no matter, since I know what I do know!" Rothadd lifted his chin with the triumph of the victorious quester.

"You followed the footprints I left in the snow?" Zargal asked with a mixture of frustration and amusement.

"Aye."

"You risked your life, then, as you believed, because you desired to see this Graschak?"

"Aye—and glad of it!"

"Then you have a disappointment in store," Zargal informed him. "I am no evil spirit, no Graschak—I'm as human as you are."

Rothadd's figure stiffened, and he shook his head in a gesture of total disbelief. "That ben't so," he insisted. "There be no mortal man the like o' 'ee upon the face of all the earth. Say what 'ee will, but 'tis certain 'ee be a Graschak! Why do 'ee deny what's plain to see?" Rothadd continued to stare up at Zargal, observing with fascination the fernlike fronds of eyelashes, the huge, dirt-caked fingernails, under which a number of small plants, sustained in the winter temperatures by the warmth of his body, had taken root, the ears as large as platters, and the vast, melancholy eyes.

Zargal could feel himself starting to redden. "You're wrong," he returned brusquely. "I am Lord Zargal of Szar, and entirely human."

" 'Ee be not a mullyin' me?" Rothadd asked.

"No. My unfortunate condition is the result of a magician's malice, nothing more."

"Then 'ee be naught but a man, truly?" Rothadd was beginning to droop.

"Truly. What you see before you is the work of King Laza of Obran."

At the mention of Laza's name, Rothadd raised his eyes. "King Laza the Enchanter?" he inquired. Zargal nodded, and Rothadd brightened noticeably. "There be magic in it, then?" he asked hopefully. " 'Tis true sorcery has made a monster of 'ee?"

Zargal frowned. "Must you use that expression?"

"Oh, aye, that must pain 'ee," Rothadd replied contritely. "But," he continued, unable to control his glee, " 'tis the work of a master magician, it is, here upon our own Wolds, and 'tis Rothadd alone has seen! Ah, this is a tale will catch Hincmar's ear!"

"Hincmar? Who is that?"

"My master."

"Did he tell you to follow me?"

"He knows naught of it."

"You are this man's servant?"

"Nay," Rothadd responded indignantly. "I be no man's servant!"

"His apprentice, then?"

"Well—so I be, of sorts," Rothadd answered obscurely. "Of sorts. A hard man he be, and solitary as an Outcottager, though he ben't a native to the Wolds. I would be apprenticed to him, but he won't give me a plain aye or nay."

"I see," Zargal said, although he didn't. "And what craft do you wish to learn?"

"Magic! Aye, Hincmar has the power, for all that he do live alone upon the Wolds like one of us. He can learn me the way of it, if he will. A hard man he be, though."

"Why don't you choose another master, then?" Zargal asked, not unkindly. He observed, without paying any particular heed, that the lights he'd noticed earlier were drawing nearer again.

"That I will not!" Rothadd exclaimed. "Hincmar be the only true sorcerer hereabouts, and he be the master I must have, or none. No one else can teach me. Why," he went on impetuously, "when I was a lad, Sym the peddler would come to our door. Sym was a man knew how to tell a tale, right enough, and 'twas from him that I first did learn o' the great sorcerers and vowed that I'd be one, too."

"You?" Zargal couldn't repress a smile.

"Why should I not? There's no cause to start a-laughin'!" Rothadd exploded.

"It's a great ambition," Zargal conceded, "but surely—surely it demands a certain amount of training and education, and it hardly seems likely that a country lad such as yourself—"

"Education! Aye, there's the rub!" Rothadd interrupted. "I knew it well, I'd never amount to a heap o' kindling without it! But there was naught that I could do, for who upon the Wolds was there to teach me? Then—two years ago, it was—Hincmar came to live by himself, far from other folk. And he was as great a magician as any of 'em ever hatched."

"Is he indeed?" Zargal was paying much closer attention now, as the possibilities of the situation revealed themselves to him. "He could, I trust, make a spell—or break one?"

"Oh, to be sure," Rothadd answered carelessly. "So I sought him out in his own cottage, but he weren't easy to see—a hard man he be. First I had to climb the wall he'd set up about the house. Then I swam across the moat. Then I pushed through the thorn hedge and made my way through the maze. After I'd won past the dogs, I came to his very door and rapped upon it loud, but he wouldn't let me in—almost an Outcottager he be. I wouldn't be put off by trifles, though," the boy continued, "and so I stayed there, on his doorstep, night and day. Every few hours or so, I did rap upon his door or window so he'd know I'd not gone away. Each evening I did shout down his chimney, just to let him know I was still there. After that, I started pitching messages down his chimney, and under his door, but he never would answer. 'Twas plain he was a-comin' around, though, for he no longer jumped up and dropped things when he did spy my face at his window, the way he had at first. At last," Rothadd went on, "in the middle of the second week, I was hunched up in the rain, a-talkin' to him through the door, for I knowed he could hear me—and he did change his mind, of a sudden like, and drew the bolt. 'Enter, boy,' he said, 'and we shall see what can be done with you.' "

"That sounds a bit sinister," Zargal remarked.

"Oh, nay—he meant nothing by it, 'twas just his way o' talkin'," Rothadd replied. "He ben't really one of us. Truth to tell, he do sound more like 'ee. But he looked me up and he looked me down, and he didn't seem much taken with what he saw until I took my hands out o' my pockets, for it didn't seem respectful to keep 'em there, and he said, 'A magician's hand—the classic shape. Perhaps there's something here after all.' Then he went on and told me that he might take me as his apprentice and he might not—I'd have to prove to him first that I do have the gift for it, else 'twouldn't be worth his care to teach me. A hard man he be."

"How were you supposed to prove that you have the gift?"

"That be just what I wanted to know! And when I did ask him, he smiled and said, 'I shall give you a simple spell, one to help your crops to grow. If there's an ounce of talent in you, you'll find a way to use it.' So he did hand me a mort o' gibberish, all writ down on paper, and I said, 'It don't make sense, I can't read it.' And he said back, 'Until you do, you'll be no apprentice of mine!' And that's how things have stood ever since," Rothadd concluded despondently. "He do let me run his errands for 'im, but he'll not teach me his art, no true magic, though I pine to death for it!"

"Where is this spell that the magician gave you?" Zargal inquired curiously.

"Here it be." Rothadd exhibited a sheet of parchment, torn and heavily creased. "I've tried and tried, but I can't make sense of it." Neither could Zargal. The sheet was covered with incomprehensible symbols, unreadable sentences, and a couple of confusing diagrams.

"Do you believe that this man Hincmar could restore me to my normal size?" Zargal asked.

"That he could, no doubt—if he be willing."

Zargal's first impulse was to command Rothadd to lead him to the magician, but of late he had begun to learn the value of self-restraint. "Will you take me to him?" he asked courteously.

Rothadd passed a doubtful hand across the back of his neck, which had grown sore from being bent backward during the conversation. "He wouldn't like me to bring a stranger," the boy replied. "He do keep himself to himself and meddles with no man."

"That may be, but this is a rather unusual case," Zargal pointed out dryly.

"Oh, aye! 'Tis grand!" Rothadd exclaimed, and broke off in confusion at the expression on the tremendous face looming above him. "I mean—anyone would want to look at 'ee. 'Tis a rare sight—" The boy was aware that he was making matters worse. "I be a-willin' to try," he concluded.

"Thank you. In what direction does his cottage lie?"

" 'Tis naught but a few miles yonder—" Rothadd's jaw dropped as he caught sight of the approaching clusters of lights.

"Then it shouldn't take long to get there. What are you staring at?" Zargal asked, following Rothadd's gaze. "Those lights? What are they, do you know?"

"Aye," Rothadd whispered. "The brain of a backward goat I do have! All this time a-jawin' here, when they be a-comin' for 'ee!"

"What are you talking about? What are those lights?"

" 'Tis the Outcottagers—a fair herd of 'em, hot upon the trail o' the Graschak. Stonn has roused 'em, and they be out for blood! 'Tis the light o' their torches 'ee do see!"

"You mean those people are looking for me? Why?"

"They think 'ee be the Graschak. After all, a lot of our crops and goods be a-missin' o' late," Rothadd reminded him delicately.

"Unavoidable." Zargal shrugged. "But I'm willing to pay for what I took."

"Ah, will 'ee, now? Well, there be some things that your gold be no cure for!"

"Then—then I suppose I must apologize," Zargal said with an effort. "Yes—that's fair. I'll do it."

"Nay, 'ee won't. Would 'ee like to know why?"

"Because it would be too demeaning?"

"Nay—because 'ee won't have the chance! I tell 'ee, man, they do take 'ee for the Graschak. Once they have 'ee, they never will stop to have a chat. Forward will come the torches, and in a trice, they'll have 'ee blazing away like a dried-out stick o' woldwidd!"

"Nonsense!" Zargal snapped. "They'll realize that I'm no Graschak as soon as they get one good look at me."

"Did *I?*"

"I see your point."

The vengeful Outcottagers were drawing ever nearer. The sound of shouting was carried on the winter wind to the ears of Zargal, who was beginning to wish he'd never been born. For a moment he considered the possibility of standing his ground and confronting his pursuers. Then he looked at the scores of torchlights dotted across the Wolds and was forced to dismiss the idea.

"Would your friend the magician be able to help?" he asked wearily, noting that his path eastward had already been cut off.

"Aye, I'll bring 'ee to Hincmar. He'll see what stuff I be made of when I do bring to him a true giant. 'Tis not just any Outcottager's son has the wit to discover a giant." Rothadd ignored the expression of disgust that passed over Zargal's features. "Nay—giants ben't a garden crop. Follow me, then."

After stowing his notes and pen away in his pocket, he set out over the rolling hills at a brisk trot, with Zargal at his side.

CHAPTER IX

Rothadd proved to be a lively companion. During the hike to Hincmar's cottage, he never once stopped talking, and Zargal was treated to descriptions of the young Outcottager's life history from the age of three onward. Zargal also acquired, in that short time, a working knowledge of the care and cultivation of the greshunk shrub, and familiarity with the breeding habits of the native Eastling goats. Young Rothadd was anything but a typical Outcottager, being far more gregarious and communicative than most. His love of books, and his passionate interest in magic, also set him apart. He seemed hardly aware, as he trotted along dispensing advice and confidences, that the being who stalked silently at his side was not only a giant, but heir to the Dukedom of Szar as well. If he remembered at all, then it simply made no impression on him.

Zargal found this treatment refreshing. It had been a long time since anyone had actually spoken to him, and it came as a surprise to realize how lonely he had been of late. The Duke's son would have been feeling almost cheerful, had he not noticed that the distance between himself and the torch-bearing Outcottagers seemed to be lessening all the time. "They're catching up," he observed morosely.

Rothadd broke off in the middle of his discourse. "Aye," he agreed with a troubled expression. "There be no mystery about it. They've spied the footprints at last, and they do trail 'ee quicker now."

Zargal suppressed a curse. "How far is it to the cottage?" he demanded.

"It ben't far off," Rothadd encouraged. "Look, 'ee. Yonder."

Zargal looked. In front of him the Wolds stretched onward—rolling hills, naked rocks, skeletal vegetation murdered by the winter, white snow, and a white moon. About half a mile away lay a dark area that looked like a black hole in the pallid landscape.

"There it be," Rothadd declared, pointing. "The wall about Hincmar's house—all o' black granite it be. And how do 'ee get black granite upon the Wolds, where all the granite be gray, I ask 'ee?"

"Paint?" Zargal inquired unworthily.

Rothadd ignored the poor-spirited suggestion. "Magic!" he declared triumphantly. "Hincmar can turn a wall o' sod into one o' granite if he choose. There ben't no end to what he can do! Oh, 'tis a wonderful thing to be a sorcerer!"

"Personally, I'm not very fond of them," Zargal said, thinking of King Laza.

The Outcottagers were starting to close in. The horseshoe of lights was beginning to tighten like a noose. Those among the hunters who were following Zargal's footprints were able to advance with alarming speed. Their voices were clearly audible now, shouting encouragement to one another and hurling threats at the Graschak.

Zargal and Rothadd hurried across the remaining stretch of woldlands that separated them from Hincmar's dwelling. As they passed over the rim of one of the steeper of the hills, a change in the quality of the shouts arising behind them served to inform the fugitives that Zargal had been spotted.

The gate in the great stone wall was locked against them, but Rothadd possessed a key. "He's given me leave to come to him this night," the boy explained, "else we wouldn't get in so easy." The door swung open, and the two of them ducked inside, then shut it again. Rothadd drew the bolt, and Zargal pushed the massive bar into place.

The moat was quiet, dark, and broad. A small boat was moored at the near shore. Rothadd was able to paddle across to the other side, but Zargal had to wade. The water was tremendously deep—at times it came all the way up to his neck—and very cold. Zargal was in a thoroughly uncomfortable state when he reached the far shore, and stood dripping and shivering as he waited for Rothadd to join him. His quilts hung in icy, sodden folds. A puddle was fast forming at his feet.

Ahead of them lay the thorn hedge and the maze. Rothadd was able to thread his way among the hostile branches with the adroitness born of much practice. For once, Zargal's great height stood him in good stead, for he could simply step over the entire barrier. Similarly, as he looked down upon the maze from above, he was easily able to pick out the correct path.

Beyond the maze, the ground had been cleared. In the middle of the clearing stood the house of Hincmar. It was only a simple cottage with walls of sod, a thatched roof, one wooden door, and two windows. One of these windows showed a light. Wisps of smoke were drifting out of the chimney. Several huge dogs roamed the clearing and bounded forward with ferocious snarls. They subsided, however, upon recognizing Rothadd, with whom they were obviously on friendly terms. While Rothadd was busy with the dogs, Zargal approached the cottage and rapped upon the door.

"Rothadd, is that you?" came a voice from within.

"No, it is not," Zargal replied. "But he's here with me."

A long silence greeted this announcement. At last the voice spoke again. "Rothadd, have you dared to bring a stranger to my house?" The accent was that of an aristocrat of Szar. The tone was one of icy outrage.

Rothadd presented himself at the door at once. "Aye, that I have," he answered resolutely. " 'Ee'll see why when 'ee do open the door."

"I have no intention of opening the door," the angry sorcerer returned. "I have told you time and again that you must never bring anyone with you when you come here. Why you have disregarded this order I cannot guess, but I assure you, it is a breach of faith that I shall not dismiss lightly. Now begone."

"Nay, there ben't no cause to boil up," Rothadd replied. "It ben't no breach o' faith—"

"Indeed not," Zargal interjected. "I asked him to bring me here to you in the hope that—"

"I will exchange no words with you, sir," Hincmar informed Zargal through the closed door. "You are uninvited and unwelcome here. I consider you a trespasser, whoever you may be. Please go."

Zargal's eyebrows drew together and he glowered contemptuously at the cottage. "With pleasure," he answered. "It's clear that you lack the power to help me." Turning to Rothadd, he added, "There's no purpose in attempting to converse with this boorish hermit. But you have tried to help me, and I shall not forget. Good-bye, Rothadd."

" 'Ee can't go!" Rothadd cried. "Don't forget—Stonn and the others be outside the wall, athirstin' for your blood."

"I'll deal with them," Zargal replied ominously.

"Wait! Let me talk to him for 'ee!" Rothadd knelt near the keyhole. Zargal watched, arms folded. "Hincmar—'ee did tell me to go to the gathering o' the Outcottagers to see what was what. Ben't that so?"

"What of it?" Hincmar returned coldly through the closed door.

"They did come together to hunt down the Graschak."

"Well?"

"But he be here!" Rothadd announced. "The Graschak, his own self! I brought him here, I did, to your very door! But it ben't no true Graschak, mind 'ee; 'tis a mortal man that do need your help. Will 'ee see for yourself now?"

"This is an absurd tale," Hincmar said. "And I have no desire to meet strangers of any description, much less this one. Now take him away. And if you ever bring anyone here again, I may not greet you with such forbearance."

Zargal once more turned to go, and Rothadd lost his self-control entirely. Leaping to his feet, he began pounding on the door with all his strength, at the same time screaming, " 'Ee must come out! The Outcottagers are nigh, and 'tis sure that blood will be spilled if 'ee don't!"

"That is no business of mine," Hincmar answered. "Go away, and leave me in peace!"

Zargal watched in fascination as Rothadd started kicking the door, which shook and creaked beneath the on-slaught. " 'Ee can't turn us away!" he cried. " 'Tis cruel!" He dealt the door another blow. " 'Ee must come out!"

Hincmar complied. He flung the door open and rushed furiously from his cottage. "Stop that!" the sorcerer com-manded, his voice shaky with rage. "Stop that at once! You go too far, boy! You've tried my patience once too often! If you think that I'm willing to tolerate this outrage, then you've either overestimated yourself or underestimated me—"

Then he broke off in mid-sentence as he caught sight of Zargal for the first time. Sorcerer and giant stared at each other in silence for a couple of moments. Hincmar was a man of middle years. Although he was attired in the sturdy and practical garments of an Outcottager, his features, speech, and bearing bespoke experience of the Court of Szar. He was tall, somewhat gaunt, and straight of spine. A thick, gray-streaked beard did not succeed in disguising a rather bitter expression. His hands, long and flexible, re-sembled Rothadd's. "What is this?" Hincmar asked, his anger replaced by interest. His shadowed eyes had come alive. "What have we here?"

" 'Tis the Graschak!" Rothadd declared with pride. " 'Tis the Graschak, the terror o' the Wolds, that I, Rothadd, Rotha's son, do bring 'ee!"

"How many times must I tell you, Rotha's son, that I am not a Graschak?" Zargal snarled. "Will no one believe me?"

"Oh, I believe you," Hincmar said. "The only surviving Graschak in the world lies hidden in the mountains nearby, and knows better than to show his face upon the Eastling Wolds. You are no Graschak, but the question remains—who, or what, are you?"

"A giant he be," Rothadd said. "A mortal man become a giant!"

"This time he has it right," Zargal said. "In fact, he ex-plains it well—a mortal man become a giant."

"A mortal man from the city of Szar, I presume," guessed Hincmar, who was still inspecting his visitor.

"Yes," Zargal replied. "I am Lord Zargal, son of Duke Jalonzal."

"Indeed?" Hincmar asked, his expression growing more

and more intrigued. "I am not unaware of happenings in the world, even here. The news was given out that the Duke's son was dangerously ill. It was later reported that he had departed from Szar under mysterious circumstances."

"That is my father's explanation, but it isn't entirely true."

"That does not surprise me."

"Why—what do you know of Duke Jalonzal?" Zargal asked.

"A great deal more than you might imagine. Proceed with your explanation."

"Very well. When my condition became a serious embarrassment to my father, he issued orders that I be confined permanently in a subterranean vault. Had it not been for the timely warning of my valet, the sentence would have been carried out. As it was, I had only enough time to make my escape."

Hincmar nodded. "Yes—that sounds like the Duke. But it does not explain how your transformation came about in the first place."

Zargal stirred uncomfortably and wrung the excess water out of one of his quilts before answering. "A magician's work. I gave offense to the wrong party. This is the result."

"A master—a master of his art!" Hincmar explained. "He has done a superb job!"

"I'm glad you like it," Zargal said bitterly.

"All question of personal inconvenience aside, Lord Zargal, you must admit this is a stupendous accomplishment!"

"Stupendous is the very word."

In his enthusiasm, Hincmar seemed to have forgotten his normal aversion to humanity. "I am lost in admiration! But I must know—who is the artist? Who has done this thing?"

"It was King Laza of Obran."

"Ah, I should have guessed," the sorcerer said. "He is even greater than I thought him. The man is a genius."

"You admire him—for doing this to me?" Zargal asked.

"I regret your misfortune, my lord, but I am forced to esteem his skill. Moreover, there must have been some reason for his action."

"Well—there's no point in going into that now," Zargal said.

"No? Just as you wish. But you are luckier than you know, young man. Had you been transformed by a lesser man, the results could have been dreadful."

"The results *are* dreadful!"

"Not at all. Such a vast increase in size as you have undergone is usually accompanied by the most horrible deformity, a result of the failure of the bodily parts to enlarge at the same rate of speed. There is normally a certain degree of malformation as well. But neither of these things has happened to you. You have grown in stature, but remain unchanged in all other respects. That is due to the exquisite skill and control of King Laza. You ought to be grateful."

"Grateful? *Grateful?*"

"Certainly. Your situation could be infinitely worse than it is. If you remain here in the wilderness, far from the noisome air of the ducal Court, in time you may learn the art of deriving the greatest satisfaction from the smallest benefits."

Zargal was beyond speech. But Rothadd, eyes shining, murmured raptly, "Magic!"

"Come, come, Lord Zargal," Hincmar advised. "Be of good cheer. You could make a place for yourself upon these Wolds, far from all taint of civilization. You'd find that it would cleanse your heart and strengthen your spirit to make a home like this one, in a place where no man comes—" Hincmar was interrupted by a loud crashing noise. There was silence for a second, and then came a tremendous volley of knocks and bangs. The sorcerer started nervously. "What was that?" he asked.

"It be the Outcottagers," Rothadd explained. "They do follow hard upon the trail o' the Graschak. When they catch him, they mean to set him alight!"

"How many are there?"

"There be dozens of 'em. Scores of 'em!"

"What—you mean there's an entire mob of your people *here?* Outside my gate?"

"I can tell 'ee, they won't stay outside for long!" Rothadd told him. "They mean to come in, they do, and your locks and bars won't stop 'em!"

Hincmar was horrified. "Invaders! Trespassers! Human beings—will I never be free of them?"

"Nay, this be no time to think o' that," Rothadd said. "What shall we do?"

Zargal had been listening to the angry exclamations of the Outcottagers, halted by the granite wall. But now he spoke up. "Rothadd assures me that you are able to break King Laza's spell and restore me to my normal size, if you choose. Is this so?"

"Perhaps," the sorcerer answered in a harassed manner. "It depends on what sort of a spell it is. Did he use any special charm or talisman?"

Zargal thought hard. He had a vague recollection of a great flash of light. As he concentrated, the hazy image resolved itself. "A ring! He used a ring."

"As I thought—a fairly straightforward procedure, as these things go. Yes, I know how to deal with your problem."

"Will you do so, then? Will you break the spell?"

"Absolutely not," Hincmar replied.

"If it's a question of payment—" Zargal began.

"You think too much of payment, my lord," Hincmar returned stiffly. "It verges on insult. We deal here with a question, not of money, but rather of ethics."

"But Zargal here means no harm by it. 'Tis like he don't know the difference," Rothadd suggested helpfully.

"Ethics? I do not understand you, sir," Zargal said.

"King Laza, a respected colleague, has performed a feat of magic. In brief, my lord, it would not be ethical on my part to meddle in the affair. There is such a thing as professional courtesy."

"Professional courtesy prompts you, then, to allow me to be burned to death before your eyes, without lifting a finger to help?" Zargal queried.

"You exaggerate," the sorcerer returned. "The Outcottagers are somewhat primitive, I grant you, but they are not bad people—as people go. Though they should not," he added, "venture to set foot on my property. That I find difficult to overlook. Nevertheless, I am quite certain that they will not actually go so far as to attack you—"

"They will, though," Rothadd contradicted. "Burn 'im

to black cinders, they will. There's naught will hold 'em now." The lad was twisting his long fingers into knots.

"I do not intend to stand here and allow myself to be slaughtered," Zargal announced grimly. "There's more than a few of those farmers outside your gate who won't go home again. But no doubt that's what is required by your code of ethics."

The sarcasm of this remark was lost upon Rothadd, but he was able to follow the general drift. " 'Ee must help!" he appealed to Hincmar desperately. " 'Tis sure to be a blood-bath here if 'ee don't!"

Hincmar shrugged. "Your personal quarrels have nothing to do with me. I want no part of them."

"Aye, but if there be a battle here, the Outcottagers and their sons will come a-gawpin' 'round to mark the spot for the next fifty year and more!"

This argument appeared to make an impression on Hincmar, and he thought deeply for a time. At last he said, "I still cannot see my way clear to undoing the work of King Laza. But this much I will do. I'll hide you from the mob."

"Impossible!" Zargal objected. "Where can someone my size be hidden?"

"It is a proven fact," the magician informed him, "that the best hiding places are those which seem most obvious. You will be out in the open, in plain sight of the farmers, and they will not recognize you. There is no time to talk. We must get to work. Rothadd, you may watch. Perhaps you'll pick up some pointers, although I doubt it."

CHAPTER X

$$\sim$$

It soon became apparent to the Outcottagers that no one was going to open the gate to admit them, and they started considering various means of breaking it down. But the gate was strong and heavy, and they had no battering ram. The wall was of granite and could not be burned. For a while they were at a loss, until at last it occurred to them to send a few of their most agile young men scrambling up and over the barrier, to draw the bar from within. This procedure took several minutes, during which time the hunters waited angrily.

When they finally gained admittance to Hincmar's grounds, it was only to find themselves blocked by the moat. This caused another long delay, and much time passed while a couple of the hunters withdrew hatchets from their belts and chopped down one of the tall trees to form a bridge across the water. The bridge proved slippery and unsteady. Halfway across, Kreenly lost his balance and tumbled headlong into the freezing moat. Since he was unable to swim, several of his friends leaped in to help fish him out. Eventually everyone reached the far shore, all of them safe and most of them uncomfortable. It put them into an even more murderous temper to find their progress once again hindered, this time by the thorn hedge.

They attacked the hedge with hatchets and knives. But the vegetation—specially nurtured by Hincmar—was difficult to handle, and many an Outcottager was streaming blood before he arrived at the next obstacle, the maze.

The walls of the maze appeared to be formed of closely planted rows of boxwood. This hedge did not yield to their blades; upon closer inspection, the men discovered that the shrubs—each branch, every twig, down to the smallest leaf —were made of bronze, painted to resemble living plants. It was actually a marvelous piece of work, but the Outcottagers were in no mood to appreciate it. With weary threats and curses, they wandered through the narrow corridors. It seemed that whenever it was possible to make a wrong turning, they made it; wherever there was a blind alley, they always found it. Many of them certainly longed to abandon the chase and go home, but they had come so far and tried so hard that they couldn't bring themselves to give up now; and so they struggled on with a dogged persistence.

In the end, through sheer chance, the wrathful Outcottagers managed to find the right path. The metal shrubbery was left behind. They reached the clearing, and there was the cottage of Hincmar, set amidst the hills. Their satisfaction at this sight was somewhat offset by the immediate appearance of the sorcerer's pack of watchdogs, which came racing toward them over the open ground with barks, growls, and unmistakably hostile intent.

The leading Outcottagers raised hatchets and knives, preparatory to defending themselves. But the dogs never attacked, for they were halted in their tracks by a single sharp command from their master. Hincmar had emerged from his cottage into the orange glare of the torchlight. His straight figure was almost quivering under the strain of enduring the presence of so many visitors. The mere sight of them seemed to crush him beneath some invisible weight. However, he advanced toward them steadily and inquired with chill, but perfect, courtesy, "Gentlemen, how may I serve you?"

The Outcottagers looked confused. Certainly they did not know what to make of the magician, who, although dressed as they were, was so clearly unlike them. There was a nervous rustling, and finally Wilpp spoke up. "Good even, neighbor Hincmar," he said.

"Good evening," the sorcerer responded, not very encouragingly.

"Nice place 'ee have here. Good soil."

"Thank you."

" 'Tisn't our usual way," Wilpp went on with a hint of apology, "to come a-stormin' in uninvited like this. We men o' the Wolds, we know the love o' loneliness. And so do 'ee, too, by the look o' your wall and moat, the thorns, the metal hedges, and the dogs. I'll take my oath, them thorns did claw at me like they had a will o' their own!"

"In a limited sense, they do. That thorn hedge is the result of some of my experiments in vegetable vitality, based on the theories of Professor Horm, late of the University of Szar. A brilliant man—perhaps you are familiar with his work?"

"Nay, that I am not—"

"Oh, 'ee do talk too much, Wilpp!" old Stonn interrupted the strained conversation. "Let's have what we did come for! Neighbor," he addressed Hincmar directly, "we seen the Graschak come in here, and we will have him!" His cohorts muttered their agreement.

"Look around you," Hincmar invited. "There is no Graschak here."

"I tell 'ee, we did see him a-comin' through your gate. Saw him plain in the moonlight, we did!"

"Moonlight will often play tricks on your eyes," Hincmar suggested.

"Nay—there's no tricks to be played on us this night," the dripping Kreenly denied. "We saw what we saw."

"I give you my word of honor," Hincmar said. "I have seen no Graschak set foot upon my property tonight."

" 'Ee lie, then," Stonn shrilled, "for we did see 'im! The great footprints do lead across the Wolds, clear to your gate, and there they stop. What do 'ee say to that?"

"That there is a sensible explanation of some kind. You've lost the trail—or made a mistake."

"Nay—'tis 'ee have made the mistake!" Old Stonn advanced with upraised torch and outthrust jaw. "For we'll not be put off. The Graschak be here, and we mean to have 'im!"

Hincmar's expression did not alter. "You are wrong," he said, "but I see that nothing I say will convince you of that—"

"Aye! Nothing 'ee do say!"

"—and therefore you must satisfy yourselves. You have my permission to make a complete search of the premises. I shall see to it that the dogs don't interfere."

"Well—that be fair," Wilpp said with relief. "We can't ask for much more than that, neighbors."

"Foolishness!" Stonn muttered. "He do know where the Graschak be, and he ben't a-talkin'. He be a wizard and shiftier nor a Turo."

"Fair's fair, Stonn," Wilpp pointed out. "If the Graschak be here, we'll find 'im right enough!"

With that, the Outcottagers commenced their search. Having ascertained that the bronze hedges of the maze were too low to provide concealment for the Graschak, they confined their investigations to the cottage and clearing. There wasn't much to see. The house itself was far too small to contain the creature they sought. They quickly found that the Graschak did not lie in wait behind the building. The hunters milled around the clearing for a time, over the hills, into the hollows, around the tree stumps. They stamped and swore, growing more frustrated with each passing moment. But they found nothing.

During this time Hincmar stood apart, separated from the others by a living wall of dogs. He seemed absorbed in his thoughts, which were obviously unpleasant ones. For a while he repeated mathematical equations to himself in a low tone. But evidently this could not keep him diverted, for he finally demanded, in a voice that brought to mind the sound of a mirror cracking, "Well, gentlemen— are you content?"

The Outcottagers paused to consider. "We won't be content afore we do find the Graschak," Wilpp answered at last, "but it be plain that he ben't here."

"Then will you be so good as to go, and leave me in peace?"

"Well, neighbor—it seems we been wrong—"

Wilpp's peaceable rejoinder was interrupted by Stonn.

"Fools! Daft fools you be, young folk that do fancy yourselves so smart! This man be a-mullyin' you! And you do swallow it like geese a-gobblin' up maize!"

"What do 'ee mean, Stonn?"

"I mean you be a gang o' cream-faced loons! All of you did see the monster a-scurryin' through that gate—saw 'im with your own eyes. And now, just because this stranger here do say 'tis so, you do believe there's been a mistake. Every jack among us has mistook, and he alone do speak the truth! Pah!" Stonn spit into the snow with great eloquence.

"Well, then," Wilpp demanded, "if 'ee know so much more than we do, then tell us—where be the Graschak? Tell us where it be a-hidin', Stonn—if 'ee know."

Stonn glared at all of them from under his bushy eyebrows until his gaze came to rest on Hincmar. Stonn slowly lifted an arthritic claw and pointed. "Ask him," he commanded. "Ask him, and don't let yourselves be put off so easy this time. He ben't one of us, so there be no trust in what he do say. What's more—he be a wizard, and they be a breed more slippery nor tallow."

"You men of the Wolds," Hincmar called out. "You have trespassed upon my land, broken in upon me uninvited, and yet I have greeted you with courtesy. I called off my dogs and permitted you to search my property. In return, I am met with accusations and insults. But I advise you to take care. My patience is not inexhaustible—and you do not know with whom you deal." The shadows seemed to gather around him as he spoke.

"Well, now—" Wilpp began, as startled as if a length of limp cord had suddenly turned into a snake in his hand. "Well, now—"

"Pay 'im no mind!" old Stonn cried. "The wizard be tricky, but the best among us be men! And now I do see the lay o' the land!"

"What do 'ee mean, Stonn? Speak up," his companions urged.

"'Tis naught so hard," the ancient informed them. "We did see for ourselves that the Graschak come in here. But now there be no one but the wizard. 'Tis plain what that means, ben't it? There be but one answer. The Graschak and the wizard—'tis certain they be one and the same!"

The Outcottagers were astounded, and stood muttering in doubt. Old Stonn remained where he was, eyes flaming, white mustache bristling, gnarled finger outstretched and pointing in accusation.

Hincmar eyed them all with disgust. "What nonsense is this?" he asked. "Regard me well. Do I resemble the creature you seek?"

" 'Ee ben't one of us!" Stonn insisted. "And we all do know that a wizard can look as it pleases 'im to look. Strange powers 'ee do have, but do 'ee be proof against— fire?" Stonn gestured with his torch, the flame of which was no brighter than his eyes.

"Leave this place and trouble me no more!" Hincmar commanded. "And woe to those among you who dare to disturb my solitude again. For I see I must take steps to protect myself."

" 'Tis too late for that!" Stonn cried out. "The Graschak be here! Hand 'im over, if 'ee be hiding 'im, or we'll know 'ee be the Graschak yourself!"

"Get off my property and out of my sight," the magician ordered, with a visible effort at self-control. "Else I'll set the dogs on you, or worse. Away!"

"Nay, then, that be the voice o' guilt, if ever I did hear it. Neighbors, we've found the Graschak, and it be a-standin' here afore us! This be where our search do end, and now be the time to act, if we be men!"

Stonn's meaning was clear as he lifted his torch once again. The Outcottagers were still hesitating in confusion. The dogs were braced, with lowered heads, raised hackles, and bared fangs. At that moment Rothadd, who had been sitting by the window inside the cottage and listening, came running out into their midst. "Easy!" he warned. "Don't go doing what you'll be sorry for, now!"

His sudden appearance was greeted with great surprise. "Why, Rothadd, lad," Wilpp said. "What do 'ee do here? Is all well with 'ee?" Wilpp cast a distrustful glance at the sorcerer.

"Aye. I did come to tell neighbor Hincmar the news o' your meeting," Rothadd informed them. "There be naught to fear here."

"Naught to fear! There do speak a gormless innocent!"

Stonn scoffed. "Lad, this stranger here be the Graschak what's pillaged our crops!"

Rothadd drew himself up to his full height. "Stonn, 'ee be woolly-headed!"

"Treat your elders with respect, boy, if 'ee know what be good for 'ee!" the choleric ancient advised.

"And so I do treat 'em, when they deserve it! But 'tis woolly-headed 'ee be if 'ee do think that neighbor Hincmar here be the Graschak!"

"A lot 'ee do know, for a mewlin' lad," Stonn sneered. "Here be no place for women nor children. If 'ee don't got the stomach for men's work, then 'ee best go, while we get on with it!"

Rothadd's chin was set in determination. "I tell 'ee, I know!" he insisted. "Because—because while all of you was off a-chasin' the Graschak, I was here with the wizard. I was here all the time, and so was he."

This inaccurate assertion seemed to convince some of the Outcottagers, but Stonn refused to be appeased. "That do prove that the wizard ben't the Graschak his own self —if it be true," he conceded. "But don't forget, neighbors —we all did see the great beast a-goin' into this place, and here he be still—somewhere."

"Mullytwaddle—you imagined it, then," Rothadd scoffed.

"Not so, lad," Wilpp contradicted gently. "We all did see it."

"What have 'ee to say to that, then, young master?" Stonn demanded in mean triumph. "Your slippery friend here may not be the Graschak, but he do know where it hides. And," he added in slow realization, "if 'ee been here all the time—then 'ee been a-helpin' our enemies!"

The Outcottagers were all staring at young Rothadd, who stood motionless in the glare of their torches, like some forest animal transfixed by the light.

"Well, Rothadd," Wilpp asked sternly, "what have 'ee to say to all o' this? Can 'ee explain it?"

"Aye—let's hear 'ee explain it, then!" Stonn urged, in obvious excitement. His hand was twitching, causing the flame of his torch to flicker and jump.

"Don't trouble to answer that, Rothadd," Hincmar advised.

"'Ee keep out of it, wizard!" Stonn was not to be diverted from his prey. "Let's have your answer, boy, if 'ee have one."

Rothadd did not flinch under the collective scrutiny. " 'Ee be gettin' old, Stonn. Can't see what's plain afore 'ee. The Graschak come in here and he ben't gone out again. But neighbor Hincmar and me never did spy 'im—we told the truth o' that. And how could that be, 'ee ask? 'Tis simple. The Graschak never did come nigh the house because—" He took a deep breath "—because he never won past the moat."

"Mullytwaddle! *We* won past the moat!" Stonn snarled. "If we could, then he could! 'Ee be a beardless, lyin' little gumfer!"

"Give the lad a chance to speak, Stonn!"

"Along about midnight or thereabouts," Rothadd said, "Hincmar and me were both a-sittin' in the cottage, alongside the fire, when all of a sudden the dogs started acting real meachy. Roilin' around they were, a-shiverin' and whimperin', with their tails tucked 'neath their rumps. Ben't that so, neighbor Hincmar?"

Hincmar did not answer. One eyebrow went up slightly.

"Well, we both got up and stepped outside to take a look 'round,' Rothadd continued, "but we didn't see nothin'. We were about to go back in when there came a hugeous splash and a terrible great howl."

"Did 'ee go to see what it was?" Wilpp asked.

"Oh, aye, for certain! We took up lanterns, we did, and bustled on out to the moat. But when we got there, friends, there was naught to be seen! The water was still a-swirlin' 'round, but that was all. There wasn't a creature in sight. 'Ee didn't see naught, did 'ee, Master Hincmar?"

Hincmar shook his head wordlessly. His eyes were still steely with rage.

"And how could we know—how could we even dream, then—'twas the Graschak his own self here?" Rothadd asked in apparent awe. "We'd never have known it if the lot of you hadn't come and told us! For which, neighbors, we do thank you most kindly."

"I see your game! The two of you be in it together!" Stonn shrieked furiously. "Sneaking little liar! Let me at 'im!" Stonn attempted to spring forward. His companions restrained him.

"Do this be the truth of it?" Wilpp asked.

"Of course it be true!" Rothadd returned indignantly. "An Outcottager I do be, and I wouldn't cause ill to my own kind. As for the Graschak—he be drowned, that's what! He be drowned and a-lyin' this minute 'neath fathoms of freezin' water. We'll never see him more."

Stonn's infuriated rejoinder was not audible above the relieved laughter of the Outcottagers. It was in vain that the old man insisted that Graschaks were supernatural beings who could not drown, that any Graschak would float. Nobody heard him. Nobody wanted to listen to objections to the explanation that suited each of them so well. Hincmar was looking at his apprentice as if he had never seen him before.

"Well, neighbor—it seems we near made a mistake," Wilpp confessed. "We ask pardon for it, and we hope 'ee won't think too hardly of us."

"Not at all," Hincmar assured him graciously.

The Outcottagers now wanted to inspect the moat. The sorcerer led the torchlight procession back through the paths of the maze until they all stood together on the shore, staring down into the still, black water.

"Only to think," one of the men marveled in a hushed voice, "the monster be somewhere down there right now, right below us."

"Only to think," Rothadd echoed gravely.

"Fools!" Stonn screamed at his companions. "Driveling numbskulls, all of you be, took in by a wizard and a half-grown lad!"

"Here, now, Stonn—"

"Blockheads!"

But nobody paid any attention to the old man. After having studied the quiet surface of the moat for a time, the Outcottagers made their way in silence back across the fallen tree trunk to the other side of the water, and from there, through the gate and onto the open woldlands. Once clear of Hincmar's property, they scattered. Each man took his lonely way back to his own home. And each vowed, in the depths of his heart, that it would be many a long day before he would subject himself to human companionship again.

Old Stonn was last glimpsed stalking rapidly away over the hills, gesticulating and talking angrily to himself.

It was dawn when Hincmar and Rothadd retraced their steps back through the maze to the clearing. All appeared deserted. There was not a sound to be heard, other than the sighing of the wind. Only the muddy imprints in the snow of scores of boots remained to mark the visit of the Outcottagers.

"You may come out now, Lord Zargal," Hincmar called clearly.

For a moment there was no response to this summons. Then the ground before them shifted and quaked. Slowly the Duke's son arose, brushing away his blanket of snow and cold dirt. With a sigh of relief, he stretched his limbs, able to move for the first time since the appearance of the Outcottagers. For what seemed an eternity, Zargal had been lying on his side, motionless, curled up beneath a thin covering of earth and slush, while the Outcottagers had stamped to and fro across his body. The art of Hincmar had lent him the semblance of one of the natural hills of the Wolds. Zargal was wet clear through, filthy, and marked with purple bruises from head to foot.

"How do 'ee feel?" Rothadd inquired anxiously.

"Damp," Zargal replied. "Cramped. Cold. Sore. Do those friends of yours happen to wear spikes on their boots?"

"Oh, aye, when the snow comes."

"I thought so. Well, no matter—it was worth it, and I'm grateful to both of you."

"We were happy to be of assistance to you, Lord Zargal," Hincmar said composedly. "It has been an interesting experience, albeit not one that I'd care to repeat."

"Nor I," the Duke's son agreed. "I don't suppose you might reconsider your decision and restore me to my natural size?"

"Out of the question, I fear. King Laza might be offended. There is such a thing as—"

"Professional courtesy?"

"Exactly. Well, the Outcottagers will not trouble you again—as long as you don't trouble them. What do you intend to do now, Lord Zargal?"

Zargal shrugged, and a small avalanche of loose dirt

cascaded from his shoulders. "Continue on my way to Obran," he said. "Perhaps King Laza may be persuaded to undo his handiwork."

"Such good handiwork—it seems a pity," the sorcerer observed regretfully.

"That is a matter of personal opinion. Have I far to travel?"

"Not far at all. You are almost upon the border of Obran now."

"I am in your debt, sir," Zargal said with formality.

"That is true, but you may repay me easily enough."

"How?"

"You will take Rothadd with you when you leave."

This cool announcement startled Zargal, and wrenched a cry of dismay from Rothadd. " 'Ee want to send me away, then?" he gasped.

"I believe that would be best, lad," the sorcerer told him.

" 'Ee don't want me here no more? 'Ee won't teach me the art?" Rothadd was crushed, and looked to be on the verge of tears. "A hard man 'ee be!"

"That's not altogether true." Hincmar spoke gently to the boy, and the bitter lines of his face softened more than Zargal would have thought possible. "Rothadd, I believe that somewhere inside you there may be the makings of a magician—I have always thought so. It would be easy for me to teach you a few simple techniques. But if I did, you wouldn't amount to anything more than a carnival mountebank. True sorcery doesn't consist of a bagful of tricks to be learned by rote; it is an art, and you must find the source of power within yourself. No one can do it for you. In that sense, you are essentially alone, and always will be."

"Then what be the use o' sendin' me away?" the boy demanded.

"You've been serving me for two years now, and in all that time, have made no progress. I think a change of some kind is indicated. Perhaps a meeting with King Laza will be just what you need. In any case, I am sending you to him. Lord Zargal, in order to return the favor that you owe me, will you take this boy with you to Obran?"

"Yes," Zargal answered without hesitation. Rothadd was gazing from one to the other and back again, in dismay.

"Good. Though I perceive that you are but slightly older

than he, you possess far more knowledge of the world than Rothadd, and may be able to look after him. Rothadd, you are willing?"

The lad squared his shoulders. "If 'ee do think 'tis the only way I'll ever learn, then I'll go, I will. But when I've been, can I come back to the Wolds again?"

"Yes—but you must make a true effort to learn what you can from King Laza of Obran, else there's no point in going. You'll promise me that?"

"Aye."

"Good. And now, gentlemen, I suggest you be on your way. The sooner you go, the sooner your purposes may be accomplished."

"But," Zargal protested, "we've had no sleep tonight. Can't we rest here for a few hours before leaving?"

"I think not. In the first place, you would do well to cross the Obran border during the daylight hours. The krorks that infest the region are dangerous enough during the day, but at night they are positively deadly. You must use every precaution when traveling through their territory, and under no circumstances must you be caught there when darkness falls. And frankly, gentlemen, it is necessary that I be alone. I have had more company tonight than I wish to endure in all the years remaining to me. I have had enough of mankind, and I must be alone."

There was no arguing with him; Hincmar was absolutely inflexible. For the last time, he escorted them to the edge of his property. "There lies your destination," he said, pointing east, toward the region of fog. "Take care not to wander from the main road, and beware of the krorks." He placed his hands on Rothadd's shoulders. "Look after yourself, my boy," he counseled unsmilingly. "Do your best, and give my regards to King Laza when you meet him."

"Aye, that I will," Rothadd promised sorrowfully.

"You know that my best wishes go with you. But take this advice as well—do not be quite so swift to trust strangers."

"Oh, there ben't no fear o' that—a true Outcottager I be!"

"Sometimes I wonder. But no doubt you will learn caution in time, if you survive." Hincmar released Rothadd and turned to gaze up into the eyes of the Duke's son. "I wish you good fortune as well, Lord Zargal," he said. "You are a somewhat presumptuous young man, but I don't dislike you: and I believe that a visit to King Laza may prove instructive to you, as well as to Rothadd. You'll keep an eye on the boy?"

"He'll be quite safe with me," Zargal assured the sorcerer.

"Hmm. Perhaps." Hincmar didn't seem entirely convinced. "Farewell, gentlemen."

"Good-bye, Hincmar. I'll be back!" Rothadd cried. "Good-bye!"

Hincmar did not stay to watch them go, but retired to his solitary cottage. Zargal and his companion set off across the short stretch of Woldlands that separated them from the misty peaks of Obran.

CHAPTER XI

Zargal and Rothadd did not make very good progress. They had returned to the road, but the ground was growing rougher and steeper all the time. Patches of ice lay in the ruts of the highway. Layers of glassy ice coated the rocks and the naked gray branches of the shrubs. The travelers' slippery path was becoming more difficult by the minute, as they passed the extreme limits of the Eastling Wolds and began their ascent into the mountains. The fog thickened and swirled around them. Sunlight faded, and finally died away. The world turned gray and curiously silent, as if the mists that blocked out the light blocked out sound as well. The air was colder at the higher altitudes, and the wind was whipping down the slopes, driving the grit into their eyes, dragging at Zargal's quilts, and chilling his naked arms and legs.

Both Zargal and Rothadd had already been tired when they left Hincmar's cottage. Since then, the battle with the uphill path and the hostile winds had tired them even more, especially the young Outcottager; and they were forced to pause frequently. By noon they had only cleared the first foothills of the mountains of Obran. Neither traveler possessed a watch, but Rothadd's growling stomach served to inform him that lunch time had come. As for Zargal, he was once again wild with hunger. There was, however, nothing edible in sight.

"I be hungry," Rothadd announced unnecessarily.

"Yes. I can appreciate that," Zargal replied.

"I could do with a bowl o' porridge," the boy mused. "Or a mess o' stewed meat and greshunki, the way my mother do make 'em. Or maybe a barley cake topped with fried apples and brown sugar—"

"Talking about it isn't going to help!" Zargal broke in, unable to endure any more.

"Aye, 'tis so. Ben't 'ee hungry, then?"

"Yes. Very," was all that Zargal trusted himself to say.

"What'll we do, then?" Rothadd inquired.

"We shall have to continue along this road until we reach civilization, I suppose. Eventually, we're sure to come to some inn, where we'll be able to buy a meal."

"Buy a meal! With what, I do ask 'ee?"

"Don't worry about that."

"I won't take part in no stealin'—"

"There will be no stealing."

"Sayin' that there's an inn to be found upon this lonely road," Rothadd asked after a pause, "where be the meal would fill up a belly the like o' yours?"

"We'll have to deal with that when the time comes." Zargal had in fact been pondering that very question, and had formed no satisfactory conclusion. "But one thing is certain—it will do us no good to tarry here." His vast stomach produced a rumbling noise like distant cannon fire, and he tightened the cord around his waist.

They trudged on in silence. The prospect before them was at once dismal and boring—slushy, rutted road and icy rocks, with all the rest of the world curtained from view by the dank, opaque fog. Rothadd was deep in thought. A variety of expressions chased across his mobile face before he inquired, "Have 'ee marked how this road do twist and turn, back and forth—first one way, then t'other?"

"Yes, I've noticed," Zargal replied absently. His mind was filled with visions of roast haunch of venison, currant jelly, and chestnut puree.

" 'Twould make more sense altogether," Rothadd pointed

out, "if we do leave this twisty way and find our own straight path up the hills."

"Good idea, but not practical," Zargal objected. "We don't know these mountains and we'd surely get lost in the fog."

"Aye, that we would, except I have this." Rothadd triumphantly displayed an antique compass in a silver and enamel case. " 'Twas my great-grandfather's, and his grandfather's before him, it was."

Zargal regarded the ancient instrument doubtfully. "Are you sure it's accurate?" he asked.

"Aye, that I am. 'Twill show us the way east, right enough."

"Too dangerous. We don't know what sort of terrain lies out there—it may be impassable."

"And if it be so, 'twill be a simple matter to return to the road again, and we'll lose naught in the attempt."

"Except time—which we can ill afford. Remember, we must be past this region before darkness falls."

"Oh, 'twill make our journey all the shorter, it will. Besides, if we do leave this road, there be a fair chance we may light upon a greshunk bush or some early winterworts. Elseways there be no tellin' when a scrap o' food is like to hit our bellies again."

Zargal could not resist. With the compass clutched firmly in Rothadd's hand, the two wanderers struck off from the winding road, maintaining a straight easterly course. At first it seemed a wise move. The ground was slippery and treacherous, but not much more so than the road. It was not long before they chanced upon an entire growth of winterwort, with which Rothadd was able to satisfy his appetite, and Zargal, fractionally allay his own. Their good fortune did not continue, though. They had come to a region of the mountains formed entirely of naked rock. Here was no covering of topsoil and no vegetation, but only granite—huge slabs of it, piled atop one another as if they'd been dropped there by careless hands. The rocks were coated with ice and impossible to climb. After having expended considerable energy in unsuccessful efforts to scale the slabs, and acquiring a number of cuts and bruises in the process, Zargal and Rothadd were forced to admit defeat.

"Enough," Zargal ordained, after a particularly painful slide down one of the steeper slopes. "This won't work. We'll return to the road and continue along our original route."

"Aye," Rothadd agreed, examining a scraped and bleeding knee. "This here be harder nor trying to climb over a hill o' greased glass. Let's go back to the road, then. Happen we'll find more winterwort on the way."

"It might not be a good idea to stop again. Remember what Hincmar told us—" It cost Zargal a great deal to decline a meal, even one that existed in theory only, but he was growing a little uneasy. "We must be well past the borderlands before darkness sets in, else we may encounter the krorks. In view of that possibility, there's something that I've been wanting to ask for some time."

"What do that be?"

"What *are* krorks?"

Rothadd considered the question. " 'Tis a hard thing to say what they be, for they be neither one thing nor t'other. They be neither all spirit nor all mortal; they be neither all animal nor all human. They ben't truly alive, but they ben't dead neither. Do that make it clear to 'ee?"

"Not very."

"They do roam these borderlands in packs. They hate all strangers, and when the darkness falls and their power be full upon 'em, they venture from out their holes and crannies and go a-huntin'. Full o' black mischief they be, and there ben't many meets 'em and lives to tell the tale."

"Yes, yes," Zargal said, "but that still doesn't tell me what they are."

"I'm a-tryin' to. It ben't like I've truly seen one, but Hincmar's a-told me o' them often enough. They be a part of all that do be magic," the boy concluded loftily. "A krork, if 'ee must know, be a kind o' half-spirit."

"What do these creatures look like?" Zargal inquired patiently.

"There's some folk do say," Rothadd declared, "that a krork goes about on two legs like a man, but do have the hair and snout and tail of a beast. And others do say that he runs on four legs, with the face of a man on 'im. Some folk tell o' krorks made o' mist and smoke, that 'ee can see clear through; but others say they be formed o' fearful strong flesh and bone. 'Tis said they be smaller nor a man, but swifter; else bigger nor a man, but slower. Either they have eyes that do see through the mist and fog, or they go a-sniffin' their way about—'tis one or t'other, for certain. That be all I'm sure of."

"Good. Now I have a perfect mental image of them," Zargal said appreciatively. Rothadd appeared slightly nettled at his bantering tone. "But there's one thing about krorks that I *am* sure of—"

"What?"

"That we don't much want to meet any."

"Oh, 'twould take a desperate gang of 'em to dare to attack a giant like 'ee be. So there ben't no need for 'ee to fear," Rothadd informed him kindly.

"I am not afraid!" Zargal exclaimed, stung in his turn. "I am the heir of Szar—at least, I was—and not subject to idle terrors."

"If 'ee say so."

"Still got your compass? We're not going to find that road again without it."

"Oh, aye, 'tis safe enough." Rothadd withdrew the compass from his pocket and flicked open the case, the better to demonstrate the antique instrument's soundness.

"The road will be directly to our west—" Zargal was saying, only to be interrupted by a cry of dismay from Rothadd. "What's the matter?"

"Grandfather's compass!" the lad replied. " 'Tis bewitched! Look here!"

Zargal looked. The compass was indeed behaving strangely—the needle was swinging back and forth in irregular arcs. From time to time it spun around in complete circles. For purposes of navigation, it was utterly useless.

"She was a-workin' perfect," Rothadd said sadly. "Always has. What ails her now, I do wonder?"

"It would be far more to the point to wonder how we're going to get back to the road again," Zargal reminded him. "We should never have strayed in the first place. I knew it was a bad idea."

"Why did 'ee agree to it, then?"

"Oh, probably because of those winterworts. Well, we've

had our winterworts—not very good ones at that. Not worth it."

"What'll we do now?" Rothadd was still staring dolefully at the crazed compass.

"Find the road again without the compass, I suppose." Zargal was making an effort to sound unconcerned. "We must simply go back the way we came. Come, come," he said, catching sight of his companion's unhappy face, "we're not so badly off as all that."

"This be my fault," Rothadd muttered. "Hincmar did right to send me away from 'im."

"Nonsense. It's not your—" Zargal broke off suddenly and listened. "Did you hear something?"

"Hear what?" Rothadd tilted his head back to stare up at Zargal's face, so far above him as to be partially obscured by the fog.

"I thought I heard a voice."

"I didn't hear a peep."

"Ssssshhh—listen!"

They listened intently. Zargal had been right. The fog was filled with whispering voices.

"Krorks!" Rothadd opined. "There be krorks here!" He looked far from displeased. The whispering started up again—a nasty, chilly sound that danced in the swirling mists.

"What are you looking so happy about?" Zargal asked.

"Nigh unto krorks we be!" Rothadd exulted. "True krorks! Not everyday creatures o' solid flesh and blood, but spirits that sometimes be there and sometimes be nothin' but fog!"

"Oh, I see—magic."

"Aye!"

The whispering voices—which sounded nearly human, but not quite—came closer. The mist darkened and pressed in upon them with an almost tangible weight. Zargal could see no living creature other than Rothadd, but was aware of a multitude of presences near at hand. "Leave us— begone!" He lifted his tremendous voice in an unearthly shout that rang for miles through the clouded mountains, echoing from the peaks and thundering across the valleys.

Rothadd had flung himself face down on the rocky

ground, his hands pressed tight to his ears. "Why did 'ee do that?" he gasped. "For mercy's sake, don't do it no more!"

"Listen." Zargal held up a finger as long as a branch. "It's stopped."

"Well, 'ee won't drive them off with naught but a lot o' noise, I can tell 'ee!"

"Perhaps not, but I rather doubt they'll attempt to hinder our departure now," Zargal returned, in the vain hope that he sounded confident. "They must be cowards, else why would they roam in packs and hide in the fog?"

"Happen 'tis just their way. But they ben't cowards— that be for mortal men, not spirits." As if to confirm Rothadd's statement, the whispering started up again, this time louder than before. The young Outcottager peered hopefully into the fog, but saw no one. When Zargal tried shouting again, the noise produced no results. The krorks obviously understood that they had nothing to fear from loud noises.

"We'll ignore them," Zargal decided. "We'll walk back the way we came until we reach the road again, and they may whisper all they please."

Rothadd bestowed a last glance upon his compass. The needle was still swerving as if gripped by a drunken hand. The boy replaced the instrument in his pocket, and mirthless laughter came rattling out of the mists at him.

"Cowards!" Zargal exclaimed, and the laughter intensified. "Come on," he told Rothadd. "Let's be on our way. As for these sneaking shadows, they are unworthy of our notice." The laughter and whispering died away. Ominous silence reigned.

" 'Ee do insult 'em!" Rothadd said in a shocked tone. "Don't go a-makin' 'em angry!"

Together they descended from the granite slabs and tried to retrace their steps back to the road. Zargal had expected it to be a difficult task, but he hadn't realized how completely they'd been relying on the compass to guide them. On the rough, uneven ground, in the fog, with no compass, they soon grew thoroughly confused. For hours they went plodding over the icy hills in search of their lost path. At the end of that time they were still lost, and had succeeded in exhausting themselves as well. Rothadd in particular was drained of energy, for he was forced to climb over obstacles that his enormous companion could clear with a single step; and he went sliding into and out of many a gully across which Zargal could easily leap.

As late afternoon wore on and evening approached, the mists darkened and the krorks grew bolder. They had never been far away from the two travelers; but now they pressed in even closer, whispering words and phrases that were never quite intelligible. Many times Zargal felt that he could nearly understand what they were saying. No matter how he strained his ears, though, he could never quite catch the sense of it.

Little by little, the krorks were increasing in solidity and substance, as if they drew their strength from the coming darkness. The fog was infested with slinking gray forms, which seemed to assume a more definite outline as Zargal and Rothadd watched. Greenish-yellow eyes gleamed through the mists. Sometimes Zargal could glimpse the twitch of a pointed ear, the lash of a bushy tail, the glint of fangs. Rothadd was fascinated, but had the good sense not to communicate his interest to Zargal. Time passed, the cold hills darkened, and the travelers continued their search.

Then, all at once, the whispering ceased and another sound took its place. Someone nearby was playing on a recorder. The music, thin and wailing, could not have been of human origin. The mere sound of it sent cold chills racing down the enormous length of Zargal's spine; and even Rothadd was looking subdued. For a few minutes the discordant tune quavered out unaccompanied. And then the krorks began to sing.

Their whispering voices rose and fell in a slow chant, in which notes of triumph were underscored by snarls. There was a chorus to the song, and each time the krorks repeated it, the mists grew perceptibly denser. The chant was growing stronger all the time, as more and more krorks joined in.

"Have you any idea why they're doing that?" Zargal asked at last.

"That I do. Hincmar's told me o' this often enough, but I didn't think I'd ever be a-hearin' it with my own ears. It be the Darkness Song o' the krorks. 'Ee see—they be creatures o' fog, and mist, and dark. When the dark do come, their power be full upon 'em. When the whole pack do sing together like they be doin' now, it pulls the mists in thicker and hastens the comin' o' the night. So 'tis like to be twilight time over all the rest o' the land, but here 'twill be black as midnight."

"And when night has fallen, what will happen then? I assume these creatures are carnivorous?"

"Come again?"

"They eat flesh?"

"Ah, nay. I tell 'ee, they be spirits o' sorts. They won't taste o' no meat."

"In that case," Zargal asked, "what have they got to gain by harassing us in this insolent manner?" The song of the krorks was now so loud that he had to raise his voice to be heard.

"They got nothin' to gain," Rothadd said. " 'Tis a matter more o' pride to 'em. These be their lands, and they won't abide no strangers to cross 'em. Also," Rothadd added, " 'ee did insult 'em back there, and they don't take kindly to it."

"I said nothing that was not true. As for these lands, they are, as far as I know, part of the domain of the King of Obran. The krorks do not rule here. If they claim otherwise, then they are liars and thieves."

Zargal spoke very distinctly, but the Darkness Song of the krorks continued without a break. After a few seconds, a stone came whizzing out of the fog and struck him squarely in the chest. Zargal cursed, and Rothadd winced, crying, "Must 'ee be forever a-blurtin' out aught that pops into your skull? 'Tis like 'ee'll make things worse!"

It was getting too dark to continue traveling. There seemed to be no chance of finding the road. The constant chanting, and the presence of the sinister, semi-solid shapes slipping in and out of the mists all around them, foiled all attempts at navigation. "We can't go on," Rothadd said, and halted in his tracks. "Best we stay here. At least we can watch the krorks until the light be gone." He seemed to find a measure of solace in this thought which Zargal was unable to share.

"You watch them," he suggested. "And I'll see what an expert suggests should be done in this sort of situation." He then withdrew from the sack that hung on a cord at his waist the old volume that Flimm had placed there—*Surviving the Wilderness: Memoirs of a Gentleman Voyager*—and began to read. There was just barely enough light left for him to be able to do so. The krorks continued their chanting song. The music rose to greet the falling darkness.

"They be a-plannin' somewhat," Rothadd remarked. "What do the book say?"

"Let's see—" Zargal read:

"To Afford yourself Protection, in a Manner worthy of a Gentleman, it is necessary to erect a Fortification in your Defense. Have your Servants, all and Sundry, hew down the great Trees that Surround you, and with them they are to construct a Stockade, not less than ten Cubits in Height, stout and strong withal. Let it be stocked within with all manner of Dainties for your Refreshment, and all manner of Weapons for your Defense; viz., Swords, Daggers, Halberds, Muskets. Let armed Servants be Stationed Without the Stockade to act as Sentries and Guards, to repel Attack. Do you retire Within, and so pass the Night. Thus will you infallibly preserve your Life, and your Honor remain Whole."

At the conclusion of this passage, Zargal hurled the book away into the fog. "What are the krorks likely to do?" he asked.

"I can't say. 'Tis sure they be no friends to strangers; and now, when 'ee do insult 'em—"

"Yes, you've already mentioned that. Well, if we must stay here, we'd best build a fire. I've a flint and steel in my sack."

"Ha!" Rothadd snorted. "Flint and steel 'ee may have, but 'ee do know naught o' fires. What will 'ee use to start a flame when all the grass and scrub be wet?"

As if in answer to Rothadd's question, the discarded copy of *Memoirs of a Gentleman Voyager* came sailing out of the mist and bounced off Zargal's chest. "This," Zargal said, retrieving the volume. He hurriedly tore a number of pages out, made a small pile of them on the ground, and found no difficulty in setting the paper alight. Rothadd pulled up handfuls of the scrub vegetation, with which they were able to maintain a smoky campfire. By this time the darkness was complete. The song of the krorks ended in an explosion of howls and snarls. After a moment the creatures began their whispering conversation again.

"I wish I knew what they were doing!" Zargal burst out, after he'd sat listening to the whispers for twenty minutes or so.

"There ben't no telling," Rothadd replied. "Krorks be like that," he added philosophically. "We must bide quiet and just take what do come."

Zargal hunched nearer the fire in a vain effort to take the chill off his exposed arms and legs. He was much too large to be able to warm all his limbs simultaneously. Instead he was obliged to toast them one at a time, and was constantly shifting his position in order to do so. As for Rothadd, he had withdrawn Hincmar's parchment from its resting place, and now resumed his attempts to master the spell. Again and again he repeated the words, each time with some new variation in pronunciation, emphasis, or gesture. The boy's powers of concentration must have been extraordinary, for the constant whispering that buzzed in the air all around them did not distract him in the least. Despite his perseverance, however, he achieved no success.

Zargal had not rested since the previous night. Now the fire was an orange blur. Rothadd's droning voice was merging with the voices of the krorks, and both were receding. Zargal's head drooped. His eyes shut, and he slept.

CHAPTER XII

Hours passed. Rothadd continued to study Hincmar's parchment. The unseen krorks clustered thickly around the fire, and their whispers grew more insistent. Zargal slept through it all. No dreams troubled him, and thus he would have slumbered throughout the night, had he been permitted to rest undisturbed. Such was not to be the case.

The Duke's son was awakened by the shock of a volley of stones thudding into his ribs and shoulders. His head jerked up, and he opened his eyes to behold Rothadd writhing and twisting in an extraordinary manner. The young Outcottager was screaming. "They be a-holdin' me! Holdin' me!"

"What is it? What's happening?" Zargal exclaimed, jumping to his feet.

"The krorks!" Rothadd stumbled this way and that, twitching and struggling. When he chanced to draw near the fire, Zargal could just barely glimpse the crouching forms at the boy's side. The air was filled with howls and demonic laughter.

"I'll help you!" Zargal promised, and took a step forward. At that moment a load of moist earth and pebbles, flung by unseen hands, landed on the fire. The flames fizzled, sank, and went out. The resulting darkness was absolute. The krorks uttered a concerted yell of triumph.

"Let me be, I tell 'ee!"

Zargal could hear Rothadd a short distance away, but he could see nothing. For an instant he hesitated, and in that instant he felt hands clutching at his naked ankles—hands that seemed almost human, but hairy-palmed and deathly cold. They grasped him very lightly, without force, as clammy as the fog, hideous beyond words. With a cry, Zargal kicked out in all directions and managed to shake himself loose. No sooner had he done so than they were back again, plucking at his limbs, dragging softly at his quilts. Frigid fingers rested lightly upon the back of his neck. A mob of weightless bodies surged all around him. He could feel their fangs pressing against his flesh, but they left no mark upon him.

Rothadd was shrieking in a panic, and Zargal could hear the sounds of a violent struggle going on. With some difficulty he made his way toward his companion, stumbling in the dark over the rough ground and hurling aside the invisible, weightless bodies that obstructed his path. He was halted when he placed his foot squarely on the hot ashes of the fire. There must have been live embers buried among them, for there was a hiss, a thick smoke arose, and the rags binding Zargal's foot glowed dull red. Fortunately, the fabric was far too wet to ignite, and the glow died out. Zargal yelped, yanked back his foot, and sat down hard.

Immediately he felt the krorks around him, clasping him lightly with their icy hands and whispering in his ear. Fear and disgust welled up within him, and his impulse was to give way to panic and run. Rothadd apparently had done just that. Zargal could hear the boy's yells receding into the darkness, with a party of krorks baying in pursuit. Once more the Duke's son pushed aside the clinging forms, pulled free of the clutching hands, and rose to his feet. "Rothadd—where are you?" he called.

"Here I be!" A faint cry came across some distance. "Help!" The voice was then drowned out by a chorus of howls.

"Stay where you are—I'm coming!" Zargal started off in the direction of Rothadd's voice, with the krorks snapping at his heels. It was not an easy progress, for he was con-

stantly bumping into rocks, sliding on patches of ice, and
tripping over the hills and gullies. Many times he fell, with
crashes that jarred the earth for hundreds of yards about.
Each time, the krorks swarmed around and over him until
the touch of their cold hands and the sound of their whispers nearly drove him mad with loathing. It was only with
an effort that he was able to stop himself from screaming.
Rothadd was making no such effort, which was fortunate,
for Zargal would not otherwise have had any idea where to
find him.

"Don't let them frighten you!" Zargal yelled, but found
himself unable to follow his own advice as he slid down
an icy slope, landed on his knees, and felt scores of hands
clawing at his eyes. A pack of the krorks could be heard
retreating again, and it could only mean that Rothadd was
still on the run. Zargal shook his head free and stood up
painfully. He was vaguely aware that he and Rothadd were
being chased and driven in a consistent direction; their
course had followed a fairly straight line. But there was no
time to think about that.

Zargal staggered on through the dark, as blind as if he'd
been born without eyes. Because of his size, he was able to
proceed over the rough terrain far more rapidly than his
companion, and eventually he realized that he'd drawn
about level with Rothadd. He could discern, by the sound
of the yells, snarls, and howls, that the youth and his entourage of krorks were approaching.

"Rothadd! Over here!" he thundered, and was rewarded
with an answering shout. Zargal tore himself loose of a
myriad of invisible hands and headed toward that shout.

But now the krorks that dogged his footsteps had
worked themselves into a state of mad excitement. Their
howls rang out, frenzied and expectant. Their jaws were
snapping audibly, and he could hear them panting and
giggling at his side. No longer did they clutch and drag at
him. Instead, they pushed, urging him on to greater speed.
The corpse-cold hands pinched, prodded, goaded. The
ghostly fangs nipped at his legs. The voices taunted and
threatened.

Zargal's mind was clouded with rage and confusion. Had
there been any foe of solid flesh and blood, he would have
turned to fight, despite the darkness. He stumbled another

few steps and was but dimly aware of the voices of all the krorks rising in a wild shriek of triumph as he suddenly lost his footing, plunged forward, and felt himself falling freely through the air.

The Duke's son had no time to be frightened. He was conscious of a vast astonishment. Then he struck the ground, pitched forward, and broke his fall on outstretched palms. It was a drop that might well have killed a man of ordinary size, but in his present state, had proved nothing more than a bone-rattling accident. Slowly he dragged himself to his knees. As he did so, there came another hellish shriek from the krorks. Something warm and heavy came hurtling down from above and landed atop Zargal, crushing him to the rocky earth once more. A strangled cry of "Be I dead yet?" served to inform him that Rothadd had arrived.

"No, you are not dead. Get off of me!"

"Do 'ee be here, Zargal?"

"Yes—underneath you. Will you get off?"

"Oh—sorry. Do 'ee be whole and sound?"

"Whole, yes—if not altogether sound," Zargal assured him gloomily. "And you?"

"Aye, I be well—I think. Where do we be, then?"

"I don't know. Quiet, now—they're here!"

The krorks—a mighty band of them, by the sound of it—had gathered together in the darkness overhead. For a short time they laughed and whispered, their voices still throbbing with excitement. Then they began to sing again. They did not repeat their Darkness Song. This time the voices soared in a kind of triumphant hymn—a slow, solemn paean of satisfied malevolence. For long minutes the chant continued. Zargal could hear Rothadd breathing in rapid gasps, whether because of terror or some other emotion, he could not judge. He himself felt little beyond amazement.

The song of the krorks rose to a crescendo—a prolonged, savage note—and then ceased. There was not another sound. Zargal and Rothadd sat huddled together upon the ground, seeing nothing and hearing nothing. When perhaps an hour had passed and the silence remained unbroken, Rothadd finally asked in a whisper, "Do they be up there yet?"

"I don't know."

"What sort o' place did we come a-tumblin' into?"

"I don't know."

"What be like to happen next?"

"I don't know!"

" 'Ee don't know much, do 'ee? 'Tis lucky I went a-fallin' on top o' 'ee," Rothadd said optimistically. "Happen I'd a-broke my neck, otherwise."

The blackness about them was intense, and they did not dare try to move. Eventually the silence of the place convinced Zargal and Rothadd that the krorks had truly departed. But they remained where they were, nursed their bruises, and waited for daylight.

Morning came at last. Rothadd lay curled up on the ground, fast asleep. Zargal was in a semiconscious state, as he had been for some hours. When he finally roused himself, it was to discover that the borderlands were once again gray rather than black. A dreary light was struggling down through the mists. All was dim and hazy, as it had been the previous day, but there was sufficient light to see by. Zargal shook Rothadd awake. Together, they examined their surroundings.

The krorks had driven them into a great pit. Around them towered sheer, inward-sloping walls of polished stone. The floor of the pit was strewn with rocks and whitened bones. Human bones lay everywhere, thousands of them, piled up like so much bleached kindling. Many were smashed and splintered. But some skeletons were whole, and lay near the edges of the pit, clawing at the stone walls with their fleshless fingers.

Rothadd's blue eyes grew round. "What sort of a hole do this be?" he wondered.

"It's a trap," Zargal responded. "They've driven us into a trap, as they've driven many others."

"What—'ee mean they did chase us here on *purpose?*" Rothadd could scarcely credit such perfidy.

"Surely."

"And then just left us here to *die?*"

"To break our bones, and then to starve to death."

"Oh—'tis devilish, 'tis wicked!"

"Yes. But fortunately," Zargal pointed out, "the krorks are not very bright. In fact, their minds must be as dim as the fog from which they came, if they imagined that such a trap could hold us."

" 'Ee know the way out, then?"

Without replying, Zargal abandoned his sitting position and rose to his full height. The top of his head was only a few feet below the opening of the hole. By stretching forth his arm, he was easily able to grasp the edge. "Deep as this pit is, I can climb out of it," he remarked, and added dryly, "Magic."

"Oh, aye, 'tis well enough for 'ee, but what about me?" Rothadd demanded.

"If I can get out, then you can get out," Zargal informed him. "Although I must confess I never foresaw the day would come that I'd be transformed into a human step-ladder." He knelt down again. Rothadd took his meaning at once. The boy was able to clamber to Zargal's shoulder with a monkey's agility. There he remained, hanging onto a giant ear to maintain balance, as Zargal carefully stood. From there it was a relatively easy matter for him to scramble along an outstretched arm to solid ground and safety. Placing his hands on the edge of the opening above him, Zargal succeeded in dragging himself out of the hole.

They sat together in the fog, their legs dangling over the edge of the pit which had lately contained them. There was no sign of the krorks. The creatures must have departed during the night, certain that their lethal purpose had been accomplished. There was not a sound to be heard.

"What do we do now?" Rothadd asked.

"We'll leave this place," Zargal answered. "Get out as quickly as we can—the krorks might always return, and I for one don't find their company pleasant."

"Oh, aye—but which way are we to go?" Rothadd cast an uncertain glance around him into the swirling mists. "We be lost, for certain."

"I don't believe we could have gone any great distance from the road," Zargal said.

"Aye, but where be the road? If only grandfather's compass hadn't gone crackbrained!" Rothadd wistfully drew forth the instrument and snapped the case open. Within, the compass needle pointed a true, unwavering north. "She's a-cured herself!" Rothadd crowed. "See, she's a-pointin' the way north again! Look here!"

Zargal looked. "It seems to be steady," he admitted, "but how do we know that it's right? It could be misleading us."

"Grandfather's compass? Nay—she wouldn't lead us astray." Rothadd seemed a trifle insulted. "I tell 'ee, 'tis cured!"

"How do you know?"

" 'Twere the fault o' the krorks!" Rothadd explained. "They be o' the spirit world, and things be twisty when they're nigh. Now they be gone, and all's well again."

Rothadd was right. Having nothing better to try, he and Zargal placed their trust in the old compass and headed in the direction they hoped was east. Shortly thereafter they reached the road and did not leave it again.

Their path took them steadily upward into the mountains. For hours they struggled on through the opaque fog, blind to their surroundings and never daring to stop for rest. Gradually, however, as they ascended, the mists started to thin out. The gray light that filtered down to them grew brighter and stronger. Soon they were able to distinguish the forms of the snowy rocks and shrubs that stood by the roadside. A little later Rothadd could discern the clear-cut features of his towering companion, whose face, far above, had been completely obscured. The world began to open out again. They were passing over a land of stark, stony hills and narrow valleys. There were no signs of human habitation, save for the ruts in the road. It was understandably not a well-traveled region.

As the fog began to lighten, so too did Rothadd's and Zargal's spirits. By midafternoon Rothadd was positively cheerful; even Zargal was gladdened when, upon reaching the summit of one of the steeper hills, they glimpsed the sun. It was a sun so dim and sickly that it resembled a full moon, and yet it was the most welcome sight that had met their eyes since leaving Hincmar's cottage.

As they progressed, the sunlight grew steadily stronger and the air cleared, until they were able to see the great surrounding mountains quite distinctly. Only the highest peaks were still blanketed in the smoky mists, merging into the smoky sky. No further obstacles hindered Zargal and Rothadd. They soon began to encounter occasional areas of cultivated ground bordering the road, though the land of Obran, mostly unfit for farming, was thinly settled.

The travelers met no one until late that afternoon. They were standing at a fork in the road, debating which path to take to reach King Laza's castle, when the question was settled by the appearance of a lone Turo tinker on his way down the mountain. While Zargal discreetly retired from view, Rothadd questioned the man, who provided directions and continued on his way. Zargal and Rothadd quickly discovered that the Turo had misguided them, either accidentally or by design, for the path led only to a deserted village on the edge of a cliff. They retraced their steps and tried the other road.

Before another hour had passed, they caught sight of King Laza's turrets outlined against the sky. The castle, in seeming defiance of the laws of gravity, was impossibly perched on the crags high above them.

CHAPTER XIII

Zargal and Rothadd spent the next several hours struggling up the mountain toward the castle. Their path was much steeper and rockier than ever before; evidently King Laza did not choose to encourage chance visitors. This fact did not escape the notice of Zargal, but certainly made no impression on Rothadd, who was now brimming with excitement and enthusiasm at the prospect of meeting the famous sorcerer-monarch.

"What do he be like—King Laza?" Rothadd inquired as he hiked along.

"Unspeakably ugly," Zargal replied.

"Aye, but what sort o' nature do he have?"

"Vicious," Zargal said. "Cruel, corrupt, and depraved. He is tyrannical, overbearing, unpredictable. Irresponsible, unjust, inhuman, and malign."

"What sort o' way o' talking do he have?"

"Arrogant, harsh, and disagreeable. To the best of my recollection."

"To the best o' your recollection!" Rothadd echoed. "How could 'ee forget? 'Tis certain 'ee do have sound reason to remember him!"

"Well—" Zargal proceeded to relate the entire tale, or as much of it as he could recall, of the disastrous night at the Peacock.

"Oh, 'tis plain King Laza be a hard man," Rothadd

131

observed at the close of the story. "Near as hard a man as Hincmar he be. But 'ee can't say 'ee didn't give him just cause to act against 'ee. Like 'ee did give the krorks cause," he added in an undertone. " 'Tis the same all over again."

"I'm tired of hearing about those krorks!" Zargal flared. "As for King Laza—I admit I offended him, and I was wrong."

"Looks like it."

"But in return, he has wrecked my entire life. The punishment is completely out of proportion to the offense. He needn't have been so touchy!"

"That be the way o' the sorcerers," Rothadd said. "There just ben't no telling about 'em. 'Ee must keep it in mind—there ben't no telling."

"It's a little late for that."

"Ah, nay. Remember, 'ee'll meet him again soon enough. What will 'ee say to him?"

"I hadn't thought about that."

" 'Ee'd do well to think about it, then. We be there, almost."

Rothadd was right. Ahead of them loomed King Laza's castle—not a rational, perfect piece of formal elegance, like the dwelling of Duke Jalonzal. King Laza's castle was the product of a bygone age, a huge stone pile, topped with a crown of twisted towers connected to one another by fragile covered bridges, studded with gargoyles, and surrounded by a crenellated wall. Its builder, some distant ancestor of the present King, had possessed eccentric tastes—and his descendants had carried on in the family tradition. The resulting edifice was a fantastic conglomeration of various additions constructed by successive rulers of Obran. But the most striking aspect of the castle was its location—for it possessed no foundation at all and stood upon a single immense rock. So delicately was the building balanced that it looked as if a strong wind might knock it from its resting place and send it toppling down into the valley, thousands of feet below.

Zargal was paying little attention to the building, for he was pondering Rothadd's last question. In all the time that had elapsed since he'd left his father's Court, he'd never actually considered what he might say when he should finally find himself face to face with King Laza. "I suppose

I must—apologize to him," the Duke's son decided. "And then I shall ask him to restore me to my normal size."

"If he do be as vicious and depraved as 'ee say," Rothadd countered, "then why should he do it? After all, when 'ee did insult him—"

"Perhaps if I offer to pay him—"

"Ha! That didn't get 'ee far with Hincmar, did it?"

"Well—well—" Zargal finally hit upon a satisfactory reply. "Laza of Obran is a king. And my father is the ruler of Szar. Therefore we have much in common, and should be able to understand each other. We shall speak as one prince to another."

"I know naught o' princes, but I do know somewhat o' magicians from Hincmar. And I tell 'ee, 'tis never a safe thing to presume upon 'em—"

"We have here a magician who is also a king—remember that. Magicians may be your specialty, but monarchs are mine. I've dealt with them all my life, and believe me, I know how to treat them. You mean well, Rothadd, but you have much to learn," Zargal concluded kindly.

"That be true. But I ben't the only one," Rothadd replied.

A warning bell sounded from the castle. Apparently the sentry had noted the approach of the two strangers, one of them a giant, and had taken alarm. By the time that Rothadd and Zargal arrived at the gate, the bolts were in place and the portcullis down. The guard on duty was one of the four lackeys who had accompanied King Laza to the Peacock Inn.

"I am Lord Zargal of Szar. My companion is Rothadd, Rotha's son, of the Eastling Wolds." Zargal addressed the sentry with great self-possession and an air of pleasant condescension. "Be so good as to inform his Majesty Laza of our arrival." He paused, awaiting reply.

The guard answered in an unintelligible foreign tongue.

"Tell his Majesty that we are here, fellow," Zargal commanded more sharply.

The guard extended his hand, pointed up at Zargal, and asked some question which they did not understand.

"Don't stand there gibbering, fellow—do as you are bid," the Duke's son snapped. Rothadd shook his head doubtfully.

Without removing his eyes from Zargal's face, the guard backed away from the gate. When he was but a few feet from the great door of the castle, he turned and dashed into the building.

" 'Ee didn't go about it in the right way, I think," Rothadd said.

"Really—how so?" Zargal had taken hold of the portcullis and was rattling it experimentally.

"It wouldn't hurt 'ee to use some of your fancy manners sometimes."

"Manners—to a palace sentry?" Zargal regarded him blankly. "What for?"

"It wouldn't be so bad a thing to get on the good side of folk for a change—"

"Possibly. But there is a natural order in the world, and it doesn't do to forget one's position."

"Aye," Rothadd agreed, "but one's position do change sudden, sometimes. 'Ee be the living proof o' that yourself. I still say 'ee ought not talk so sharply to the sentry."

"The sentry is obviously a slow-witted lout and of no importance. I don't approve King Laza's choice of servants."

"Indeed? Perhaps I'll be able to change your mind about that, Lord Zargal." Zargal and Rothadd both started. Unnoticed by either, King Laza had emerged from the castle. He now sat just behind the portcullis, ensconced in his wheeled chair, looking at them with a smile that contorted the muscles of his dreadful face. The great silver lizard crouched on the ground beside him.

For a moment Zargal could think of nothing to say. Rothadd was simply staring, openmouthed. King Laza regarded them with an air of pleased expectation. "I'm delighted that you've come," the King went on helpfully. "I receive so few visitors these days. And you have brought a companion as well—a young Outcottager, I presume. What is your name, lad?"

The boy gulped. "I be called Rothadd, your Majesty."

"Rothadd—ah, yes, a fine old name in your country. Well, gentlemen, you are both quite welcome. Please do overlook the discourtesy of my guard—he is unaccustomed to strangers," Laza apologized smoothly. "Bibka, admit our visitors, if you please."

The lizard flashed a distrustful glance at Zargal, but did as she was asked. After slipping the bolts, she grasped the portcullis chain in her teeth and hauled mightily upon it. The portcullis rose and remained in place as the lizard deftly affixed the chain to a hook sunk deep into the stone.

"Excellent. Gentlemen, enter freely," the King invited.

But Zargal's entrance was far from free. Despite the great height of the castle gate, it was still much too low for him, and he was forced to get down on his hands and knees and crawl through, with Rothadd following in his wake. Once inside the courtyard, Zargal quickly rose to his feet in a belated effort to appear dignified.

"You must be weary after your long journey," the King said. "No doubt you could do with some refreshment?"

"Oh, aye!" Rothadd agreed.

"And you, Lord Zargal? You are perhaps a bit hungry?"

"Thank you—no," Zargal returned, with rigid courtesy.

"Indeed?" The King's eyes glinted with amusement. "You are quite certain?"

"Quite."

"A pity!" Another glint came from the shadow of the King's wide-brimmed hat. "My chef is to be denied the honor of entertaining you. He will be most disappointed!" Zargal said nothing. "But you, lad," King Laza said to Rothadd. "You have an appetite, I'm sure. Go into the castle, and the lackeys will provide for you. Refresh yourself, lad—and after that, we shall talk."

King Laza's manner did not brook contradiction, and Rothadd departed without argument. Zargal gazed after him longingly as King Laza turned back to him.

"And now we are alone, my lord. It grieves me that you seem disinclined to accept my hospitality. Yet I'm certain that you'll consent to remain here as my guest for at least a little while. After all, you've come such a long way from Szar."

"I should be honored, your Majesty."

"Excellent. Actually," King Laza confided, "I've been expecting you for some time."

"Oh?"

"Yes. Last night, various disturbances in the borderlands were reported to me by my agents, and thus I surmised that you were on your way."

It was on the tip of Zargal's tongue to ask if King Laza's agents included any of the krorks, but he refrained, contenting himself with a brief inclination of his tremendous head.

"And you have arrived at last!" King Laza continued, with the utmost graciousness. "We shall do our best to make you comfortable, my lord. This evening, a tented enclosure will be erected for you out here in the courtyard. I should much prefer, of course, to invite you into the castle, but under the circumstances, that is hardly practical, I fear." King Laza's venous eyes traveled slowly up Zargal's giant figure, then he lowered them regretfully, with the air of a host reluctant to call attention to his visitor's infirmities.

The Duke's son found King Laza's manner infuriating, and it was with increasing difficulty that he managed to control his temper. However, his boyhood training at the Court of Jalonzal stood him in good stead now, and he was able to reply with an appearance of unconcern. "The fact is, your Majesty, my visit to Obran is not purely social in nature."

"No?" One of the King's eyebrows lifted. The other, on the paralyzed side of his face, remained still. "You surprise me, my lord. Am I to understand that you have come as the Archduke Jalonzal's emissary upon some business of state?"

"I bear no word from the Duke. I bring you a message of my own."

"And that message is—"

"An apology," Zargal said, with all the forthright charm he could muster. "I have wronged your Majesty."

"To what do you allude, my lord?"

"Do not jest with me, your Majesty! You cannot pretend to have forgotten my insults to you at our last meeting. I bitterly regret my words."

"Yes—yes, I'm sure you do," the King answered.

"What I said to you that night was very wrong—"

"It was undoubtedly a mistake," the King agreed.

"—and I have never been at peace with myself since then."

"I believe that."

"And therefore, your Majesty," Zargal concluded, "I

have journeyed from Szar in search of your pardon, which I pray that you will not withhold from your humble servant." He performed a bow that was easy and graceful, despite all his size.

Bibka uttered a low hiss, and her tail twitched.

"Ah, Lord Zargal, that is a most handsome apology, and aptly delivered." The lines around the King's mouth deepened, and his lips turned down at the corners on the good side of his face. "Who could doubt the sincerity of such elegantly expressed sentiments? Who, indeed, could resist them? Consider my pardon freely granted."

"Your Majesty is most generous—I don't deserve it—"

"But you do, my lord. You do."

"Had I realized whom I offended that night—"

"I'm sure you would not have done it, for your life! Be at ease, my lord. Our quarrel was rooted in misunderstanding. I have forgotten it."

"But, as you can see," Zargal pointed out delicately, "I cannot hope to forget."

"My lord?"

"I am burdened with a perpetual reminder," Zargal explained, encouraged by the seeming success of his tactics.

"Ah, you mean your increased size," the King replied, enlightened. "That is a great misfortune, my lord—a great misfortune."

"A misfortune which I hope your Majesty will soon correct, in view of the renewed friendliness of the relations between us."

"Nothing would give me greater pleasure!" King Laza exclaimed. "I am essentially of a kindly nature and rejoice in the opportunity of doing good for others."

Zargal waited hopefully.

"Yes," the King went on benevolently, "for my own part, I'm only too happy to overlook your past offenses. I'm willing to pardon and forget the public insults you heaped upon me, unforgivable though they were. I bear you no grudge—none whatever!—and would be delighted to remove the spell and restore you to your former condition. How unfortunate it is that there is more to be considered here than my own personal feelings!"

"What do you mean?" Zargal demanded warily.

"Alas, my lord, I am a monarch, and have a duty to the

people I rule. I am forced to uphold my dignity at all cost, not so much for my own sake as for theirs."

"You mean you refuse to undo the spell!" Zargal translated.

"The trust of the people of Obran rests in me. Do these good folk not deserve better than a King who permits himself to be humiliated before a rabble?" The gravity of King Laza's voice was belied by the sardonic red spark in his eye. At his side, Bibka puffed and snorted.

Zargal was tempted to suggest exactly what might be done, collectively, to the good folk of Obran, but he decided that such a course would be unwise. Common sense told him that the King was making a fool of him, but he didn't know quite what to do about it. He couldn't afford to anger the sorcerer again.

In a last attempt to save face, Zargal stammered, "Surely, your Majesty—surely there is some restitution which might be made—" He paused and regarded the King, who said nothing "—which will satisfy the honor of all parties and yet make it possible for you to restore me to normality."

"Ah? You interest me, Lord Zargal. What do you have in mind?"

"A—a public apology, perhaps?" Zargal floundered. "Before the assembled citizens of your realm? Would that suffice?"

"My lord, I should never demand such a sacrifice of you!" the King assured him charitably.

Zargal was sick of being toyed with by his powerful adversary. Moreover, he was exhausted, starving, utterly wretched, and beginning to grow desperate as well. Now he burst out, in the same words he had once used to Professor Horm, "What do you want of me?"

"I want nothing. On the contrary, it's you who have come to me, asking favors."

"King Laza, let us be direct with one another. Do you intend to leave me in this condition permanently?" Zargal's voice was expressive of his misery.

But King Laza was not easily moved. "Your offense was rank, and deserved extreme punishment. And yet I am not a vengeful man." Zargal was by this time too dejected to point out the obvious falsity of this claim. "As I hark back to the events of that night, I seem to recall—yes, I'm sure of it—I told you then how you might redeem yourself in my sight. Do you remember this?"

"Not really," Zargal answered uneasily.

"You were to spend five years—" the King prompted. "Is it coming back to you now?"

"No!" Zargal replied, looking trapped.

"Five years as a servant in my castle," King Laza pronounced. "At the end of that time, provided you give satisfaction, all debts will be clear."

"Such work is beneath a gentleman!"

"You refuse? I understand perfectly. You wish to seek some other savant who will undo my work. In that case, I wish you the very best of luck. You will need it."

Zargal cast his eyes hopelessly around the empty courtyard. For a moment he did consider the possibility of looking for help elsewhere, but was forced to dismiss the thought. His encounter with Hincmar had convinced him, once and for all, that his only hope lay in King Laza of Obran. "Five years is a long time!" he protested. "Must it be five?"

"Five years," the King repeated inexorably.

There was no way out. Zargal did not trust himself to speak. Gritting his teeth, he nodded once.

"Excellent!" the King approved with one of his nightmare smiles. "I'm delighted that this little matter has been settled to our mutual satisfaction."

"King Laza, I shall do as you ask, because you leave me no other choice. But permit me to say that I do not feel you have behaved as a man of honor."

Bibka immediately let out a roar, sprang forward, and sank her fangs into Zargal's ankle. A man of average size would have been left crippled for life by the attack, but to Zargal it was only a painful nip. He kicked the creature aside violently. Bibka flattened herself to the earth, snarling.

"I loathe discord. It distresses me," King Laza mused. "Lord Zargal, if you are to remain here for the next five years, you really must make up your mind to live in peace with the other inhabitants of the castle. Moreover—" His tone altered dangerously. "You had best learn at the outset that I do not tolerate insolence from the members of my household staff. I should think I'd already made that clear to you. You will find me to be a just master, but not indulgent."

Zargal opened his mouth—and shut it again.

"I believe we understand each other," the King said, once more amiable. "And now, as you must be eager to assume your new position, there is no time to be lost!"

"No time to be lost?"

"Come, come, my lord, don't look so suspicious. I am about to help you. That is what you came here for, isn't it?"

"Yes. I only hope that your idea of helping coincides with my own."

"I intend to reduce you in size," the King declared, a bit irritably. "I have no patience with quibbling." From somewhere beneath the folds of his enveloping cloak he produced a flask of some quivering, metallic, liquid substance. "Drink it," he commanded.

Zargal took the flask and examined it. The heavy liquid within resembled quicksilver, but for an odd iridescence which that element never possessed. The shining surface reflected a variety of colors that changed with each shift of the flask. "What is it?" he asked.

"A cure, of sorts. Nothing beyond that need concern you."

"You're in the habit of carrying cures on your person?"

"Did I not explain," the King remarked with some amusement, "that I was expecting you?"

"And now you ask me to drink this, without knowing what it is?"

"That is entirely up to you. Drink it or not, but choose quickly. This argument begins to weary me. Another moment, and I may decide to withdraw the offer."

This threat produced instant results. Without further ado, Zargal lifted the flask and drained the contents in a single swallow, without allowing himself to taste it. For a moment nothing happened. Then the Duke's son was seized with a series of cramp and pains that convulsed his entire gigantic frame. He was certain that he'd been mortally poisoned, for his every vein seemed flooded with acid, and a red mist was burning before his eyes. Through the mist he could still discern the horrible face of King Laza, who was watching him with great interest. Then all vision faded away. The lizard Bibka had just enough time to draw her master's wheeled chair safely out of the way before Zargal's body crashed to the ground like a tree struck by lightning.

CHAPTER XIV

The Duke's son had no idea how long he remained unconscious. When he finally awoke, it was to find himself lying in a large, cold, stone room, with Rothadd kneeling at his side. The Outcottager lad had been watching anxiously and now heaved a sigh as Zargal's eyelids slowly lifted.

"How do 'ee feel, then?" Rothadd asked.

"Tired," Zargal murmured. Memory returned to him. "What did he do to me this time?" He raised himself up on one elbow. "Where are we?"

"Easy!" Rothadd warned. " 'Ee be all right, no fear!"

"What happened? The last thing I remember is drinking that silver poison."

" 'Twas no poison, else 'ee'd not be alive to tell of it," Rothadd pointed out logically. "Well, I didn't see it. I was in here, a-fillin' myself with bread and cheese. The first thing I did know, I looked out the window, and there 'ee were, a-lyin' flat on the ground, like as if 'ee'd been brained—"

"What was the King doing?"

"Nothing much. Just a-sittin' there with his lizard, the both o' them looking at 'ee like it were something they wanted to remember. So naturally, I jumped up, and left

141

the bread where it was, but put the cheese in my pocket. I
wish now that I'd a-took the bread as well, it was new-
baked, and—"

"Yes, yes. Then what?"

"Then I went a-runnin' toward the door to go out and see
if 'ee were dead, and I met King Laza comin' in. He
stopped me and said, 'No fear, lad, your friend has not
been harmed—' "

"Ha!"

"And he said that now would be a good time for us to
have a chat. I wanted to go out to the courtyard, but he
wouldn't hear of it. So we did talk."

"What about?"

"Oh, he asked me all about myself, and I told him o'
how I met 'ee, a-thinkin' 'ee were the Graschak, and how
I did take 'ee to Hincmar. And then I did tell him how
Hincmar had sent me to 'im, and he answered, 'I am happy
to receive you. The least I can do is to extend that professional courtesy to Hincmar—as he has so obviously extended it to me.' I think he may have been talkin' about
'ee," Rothadd guessed, "but I ben't sure."

"I am."

"Maybe. Anyway, he said I could stay, and welcome.
After that he took himself off with his lizard, and I went
out to see to 'ee. 'Twas plain at once 'ee weren't dead. 'Ee
were a-lyin' on the ground, still and quiet, but ever so
often 'ee'd give a sort of a twitch, like neighbor Woonly's
daft boy. First one arm would go, then t'other; then your
legs; then 'ee'd flop around some, and—"

"I see. What happened next?"

"Why, then it grew interestin', it did. 'Ee just lay there,
but grew smaller and smaller, like 'ee were a man of ice,
a-meltin' in the sun. A rare sight it was. After 'ee did
shrink small enough, the King's men came out and carried
'ee down here, with me a-followin' after. Last night, that
was. That be all of it."

"Where are we?" Zargal was still somewhat confused. He
was lying on a pallet near an immense fireplace. Great iron
pots and pans hung on all four walls.

" 'Tis the kitchen, by the look of it," Rothadd answered.

"And," Zargal marveled, as the meaning of it all began

to sink in, "I'm cured? I'm no longer a giant? I'm a normal human being again?"

"Well—" Rothadd waffled uneasily. "Well, now—"

The boy's manner alerted Zargal to the fact that something was amiss. "What is it? Something's wrong, isn't it?" he demanded. "What's happened?"

"Well, Zargal, 'tis certain 'ee be much better off now than 'ee was. Much."

"What are you trying to say? Why are you looking at me like that?"

Rothadd hung his head and said nothing. Zargal looked down at himself. He could see at a glance how much he'd changed, how much smaller he was. He now lay buried beneath the quilts, which had formerly failed to cover his long limbs. He was able to observe his surroundings from a human vantage point. The ceiling of the room was well above him, and Rothadd no longer appeared dwarfish. Yet something was surely wrong.

" 'Ee know," Rothadd chattered in an attempt to soothe him, "this be the first time ever I did see your face close up. 'Tis the same as I thought, only not the same, somehow—"

Zargal was paying no attention. With some effort, he managed to pull himself to his feet—and perceived at once the cause of Rothadd's discomfort. King Laza's cure had undoubtedly done him great good—he had shrunk considerably. But he had not been restored to normal human condition. He was still at least half again his true height, and the top of Rothadd's head didn't reach as high as his chest. Zargal blanched with fury and frustration. "I'll kill him!" he exclaimed. "Where is he? Take me to him!"

"Easy, now, Zargal!" Rothadd pleaded in alarm. "Stop and think, now!"

"No. He's played his last wizard's trick on me. Take me to him. Now!"

" 'Ee be a-crazed! 'Ee can't touch him!"

"He is toying with me. He's made a mockery of me!"

"Well—'ee did the same to him, didn't 'ee? In the tavern?"

"He's broken his promise. He obviously has no intention of restoring me—"

" 'Ee don't know that."

"He has a mind as misshapen as his features." Zargal's own features were somewhat twisted with rage and distress. "He doesn't deserve to live."

"It ben't your right to say so!" Rothadd was growing distressed himself.

"I see now that my own life is ruined, beyond hope of recovery." Zargal had regained some measure of self-control, and he spoke slowly and clearly. "But I'll bring him down as well. You may be certain of that."

" 'Ee mustn't say so!" Rothadd insisted. " 'Twas this mad humor got 'ee into this fix to begin with! If 'ee do harm the King, then there won't be anyone to take the spell off 'ee, I can tell 'ee that. 'Ee'll stay as 'ee be now forever!"

"It looks as if I'm to stay as I am forever in any case."

" 'Ee don't know that. Happen King Laza hasn't shrunk 'ee all the way back, so as to make sure 'ee won't run off afore your five years be up."

"He could have had my word on it. He ought to know that my word is to be trusted."

"How do he know that, then? 'Ee don't trust *him*, do 'ee?"

It was becoming apparent to Zargal, even in his excited state, that Rothadd was not an easy person to quarrel with. The Duke's son was too intelligent himself to fail to recognize a reasonable argument when he heard it.

Noting Zargal's hesitation, Rothadd followed up his advantage. "King Laza be your only hope," he pointed out.

Zargal did not dispute this, thus revealing that he was not quite as devoid of hope as he had claimed. He was still endeavoring to master his outrage when the kitchen door opened.

The man who stepped into the room was short, slight, and balding, with a very thin face crowded with large features. He was attired in the black and white livery of King Laza's household servants, and his coat was handsomely trimmed with silver galloon. Over his arm he carried a similar suit of livery, minus the decoration, and a pair of very large shoes. Briefly he paused, startled at the sight of Zargal. Then he advanced into the room with small steps and inquired in a high, penetrating voice, "Which of you two lads is to be the new scullion?"

For a moment there was a terrible silence, and then Zargal asked, with restraint, "I beg your pardon, did you say—scullion?"

"That is correct."

"No, I think not. Surely you can't mean a scullion?"

"I assure you, that is what I mean. And I think I should remind you," the man added, his high voice taking on nasal overtones, "that it is by no means your place to contradict me. Do you know who I am?" Zargal shook his head. "I am Guggard, the major-domo of the King's household. If that term is unknown to you, you may think of me as the steward. I am in charge here."

"I see," Zargal answered coldly. "And do you know who I am?"

"Are you not Zargal, the new scullion?"

"It's true that King Laza has engaged me—"

"As the new scullion," Guggard completed. "Though why he should have done so is beyond me—a great, hulking lout like you, and probably clumsy into the bargain. Well, I suppose I must accept his Majesty's decisions."

"Now listen, Guggard, or whatever your name is—"

"It's 'Master Guggard' to you, boy," the major-domo admonished, cracking his knuckles for emphasis. Zargal and Rothadd both started at the sound. "His Majesty warned me that you might prove impertinent to begin with, but I'll wager I know how to deal with you. Put this on." He tossed the suit of livery to Zargal. "It's obvious," he said, eyeing Zargal's tattered quilts, "that going into service is a step up in the world for you. I hope you are properly appreciative."

"Hang on, now," Rothadd warned Zargal in an undertone. "This ben't the time to say nothin'!"

Zargal loked as if he were about to explode, but followed the advice and struggled into the livery. King Laza must have provided it especially for him, for it fit perfectly.

"Are you Rothadd?" Guggard asked the young Outcottager. Rothadd nodded. "His Majesty desires to see you immediately."

"What for, then?"

"I do not know. It is not my place to ask questions. Nor is it yours."

"Maybe so. But I ben't a servant here," Rothadd reminded him defiantly. Guggard pointed regally at the door. Rothadd exited with reluctance.

Guggard turned his attention back to Zargal, who had finished dressing and was examining the servant's garb with disgust. "How——" Guggard began, and broke off to command, "Have the goodness to look at me when I'm speaking to you, boy! How did you happen to grow to that ridiculous height?"

"That is not a matter I choose to discuss with you," Zargal returned.

"Insolence will not be tolerated here." Guggard popped his knuckles again. It was evidently an ingrained habit. The knuckles of both his hands were huge, protuberant, and inflamed. "Were you born that way, or did it happen to you late in life?"

"Some have greatness thrust upon them," Zargal replied glumly.

"Eh? Well, I daresay you're to blame for it," Guggard decided, surveying him with more than a shade of suspicion. "These things don't happen accidentally; it's not natural. I shall be keeping an eye on you, boy. As long as you are here, in the service of his Majesty, it's up to me to see that you do an honest day's work. You will begin now. I shall supervise."

Zargal looked around the kitchen, at a loss. "Well? What am I expected to do?" he asked.

"What are you to *do*? What are you to *do*? Do you mean to stand there, looking at this room, and actually ask me what there is to *do*? I see now why you are so huge—all of your vital energy was used to develop your body, and not a shred of it went to your mind!"

"I've never done this sort of work before," Zargal said, keeping a tight rein on his temper.

"I see. Then I must deal with your deficiencies as best I may." Guggard cracked his knuckles. Zargal was already beginning to loathe the sound. "Keep in mind, boy, that there is always a right way and a wrong way of performing any task. You are now going to learn the right ways. I shall instruct."

Guggard loved to instruct. In fact, he was so fond of it that he never stopped advising, correcting, and criticizing. Moreover, he was imaginative, and never at a loss to think of something for Zargal to do. Thus, Zargal started off by learning how to clean the floor, how to sweep the flagstones, always sweeping from left to right, how to mop and dry, and how to apply wax in the correct circular patterns. Next he proceeded to the great fireplace and learned how to remove ashes and cinders, how to polish the andirons, how to shine the tiles, and in what order. From there he continued to the great washtubs and learned all the best methods of cleaning dishes, platters, goblets, pots, and pans. Zargal learned how to whet knives, draw water, and chop wood. He learned the right way of peeling potatoes, turnips, and carrots—Guggard preferred that the peel be removed in one continuous strip. He learned how to chop onions, garlic, leeks, chives, scallions, and shallots—there was a different technique for each vegetable. He learned how to pluck chickens and scale fish, render fats and turn the spit, baste the meat and stir the kettle. He also received some instruction in the arts of soap-making and candle-dipping, but only on a very basic level—Guggard did not judge that his pupil was yet worthy of assuming these duties.

The major-domo decided within the first few hours that the new scullion was a hopeless case. It was obvious from the beginning that Zargal possessed none of the qualities of a good servant. He did not have even the most rudimentary understanding of the correct procedures involved in operating a palace kitchen, and displayed little enthusiasm for learning. It was apparent that he did not really put his whole heart into scrubbing and scouring. His attempts at dusting and mopping were downright lackadaisical, and he had an annoying way of staring out the window at the courtyard in a brooding manner for whole minutes at a time. His gigantic size was glaringly unnatural. Worst of all, Zargal didn't know his place, and seemed unaware of the difference in station between a scullion and a major-domo. He did not address Guggard with that admiring respect which was so clearly due the steward of a King's household. It was hard to put into words, but somehow the new scullion's manner seemed devoid of appropriate humility.

He didn't take kindly to instruction, either. Once, when he had waxed all the wooden stools and benches in the room, using colorless wax rather than the correct amber-glow wax, and Guggard suggested that he do it all over again, Zargal had exhibited an unbecoming resentment. Another time, when the major-domo ordered him to roll the thick slime cleared out of the grease-trap into spheres of uniform size prior to discarding it, the scullion ventured to object and had to be severely reprimanded.

Even more objectionable than his impertinence, however, was his habit of asking questions. He asked numberless questions about King Laza, his customs, pastimes, likes, and dislikes—things that a newly engaged scullion had no right to know.

"You remember your place, boy," Guggard advised and cracked his knuckles. "I shouldn't ask so many questions, if I were you."

Zargal ignored this sound advice—Guggard couldn't help but notice the scullion's indifference to even the best of advice, and it vexed him. Outside one of the kitchen windows stood a great pot into which were thrown the entrails of all the fish, poultry, and game that King Laza's household consumed at mealtimes. Guggard set Zargal to work cleaning the pot, and felt better.

By the time that evening had come, Zargal was exhausted. In the past, he'd been quite capable of riding or hunting all day without ever feeling tired, but one day of kitchen work had completely drained him. The strain of enduring Guggard's presence and conversation was partially to blame. Another problem was hunger. Zargal soon discovered that King Laza's cure had reduced his appetite to a more or less manageable level, but he was still intensely hungry all of the time. After what seemed like an eternity of waiting, the dinner hour finally arrived. It was Guggard's opinion that scullions were meant to dine on bread, goat cheese, and gruel; and bread, goat cheese, and gruel were what Zargal received. The Duke's son had no objection at all, and proceeded to devour every morsel in sight.

"A greedy one, aren't you?" Guggard asked.

"You've your master to thank for that," Zargal replied.

Guggard's lip curled. "It never does good to blame others for our own failings, boy," he admonished. "That's an important lesson, and I hope you'll remember it."

Zargal ceased chewing and studied his overseer. "Haven't you any duties," he asked at last, "that take you out of the kitchen?"

"By no means! I remain here with you during your period of training. I'll correct your faults, deal with your inadequacies, and render you fit to serve in the kitchen of a king. It will be a hard struggle—you're very unpromising material—but in the end, I'll succeed in making a decent scullion of you. For that service, I shall expect no repayment other than your thanks." Guggard smiled condescendingly.

Zargal made an almost imperceptible brushing gesture, as if to repel some buzzing insect. "Will that take long?" he inquired.

"As little time as possible. I hope you'll keep in mind that every moment I spend here working to improve you is time robbed from far more significant activities!"

"I wouldn't want to be responsible for that," Zargal said with utter sincerity.

"His Majesty Laza has commanded, and I obey. If he wishes his major-domo, the superintendent of all his household staff, to spend entire days schooling an oversized kitchen lackey, who am I to question his orders?" Guggard shook his head. "But I don't understand it. It's not right." He popped his knuckles furiously. The room seemed to be full of cracking twigs.

Rather than answer, Zargal began shredding a hunk of bread into crumbs. He was doing his best to keep his attention fixed exclusively on this task, until Guggard commanded, "Stop that, boy. You irritate me!" His voice had grown more nasal. "You were brought here to keep this kitchen clean, and you scatter crumbs all over the table! Shame!"

The Duke's son felt as if he were being attacked by a gnat. But remembering that he would be here for the next five years and that it would make things harder if he quarreled, he stopped tearing the bread and said evenly, "You call yourself the head of the King's household staff. I've seen no servants or guards, but for the sentry at the gate. Where are the others?"

"The others? You ask of the others? No doubt they are

at work, attending to their own affairs, boy. As we all should do."

"Yes, but where? How many servants do you supervise?"

"Why, all of them, of course. Did I not explain that I am the major-domo? Are you a little slow of understanding, boy?"

Zargal persisted. "How many servants are there in the palace?"

"There are his Majesty's four lackeys, Vaxil the chef, who is sick in bed today, and yourself. I am in charge."

"That's all?" Zargal asked, amazed. "In a castle of this size—the castle of a king—there are only half a dozen servants? Why, any nobleman of Szar would have at least three times that number!"

"Sham and show!" Guggard scoffed, but he seemed uncomfortable. "Frills and feathers! Six are all that's needed. It shows a certain vanity in you to expect anything more."

"Six are not enough," Zargel declared. "Have there never been any more?"

"In the old days, of course—" Guggard said and stopped. "They're gone now," he added after a short pause.

"Why?" Zargal asked curiously. "Why did they all leave? Were they mistreated?"

"Certainly not! King Laza desired them to go, so they went."

"Why did he dismiss them?"

"That is no concern of yours!"

"But who attends to the needs of his courtiers?"

"His Majesty keeps no court."

"A king with no court? How can that be?"

"This discussion is ended. Ended!"

"I see. You don't know the answer," Zargal said.

"I've had enough of your insolence, boy!" The popping of Guggard's knuckles now resembled a tiny firing squad. "You ask too many questions! I knew as soon as I saw you that you'd be a problem, what with the idiotic size of you!"

"Why shouldn't I ask questions?" Zargal fired back. "What harm does it do?" He was finally losing control of his temper. "I'm sick of your niggling, you insufferable flunky!"

Guggard's eyes bulged and his narrow face reddened. For a moment he seemed incapable of speech. This effect did not last. "This—is—impossible! Intolerable! That a scullion should speak thus to me! To me! Such a thing cannot be!"

"You'll have five years to get used to it!" Zargal told him hotly. Five years—the thought of it put him into a rage that no remark of Guggard's could possibly have aroused.

"We'll see about that, boy!" the major-domo shrilled up at him. "We'll see who has to get used to things around here! We'll see if you're still such a firebrand after you've spent the rest of the evening cleaning out the servants' latrine in the courtyard! See how you like *that!*"

"I refuse. I'll do no such thing!"

"You have no choice. You are a scullion, and I am the major-domo. You have to do what I tell you." Guggard smirked. "So you might as well get started."

"I will not!"

"Oh, yes, you will, boy! His Majesty has put me in charge here. If you don't obey, you'll answer to him. And whatever grand ideas you may have, you'll find that his Majesty didn't bring you here to lead a life of ease and luxury!"

"Ease! Luxury!" the Duke's son spat. "I'll answer to him, all right! And he'll answer to me. He has much to answer for!"

CHAPTER XV

Zargal was so thoroughly infuriated that he had lost all thought of possible consequences. He flung himself out of the kitchen, then stormed off down the corridor in search of the King of Obran.

It was a very large castle, and Zargal wasn't familiar with it. He had no idea where he was going and rushed up and down spiral staircases, through room after quiet room, without meeting a soul. The place was vast and seemingly deserted. The Duke's son sped along endless stone galleries, hung with tapestries and lit with wax candles. He passed through ballrooms, council chambers, banqueting halls, and antechambers, all glowing with candlelight, all beautifully furnished, and all empty. Zargal simply went slamming through the rooms in ever-increasing frustration. He had no specific plan in mind, but was in a mood for violence.

It wasn't until he reached the second storey of the great east wing of the castle that he finally encountered signs of a human presence. Upon reaching the head of the stairs, he turned to the left and stalked toward the door at the end of the corridor as if drawn there by instinct. For just an instant he paused, casting his eyes around the hall in search of something to use as a weapon. There was nothing to be found, and he resumed his advance.

Now his ears were caught by the sound of music, music that grew stronger as he neared the door. Someone on the other side was playing a stringed instrument, and there came the sound of a human voice singing. It was a remarkably lovely feminine voice. The song was an ancient and mournful Obranese ballad. Something—perhaps the voice, perhaps the song, or else the combination—was exercising a curiously soothing effect on Zargal's nerves, and he could feel his anger start to ebb. That wouldn't do, so the Duke's son mentally listed all the outrages he had suffered at King Laza's hand. He was still in a state of high indignation as he kicked open the chamber door.

The room beyond, which was the King's private dining hall, was small and very richly furnished. Magnificent tapestries clothed the stone walls. Two silver-gilt candelabra, sitting on the marble tabletop, cast their warm light. The carved chairs were covered in amber velvet, which repeated one of the dominant colors in the tapestries. All four lackeys were in attendance. One of them was carving a roast fowl for Rothadd, who sat attired in a new and handsome suit. In the middle of the room stood a girl in green, presumably the singer, who turned her head and stared as Zargal entered.

Zargal noted all of this but dimly. He had eyes only for King Laza, who sat with his lizard coiled on the floor beside him and nothing more than a goblet of mineral water on the table before him. The King was, as usual, wearing a wide hat that shaded his face. Zargal paused, breathing heavily.

"Well. My Lord Zargal," the King said with every evidence of good will. "This is an unexpected pleasure! All the more unexpected," he added significantly, "in that you have not been summoned."

The Duke's son ignored the implied rebuke. "Traitor!" he cried. "You have played me false! Liar!"

The girl in green caught her breath. The four lackeys looked dazed. Bibka uncoiled herself. Rothadd was making desperate signals to him.

Zargal paid no heed. "Traitor!" he repeated.

King Laza showed no sign of anger. Only his face, under

the shadow of his hat, was more impossibly ugly than ever. "You've insulted me in the past," he said quietly, and for once the tinge of amusement was absent from his voice. "Behold the result. Now you repeat your error. You learn slowly, my lord. What will it take to teach you?"

"You have broken your word to me," Zargal accused, "and I despise you for that. Magician you may be, but I will say it."

"Indeed." King Laza stared thoughtfully at him for a time. For that matter, everyone in the room was staring at him. Rothadd was literally wringing his hands. The King seemed to conduct a brief inward debate, then said, "Before I decide how to deal with you, you will explain yourself."

"Explain? Surely there is no need! Is the very sight of me not sufficient explanation? You promised me a cure. Is this the way you keep your promise? You are forsworn, sir!"

"Zargal! For mercy's sake, hold your tongue!" Rothadd pleaded.

King Laza stopped him. "Enough, lad. I shall attend to this. You have a poor memory, my lord," he told Zargal. "If you will recall, you've agreed to serve me for five years. At the end of that time, providing you give satisfaction— I would advise you to keep that condition in mind—at the end of that time, and not before, your debt will be clear."

"You led me to believe you would cure me at once."

"That is false. If it is what you chose to believe, you deceived yourself."

"Do you imagine that I will endure this for five years? I have no patience!"

"Quite right, Lord Zargal. And mine is wearing thin as well."

"Zargal!" Rothadd cried desperately. "Will 'ee get out o' here while 'ee can? Crackbrained, 'ee must be!"

"I demand satisfaction, your Majesty!"

Rothadd choked helplessly.

"Lord Zargal." The King's eyebrow arched in genuine disbelief. "Am I to understand that you are offering me a challenge? You actually wish a duel?"

"You may pick your weapons, your Majesty."

The King hardly responded to the invitation as Zargal

had hoped. He leaned back in his chair and burst into prolonged laughter. As Zargal stared in bewilderment, and
Rothadd looked relieved, Laza continued to chuckle.

"I'll have no more of this!" It was the girl in green who
now spoke up unexpectedly. "No more! What are you
about, sir? First you insult my father, and now you seek to
murder him!"

Her father! Zargal turned and looked at her closely for
the first time. The young lady was light and slender, and
no more than eighteen years old. She had been blessed with
springtime coloring—leaf-green eyes that now flashed warn-
ingly, and a splendidly unruly crown of pale gold curls.
Her small hands were clenched around the neck of a
kleveen—the traditional stringed instrument of the Obranese mountaineers. Surely such a creature could not be the
daughter of King Laza!

"This is an affair of honor," he told her briefly. "A duel
is indicated."

"Honor! Ha! You are a bully, an assassin!" Her cheeks
were flushed; she looked thoroughly angry. Curiously
enough, her voice was so musical that the insults lost their
bite. No matter what she said, the effect was pleasing. Zargal was at a loss to explain it.

"You are hardly aware, madam," he began, "of the
facts—"

"It is enough for me to know that you—so great and
strong and young—desire to fight my father, who obviously does not possess good health! Have you no sense of
decency, sir?"

King Laza had stopped laughing, but a smile still bent
one side of his mouth. "I am much to blame," he confessed
gracefully. "Lord Zargal, I beg leave to introduce my
daughter, Princess Bellora. She is overly concerned for my
welfare. My dear, our young friend seems to have lost his
voice, which is a pity, in view of his many interesting ob-
servations. This is Zargal, our new scullion."

"A scullion—oh!" she exclaimed.

"He is also," the King continued, "the heir to the Dukedom of Szar."

"Oh? I see. I thought his speech was a little unusual for
a scullion."

Zargal had the now-familiar feeling that he had once

more lost control of the situation. "I have challenged your Majesty," he said. "I see no cause for merriment in that. Her ladyship's point, however, is well taken. Under the circumstances, I am willing to engage whichever member of your household your Majesty deems fit to select as a champion."

"And if I simply decline your challenge, my lord?"

"Then the world shall know of it and judge."

"So. Knowing who I am—and what my powers are— you are quite determined, young man, to go ahead with this?"

"I am."

"Then so be it. You will have your desire." King Laza's expression was unreadable. "You have chosen your course." The King spoke calmly and seriously, without anger and without mockery. Somehow this response was far more alarming than any gust of rage. His words were leaden with finality.

"Your Majesty—Zargal here doesn't know what he's a-sayin' to 'ee—" Rothadd appealed.

"He has said it. What's done is done," the King answered, with a chilling hint of regret.

"Father," Princess Bellora cried, "you don't mean to fight this—this giant?"

"My dear, the poor wretch has been foolish enough to issue a challenge which I may not refuse. I'll take him at his word, however, and appoint a deputy to fight in my place." For various reasons, the Princess, Rothadd, and Zargal all brightened at this decision. Only the four silent lackeys looked glum. Presumably it was one of them who would have to fight the enormous stranger. "Lord Zargal," the King said formally, "as the challenged party, I waive my right to choice of weapons. What do you favor, sir?"

"Swords," Zargal answered. He was a notably fine swordsman. "Who is to act as your Majesty's proxy?"

"My servants do not assist me in such matters," King Laza replied. "I call upon a friend for that. I name as my second—if she is willing—the slatku Bibka."

At mention of her name, Bibka raised her head with a look of unmistakable eagerness. A globbering sound escaped her throat, and she took a step in Zargal's direction.

The Duke's son was taken aback. "A lizard? I'd assumed

that your Majesty's place would be taken by a human substitute. I'm not certain that honor will be satisfied—"

"You declared your conditions, my lord, and I accepted them," the King replied. "The slatku is your opponent. That is my decision."

Bibka's eyes had gone red. Tremors ran along the muscles of her long back, causing thousands of silver scales to flash gold in the light of the candles. Evidently the lizard recalled Zargal's behavior in the courtyard and was looking forward to a rematch. Zargal, albeit oversized, was by no means the giant he had been then.

Zargal regarded the great lizard, whose eyes were fastened on his throat. Once again, King Laza had placed him in an impossible situation; but there was no denying the fact that he'd asked for it. "Very well," he heard himself saying. "When and where shall the match take place?"

"Here and now."

"Here? Now?" Events were moving along too rapidly. Zargal felt as if he were being pulled out to sea by a strong undertow.

"Your Majesty," Rothadd interjected, "it ben't fair. He has no sword—"

"Father," the Princess began, "this is too rash, too unadvised, too sudden—"

"Enough. I am through with games and trifling," the King said. "This lord has insisted upon a duel. Very well, his request will be fulfilled, and at once. Lord Zargal shall be supplied with a sword." Laza nodded to one of the lackeys. The fellow drew his sword and handed it to the reluctant Zargal. It was a plain, heavy weapon with a very keen edge. To one of Zargal's size, however, the blade seemed pathetically short. At a sign from their master, the servants began to shove the table and chairs away from the middle of the room to create space. Zargal looked on without enthusiasm.

"My Lord Zargal, advance to the center, if you please," the King directed. "Bibka," he addressed the hissing creature, "be so good as to join him. There will be no further delay."

Bibka needed no urging, and stalked forward to face her foe. Seeing no help for it, Zargal stepped forward to meet her, his borrowed sword poised in readiness. Never again, he reflected, would he be so thoughtless, so hasty, so down-right stupid—if he survived to profit by the lesson.

"Let the duel commence," King Laza commanded re-morselessly.

The words were no sooner out of his mouth than the slatku launched herself in a prodigious leap straight up at Zargal's throat, far above her. Every tooth was bared, her eyes burned crimson, and she was a terrifying sight. But Zargal had no time for terror. Bibka's entire weight struck him full in the chest and sent him hurtling back across the room. Her claws were digging into his shoulders, and she was clinging to him as she ravened at his throat. There was no room to employ the sword.

Zargal flung up his hand, grasped the lizard's broad snout, and managed to shove her away from him. She dropped to the floor, snarling horribly. Zargal took a step backward and at the same time brought his sword forward. When Bibka leaped again, she was met with the steel point. Following up his advantage, the Duke's son dealt half a dozen quick, fierce slashes at the slatku's flat head. Unfor-tunately for him, she was so solidly protected by her metal-lic scales that the sword blade failed to injure her.

Zargal's slashes and thrusts could not wound Bibka, but they were enough to prevent her from launching another upward attack. Now she changed her tactics and went for his legs, seeking to throw him off balance. Hissing and puffing, she worried at his ankles, tearing at his white stock-ings, which were rapidly turning red. Zargal tried to wrench himself loose, but found that his opponent was fearfully strong; whereupon he slid the edge of his sword between her clenched jaws and sawed away until the unprotected skin around her mouth was as bloody as his own ankles. Bibka's blood was a thick, pinkish fluid. The taste of it seemed to drive her to new heights of rage. With a vicious snarl, she released her hold on Zargal, dropped back a few paces, and charged.

The Duke's son stood his ground before the attack, rain-ing blow after blow down upon the slatku's head and body. None of them seemed to hurt her much, but at least they forced her to keep her distance. Zargal's mind was working furiously. He was not able to harm Bibka, and could only just manage to hold off her attack, at the cost of tremendous effort. At the present rate, he would exhaust himself, and he would then be helpless. The Duke's son suddenly sprang to the table, grasped one of the candelabra, and thrust the flaming candles straight at Bibka's eyes. The lizard hastily retreated. The Duke's son was conscious of the sound of yelling, and vaguely realized that Rothadd was cheering him on.

When Bibka once again charged, Zargal swept the candelabrum forward in a wide, attacking arc—and all of the candles extinguished themselves in the resulting wind. Bibka leaped toward him, undaunted and untired. Zargal pitched the great candelbrum at her, and it crashed down on her shoulders. The slatku hardly seemed to notice, and kept coming. The Duke's son brought forth his useless sword again as his enemy sprang. The point struck her breast, but such was the strength of the slatku's armor that Zargal's blade gave way, snapping in two and leaving the Duke's son altogether defenseless. Bibka sank to the floor, unharmed. She seemed to understand the situation, and paused a moment as if savoring it.

"Your Majesty!" Rothadd cried. " 'Ee must stop this!"

"Yes, father," Princess Bellora agreed, "it really isn't fair at all!"

King Laza didn't reply.

Zargal began to edge back in the direction of the table. His aim was to seize the one remaining candelabrum. If he could not succeed in blinding the lizard, then he might at least manage to plunge the room into darkness and put an end to the fight that way. As if she realized his intentions, Bibka moved swiftly to intercept him. With one powerful, unforeseen lash of her tail, she swept his feet out from under him.

Zargal went down in a heap, still clutching the stump of his sword. In an instant Bibka was upon him, and her tail, with a serpent's life of its own, went twisting around his neck. Struggling was obviously useless; in any case, he had little strength left for it.

Bibka was hissing to herself and she tightened her strangling grip on Zargal's throat. As he lay upon the floor, the Duke's son became aware of voices arguing. Rothadd and Princess Bellora were pleading with King Laza to spare his life.

Zargal was pulling and tearing vainly at the reptilian tail that encircled his throat, but he wasn't able to budge it, and his strength was all but gone. Bibka was crouched upon his chest, peering closely into his face. Releasing his grip on the lizard's tail, Zargal attempted to gouge at her eyes, but she was able to evade the attack easily.

Something that Rothadd or the Princess said must have been effective, for King Laza suddenly issued a brief command. Bibka's hisses increased in volume, her scaly lips drew back from her fangs, and she reluctantly loosened her grip, then unwound her tail completely from around her enemy's neck.

Zargal lay where he was, gasping. After a moment, the King addressed him curtly. "Get up."

Zargal rose, clutching his aching neck. Bibka returned to her place at her master's side and crouched there, her forked tongue flickering.

"Well, Lord Zargal," the King inquired with elaborate courtesy, "is honor satisfied?"

Zargal opened his mouth to answer and found himself incapable of uttering a sound.

"Have no fear," the King assured him. "Your powers of speech will return soon enough. You're not seriously hurt. That is entirely due to the pleas on your behalf of Rothadd and my daughter. Had it been left to my choice, or to Bibka's—" He did not need to complete the sentence. "You have escaped unharmed, this time," the King went on, blandly ignoring the network of bleeding cuts, scratches, and bites that marked Zargal's legs, neck, and shoulders. "But I must warn you, my patience is at an end. If you cause one more disturbance here—" Again he did not need to complete the sentence. "I hope you understand that I mean what I say."

"I don't doubt for a moment that your Majesty is in earnest," Zargal replied, with great difficulty.

"I advise you to remember it. And now, if I am not mistaken, Master Guggard has work for you. I strongly suggest that you go do it."

Without another word, Zargal turned and slowly limped out of the room.

CHAPTER XVI

⌒

Zargal spent the next several hours cleaning out the servants' latrine in the courtyard of King Laza's castle. His state of mind was indescribable. When at last he finished the task, it was quite late, and Master Guggard had retired for the night. Upon returning to the darkened kitchen, Zargal was startled to find Princess Bellora awaiting him. The fire had sunk low, and the girl's face was in shadow, but there was no mistaking the graceful, green-clad figure, or the crown of pale curls.

Tired as he was, Zargal performed his best bow. "Is there anything your ladyship wishes?" he asked impassively.

"Well—yes," she answered, in that irresistibly musical voice. "I wish to know what, exactly, you are doing here."

The question startled Zargal, but he concealed his surprise. "I'd thought your ladyship was already aware that I am a scullion."

"But you are the heir of Szar?"

"I was once."

"Then you are the most unlikely scullion the world has ever seen!"

"I think Master Guggard agrees with you," Zargal said.

"Oh, yes. He certainly would!" Bellora laughed. "Poor old Guggard! You must be driving him mad!"

"Not so, your ladyship. He's driving *me* mad."

"I can imagine! Does he crack his knuckles at you?"

Zargal nodded, but regarded her doubtfully. "I can't help but fear that his Majesty would be displeased to know of your ladyship's presence in the kitchen."

"Yes, I'm sure he would be," Bellora agreed, "but he won't find out about it."

"Indeed? King Laza seems to have a way of finding out about things," Zargal observed.

"Yes, he does, but he's busy right now," Bellora said with disarming candor. "He's shut up in his laboratory with that boy Rothadd. Father likes Rothadd and has made him his new apprentice."

"Good." Zargal was pleased. "That will make Rothadd happy."

"Rothadd's your friend?"

"Yes. Yes, he is."

"And my father is *not*, I notice," Bellora commented. She knelt on the floor, heedless of her brocade gown, and stretched out her hands toward the dying fire. No lady of Duke Jalonzal's Court would have dared to behave so naturally.

"No, definitely not," Zargal admitted.

"Now, there is something I must know," the Princess said earnestly, with a slight frown. "My father—is he responsible for what has been done to you? Was it he who made you that size?"

"It was." He, too, knelt by the fire.

"And why? He must have had a reason; he's not a bad man. Why did he do such a thing?" She was gazing searchingly up into his face.

Zargal found himself telling her the entire story of his first meeting with King Laza, and what had happened afterward. Bellora listened quietly until he got to the part about his meeting with the Turos, whereupon she began to smile. And by the time he described his first encounter with Rothadd, she was chortling aloud. Zargal found himself laughing with her, although it had never before occurred to him to regard his mishaps as amusing in any way. When he got to the end of the story, Bellora's expression was once more grave, although her eyes were alight with a deviltry that recalled King Laza's. It was their one point of resemblance.

"You should never have done it!" she exclaimed. "It was madness! My father is not to be trifled with. When I think what might have happened!"

"Isn't what *has* happened bad enough?"

"You insulted him, sir," the girl pointed out. "You cannot say that you don't deserve punishment."

"I admit it. But—five years! Think of it! To remain as I am, in this monstrous condition, for five years!"

"Well—yes," she conceded. "That is severe. Very severe indeed."

Zargal was feeling calmer, more at peace, than he had since the night his misfortunes began. He had a vague notion that the sound of her voice had something to do with it.

"I think," Bellora said, "that I ought to speak to father about this. He's really being too hard. Mind you—you did offend him, and he's not likely to forget that. But he shouldn't be quite so harsh. Setting a creature like Bibka on you was really going too far! I'll tell him."

"Thank you. That could mean everything to me."

"I'll do what I can, but don't hope for too much, Lord Zargal. I'm afraid you may be scrubbing pots and pans for some time to come."

"If pots and pans are all I have to scrub, I'll count myself lucky," Zargal said, thinking of the servants' latrine.

"Oh?" The Princess' brows lifted quizzically. When Zargal failed to enlarge upon his answer, she rose to her feet. "I must leave now," she announced. "If father knew I'd come down here, he might do something unpleasant."

"What, you mean he'd punish you?"

"No, I mean he'd punish *you*."

"Yes, that sounds like King Laza."

"Before I go, I want to give you these." She handed him a small vial of ointment and a roll of bandages. "They'll help your cuts and bites to heal. I'll speak to my father about you as soon as the time seems right. Until then, be certain that you cause no disturbance here—he'll be *very* angry if you do. He has warned you, remember."

"I'll certainly remember. Will you come back here again, when you can?" Zargal asked.

"Indeed I will. I want to hear all about your life in Szar."

"But I shouldn't wish you to risk your father's anger on my account."

"Oh, I'll see to it that he doesn't find me out. And to think I'd been expecting such a dull winter!" With that she was gone, leaving Zargal staring after her.

Princess Bellora was true to her word—she did intercede with her father on Zargal's behalf. However, King Laza proved stubborn, and Zargal remained in the kitchen, scrubbing pots and peeling vegetables under the unfriendly eye of Master Guggard. Guggard's authority was shared by Vaxil the chef, a morose and sullen individual. Vaxil did little to anger Zargal and, indeed, rarely addressed him. The chef spent much of his time constructing marvelous sculptures of marzipan and spun sugar, which King Laza invariably declined to taste. It was perhaps this fact that accounted for Vaxil's low spirits.

Zargal had grown cautious and no longer quarreled openly with the major-domo. As a result Guggard concluded that his program of instruction had been successful and that Zargal was thoroughly subdued. Guggard was wont to congratulate himself on his triumph, but he was quite mistaken. Zargal was not at all subdued, but was biding his time in silence and quietly plotting revenge. His efforts at self-repression, as he polished tiles and listened to Guggard's noxious chatter, were superhuman, but he realized that he could not continue thus forever. Sooner or later, the explosion was bound to come.

The days passed slowly, and Zargal's life settled into a routine—not a happy one. Although his work kept him busy most of the time and he had few leisure hours, he was hopelessly bored, for his tasks were dreary and repetitive. The hard manual labor kept him tired most of the time, and he was always conscious of his unnatural height. Zargal's existence would have been entirely miserable, had it not been for the frequent visits of his two friends, Rothadd and Princess Bellora.

Unlike Zargal, Rothadd was enjoying life in Obran. King Laza had taken a fancy to the young Outcottager, and the two of them spent much time together. It was not an uncommon sight around the palace to see King Laza, ensconced in his wheeled chair, being drawn along the corridors by his great lizard, with Rothadd walking at his side—the two of them usually engaged in lively conversation. King Laza was heard to laugh often, and treated the boy with every mark of favor. Rothadd's days were busy, and he was learning much. Association with the King of Obran was gradually broadening his outlook, as he discovered more and more of the world beyond the Eastling Wolds.

Moreover, Rothadd was learning about the art of magic. He was permitted to assist in some of the King's simpler experiments, and was present as an observer at many more. By dint of much observation, Rothadd was beginning to grasp the basic principle that the sorcery he wished so ardently to master was not a simple matter of imitation and memorization.

True magic, as opposed to mere parlor tricks, demanded a certain force that could come only from within—a power of imagination so strong as to color and influence not only the mind of the magician, but the real world surrounding him as well. At the lowest level, this power involved illusion, which was not a difficult art to acquire. A more accomplished sorcerer possessed the power of transformation, and the changes he effected were real, not illusory. The greatest of the magicians, the few true masters, possessed a supreme power of creativity, which was a gift that was present at birth, or else never appeared.

King Laza possessed the creative genius to a certain degree—enough to make him an immensely formidable sorcerer, albeit not among the truly great ones of history. It was at this point very unclear what abilities Rothadd had inherited. So far, he had perfected a few clever illusions which hardly went beyond elementary conjuring, but this meant little—magicians' gifts often manifested themselves relatively late in life.

One thing was certain, though: if Rothadd should fail to learn magic, it would not be for want of trying. The boy was tireless in his efforts. Rothadd had studied the spell Hincmar had given him so often that the parchment had grown as thin and brittle as ancient leaves. The writing was smudged, the diagrams dim and faint. Not a single day passed but Rothadd attempted the incantation, droning out the senseless syllables again and again without success.

No crops sprang up at Rothadd's command, but the results he sometimes obtained were interesting enough to lend him the will to continue trying. Once, when he spoke the words, the snow suddenly melted away from the ground before him, leaving a small patch of earth brown and bare. Another time, there came the sound of a voice from underground, screaming curses and accusations, a most disturbing manifestation. And one time Rothadd thought he'd actually succeeded, for wheat sprang out of the earth as if escaping prison. But when he reached out to grasp it, his hand passed through the stalks; it had been an illusion only.

Rothadd felt, however, that he was on the right track, and discussed the matter at endless length during his frequent trips to the kitchen to visit Zargal. Sometimes Rothadd descended to the scullery in the company of Princess Bellora. But more often than not, the Princess came by herself.

Bellora's visits were not as frequent as they might have been, because King Laza very definitely disapproved. Early on, he had learned of his daughter's sorties belowstairs. He had not gone so far as to forbid her to continue. His solution to the problem had simply been to instruct Master Guggard to load Zargal with so much extra work that the scullion would have no time for visitors. The Princess, however, was not easily discouraged. As often as she was able, she would steal quietly down to the kitchen, where she would find Zargal alone, peeling turnips or raking greasy ashes, and the two of them would talk and laugh by the hour. Sometimes when Master Guggard or Vaxil the chef ventured into the kitchen while Bellora was there, the girl would haughtily order the intruder to depart. These incidents delighted Zargal, but invariably resulted in an even greater work load, which often kept him up far into the night.

As for Bellora, she soon found that a visit to Zargal was mysteriously apt to coincide with some command from her father, who acted as her tutor, to study a three-volume work on the subject of trade regulations in ancient Dizna; or to memorize large portions of the epic Lay of Refiu, in the original High Strellian. Bellora noted the connection, but did not let it stop her.

It was obvious from the first that Princess Bellora was

not an ordinary girl, but no daughter of King Laza of Obran would be. Her most remarkable feature, which Zargal had noted at once, was her voice. The Princess' voice was an instrument of power; the sound of it could lull anger and pain, promote contentment. It was a subtle influence, uncertain and transitory, over which the young girl lacked control. But the power undoubtedly existed, for the voice was a hereditary characteristic of the Varingians, the royal house of Obran, and could be traced clear back to the founder, Cramarius. The voice was, in fact, one of the causes of the House of Varingia's original rise to the throne of Obran. Cramarius had used it to woo the mob to his support at the time he usurped the crown. In his younger days, King Laza had made good use of the gift in his dealings with foreign dignitaries, though later on the voice had passed from him.

Princess Bellora was no sorceress—her father had decided at her birth that she would lead a happier life without magic, and had not instructed her in the art. Thus she possessed little control over the extraordinary voice; and the most noteworthy effect of it was that nearly every young man who heard Bellora fell in love, and insisted upon becoming her suitor.

The castle grounds were, despite the efforts of the sentries, constantly infested with lovesick young Obranese noblemen who had somehow glimpsed the Princess and heard her voice. It seemed that nothing could keep them away. As the weeks dragged by, and the entire land of Obran froze over and lay inert, encased in its armor of ice and smothered beneath its blanket of snow, the young suitors persisted in their quest. The roads and mountain trails were nearly impassable, but still they came. Some froze to death, and avalanches buried the unfortunate. Despite the perils of the journey, however, they came and camped outside the castle walls, quarreled among themselves, and tried to think of ways of getting to Bellora.

Periodically, rocks would come flying over the wall into the courtyard, and there were messages attached to them, usually addressed "To the Divine Princess." Sometimes a young earl or viscount would manage to scale the wall, plant himself beneath the lady's window, and serenade her in a longing tenor. Once in a while one would even gain access to the castle itself and skulk through the vaulted corridors in search of his beloved, only to be discovered and ejected—painfully—by Bibka.

Princess Bellora regarded her suitors with a mixture of amusement and embarrassment. Zargal detested them all. He was actually in a much worse case than all the rest of the young men, for he had come to know her nature and would undoubtedly have loved her even if she had not been born with an extraordinary voice. But he imagined that his great size must make him ridiculous in her eyes. In any case, a scullion did not aspire to the hand of a princess of Obran.

Zargal expended considerable time and effort in trying to devise some way of getting rid of the unwelcome suitors. No practical method suggested itself to him—but something else did. He finally came up with a scheme for using the suitors to deliver himself, once and for all, from the power of King Laza.

"I have an idea," Zargal said to Rothadd. It was late at night, and the two of them were sitting by themselves beside the great fireplace in the kitchen. The fire had died hours ago. Guggard and Vaxil had long since retired, but Zargal was still scouring the cutlery. It was freezing cold in the great stone room. Rothadd did not feel the chill, for he was attired in a heavy, fur-lined mantle, the gift of King Laza. Zargal was not thus fortified and was shivering miserably. "An idea," he repeated.

"What do that be?" Rothadd asked, a little apprehensively.

"I have a plan that should get me out of this place."

"Oh, aye, there ben't no one to stop 'ee from goin', if 'ee have a mind to be a giant forever," Rothadd observed.

"No. When I leave this castle, I'll be restored to my own proper size."

"Your proper size? 'Tisn't like. King Laza won't do it for 'ee—and 'ee do know that I can't, as yet."

"Yes, yes, I know all that. It doesn't matter. I plan to cure myself."

"Mullytwaddle! 'Ee know naught o' magic. 'Tis pure moon-schemes!"

"You think so, eh?" Zargal inquired grimly.

"Zargal! What do 'ee be a-thinkin' of? Has 'ee not learned your lesson yet?"

"You recall that silvery liquid that his Majesty gave me to drink the day I arrived here," Zargal said, ignoring Roth-add's question.

"Oh, aye. Knocked 'ee over like 'ee was pole-axed."

"Yes, but it reduced my stature, didn't it?"

"Aye, shrank like wet woolens, 'ee did. But what of it? 'Ee didn't shrink down quite enough, did 'ee?"

"No, I certainly didn't," Zargal said. "And I can think of only one explanation for that—he simply did not give me as much as I needed. Now, Rothadd, I'm asking you this because you've been studying magic and know some-thing of King Laza's methods. If I drank more of that silver liquid, would I not shrink still further, back to my own normal height?"

"There ben't no tellin'," Rothadd answered. "It isn't sure."

"But it's possible?"

"Well, when 'ee put it like that—aye. 'Ee might."

"Right. That's what I'm going to do, then. I'll drink some more of it."

"Zargal!" Rothadd exploded. "I never did meet up with the like of 'ee! 'Ee can't do that!"

"Watch me."

"Oh, aye, I'll watch 'ee kill yourself, or worse!" Rothadd leaped to his feet and began pacing energetically around the room. "There ben't no tellin' what might happen to 'ee if 'ee do drink more o' that stuff! Anything might happen! A mad notion it be!"

"Not at all. A few swallows of that liquid made me smaller. A few more swallows will make me smaller yet," Zargal returned calmly. "Isn't that logical?"

"Aye. Aye, so it be. But there's one thing I do know. Magic ben't always logical!"

Zargal shrugged.

"Zargal. 'Ee must listen to me for your own good. 'Ee must forget these crazy schemes. King Laza will help 'ee in his own good time."

"King Laza's own good time is not quite good enough. I'm sorry, Rothadd. My mind is made up."

"Well, 'ee can just unmake it, then! Zargal, stop and

think, now. How will 'ee know how much to drink? If 'ee do take too much, 'ee may shrink down to a midget—how would 'ee like that? Or 'ee might be so small, 'ee'll disappear altogether! Now, ben't that logic ,too?"

"Yes, but I'll just have to be careful about how much I swallow," Zargal mused.

"How can 'ee be careful when 'ee don't know anything about it? Oh, 'tis sure 'ee'll get yourself killed, or worse! Much worse!"

"Well, I'll just have to take that chance."

"There ben't no talkin' to 'ee! Of all the crack-brained—" Rothadd stopped, as a reassuring thought occurred to him. "But there ben't no cause to fear. Why, 'ee won't be a-drinkin' o' that potion, even if 'ee have a mind to it, for it be locked up in King Laza's workroom, and King Laza do keep the key with him day and night. So 'ee won't be a-goin' in there for aught, not unless 'ee do go to the King and talk 'im into a-givin' 'ee the key. And I can wish 'ee good luck for that."

"Thank you, but it shouldn't be necessary. I already know how I'm going to get into that workroom."

" 'Ee do! How?"

"Ah." Zargal smiled. "That's where Princess Bellora's suitors come in." Ignoring his companion's violent protests, he picked up the knives and spoons and resumed scouring.

CHAPTER XVII

It was two days later, and the young Count sa Wenilow, scion of one of the great old noble houses of Obran, was hunched up on the ground beside a small campfire, just outside the castle wall. The snow lay thickly all around him, and the wind was shrieking in his ear, but sa Wenilow paid no heed. He was completely enveloped in a great fur rug that protected him from the weather and he was engaged in writing a poem. It was a lyric addressed to the Princess, in which the Count compared the agonies of his current frostbite to the agonies of his unrequited love.

Sa Wenilow was a noted amateur poet, and he was in the habit of attaching his literary efforts to stones and tossing them over the castle wall at least several times a day. He had never received any answer, but had not yet given up hope.

How could he guess that as often as he offered up his verses, Zargal would collect them as they lay in the courtyard and carefully consign them to the kitchen fire? Zargal, nursing a special grudge against Bellora's suitors, took particular care that their amorous messages should not reach her. It might have been different had he felt he had the right to add his own suit to the others.

It came as a great surprise to Count sa Wenilow when he was interrupted in the midst of his composition by the arrival of a message from the other side of the wall—the first he had ever received. The parchment-wrapped stone thudded into the snow a few feet away from him. The Count rose, burrowed down after it, and eagerly returned to the campfire to read.

"To a most Noble Suitor," the message ran.

"Your Pleas have moved my Heart more than you can know. Pray do not take it ill that I have long maintained Silence. If I have followed a Course so uncivil, do you set it down to Modestie, and never to Inclination. I own 'twould be a thing most barbarous to deny that Y^r Lordship's Constancy is deserving of Reward. Therefore, come this Night at ten of the Clock to the small Door in the west Wall of the Castle. This you will find unlocked. Enter the Courtyard, and be judged according to y^r Merits. Until then, I bid you Adieu."

The young Count's face lit up with rapture. Although the note was unsigned, he did not for a moment question from whom it had come. The fact of the matter was, however, that the signature was lacking because Zargal, the author, had not been able to bring himself to stoop so low as to forge the Princess' name. Similar notes had been tossed over the wall at suitable intervals to no less than half a dozen suitors. But sa Wenilow knew nothing of all this.

"She shall not find me wanting," he muttered, and returned to his poetry with fresh enthusiasm, intent on presenting a new rondeau to his lady at ten o'clock sharp.

That night, Zargal stood waiting in the hallway outside King Laza's workroom. This was a huge chamber, taking up nearly a quarter of the space on the castle's second storey, and kept locked all the time. The door was massive, the locks unbreakable, and King Laza kept the key with him at all times. The windows, although numerous, were all mullioned in stone, and thus afforded no space large enough to admit the passage of a human body—most particularly not a body the size of Zargal's.

It was now slightly past ten o'clock. King Laza had been in there working for about two hours. The castle ser-

vants were off about their tasks. Zargal, who was supposed
to be cleaning out the cracks between the stones of the
kitchen floor, had given Vaxil the slip, and had been hiding
out on the second storey since dinner time. Rothadd was
shut up in his own room, down the corridor from the
King's laboratory, practicing Hincmar's incantation. Rothadd had been observing Zargal's activities with a suspicious
eye for the past couple of days, but Zargal felt confident
that the Outcottager lad would not betray him. Princess
Bellora was nowhere in evidence.

Zargal's ears ached with listening. He was in a state of
extreme nervous tension, and it seemed to him that he'd
been waiting forever. For the past two hours the only
sounds he had heard had been the creak of King Laza's
wheeled chair, the clatter of Bibka's talons on the stone
floor, various unidentifiable hisses and thumps, and once
the sound of glass breaking. Then, when Zargal was beginning to think that his plan had not worked after all, he
heard angry shouts from the courtyard below, accompanied
by the clash of steel. Zargal raced to a window and gazed
down at a scene illuminated by torchlight.

Six of Princess Bellora's aristocratic young suitors were
assembled there. In addition to Count sa Wenilow, Zargal
had flung invitations to a pair of barons, a viscount, an
earl, and the second son of a duke. All of them had answered the summons, passed through the little portal that
Zargal had left unlocked for them, and arrived at about the
same time. Now, upon encountering one another, the hot-
tempered young men had naturally enough begun to
quarrel. Two pairs of the suitors had engaged each other
with swords, while the remaining two stood on the side-
lines, yelling encouragement.

As Zargal watched, all four of the King's lackeys
emerged from the castle and bore down upon the com-
batants, their own blades drawn. Soon the incomprehensible exclamations of the foreign lackeys were blending
with the shouts of the suitors. Master Guggard came out
and shrilly commanded the fighters to put up their swords.
They ignored him. At this moment, one of the barons managed to prick Count sa Wenilow slightly in the left arm,
and a small stain of blood appeared on the Count's sleeve.
Guggard's scandalized screeches took on a note of frenzy.

The last two of the six suitors attacked each other. The noise rising from the courtyard was now deafening, and Bibka the slatku responded to it with hoarse roars which sounded clearly through the closed door of King Laza's workroom.

Zargal abandoned his post by the window and quickly ducked around a bend in the corridor, concealing himself from view. An instant later, the workroom door groaned open, and the King and the slatku appeared on the threshold. Bibka was vibrating with excitement, her breath coming in short, rapid hisses. King Laza, on the other hand, simply looked annoyed at the interruption. At a word from her master, Bibka eagerly began dragging the chair toward the broad staircase, along one side of which a smooth ramp had been built for the King's convenience.

As soon as they were out of earshot, Zargal approached the workroom and found the door ajar for the first time since he had come to the castle. Quickly he slipped inside and glanced around him.

Light was supplied by a multitude of torches that burned in the brackets affixed to the walls. The chamber was full of tables, cupboards, cabinets, and shelves—all of them crammed with the King's rare equipment. One entire wall was set aside for a collection of ancient books, maps, and portfolios. Upon the vaulted ceiling was painted a great map of the heavens, showing the constellations, and marked with many symbols that Zargal did not recognize. Several glass-fronted cases were filled with delicate instruments of great fascination. And there were scores of shelves with literally thousands of jars, bottles, flasks, retorts, and misshapen containers of every description.

Zargal could see at a glance that his job would not be an easy one, and he suspected he might not have much time. Without any further delay, he commenced his search, examining jar after jar, peering in at an endless assortment of liquids, powders, crystals, dried plants, stones, mummified insects, preserved entrails, pods, seed, teeth, bones, and bits of strangely hued bark.

So absorbed was he in his task that he was not aware of another presence in the workroom until he heard a light footstep directly behind him. Zargal caught his breath sharply and wheeled around to confront his discoverer. His threatening expression vanished when he found himself face to face with Princess Bellora.

"Zargal," she said calmly, "perhaps you would be so good as to explain what you're doing in my father's workroom? You must be mad. Have you any idea what he'd do if he knew you were here?"

"I think I might hazard a guess."

"Well, then! Come out of here at once, before you're discovered. What are you standing there for? Come along!"

"Impossible, your ladyship."

"Impossible! What are you talking about? I don't understand you at all, Zargal. I think your wits are beginning to fail."

"If that were the case, then I'd never have managed to get into this room in the first place."

"Ah, bah! There was some sort of uproar going on in the courtyard, father went to investigate, and he carelessly left this door unlocked. That was simply a stroke of luck."

"Indeed?"

"Certainly! If it hadn't happened that there was a disturbance just now—" Bellora paused and regarded him closely. "Zargal—did you have something to do with that?"

"Am I responsible for the ardor of your ladyship's suitors?"

"Bother my suitors! What are you doing in here, anyway? What purpose do you think it serves to tempt father's anger again?"

Zargal gazed down into the worried green eyes, which had grown as dark as moss. "I would take any risk," he said slowly, "chance any punishment, and think it well worthwhile—to become a normal man once more. To lead the life of an ordinary human being, to own the hopes and dreams of happiness that other men possess. That's what I am seeking in here, Princess. Your father may blast me from here to the Sea of Ice if he chooses—but he can't stop me from trying."

Bellora was silent for a few moments, and at last answered softly, "He *has* been too hard on you, much too hard. But what can you hope to find in here that will help you?" Seeing Zargal hesitate, she added, "I won't breathe a word of it."

"Somewhere in this room," Zargal said, his eyes leaving

her face for the first time since she had appeared, and
roaming restlessly around the chamber, "his Majesty keeps
a flask of silvery liquid, which will reduce my size—if I
can only find it."

"You mean, you actually plan to drink out of one of
these bottles?"

"Yes."

"Oh, no! That's sheer folly! I won't allow it!"

"You mean that you intend to summon your father?"

"No. If I did, you might be beter off swallowing poison.
But only consider! Think of what you're doing! What if
you are deceived and drink from the wrong bottle? Or
drink too much and die of it?"

"That would be better than staying as I am. But I doubt
that it would kill me."

"Is it so very terrible here?" Bellora asked. "Can you not
bear with my father for five years? That's not a lifetime."

"Perhaps. But I don't intend to put it to the test. I won't
consent to remain in this condition if there's anyhing in the
world I can do to change it."

"Stubbornness—that's all it is! Unnatural stubbornness!"

"Just so. Everything about me is unnatural at the moment. That's what I'm trying to correct."

"It's hardly the time or place to play with words! Zargal—" She tried another approach. "Did you not promise
my father you'd remain with us for five years?"

"I made no such promise. We agreed that he will cure
me if I pass five years here as his servant. But if I'm able
to cure myself, then I don't see that I'm under any obligation to stay."

"You chop logic finely, sir. Zargal, I beg you—don't do
this thing."

"My mind is already made up," Zargal replied, resisting
her voice with difficulty.

"You don't know how I'd feel if something dreadful
happened to you."

"But how would you feel if something good happened to
me?"

"Oh, can't you see that it's simply not worth the risk?"
she cried.

"It is to me."

The Princess bowed her head. After a moment Zargal

returned to his search. As if in challenge to his resolution, the flask he sought appeared within seconds. There could be no mistake—it was the same glass bottle that Zargal remembered so well, half full of the silvery liquid, with that unique rainbow sheen. Zargal withdrew it very carefully and held it up to the light. The substance within, whatever it was, was perfectly opaque. He weighed the flask in his palm, as if estimating how much to drink, and looked at Bellora. She was watching him with wide eyes, her hands clasped, her lips compressed into a thin line. As she met his glance, she gave an imploring shake of the head. Zargal turned away, pulled the stopper, lifted the flask to his lips —and then froze, startled.

From somewhere nearby came the sound of screams. They were not rising from the courtyard, but came from within the castle itself. Someone was yelling desperately for help. The voice was recognizable as that of Rothadd.

Zargal and the Princess stood as if transfixed. Zargal's eyes flicked to the possible cure he held in his hand. He wavered momentarily, then replaced the bottle on the shelf and raced out into the hall, with Bellora at his side. The screams grew louder and more panicky as they neared Rothadd's room. Within seconds they reached his door, flung it open, and paused on the threshold, astounded at the sight that greeted them.

Rothadd had sunk hip-deep into the stone floor. It was an impossibility—the floor was made of large blocks of gray granite, as solid as the mountains themselves. Yet Rothadd was being absorbed into the stone at a rapid rate. He was sinking lower by the second.

"It's a-swallowin' me alive!" Rothadd cried in terror. "Help!"

Zargal at once stepped forward, hand outstretched to aid his descending friend, only to be halted by another shriek from the Outcottager lad.

"Take care—'ee must not come too close, else it'll get 'ee, too!"

Zargal placed one foot gingerly on the floor near Rothadd, felt himself beginning to sink into the icy granite, and withdrew to safer ground. Rothadd continued to go down quickly. He was now chest-deep into the floor. Zargal flung himself down on his stomach and again extended his hand.

"Take hold of me and I'll pull you out," he directed.

Rothadd instantly complied. But when Zargal attempted to fulfill his promise, he discovered that Rothadd was well and truly embedded in granite. Try as he would, Zargal could not budge him. When he exerted all his strength, the only result was that Rothadd's howls of fear turned to screams of pain. " 'Ee be a-tearin' my arm off!" he shrieked.

"There's nothing else to be done!" Zargal muttered in reply, pulling as hard as he could. It did no good. Zargal was aware of the steady dragging force of the stone, against which he was now exerting all his power. By pulling with every ounce of strength that he possessed, he was only just able to prevent Rothadd from sinking any further. But it was a tremendous effort, and he didn't know how long he could continue.

"Let me help!" Bellora offered. Crouching down upon the safe portion of the floor, she stretched out a hand to Rothadd; but since her reach was so much shorter than Zargal's, she couldn't touch him.

"Your father!" Rothadd gasped. "The King! King Laza!"

"I'll get him!" the Princess cried. Springing to her feet, she was out of the chamber with the speed of thought.

Zargal maintained his desperate grip. His right arm felt as if it were being stretched to new and disproportionate lengths by the relentless pull of the stone. He wondered how long it would take Bibka to draw the King's chair up to Rothadd's chamber. If she didn't hurry, then young Rothadd was going to become a permanent addition to the castle of Obran. "How did this happen to you?" Zargal asked Rothadd, in an effort to take his mind off these alarming thoughts.

"I ben't sure," Rothadd answered in a hoarse voice. "I was in here, a-speakin' the words o' Hincmar's spell he did give me, as nice and careful as 'ee please, and nothin' happened—same as ever, as I did think. There was a funny sour smell in the room, but I did think naught of it. So I did finish, 'ee see, and took a step forward, and then I went a-sinkin' down into the floor as if it was made o' dough— but that wasn't the worst of it, for it was a-suckin' me down like it was hungry—"

"Well, don't worry," Zargal told him. "King Laza will be

here to help you in a minute or two, and I'll hold you where you are until he comes." Zargal spoke with an air of confidence, but in fact it felt to him as if the pull on Rothadd's body were growing stronger all the time. For a second his hold weakened, and Rothadd immediately sank another inch. Zargal himself was hauled slightly closer to the danger area.

"Can 'ee not hold me?" Rothadd cried.

"Yes, of course. Don't worry. Are you in any pain?"

"Nay, I ben't, except for my arm 'ee have. I think 'tis broke."

"No, I'm sure you're all right."

Zargal had perhaps spoken too soon, for he felt a sudden tearing sensation, and shooting pains from wrist to shoulder. Rothadd yelped and sank deeper into the floor, while Zargal slid a few inches nearer.

" 'Ee'll be a-pulled in yourself, at this rate," Rothadd said. "Best 'ee let me go, then."

"Nonsense, I'll do no such thing," Zargal replied, wondering if his shoulder had been dislocated yet. He attempted to tighten his grip on Rothadd, but found that the muscles in his hand had grown unmanageably stiff. Sweat had gathered on his forehead and was beginning to trickle down into his eyes. Zargal rested his head for a moment on the cold floor, but raised it abruptly when he felt himself beginning to slide forward again. He tensed, increased his backward pull, and managed to come to a jerky halt.

Rothadd let out an involuntary squawk of pain. The Outcottager was now neck-deep in granite, with only the one arm that Zargal still held exposed to the air, the other engulfed. He had the look of a disembodied head resting upon the floor, blue eyes glassy and staring, and complexion so pale that his freckles seemed to stand out from the rest of his face. "A dead man I do be," he said.

"That's not true," Zargal told him. "Don't even think it."

" 'Ee can't hold me up forever."

"I won't need to. The King will be here any second."

"Nay, he can't get his wheeled chair up here quick enough. And so I must now bid 'ee farewell, for 'ee be a good sort, Zargal, underneath it all. If 'ee have high ways and don't know how to talk to folk, that be the fault of your breedin'. 'Ee best take my new mantle his Majesty did give me, for 'tis cold down in the kitchen, and I have no use for it, now that I be a dead 'un."

Zargal attempted to contradict him, in vain. Somehow or other, imperceptibly, the Outcottager had sunk to chin level.

"This all be the fault of my passion for the magic art," Rothadd said sorrowfully. "It wasn't my place to look so high. They all warned me 'twould lead to a bad end, and so it has."

Zargal began to argue the point, but the argument was cut mercifully short by the arrival of King Laza, Bibka, and Bellora. For once, Zargal was pleased to see the King.

Laza regarded the two of them for a moment before he spoke. "Really, Rothadd!" he exclaimed in amused exasperation. "How could you be so careless? You've been fiddling around with that spell again, I presume."

"Aye," Rothadd admitted.

"What did I tell you about that?"

"Well—'ee did tell me I must be careful."

"I was a little more specific than that, as I recall. I told you—" A note of severity crept into the garbled voice. "I told you to be very careful of your pronunciation. By the look of things here, you did not take my warning to heart."

"It be hard to mind everything at once," Rothadd replied.

"But you must. There's no other way. Lad, that infernal Outcottager accent of yours will be the death of you yet. We must do something about it."

" 'Tis the way my father do speak!" Rothadd expostulated. "It be good enough for him and good enough for me!"

"Not if you wish to become a sorcerer, it isn't. These spells require at least some purity of diction—"

"Father," Bellora interrupted, "I don't think that this is the time or place to discuss the matter. Zargal can't hold him much longer."

"Ah, yes. He does look a little uncomfortable. Lord Zargal," the King inquired blandly, "I hope we haven't inconvenienced you?"

"Not at all, but I fear that Rothadd may be somewhat inconvenienced."

"Quite possible. He was disgracefully careless, but we

shall not let him suffer the consequences of his folly this time." King Laza made a sign to Bibka, who drew his chair into the center of the room. There he whispered some words, too softly to be overheard.

"My Lord Zargal," he ordered, "remove our friend from the floor, if you please."

"I haven't the strength," Zargal answered.

"You may be surprised, my lord. Try."

Zargal mustered up all his remaining strength to give one long, last haul. To his amazement, Rothadd flew through the air and landed on his stomach with a plopping noise. For a few moments he lay where he was, breathing heavily. There was a deep depression in the stone where Rothadd had so nearly been entombed, but it smoothed itself as they watched. When Bellora stepped forward and lightly placed her hand on the treacherous spot, she found it to be as firm and impenetrable as all the rest of the floor.

"Well, Rothadd," King Laza said, "I hope you have learned a lesson. When dealing with magic, one must never act or speak in haste."

"Oh, aye, your Majesty," Rothadd agreed, bouncing to his feet. He was massaging his arm and shoulder, still sore from the recent ordeal. Other than that, he had obviously sustained no ill effects. " 'Tis true, that is, and I be sure to keep it in mind for next time."

A short time later, King Laza creaked down the corridor and paused outside his workroom, whose door was still unlocked.

"Left unguarded for so long?" he said aloud. "A mistake." Bibka snorted in agreement.

Once they were inside, Bibka's tail began to twitch, and her head, on its flexible neck, went twisting in all directions as she scented the air in the closed room. The King, observing her behavior, took a deep breath. With his sharp senses, heightened to compensate for his physical inactivity, he was able to pick up a very faint fragrance, which he easily identified as his daughter'e perfume. King Laza's practiced eye ran swiftly over the chamber, coming to rest on a silvery flask, which he regarded with interest, noting that it was not in its usual place. Once or twice, the King nodded thoughtfully to himself.

CHAPTER XVIII

~

For some time following the night of his interrupted raid, frustration made Zargal sullen and irritable. But shortly his mood improved, for no one who listened to the voice of Princess Bellora was able to stay ill-tempered very long, and Zargal heard it often. The Princess was fond of his company, which was not surprising, since she brought out the best in him, and he was generally on good behavior in her presence.

Zargal came to think less and less about escaping from the castle. His unnatural size was still a great burden to him, but not as unbearable as it had been. His appetite was still immense, but not intolerable.

His precious hours of spare time were happily spent in the company of Bellora or Rothadd. With the exercise of a little caution, he could usually avoid encountering King Laza; the castle was huge, and the King rarely descended to the kitchen. Guggard was annoying, but Vaxil the chef rarely bothered him, and the four lackeys couldn't speak to him at all. As winter dragged on its gray and white way, Zargal allowed himself to drift as aimlessly as the snow.

Then Princess Bellora began complaining of ill health and, more unusual for her, ill spirits. In fact, she did not look well at all; her fair complexion went pasty, dark rings circled her green eyes, her movements grew listless, and she wilted like a tired rose. Her visits to Zargal grew less and less frequent, until they stopped altogether, to Zargal's dismay. The King's servants were informed that her ladyship was ill. No other news was forthcoming.

Zargal questioned Rothadd, but found that the Outcottager was equally mystified. "I ben't—I have not seen her," he corrected himself carefully, as the King had instructed him. "I do not know what her sickness is."

At Zargal's request, Rothadd sought out King Laza and asked for an explanation. But Laza, usually friendly and indulgent, did not prove so in this case. He ordered the Outcottager from his presence, and Bibka roared so dreadfully that Rothadd did not pause to argue.

A deadly gloom descended on the castle. King Laza now kept almost exclusively to his own apartment, scarcely touching any food. Vaxil's usual melancholy now verged on desperation. The four lackeys huddled in corners and whispered together. Guggard grew more irritable. But Zargal, lonelier and more heartsick with each passing day, was finally forced to turn to the major-domo, lacking any other source of information.

"What ails Princess Bellora?" he demanded. He hadn't meant to ask Guggard; but finding himself alone in the kitchen with the major-domo, it just slipped out. "What ails her ladyship?"

Guggard was displeased, and his face showed it. Months had gone by since Zargal's arrival, but he had not reconciled himself to the giant's presence. "Princess Bellora is ill," he replied shortly.

Zargal had become comparatively adept at holding his temper. "I was aware of her ladyship's illness," he replied carefully, "but wished to learn the nature of it." His manner, although outwardly respectful, conveyed the subtle hint of disdain that Guggard found maddening.

"It's not your place to be asking questions about the Princess, boy," Guggard snapped. "You forget yourself."

"Yes, Master Guggard," Zargal said. "But I'd have thought that a loyal retainer would be concerned for the well-being of all members of the royal family. I see I'm mistaken."

Guggard's face reddened. "It's one thing to be concerned for their well-being, boy. It's quite another to start asking personal questions about your betters!"

Zargal allowed Guggard to stew in silence for a while and then inquired, "Does she show any signs of improvement?"

Guggard took his time about answering. "I assume you refer to her ladyship?"

"Yes," Zargal said. "I do."

"Then you should say so. Has anyone ever told you that you don't express yourself very well?" When Zargal failed to rise to the bait, Guggard added, "Mind that potato, boy! You're not getting the peel off in one strip."

"Has the Princess shown any sign of improvement?"

"That's a delicate question, boy, and would require a lengthy explanation."

Zargal perceived that Guggard knew nothing. "Have you seen or spoken to her ladyship at all these past several days?" he asked, as a last resort.

"When are you going to stop asking questions all the time? When will you cease?"

"When I'm properly answered."

"I thought you'd finally learned your lesson, boy. I thought that I'd finally managed to train the insolence out of you!"

"You were wrong!"

"You're going to change your habits, boy! You're going to mend your ways! I'll see to that personally. Perhaps I'll begin by having you clean out Bibka's kennel."

Zargal had had it by then. "Perhaps I'll begin by throwing you down the stairs!" he flared.

"You—dare!" the major-domo gasped. "You dare! We'll see what his Majesty has to say about this!"

Master Guggard stormed out of the room in a fit of petulance.

Zargal sat staring blindly into the fire for a time. Then he nodded. "Yes, we *will* see what his Majesty has to say."

Rothadd was not there to dissuade him. Zargal arose slowly, left the kitchen, and made his way through the halls of the castle as silently as a rising mist. The stillness of the place was unsettling. Zargal stole up the great staircase and turned toward the east wing. As he went, he was reminded of the time, months before, when he had crept through his father's palace and had succeeded only in making an outcast of himself. He earnestly hoped that this night's venture would prove more rewarding, but was far too intent upon his purpose to worry about it much.

In due course Zargal arrived at King Laza's apartment. Drawing a deep breath, he rapped on the door. The sound echoed through the granite hall with false authority, but there was no response. After a moment Zargal knocked again, and this time he was answered.

"Go away," King Laza commanded from within, without any particular expression.

Zargal knocked harder.

"I said, go away." The King's voice was still neutral, but this time it was accompanied by a low, murderous snarl from Bibka.

Calling upon all his courage, Zargal knocked once more.

"Who is there? Identify yourself!"

Without speaking, Zargal twisted the handle, pushed open the door, and stepped into the room. King Laza was sitting with his back to the fire. His eyes had been downcast, but at Zargal's entrance he lifted his head and stared at the intruder. King Laza had never looked so dreadful. He had something of the appearance of a partially decomposed cadaver, lately arisen from the grave. His hands, resting upon the arms of his chair, were contorted and stiff, like grotesque sculptures. His bloodshot eyes burned with all the portent of a red sun in the morning, but their expression bespoke grief amounting to desperation.

"I thought it must be you," the King said, with none of his usual sardonic courtesy. "Who else would dare disturb me now? Leave my presence."

"I have a question for your Majesty."

"I will not hear it. Get out." Bibka underscored the command with a hiss that came from deep inside her.

Zargal did not move. "I have come to inquire after the health of your daughter," he said.

Not a muscle twitched in the ghastly face opposite him, but Zargal had to check an impulse to take a step backward. "You come here to me, hoping to satisfy your idle curiosity? Get out!" King Laza's voice rang clear and sharp with fury. "Before I forget myself entirely, get out of my sight!"

"Your Majesty is mistaken. I ask no questions in idle curiosity," Zargal said. "I ask because I love her, and fear for her—as you do. As you suffer when harm befalls her, so must I."

For a time, King Laza made no reply to this. "You love her?" he asked at last. "So do many others."

"Of course," Zargal said simply. "Who would not?"

"Yes, I might have expected it," the King said to himself.

"She's ill?" Zargal asked. "May I know if she's in danger?"

"You are better off not knowing. I wish I did not."

"What do you mean?" Zargal cried. "What's wrong? Can't you help her?"

"No. I cannot."

"Then I will!"

The King's lips twitched in something that might have passed as a smile. "I believe you would. But my daughter is beyond our help. There's nothing you can do."

"That can't be true!"

"It is true. Love will not serve her. You and I are equally powerless, my lord."

"I must not believe you," Zargal said.

"Words will not convince you? You require proof? Then come with me," the king commanded. "Come with me now."

Zargal followed the King out of the room and along the hall to the stairs, which they ascended together—Zargal making use of the stone treads, while Bibka hauled her master's chair up the smooth ramp to the third storey.

Zargal wondered where they were going, but did not ask aloud, and Laza spoke no word. The silver lizard was obviously very familiar with the route, for she proceeded on her way without guidance and without faltering.

At the end of the gallery on the third storey was a narrow, steep flight of stairs that led up to the fourth floor of the castle—a floor full of small chambers originally intended for the use of a full staff of servants. Nobody used it now. The stairway had nonetheless been provided with a ramp, and now Bibka had to strain every muscle to pull the wheeled chair up the sharp incline. Zargal had never visited the fourth storey before. He was becoming more and more mystified and noted that his companion's expression grew grimmer as they proceeded.

The fourth floor was the site of the various entrances to the group of eight high, thin towers that soared grandly above the main body of the castle. Each of the towers was composed of a number of hexagonal rooms, built one atop the other. The only means of access to the upper chambers was by way of the staircases which spiraled their way up the inner surfaces of the tower walls. It was unthinkable that Bibka, despite all her strength, could drag the crippled King up such stairways. Laza, however, was not to be put off by obstacles. King, giant, and lizard passed together into the base of the southern tower, and Zargal received another surprise.

In this tower, the platforms which had formed the floors and ceilings of the successive chambers had been removed. The niches in the walls, which had once received the huge supporting timbers, were still there, but now empty. The walls were pierced at regular intervals by deep windows, like tunnels in the stone, and there was an incongruous vertical row of forsaken fireplaces set into one of the six granite faces. Near the very top was a small, arched opening in the wall, and beyond it, darkness. It was freezing cold.

For the first time since he had left his apartment, King Laza spoke, in a low voice, to himself. His words were indistinguishable, but their effect was startling. The entire floor began to rise, slowly and jerkily at first, then with increasing speed. Zargal was unprepared for this and came close to losing his balance. But neither Laza nor the slatku was at all affected. The rise of the floor was accompanied by a high-pitched whine, and the air in the tower went heavy and stale. Then the ascent slowed, and the floor came to a halt, tipping sickeningly.

They were now level with the dark opening in the wall, and Zargal could see that it led out onto one of the covered bridges that connected all eight towers known as the Crown with one another. King Laza immediately started out across the bridge, with Zargal close behind him. The Duke's son had to duck down low to pass through the arched doorway. The bridge itself was narrow and unsteady. It swayed and trembled under the onslaught of the tremendous winds that howled over the peaks of the Obranese mountains. Zargal wondered if the structure had been designed to support so much weight—a man in a heavy wheeled chair, a full-grown slatku, and a human being of excessive size. He felt a distinct surge of relief as they left the bridge behind them and passed into another tower. Zargal's relief came too soon, however, for the little party had to traverse three more shivering bridges in order to reach the northernmost tower of the Crown.

They had arrived at the top room of the northern tower; the highest, most isolated point in the castle, from the windows of which it was possible to look out over endless stretches of frozen mountains, dotted with ice-bound villages, all the way off to the misty regions that marked the frontier. Within the hexagonal room, the air was warm and comfortable, for a large blaze was crackling in the fireplace. In the center of the floor, on a dais, stood a bed hung with dark velvet, wherein reposed Princess Bellora.

Bellora was unconscious, motionless as a dead thing. Her skin had taken on a dreadful grayish tinge, and her entire figure seemed somehow to have shriveled. Most alarming, however, was an indefinable transformation. She looked as if she were undergoing some process of change—as if her muscles were loosening and softening, her flesh losing its tautness, her very bones subtly starting to shift. She might almost have begun to decay, though yet alive. All of the Princess that remained unchanged was the fair hair that went twirling over her pillow.

"She's dying." There was no doubt in Zargal's mind. "She is dying."

"No," King Laza said. "She will live."

"You're certain? She'll recover?"

"She will live. But she will not recover." The King was watching his daughter. He did not look at Zargal.

"What do you mean? Stop talking in riddles, man!"

Laza let the impertinence pass. "I mean," he answered tonelessly, "that she will not die, but the effects of this illness will remain with her all the rest of her life."

"What effects?"

King Laza did not answer, but seemed to draw in on himself, his figure contracting in the wheeled chair.

"But you are a great sorcerer!" Zargal exclaimed. "You have immense forces at your command. Surely you can help her?"

"No more than I could help myself when it happened to me."

"To you—?" Zargal asked, with his first horrible suspicion.

"Yes, to me. To my father before me. To my father's grandfather—and so on, through the generations. Our family bears a curse, which has now struck my daughter."

"You mean that this sickness which has come to Bellora is the same that made you what you are?"

"Yes. You and the other young fools who cluster around my gates claim to love her. Will you still love her, my lord, when she resembles me? Or will you perhaps suggest that we put her on exhibit in a cage and charge admission?"

Zargal had only a hazy recollection of the fatal words he had once spoken to King Laza. "You have the power," he said. "Power! It should be a simple matter for you to cure one sick girl."

"Not this sickness."

"Have you tried?"

"Of course I have tried! Every night for weeks past, I have been here with my spells and potions. Nothing helps her! Haven't I made it clear to you that this is no ordinary malady? It is a curse that has blighted the lives of scores of my ancestors, has made me as you see, and is now destroying my daughter. The curse of the Varingians! You desired to learn what troubles the Princess. Now you know —you see it at work before your very eyes! Are you content?" For the first time since Zargal had met him, King Laza's voice was raised, and his composure shattered. For once he was turned toward the window, and the dull light that filtered into the room was playing full on his monstrous face.

After a moment's thought, Zargal said, "If you mean what you say—that your family suffers under a malediction of some kind—then somebody must have pronounced it in the first place."

"A reasonable assumption, my lord."

"Who could have had such strength? Who was the sorcerer whose work you—of all people—can't undo?"

King Laza expelled his breath in a short sigh. "I'll tell you," he said listlessly. "Why not, after all? How much do you know of the history of the House of Varingia?"

"Only what any schoolboy would know," Zargal answered. "Your ancestor Cramarius acceded to the throne generations ago. Since then, a member of your family has always ruled Obran. Varingians have long been noted for their skill in magic and alchemy, but you are commonly regarded as the greatest of your line in that respect. The rulers of Obran have traditionally had little dealing with the outside world and are considered somewhat mysterious and frightening. In this, too, your Majesty has well upheld the custom of your House. That is the extent of my knowledge."

Laza nodded. "All perfectly accurate," he said, "as far as it goes. But have you any idea how Cramarius first obtained the throne?"

"I've been taught that it is a mark of ill breeding to inquire too deeply into the origins of any ruling House."

"Ah, very wise. Very wise indeed," the King said, with a touch of his accustomed sarcasm. "But we shall ignore that gentlemanly code for the moment. My ancestor Cramarius, an independently powerful Obranese chieftain, made use of his army and his irresistible voice to depose the ruling monarch and seize the crown for himself. The sovereign of Obran at that time was Queen Godescalc.

"Godescalc's family, the Lodiae, reigned here for at least a thousand years prior to the rise of the Varingians. This particular ruler was called the Raven of the Mountain and sometimes Black Godescalc—partly due to the color of her hair and partly due to the color of her heart. She was not a popular ruler. Cramarius was acclaimed a hero by the people of Obran, and Black Godescalc was forced to flee the land. That ought to have been the end of the story, but it was not."

"The deposed Queen cursed Cramarius?" Zargal guessed bleakly.

"Yes. Although she had been defeated, she was still a great sorceress and a witch. The night before Cramarius stormed the castle, she made her escape, somehow slipping through the ranks of the surrounding army. When the troops entered the next morning, they were met with no resistance, and the Queen was gone. During that night, though, she must have come close to Cramarius, for shortly thereafter he began to change."

"He was afflicted as you are?" Zargal asked.

"Undoubtedly. As one chronicler of the day put it, 'By the devilish agency of the witch and traitress Godescalc, our King was transformed and thenceforth shunned the sight of men.' Bad luck for Cramarius, certainly, but even that was not the worst of it."

"She cursed his descendants as well?"

"She did. Cramarius' son inherited the sickness, and so did his granddaughter, and many others thereafter. No one has ever discovered a cure."

"Then," Zargal cried, "if you know so well that your blood is poisoned, why have the members of your family continued to beget heirs? How can you do this to your sons and daughters? How could you do it to *her?*"

"That's where Godescalc was truly ingenious. The action of her curse is unpredictable. It strikes at random, and many rulers of our House have escaped unscathed. Many have led happy and normal lives. Sometimes generations have passed, and we have begun to hope that we are free at last; it's easy to deceive those who wish to be deceived. Godescalc extended just enough hope to prevent us from voluntarily ending our line. As for my daughter—I've prayed for eighteen years that she might be spared, but—" Laza shook his head. "She is doomed."

"I don't understand!" Zargal objected. "You are such a great sorcerer yourself—why can't you undo this work?"

"Because I don't know how it was done! Without that knowledge, I could concoct a thousand cures and never find the right one. With a simple spell, any competent magician may deal—for example, Rothadd's friend Hincmar could easily have helped you, had he not wished to avoid offending me—"

"If he had helped me, would you have been offended?"

"Not particularly. It's a matter of such complete unimportance—"

Zargal was too worried to lose his temper. "You truly

believe that this curse may be lifted only by the sorceress who pronounced it?"

"I'm almost certain of it."

"And she has been dead and gone for hundreds of years."

"Oh, no," King Laza said. "She is, I believe, still alive. She is a sorceress, remember. There are ways of prolonging life almost indefinitely. Most magicians eventually conclude that it is unwise to do so. But Godescalc is different."

Zargal did not pause to inquire what reasons could possibly prevent a magician from seeking eternal life. "If she is living," he realized, "then there's still hope. She could help."

"I daresay she could. But you'd best dismiss that thought from your mind. Godescalc lives as an outcast and an exile because of Cramarius. She has every reason to hate his descendants. And I can assure you, she would never voluntarily consent to help us."

"Then her consent need not be voluntary," Zargal snapped. "Seek her out, take her prisoner, bring her back here—and I'll wager there are ways of persuading her to cure the Princess."

"Seek her out—take her prisoner?" the King echoed. "If it were as easy as all that, do you suppose that it wouldn't have been done long ago? Don't think it hasn't been tried. But Godescalc is far too clever to permit herself to be taken unaware. When she fled Obran centuries ago, she made her way into the heart of the Elg. Are you acquainted with that region?"

Zargal nodded. The Elg was a great expanse of trackless swampland that lay outside the boundaries of Obran. The place had a bad reputation. Travelers were wont to go wandering in and not come out again.

"She hid herself away deep within the Elg. She contrived a system of traps and pitfalls that protects her on all sides. A number of my ancestors—including Cramarius himself—sent regiments of guards in to search for her. The guards were never heard of again. They vanished without a trace. In my younger days, I even attempted an expedition myself—and failed."

"Perhaps you could send the Queen an offer of payment," Zargal suggested. "If she won't bend to steel, then maybe you should try gold."

"That's a foolish thought. Use your head, lad! Of what possible use would money be to someone living alone in a swamp?"

Zargal was forced to admit the truth of this. "In that case, you might extend her an invitation to return to Obran and live in safety."

"Worse and worse. Does it really seem likely to you that Black Godescalc would agree to return as a subject to the land she once ruled as Queen?"

Zargal and King Laza both stood in silence for a while, regarding the Princess as if they sought the answer to their problem in her face. Outside the tower window, the wind screamed and threatened. Inside, the log in the fireplace cracked, sparks flew, and the fire started to sink. Without being bidden, Bibka trudged across the room to the wood-pile, seized a fresh log in her jaws, and replenished the blaze.

"Why have you shut her up in this tower?" Zargal asked.

"She will not be seen here. She will be grateful."

There was another period of silence, and this time the King was studying Zargal in an expectant manner. At last the Duke's son said cautiously, "I can think of only one offer that might tempt her. If she could return to Obran and resume her position as Queen, perhaps she would be satisfied. Had that thought ever occurred to you?" He chanced a look at the King, whose face was totally unreadable.

"Am I to understand that you are urging me to abdicate?"

"To end the curse," Zargal said, "and save your daughter. For her sake! Godescalc is the rightful Queen. Let her have the throne back to save your daughter and all your descendants!"

The King's face was still expressionless, but somehow Zargal knew all at once that this wasn't a new thought to him at all.

"There may be something in what you say," King Laza answered slowly. "But there yet remains the problem of conveying such an offer to Godescalc. Even if I were willing, I couldn't go myself. And who else would dare to venture into the Elg? Who would risk so much for Bellora's sake?"

"I would," Zargal replied instantly. "I'll do it."

"I accept your offer," Laza responded with equal speed. "You will start early tomorrow morning. I shall provide you with maps and written instructions at that time. My lord Zargal, I should like to thank you for this unexpected generosity."

"Unexpected?" Zargal repeated, as the truth dawned on him. "Isn't this what you brought me up here for?"

King Laza did not answer.

CHAPTER XIX

Dawn was just starting to break when Zargal was awakened by a hand on his shoulder and a familiar voice. "Get up—it be time for us to go!" He opened his eyes and sat up, instantly wide awake. Rothadd was standing beside his pallet, and the Outcottager was bundled up in his fur-lined cloak, a muffler and boots.

"What—are you coming with me?" Zargal asked in surprise.

"Oh, aye. The King did tell me of your mission, and asked if it would suit me to go along, too. 'Tis sure I wouldn't turn down a chance like that!" Rothadd said with great good cheer.

"Hmmm. Did he tell you what you may be letting yourself in for?"

"He said I might get a glimpse of Queen Godescalc, and that be enough for me. Besides," Rothadd added, "if there be a way of helpin' the Princess, I wouldn't say nay."

"You're a brave fellow," Zargal said, "and a good friend. I'm glad you're coming. The truth is, I wasn't looking forward to making the trip by myself."

"Well, now, truth to tell—" Rothadd flushed slightly. "—I won't be the only one a-comin' with 'ee—with you."

"The lackeys aren't coming, surely? Don't tell me, please, that the King is sending Guggard along?"

"Oh, nay, it ben't—isn't—that. 'Tis a gaggle of her ladyship's suitors. His Majesty did ask 'em to help, and they be willin'."

"Oh, no!"

"Aye. King Laza do say, the more that go, the more like it be that someone will succeed. So he did send word to all of those sitting outside the walls."

Cursing under his breath and feeling betrayed, Zargal flung his cloak around him and snatched up the sack of belongings that he'd packed the night before. Together he and Rothadd hurried through the halls and out into the windswept courtyard, where they found King Laza, Bibka, and a little group of four young men. Off to one side stood a huge, old-fashioned sleigh—a massive wooden affair, heavily carved, the front built up like the prow of a ship. At the arrival of Zargal and Rothadd, all four of Bellora's suitors turned and stared, then looked away again. Clearly they were startled at the appearance of a near-giant in their midst, but considered it undignified to admit their astonishment.

"Good! We are all assembled," King Laza announced, his voice unusually distinct, his visage completely shaded by his hat. "I shall not waste words or time. Our purpose is already known to you all. The Princess Bellora is ill, and it is my belief that she can be aided only by Lady Godescalc, currently residing in the Elg. You, my lords, will convey my request for assistance and my offer of terms to the Lady. The documents will be carried by Lord Zargal."

The King drew forth a heavy gray envelope which bore the royal seal. This he placed in Zargal's hands, while the suitors murmured among themselves. "Lord Zargal is acquainted with the terms I present to Lady Godescalc. If she chooses to accept them, she may accompany you on your return journey. If she does not accept, there will in all probability be no return journey."

The suitors were whispering and casting hostile looks upon Zargal. At length one of them spoke up with polite distrust. "We are not acquainted with Lord Zargal, his station, or his lineage. We note he wears your Majesty's livery, and are forced to question his rank. We request your Majesty's assurance that he is of fit quality to join our party."

"Lord Zargal is only son to Jalonzal, Archduke of Szar," the King replied with a touch of impatience. "And therefore, the equal or superior in birth to any of you. Will that suffice?"

There was another quick conference. "We will acknowledge the quality of Lord Zargal." Zargal glowered at them. The air was frosted with mutual antagonism.

"I think it only fitting," the King said, "that the six of you should be introduced to one another at this time. The two strangers among us are Lord Zargal of Szar and his companion Rothadd, Rotha's son, of the Eastling Wolds."

"Well-met, lads!" Rothadd smiled. No one replied.

"The rest of you," King Laza continued, "are gentlemen of Obran. We have with us Count Emce-Slatermul." The Count must have been Bellora's wealthiest suitor. He was dressed warmly against the cold, as all the others were. But the fur that lined his cloak was sable, and his gloves were trimmed with klaxin, dyed blue. His sword hilt was solid gold, set with bluish pearls, his doublet a mass of gold embroideries. It was all a little overdone, but there could be no doubt that Emce-Slatermul was a man of substance. The Count was of short stature and very powerful. He had dark hair and a dark, square face, with a determined chin. At the moment, he was looking impatient.

"The Marquis sa Relmer." Sa Relmer, thin and intense, had been lurking outside the walls of King Laza's castle longer than any other suitor. Despite his noble birth, his life had been filled with problems and disappointments. Sa Relmer had decided long ago that marriage to Princess Bellora would put an end to his troubles once and for all. He had been pursuing her tirelessly ever since.

"Crumer Paskha of Olbiord." Crumer, youngest son of a duke, had grown up fun-loving and spendthrift. He had once imagined that marriage with the King's daughter might repair his wrecked fortunes. Upon meeting Bellora, however, and hearing her voice, his motives had changed; he forgot all about his fortunes and thought only of the Princess herself. One of the most enterprising of the young men, Crumer was the only suitor who had ever thought of using trained birds to carry messages to his beloved—a scheme he was forced to abandon when the birds all flew south for the winter. His mind was inventive, his energies boundless.

"Count sa Wenilow." The Count, fair, slight, and rather delicate, was surveying the castle with a yearning expression, obviously trying to locate the window of Bellora's chamber. His hands were gloveless, his fingers ink-stained, and his pockets bulged with unfinished poems. Despite his otherworldly look, sa Wenilow carried a sword as sharp as that of anyone else.

The names of the four suitors were familiar ones to Zargal, for he had seen them many times, affixed to the love letters flung into the courtyard. He felt, in fact, as if he knew all four young nobles. But they obviously looked upon him as an interloper, and an odd one at that.

"The Princess' illness," King Laza was saying, "grows worse with each passing day. For that reason, it is essential that you proceed to the Elg with all possible speed. The mountains are frozen now, the roads dangerous, and traveling is difficult. Therefore, I've provided you gentlemen with the most effective means of transportation possible at this time of the year." The King's suave gesture directed their attention to the antique sleigh. "The six of you will ride in this."

"A sleigh, sire?" Count Emce-Slatermul asked in disbelief. "Where is the team of horses that could draw it down the mountain in this weather?"

"There will be no horses," the King replied. "This is no ordinary sleigh. It's my own invention. Once you've entered this vehicle, it will bear you at high speed down the mountains, across the foothills, and onward to the outermost reaches of Obran, where the Elg begins. It cannot, unfortunately, carry you any farther than that—the runners won't pass through the undergrowth, and the trails are far too narrow. By the time you reach the edge of the Elg, however, the actual distance that remains for you to travel is not great. The sleigh has been provided with food, lanterns, blankets—everything that should ensure your comfort and safety. There's a chamber pot with a spell to make it self-cleaning onto the road behind you. I don't think you'll find the first portion of your journey unpleasant."

"Have you given us a map?" Zargal asked. "And will you tell us how to guide the sleigh?"

"That won't be necessary. The sleigh will carry you by the shortest route to the edge of the Elg, and there it will stop. You will leave it there and proceed the rest of the way on foot, as best you can. At such time as you wish to return, you will re-enter the sleigh, issue one order—'Go' —and it will bring you straight back here."

"But if we should wish to stop along the way?" the Marquis sa Relmer asked dubiously. "How do we stop?"

"Let us hope that the necessity doesn't arise," the King replied. "Gentlemen, if you please."

The six young men climbed cautiously into the waiting sleigh. There was some slight awkwardness over who should precede whom. Count Emce-Slatermul sprang in first, with the air of a conqueror, and nobody opposed him. Then the Marquis sa Relmer, Crumer Paskha, and Count sa Wenilow all stepped forward at once, paused, and instinctively reached for their swords. While they stood bristling and eyeing one another, Rothadd seized the opportunity to slip unobtrusively into his seat. Then the voice of their sovereign rang out and put an end to the dispute, whereupon they entered in order of rank—the Marquis, the Count, and then Crumer Paskha. Zargal entered last. Somewhat altered by his months of servitude, he had automatically allowed the others to go before him. The sleigh creaked dolefully beneath his great weight, and the other occupants, excepting Rothadd, observed him with disfavor.

"Your Majesty!" Rothadd called. "Can 'ee not give us some notion which way to go once we do reach the Elg?"

"No," Laza replied.

"But how will we know where we be, then?"

"You must find your own way, lad."

"Can your Majesty not give us some idea what to expect?" Crumer asked.

"Trouble, danger, and immense difficulties," Laza told him. "Mud, quicksand, mists, and insects. Confusion, boredom, and inconvenience. Not to mention whatever unnatural obstacles Godescalc may place in your path."

"These are trifles which shall not hinder me," Emce-Slatermul proclaimed. "Danger is my recreation."

"I hope that is true," King Laza said somberly. "Gentlemen, the time has come for you to be on your way. I would not wrong your quality by speaking to you of a reward—true gallantry scorns material returns." The delicacy of this sentiment was much appreciated by the occupants of the sleigh. Only Zargal noticed the flash of sarcasm that accompanied it. "I shall merely promise that the man who succeeds in this mission will know my deepest gratitude—and that of Princess Bellora. I can say no more." The young rivals nodded in comprehension and regarded one another with increased hostility. "And now, may good fortune attend you all! My hopes go with you. Gentlemen, farewell!"

Laza uttered a command, and the sleigh shuddered as if awakening from a deep sleep. He spoke again, and it began to move.

CHAPTER XX

The sleigh moved slowly at first and then began to pick up speed. Zargal glanced back over his shoulder at the courtyard. King Laza was still sitting there watching them go, and his shrouded figure was growing smaller by the second. Once only, Laza raised a hand and waved, then allowed it to fall heavily into his lap. Zargal turned to the front again as the sleigh passed under the raised portcullis and began its descent of the mountain.

The paths leading down from King Laza's castle were immensely steep and rocky. They were difficult to travel at the best of times, and now, encased in ice, they were well-nigh unnavigable. It had been Zargal's natural expectation that the vehicle Laza had provided would maintain a slow and careful pace, but he soon discovered how mistaken he was. Once out of the castle yard, the sleigh went faster and faster, until the six passengers were whipped raw in the wind of its passage.

A couple of hundred yards from the castle wall, the path took its first great plunge. So sharp was the angle of incline that the young men in the sleigh momentarily imagined they had skidded over the edge of a precipice and were falling freely through space. Zargal's stomach seemed to have risen several inches nearer to his throat. His eyes snapped shut of their own accord, and he was clinging desperately to the side of the sleigh, expecting the fatal crash to come any second. A faint cry escaped him, but was lost in the rush of the wind and the rattle of the sleigh's antique timbers. No crash came, however, and Zargal opened his eyes again. Beside him, in the other seats, all his companions had attached themselves to anything immovable that they could lay hands on. The sleigh was whizzing down the dangerous path at a horrifying speed, but the actual sensation of movement was not unpleasant. The vehicle had settled into a steady, rocking motion. Although its joints screeched as if ready to split apart, the sleigh's speed continued to increase.

As Zargal's alarm gradually receded, he began to pay attention to his surroundings. The sun was now rising, and the eastern sky was glowing pink and gold. Every rock, bush, and tree bore a thick layer of transparent ice. In the early morning light, all the stark landscape seemed fashioned of brittle glass that shattered as the metal runners of the sleigh passed over at lightning speed.

Morning wore on, and the pink glow turned to gold as the sun climbed higher in the sky. The light reflecting off the snow became so blinding that Zargal was obliged to shield his eyes against it. For once, the peaks of Obran were free of mist. The sky was a winter's pale blue, and the jagged white mountains flashed like monster icebergs on all sides. The wind was a spear flung in their faces; had it not been for the furs that King Laza had provided, the travelers would have suffered extremely from the cold.

There was not much conversation in the sleigh. Zargal and Rothadd occasionally addressed each other, but that was all. Around midmorning, however, the six of them overcame their mutual hostility to such an extent that they agreed it was time to breakfast. There were several sacks of provisions lying on the floor. They opened one and discovered that King Laza had been generous. He had provided them with a number of Vaxil's choicest items: a small keg of double-strength ale; steamed fruit bread and butter; sharp cheese; a beef, mushroom, and oyster pie; pickled skorns; and one of Vaxil's amazing desserts—a marzipan replica of the sleigh in which they rode, tinted with vegetable coloring and decorated with blanched almonds, slivered blifilnuts, and candied fruits. There was more than enough, in fact, to satisfy the appetite of everyone present except Zargal, who had long ago given up all hope of satisfying his.

As the hours passed and the sleigh continued its mad rush down the mountainside, the young men grew accustomed to the motion, paid little further attention to it, and began to seek diversion. Rothadd removed Hincmar's parchment from his pocket and began muttering inaudibly to himself. Count sa Wenilow started to work on a poem. Count Emce-Slatermul withdrew a handkerchief and polished his sword. Crumer Paskha took up the pack of cards that he never traveled without. The Marquis sa Relmer lost himself in a book. Zargal opened up the map that had been left lying on his seat in the sleigh and traced their probable route. All known roads, he noted, stopped short at the boundaries of the Elg, a large, irregular region which had been filled in solid gray.

Time passed very slowly, and the various diversions palled. Despite the extraordinary nature of their conveyance, the young men were finding the trip dull. Eventually, out of sheer boredom, they began to talk to one another. Count sa Wenilow recited poems. Sa Relmer discussed his tragic love life. Crumer Paskha told jokes. Rothadd sang a medley of Outcottager ballads. Count Emce-Slatermul treated them all to a description of the valuables contained in his mansion. Zargal gave a rather humorous account of his fight with Bibka. A while later, the conversations died away again. They watched the sun sink out of sight behind the mountains and dined on Vaxil's cold galantine of swan, all done up in fantastical puff paste. Darkness fell. Lulled by the ceaseless rocking motion, they dropped off to sleep one by one as the sleigh raced on through the starless night.

The sunlight was already glaring on the snow the next morning when Zargal and the others awoke. There was no way of telling how far they had traveled while they slept, but if the sleigh had not paused or slowed, then they knew they had to have come very many miles. The path had widened into a lane. The second day passed much like the first. But the travelers were starting to grow uncomfortable, for the sleigh, although large, did not give them any room to move around. They were all sick to death of sitting still; their limbs were starting to ache, and their muscles were cramped. Several times Emce-Slatermul inquired in a strained voice why Zargal had to take up so much space. Zargal did not answer, and shot a warning glance at Rothadd when it appeared that the Outcottager was on the verge of doing so.

Toward the late afternoon tempers were growing short, and once or twice there were angry words. In order to distract his mind, Zargal turned to observe the landscape flashing by and recognized with surprise what a great distance they had covered. The sleigh had left the mountains behind and was now whizzing over the southern foothills. Its motion had become much gentler as the steepness of the road decreased.

What startled Zargal most, however, was the difference in the weather. Down here at the lower altitudes, the seasons were already beginning to change. The air was milder; the winds that buffeted the travelers were cold and biting, but no longer excruciating. The ground around the sleigh was soggy with melted snow, and it gave off a moldy smell. The sky was as gray as stone, and a thin drizzle lightly touched the heads of the travelers. Winter was finished here. The land was in the midst of those dank, grim days which come between the disappearance of the last snows and the first appearance of spring greenery.

As the countryside changed, and the sharp elevations smoothed themselves into rounded hills, the velocity of the sleigh increased. The fact that the runners were now passing over half-frozen mud made no difference; it went faster all the time. The joints were shrieking in anguished protest. When the vehicle encountered even a slight bend in the path, Zargal could feel it skid perilously around the curve on its one outer runner. He began to experience misgivings once again.

Matters were not improved when the Marquis sa Relmer, who had been sitting in more or less the same position for the past six hours, was seized with a sudden muscular spasm in the left leg and started twisting and rocking violently in vain efforts to ease the afflicted member. Sa Relmer's struggles threw the sleigh off balance and sent it careening wildly from one side of the road to the other, in constant danger of overturning. The passengers would gladly have stopped then and there, but lacked the capacity, and were forced to content themselves with screaming at the Marquis to sit down and keep still. By dint of much massage, sa Relmer's cramp was finally relieved. The sleigh stopped pitching, righted itself, and resumed its straight course.

"I'm sorry," sa Relmer apologized uncomfortably. "I couldn't help it. I have bad legs. In fact, I've always been quite delicate. Right now I'm feeling extremely nauseous and it's quite likely I'm going to be sick any second—"

"Do it in this, then." Emce-Slatermul thrust forward the porcelain chamber pot. "Or better yet, do it over the side. Otherwise, *you* go over the side."

Zargal said nothing, but privately he agreed with the Count. The sleigh hastened on.

By late afternoon of the fifth day, things had come to a bad pass with the travelers, who were going out of their minds with boredom and had all decided long since that they couldn't abide one another. Count sa Wenilow had suggested at one point that they try to stop the sleigh, get out for a few minutes, and stretch their limbs. The others agreed, and Rothadd attempted a variety of incantations and commands.

The sleigh did not even slow down, much less stop. It had carried them out of the mountains and foothills and was now hurtling down a wide, sloping piece of terrain. The relative flatness of the land was a clue that they were nearing the end of their journey, for this long slope—the Gluis Appli—lay near the southern boundary of Obran and bordered on the great Elg. None of the men, however, was proficient in geography. All they knew was that the trip seemed to be lasting forever and that they had no control whatever over their vehicle.

It was purely in the hope of helping matters that Crumer Paskha finally suggested that they all join him in a game of Antislez, an ancient game, familiar to them all. The Obranese deck contained a larger assortment of face cards—the king, the queen, the prince, the princess, the duke, the envoy, the executioner—and included a single odd card of great power, the Black Sorceress. The object of the game was to build up an entire royal household by deceiving or forcing the opponents into discarding the cards one needed. The black sorceress could simultaneously retain her own identity and take on that of any other card.

There was some disagreement over stakes. Those proposed by Emce-Slatermul were so high that he could find no takers. Sa Wenilow and sa Relmer were both well-supplied with gold, but were moderate gamblers. Crumer Paskha was a little short of cash. Zargal still retained the twenty-eight grinlings that he had carried away from Szar, and he divided these with Rothadd, who had only a few silver coins of his own.

The game began, and conversation ceased as the young men became absorbed in play. At first Emce-Slatermul won steadily. His luck was almost supernatural. Again and again the black sorceress was dealt to him; and although he was not a subtle player, the power she lent enabled him to triumph repeatedly. For a while the only sound to be heard was the Count's immoderate laughter as he pocketed his winnings. It was his opinion that he was a born conqueror, and he never failed, as he won each hand, to let his fellow travelers know it. Eventually, however, his luck changed. The black sorceress capriciously abandoned him; shortly thereafter his winnings did likewise. Emce-Slatermul laughed no more, and his expression changed.

Zargal was an excellent player, his upbringing in the Court of Jalonzal standing him in very good stead. He was not, however, a match for Crumer Paskha, who seemed touched with a kind of genius. Together, Crumer and Zargal quickly demolished Rothadd and then began relieving Emce-Slatermul of large sums. Zargal won substantially, but Crumer was acquiring a fortune. The Count's face darkened perceptibly, although he was clearly trying to assume a careless attitude.

At the end of a couple of hours both sa Wenilow and sa Relmer had lost as much as they would permit themselves, and both quit, leaving Crumer, Zargal, and Emce-Slatermul to continue the game. Zargal lost some to Crumer, but more than made up for it with what he won from the Count. It appeared that Crumer could not make a false move. In addition to his own natural talent, he was now being aided by the black sorceress, who seemed disposed to side with those who needed her least. Crumer, in high good spirits, was dazzling his fellow travelers with a display of spectacular shuffling tricks when Emce-Slatermul suddenly exclaimed, "I saw that, sir! Do you think me blind, sir?"

Crumer stopped shuffling. "What do you mean?" he asked, mystified.

"I mean that you are light of finger, sir—in every sense!"

"Would you care to explain that statement, my lord?" Crumer demanded menacingly.

"Does it require any explanation?"

"Are you suggesting—?" Crumer began whitely.

"Yes! You slipped a card up your sleeve just now. You are a cheat, sir!"

With a great effort of will, Crumer Paskha maintained his self-control. "Would you like to inspect my cuffs and shirt sleeves, Count, so that your suspicions may be quite set at rest before I cut your throat?" he inquired and drew back his sleeves, which were in fact entirely empty of anything other than his arms.

"Bah—you've slipped it back into the deck," Emce-Slatermul insisted sullenly. "I saw what I saw."

"That's a lie!"

"You slippery blackguard, nobody calls Emce-Slatermul a liar!"

"Why, you gaudy, overbearing, overdressed, upstart vulgarian! Why do you gamble if you can't lose like a gentleman?"

"Do you suggest I'm not a gentleman, sir?"

"You are the true heir to your grandsire the merchant, sir!" Crumer sneered.

"And you are a lying cheat!"

This was more than Crumer could endure. With an enraged snarl, he drew his poniard and flung himself upon Emce-Slatermul, who sat facing him. The Count drew his gold-hilted dagger and returned the attack vigorously. Within the cramped confines of the sleigh, the young men had no room to maneuver. Their blades were useless for the moment; but with their free hands, they smashed and tore at each other murderously.

At length Emce-Slatermul was able to obtain a strong hold on Crumer's throat, and started squeezing with all the strength of his left hand. Angrier than ever, Crumer simultaneously brought his knee up into the other's midriff and poked stiffened fingers into his eyes. Emce-Slatermul released his hold and began raining vicious blows upon Crumer's back and ribs. Crumer's knife went plunging toward Emce-Slatermul's throat. The Count dodged the blow, but lost his grip on his own dagger, and the weapon went spinning off over the side of the sleigh and down onto the ground. Emce-Slatermul gave a raging bellow and redoubled the fury of his blows.

The combat was rocking the sleigh badly. It was skidding and swerving each time Crumer or the Count landed a good punch. Matters grew even worse when the two of them, locked together, slid off the seat and down onto the floor, where they continued to thrash and struggle. The sleigh was bucking in an odd, uneven manner, like a terrified horse. Periodically, as the fighters rolled from one side to the other, the sleigh tilted and skittered along on one runner for hundreds of yards at a time.

The other travelers were powerless to interfere. Each time one of them made a move to separate Crumer and the Count, the sleigh tilted more alarmingly than ever and raced off at an angle toward the side of the road. Once, when Zargal attempted to shift his huge form, the sleigh plunged so violently, the joints shrieked so hideously, that he was forced to sit down again. There was nothing that any of them could do but yell. They did so with much fervor, but no results.

Suddenly the travelers encountered the first other human beings to cross their path since the journey began. A couple of boat-shaped caravans were making their way up the broad slope of the Gluis Appli, containing a small band of Turos headed toward the foothills of Obran. Zargal caught only a fleeting glimpse of gaily painted wagons with figureheads, bony horses, and a number of dark, astonished faces. As for the Turos, the sleigh had hardly flashed upon their vision before it drew level, passed them, and whirled away down the lane. The Turos paused where they were, staring.

Emce-Slatermul had finally succeeded in gaining possession of his opponent's dagger. The Count was now kneeling atop Crumer Paskha's chest, exerting every ounce of his strength to bring the blade within striking distance of his enemy's nostrils, which he desired to slit. For his part,

Crumer was grasping the Count's wrist with both hands and howling imprecations. The sleigh was pitching and veering perilously. It was continually on the verge of running clear off the edge of the road.

Rothadd, perceiving that Crumer Paskha, whose card tricks he had enjoyed, was in danger of immediate mutilation, could contain himself no longer. With a cry, he flung himself upon Emce-Slatermul and grappled for the knife. The Count threw him off, and Rothadd bounced heavily against one of the empty seats. The sleigh bucked, teetered, and sped on one runner toward the edge of the road. This time it collided with a large rock. There was a terrible sound of metal scraping on stone. The sleigh spun completely around, joints screaming; then it turned over, rolled off the road, and came to rest on its side, only a few hundred yards from the watching Turos.

The six young men tumbled out onto the damp slope of the Gluis Appli and lay where they had fallen, partially stunned. Count Emce-Slatermul and Crumer Paskha were still locked together. The others had been scattered over the area of several yards. Only the Marquis sa Relmer remained near the sleigh, still tangled among the furry rugs, sacks, maps, and lanterns that had spilled forth at the moment of collision.

Zargal lay motionless for a time, his eyes closed, his mind empty. Eventually he was forced to notice that the frigid moisture on the ground was seeping through his livery. Nearby, someone was moaning, and he could hear the sound of footsteps and low voices. Zargal opened his eyes reluctantly, raised his head a little, and looked around.

The footsteps and voices belonged to the Turos, whose caravans had drawn near while the travelers lay dazed. The Turos had alighted from their wagons and were now clustered around, whispering to each other in their own language. One of them walked over to the sleigh, passed a hand over the gilded carvings, and made an unintelligible comment. Another peeked cautiously into a gaping sack and lifted out one of Vaxil's bouquets of red and yellow marzipan roses, which he regarded in disbelief.

Noting that Zargal had begun to stir, one of the Turos, a middle-aged man with liquid black eyes and a kindly expression, knelt beside him and inquired, "How d'ye fare, young sir?"

"I'm well enough," Zargal answered, looking around to see if his companions could say the same. Rothadd had sat up and was feeling himself for bruises. Crumer and the Count were making feeble efforts to disengage from one another. The moans that Zargal had noticed were growing louder. They came from the Marquis sa Relmer, who lay struggling weakly.

A couple of Turo lads instantly went to the Marquis' aid and began removing the paraphernalia in which he was enmeshed, whereupon it was discovered that sa Relmer's ankle was pinned beneath the overturned sleigh. The man who had addressed Zargal, and who was evidently the Turos' leader, issued a quick command. All the members of the band—some fourteen adults and children—flocked to the sleigh and, at another word from their chief, lifted the vehicle off sa Relmer and set it upright again. The Marquis did not rise. It was only too evident that his leg had been broken.

"Ah, this is a sad accident!" the Turo leader sympathized. "This is a great misfortune, it is!" He had a slow, gentle manner of speaking.

The travelers were hauling themselves to their feet and shakily drawing near their injured comrade. Sa Relmer was entirely conscious, and in considerable pain. "I can't get up!" he cried. "I can't get up! What's to be done?" He looked imploringly from one face to the next. Nobody answered him. For the moment, no one had a word to say.

The Turo leader looked at them with his wise, dark eyes. "You young lords have had a bad time of it," he observed. "It's close on sunset now. Best you rest a little, have a bit to eat, camp here tonight with us—and there'll be time enough tomorrow morning to decide what's to be done. We Turos are poor folk, young lords, and haven't got much cheer to give ye. Such as our hospitality is, though, I offer it to ye freely."

"That's very kind," Zargal said. "But we will be glad to reward you."

"Oh, no need, young lord. I can see you're uneasy in your mind, but there's no need for that, either. There's many a Turo will aid neither man nor beast, excepting he gets payment, and it's that which has given our people a bad name. But it isn't *our* way. I'm called Fulkar. This is my family I've got here with me. And we'll be happy to do what we can for ye, with no talk of payment." Fulkar spoke with such an independent air that it was impossible to doubt him, and Zargal began to repent of his suspicions.

The Turos were kindness itself. As it was now approaching sunset, they went about tending to their horses, building a fire, and setting out the evening meal. One of the young women ministered to the Marquis sa Relmer. She improvised a rough splint for his injured leg and helped the unhappy suitor to a comfortable place near the fire. When all was ready, the entire group sat down in a large circle to eat, drink, sing, and exchange stories, as the sun sank out of sight below the horizon.

The Turos were all master storytellers, but Fulkar was especially eloquent. With his slow, unhurried manner of speech and his colorful choice of words, he was able to keep his listeners enthralled. Fulkar spoke of Turo legend and history. He spun tales of travel, of adventure in foreign lands, and of men's extraordinary exploits. But his true talent lay in the telling of ghost stories. As Fulkar sat there with the firelight glowing red upon his face and brightening his deep eyes, he hypnotized his followers and guests alike with descriptions of haunted palaces, monsters of the marshlands, uncontrollable walking corpses, and troublesome ghouls.

At last he turned to Zargal and said, "Now, if I don't miss my guess, young sir, you come from out of the city of Szar." Zargal admitted the truth of this. "Ah, yes, I could tell by the talk of ye. Well, we've just come from your homeland these three weeks past, and there's trouble of the spirit kind brewing there. Do you know of it?"

"What do you mean?" Zargal asked skeptically.

"Well, then—" Fulkar proceeded to describe an obviously accursed spot situated along the great highway leading to the southeastern gate of Szar—a haunted vegetable field, the property of a University Professor who had died under mysterious circumstances. "Aye," the Turo said. "Months ago, he was found lying there in his field without a mark upon him, but cold and dead! He'd never been sick, he had nothing worth stealing, but there he lay, stiff and stark, not touched with bullet or blade or rope, nor yet any bruise upon him. The ground around the body was soft and wet, but there was nary a footprint to be seen. There was nothing there, mind you, but a field of vegetables, sleeping in the sun. Squashes, they were. And yet the Professor hadn't died natural. Anyone could see by the look on his face—as if he just busted with astonishment and spleen!"

"About that field—" Zargal said.

Fulkar was not about to lose the thread of his story. "And if the old Professor's death won't convince ye there was queer work afoot," he continued, "then let me tell ye some more, because that wasn't all of it!" And he told stories of the many unfortunates who had died amidst the squashes during the last several months—the travelers, the beggars, the merchants, the strolling players, and the Turo lass who had been discovered with a half-eaten red squash clutched in one hand and a look of horror frozen upon her features.

"Now what does all this mean?" Fulkar asked in conclusion. "What's behind it all? A ghost, that's what. That field is haunted. There's no two ways about it! What else could possibly explain it? What else could it be but spirits?"

"Squashes!" Zargal broken in. "It's not spirits, it's those squashes!"

"What?"

"That Professor—Professor Horm—created a species of vegetable capable of killing human beings. The squashes got Horm, and now they're murdering others as well."

"That can't be, young sir," Fulkar assured him kindly. "It's out of the question."

"Why?"

"Because vegetables don't kill people. At least, not unless somebody's put poison in them. Is that what you're trying to say?"

"No. I speak literally. Those plants are dangerous, and people must be told. Will you be traveling back to Szar?"

"Not until sometime next year. But I don't really think you need to fear the vegetables, young sir, when it's the angry ghosts have made their presence known—"

"I tell you it's those squashes," Zargal insisted. "If you can believe in angry ghosts, why shouldn't you believe in angry squashes? In any case, we must think of a way of getting word to Duke Jalonzal."

"Oh, young sir," Fulkar said with a gentle laugh, "it's no easy thing to catch the ear of the Archduke Jalonzal."

"I have a feeling I could catch his ear," Zargal said grimly.

"Ah, but the Archduke pays heed to no man these days, now that he's so taken up with his wedding plans."

"His wedding plans?" Zargal repeated, inexpressibly shocked. *"His wedding plans?"*

"Oh, yes. Well, he hasn't much choice, now, has he?"

"What are you saying?"

"Ever since the disappearance of Jalonzal's son, there's been no heir to the Dukedom," the Turo explained. "The Archduke is still in his prime, isn't he? So there's time and reason for him to marry again."

"I see. Who is the future Duchess?" Zargal asked, with a slight twist of the lips. Out of the corner of his eye, he saw his companions looking on in fascination.

"There's been no official proclamation as yet, but it's certain to be Jeria of Strell."

"Jeria of Strell!" Zargal echoed, appalled again. "That can't be! She's young enough to be his daughter. Why, at one time there was even some talk of betrothing her to Jalonzal's son," he concluded on a careful note.

"That's true. It came to nothing, though. The Duke's son was too wild, and Jeria's father wouldn't have it. She was then betrothed to a young nobleman of her own country, a lad of her own choosing. When Jalonzal's proposal came, though, the Talgh of Strell insisted on the higher match for his daughter, so that's that."

"Poor Jeria!" Zargal murmured. "I met her once. She deserves better!"

"Well, it can't be such a bad thing to be a duchess," Fulkar said. "There's something in that. And great folk don't wed for love, I'm told. Anyway, the wedding isn't until spring."

"You seem well-informed," Zargal said, not altogether approvingly. He was still trying to digest the Turo's news.

"Aye, surely. We Turos travel the world over, see all, meet everyone, learn all happenings, and make friends wherever we go. It's a free and joyous life we lead. But what of yourselves, young lords? Where might you be journeying, in a sleigh that needs no horses?"

The travelers gave a somewhat shortened account of their mission. It was now late, and the young men were all exhausted, especially the poor Marquis. Nevertheless, in the interests of good-fellowship, Rothadd went so far as to provide a sketchy explanation of the magic sleigh that so obviously intrigued the Turos. Crumer Paskha rummaged around in the depleted food sacks and came up with a couple of bottles of superior brandywine, with which they were able to drink a boisterous round of healths.

After that, amidst many expressions of gratitude and promises of eternal friendship, they all composed themselves for slumber. The Turos helped to lift sa Relmer into the sleigh, where he was able to stretch out on a padded seat, then retired to their caravans. The remaining young men wrapped themselves in King Laza's furs and lay down on the ground.

"We'd better get the Marquis to a doctor," Rothadd said.

"There's time enough to think of that tomorrow," Emce-Slatermul decreed. "Right now I'm tired and I want to sleep."

"Maybe the Turos will be able to look after sa Relmer," Count sa Wenilow murmured sleepily. "They seem very helpful."

"I wonder what's going on in Szar," Zargal mused. "Duke Jalonzal to marry!" Nobody replied. Silence reigned, and soon they slept.

CHAPTER XXI

In the dead of night, the peace that lay over the Gluis Appli was shattered by the sound of human yells. Zargal and the others managed to struggle back to consciousness, tired as they were. In the moonlight that flooded the slope they beheld a curious sight. The great sleigh, King Laza's magic conveyance, was packed with people. All fourteen of the Turos had quietly squeezed themselves in while the rightful owners slept. They were sitting so close together that their dark forms presented a solid mass. A few of them were engaged in restraining sa Relmer, who still occupied one seat. The Marquis had awakened during the Turo invasion and had started to shout a warning. The Turos quickly silenced him, but the damage was done.

The five victims were all at once wide awake and they began running toward the sleigh. Fulkar was speaking aloud, exhorting the vehicle to move. His followers started gabbling excitedly in their own dialect. Sa Relmer managed to shake his head free for an instant to shout. "They're stealing the sleigh!"

Zargal, Rothadd, sa Wenilow, Emce-Slatermul, and Crumer had all drawn their weapons, presenting a frightening spectacle to the Turo band, which included a number of children. Zargal, in particular, was an alarming sight, looming high above them all. One or two of the young mothers began to scream.

Fulkar, with great coolness, continued his efforts. Just as the five young men drew near, he happened to pronounce the word "go," and the sleigh obeyed him. Slowly the great wooden vehicle hitched itself around until it was facing north. Rothadd was so near that he had to dodge back to avoid the slicing runners. Then, with the Turos cheering, sa Relmer yelling uselessly, and the other five screaming threats, the sleigh headed away up the Gluis Appli, back in the direction from which it had originally come. For a few seconds the stranded men ran after it, but pursuit was hopeless; King Laza's sleigh was far too speedy.

Seeing this, Fulkar leaned out over the back and called, "You wanted to reward us, young sirs, and this will do handsomely! Many thanks!"

The Marquis sa Relmer continued to yell as the sleigh drew rapidly away. For a while his companions could hear his cries echoing through the night, growing fainter all the time. At last they could hear him no more, and the sleigh itself was lost to view. Count Emce-Slatermul flung his sword to the ground and cursed passionately, while the others simply looked stunned.

"Never trust a Turo," Crumer said, after a long silence. "A Turo always plays with loaded dice."

"Well," sa Wenilow pointed out philosophically, "at least this solves the problem of what to do about sa Relmer. Poor fellow!"

"Yes," Emce-Slatermul said, brightening. "This gets him off our hands—poor fellow! That's one down."

"A sorry coil it be," Rothadd said. "And to think that they made off with the magic sleigh, and naught to trouble 'em! It doesn't seem right!"

"They may find something to trouble them when that sleigh finally reaches its destination," Zargal reminded his companions thoughtfully. And then, as Rothadd stared at him blankly, he said, "Remember what the King told us."

Rothadd thought for a moment and then began to grin. "They be a-hurrying back to King Laza's castle!" he chortled. "And there is naught they can do to stop themselves!

Oh, a fine thing it would be to see their faces when they arrive and the King greets 'em!"

This pleasant thought afforded the travelers a certain consolation. After some further consultation, they agreed to get what sleep they could for the rest of the night and head off toward the Elg in the morning. Fortunately, they still had a map, and Rothadd's compass. They did not, however, have either of the Turos' two horses. With the intention of forestalling pursuit, Fulkar and his people had set the beasts loose and driven them off. It would be necessary to complete the rest of the journey on foot.

Without planning to, the travelers slept late the next morning. They were all tired, and there came no sound to disturb them. Zargal awoke first, roused by the pangs of his usual hunger. He soon discovered that the Turos had made off with the entire remaining food supply, with the exception of Vaxil's marzipan sculptures, which were evidently deemed suspect. Zargal awakened the others and they had a dreary breakfast. Emce-Slatermul persisted in extolling the glories of the morning meals he enjoyed at home—the exquisite crescent rolls, the butter, the honey, the fruit preserves—and Rothadd countered with descriptions of his mother's barley mash. All this had the effect of plunging Zargal into deep gloom as he munched his marzipan.

When breakfast was over, the travelers got to their feet and walked—and walked—and then walked some more. It seemed to them that the Gluis Appli was infinite. The broad, bare slope would go on unrolling itself before them to the end of time. There was nothing to be seen but soggy earth, a few patches of dirty snow, last year's dead grass, gray rocks, and dull pewter sky. A light mist had arisen to add a finishing touch to the general desolation. They saw no other human beings that day, no animals, no birds.

In the late afternoon it began to rain, a heavy, cold rain that plummeted down upon the unprotected head of Zargal, who alone among the members of the company lacked headgear. Rothadd always carried a large square of oiled cloth with him for just such emergencies, and he was able to fold it into a kind of hood, Outcottager-style. Zargal simply took up an extra blanket and draped it over his

head. He plodded on, while the blanket grew heavier and
heavier as it became sodden with rain.

Evening brought with it more rain and a cold breeze
from the north. When it was too dark to continue traveling,
the little band halted and endured a marzipan dinner,
washed down with rainwater. There was no possibility of
building a fire. After they had eaten, they wrapped themselves up as best they could and stretched out in the open
upon the watery Gluis Appli. Zargal did not really expect
to be able to sleep in such a place; it was far too uncomfortable. "I'm very tired," he told himself, "but not at all
sleepy." Shortly thereafter he drowsed off and did not
wake until nearly dawn.

It had not yet grown light when the travelers resumed
their march. Again they hiked for mile upon mile. But this
time there was not a man among them who could fail to
see that they were drawing near their destination. The land
was changing. The little dips and hollows that marred the
smoothness of the slope were filled with standing water.
The dead grass still lay long and yellow upon the ground,
but now there was other vegetation as well—senex reeds,
water-loving swampfrets, dormant mabkins, and an occasional leafless tree, sheathed in moss. The ground was softer,
muddier; it sucked at their feet as they walked, with hungry
squelching sounds. The footprints they left behind them
were filling with water. Once in a while they could hear
the distant cackle of a swamp bird, and once a small brown
snake glided across their path and disappeared into the
moldering grasses.

At last they reached a spot where they could look back
to see that the mountains of Obran had disappeared into
the mists. Before them, in plain sight, lay the bottom of the
Gluis Appli. The sloping land leveled off. Not far beyond,
the trees grew so dense and dark that there could be no
doubt that the Gluis Appli had ended and the Elg begun.
They kept walking and soon, without sudden change or
fanfare, they found themselves traversing the swamplands,
where the trees dripped with grayish moss, and a million
tiny, free-floating plants dotted the black water like bright
green stars in a midnight sky. The branches were bare and
dark. The tree trunks were charcoal-colored and coated
with grayish slime. The wind sighed through the trees, the

birds called sadly to one another, and the water in the deep pools lapped against the muddy shores. From time to time a strange, far-off cry shivered through the air. It did not sound as if it came from human or avian throat.

Having crossed over into the Elg, the travelers were somewhat at a loss, for no one had given them any instructions as to how to go about finding the dwelling of ex-Queen Godescalc. "You must find your own way," King Laza had said, and left it at that. But there were no clearly marked trails, and the Elg was huge. She might be anywhere.

After many hours of walking deeper and deeper into the heart of the swamp, through endless stretches of murky woods, past countless identical, stagnant ponds, the young men began to suspect that they might be lost. It was not a fear that any one of them cared to voice, but it troubled them all equally. At last they paused to rest and to bolt their marzipan—the last remaining fragments of it.

"I hate marzipan," Emce-Slatermul said.

"What's to do, then, lads?" Rothadd asked, ignoring the Count's complaint. "Do any of you have any thoughts?"

"We could go our separate ways," sa Wenilow suggested. "Each man on his own. We could cover five times as much territory that way, and thus there's five times as much chance that the lady will be found."

"Too risky," Crumer Paskha objected. "No. Definitely not. We don't know what dangers we might encounter here. After all, his Majesty indicated that Godescalc may set obstacles in our path, and we'll be much better equipped to deal with them if we remain together."

"Oh, well, if you're *afraid*, sir—" Emce-Slatermul began.

"Crumer's right, you know," sa Wenilow broke in. "It's always best to stand united. It reminds me of that play I once read, the one in which an old king plans to divide his kingdom into three parts—"

"I know the one—it has an absurd plot," Emce-Slatermul cut him off, his square face flushed with ill temper.

"Queen Godescalc came to this place fleeing her enemies," Zargal mused. "She'd have wanted to protect herself as much as possible. Doesn't it seem likely, then, that she'd have hidden herself away deep in the very center of the swamp?"

"Could be," Crumer conceded.

"We know that we're heading toward the center if we continue traveling south. We have Rothadd's compass to guide us. As I see it, we must keep searching and hoping. There's nothing else to do."

"Searching and hoping! That's easy enough to say, but what do we do about food?" sa Wenilow asked uneasily.

Zargal was at a complete loss for an answer, but Rothadd was not. "Oh, there be—there *are* ways. There are dried pods here. I've seen 'em. The swampfrets will make good eating, mark you. There are roots to dig, like as not. We won't starve, lads."

"I think I'd rather starve," sa Wenilow said almost inaudibly. "I don't like this place." And indeed, the watery Elg seemed to be affecting the young Count's spirits as the blizzards of Obran never had done. His gray eyes wore a strained, haunted look.

The others received Rothadd's information with a distinct lack of enthusiasm. "But that's no fare for *gentlemen!*" Emce-Slatermul complained with a meaningful sneer in the Outcottager's direction.

Zargal had conceived a particularly pronounced distaste for Emce-Slatermul. "We have little choice," he observed. "Unless, of course, you would like to give up and go home, my lord?"

"Emce-Slatermul does not give up! Never, sir!"

"Then we'd better be on our way again," Zargal said, thinking of Bellora.

They rose and struggled on through the swamp. It grew darker as they progressed, for the trees were denser. The mud was deeper, too; they were sinking in up to their ankles. The travelers had now attracted the attention of the insect population of the Elg. Fortunately, the spring weather had not arrived, and the creatures were not yet out in force. Nonetheless, the men moved in a cloud of gnats, flies, and gegrims, which buzzed and stung and gave them no peace. Much worse than the physical discomfort was the uncertainty, for none of them had any idea if they were heading in the right direction or not.

"I'm glad that Godescalc lives in this place," Crumer said. "It serves her right."

They wandered blindly on. Time passed, and the insects

grew sparser, but the trees grew thicker. It was exhausting to fight through the muck, the ooze, and the rotting vegetation. The air was dank and filled with unspeakable swamp odors. Darkness had hardly begun to settle when the tired band halted and made its inadequate camp atop a fairly solid tussock of dead grass. The tussock was surrounded on three sides by black water in which the algae thrived. This time the travelers were able to build a small, smoky fire, but it did them little good, for their clothes had been soaked, during the course of their ramblings and would not dry out fire or no. Rothadd unearthed some roots which were edible, though tough and tasteless. After having eaten, they lay down to sleep. By coincidence, or perhaps because of the evil miasma of the place, the five of them were plagued with bad dreams and visions all through the night.

The next morning Zargal awoke suddenly, feeling ill at ease and uncomfortable. As soon as he looked around, he knew why. The entire tussock on which they lay was alive with tiny, leaping, brownish-olive forms. Rothadd, Crumer, Emce-Slatermul, and sa Wenilow were all still asleep. Their reclining figures were covered from head to foot with the hopping, crawling creatures. Hundreds of thousands of them formed a living blanket that seethed over the entire patch of solid ground. Thousands more darted through the dark water toward the tussock. They appeared to be seeking the travelers. Zargal himself was infested with them—they were crawling over his limbs, hopping across his face, hiding in his hair. A shrill peeping sound filled the air, the concerted utterance of countless tiny throats.

With an exclamation of disgust, he leaped to his feet and began batting frantically at the bodies that swarmed around and over him. They were not so easy to brush off, however. They clung stubbornly, and many sought refuge beneath his clothes. Zargal paused a moment to take a closer look at the creatures and found that they were miniature toads, amazingly small, each perfect in every part, with minute webbed feet equipped with almost-invisible suction disks. Each toad had a group of emerald-green specks in the center of its forehead. Such a toad, lurking in the dark water with its head slightly raised, would blend in perfectly with the green floating plants of the swamp.

Zargal's cry and movement had awakened his companions. It took a few seconds before they realized what was going on. Then each man in turn sprang to his feet, to begin dancing around wildly and beating at himself in vain efforts to dislodge the clinging toads. More and more of the little creatures were bouncing out of the water onto the tussock. As soon as they hit solid ground, they headed straight for the human beings, advancing in long, high leaps, remarkable for animals of their size. The peeping sound increased in volume and took on a shriller note.

Zargal was being driven insane. The toads were crawling around by the hundreds beneath his suit of livery. Many more were clinging to his face with their suction pads, squatting on his eyelids, his lower lip, and the bridge of his nose. Several were attempting an exploration of his nostrils. Others sought to invade his ears. He could not open his mouth without ingesting toads; most he managed to spit out, others he involuntarily swallowed. He could feel them tickling all the way down his throat.

"Let's get out of this!" he yelled to his companions. "Let's—" He stopped abruptly and choked as two or three toads popped into his mouth. Pausing only long enough to spit them out again, he dashed away through the mud and water. The entire band of toad-ridden travelers went blundering on for a least another mile before they felt it was safe to stop. They had come to another fairly large patch of ground—somewhat slimy with algae and gray moss, but solid. Here they paused once more and began plucking the clinging toads off each other and tossing them away into the water. Even then the toads did not swim off, but remained close at hand, making frequent efforts to regain the shore.

"What's the matter with those animals?" Crumer Paskha asked. "Are they trying to eat us or what?"

"I don't think so," Zargal answered as he carefully pried a toad out of his ear and set it aside. "Not one of them has bitten me. I can't imagine what they're up to."

Emce-Slatermul did not speak. His magnificently sable-trimmed costume was coated with mud and swamp-ooze. The gold embroideries were totally obscured. Several toads sat croaking in his damp hair, and he was engaged in yanking them out and trampling them viciously underfoot.

"There's no need for that," sa Wenilow remonstrated

mildly. "They haven't done us any harm. You shouldn't kill them."

"If you have a weak stomach, sir, then look away," the Count replied. "Do you think I'm going to sit here and allow these slimy little vermin to crawl all over me?" He emphasized the question by squashing another toad.

Sa Wenilow flinched and paled slightly. His nerves did not seem to be in a very good state.

Zargal was examining one of the little animals which clung to his index finger. He noted the pattern of green specks upon the face and the tiny, stiff spikes that stood out at the base of the backbone. "I've seen pictures of toads like this," he recalled. "Somewhere, in some book. I seem to remember something about them . . . I wonder why they keep after us this way?" The toads that they had flung away were already returning, and others had joined them. Their number was rapidly increasing.

"Happen they do like us," Rothadd said, tranquilly lifting a handful of the creatures out of one pocket.

"What?" Crumer demanded.

"Well, use your noddle, lad! They ben't out for our blood, 'tis certain. And yet they won't leave us alone. All over us, they be. Now why is that, except that they like us?"

"Why *should* they like us?" sa Wenilow asked.

"Because we're essentially lovable," Zargal suggested, with no conviction whatever.

"Happen 'tis just their way to like people."

It didn't seem unlikely that Rothadd was correct, for the toads actually were exhibiting every sign of frenzied affection. They crowded in close to the travelers, as if their little lives would be enriched by the touch of humankind. Apparently all they desired was nearness. They sought nothing more than to cling to human limbs and listen to human voices.

"They do like people," Rothadd repeated.

"Then what they lack in good judgment, they make up in good nature," Zargal said, with a glance at Emce-Slater-mul, who was still busily trampling any toad he could catch.

This remark passed over Rothadd's head. The young Outcottager was studying one of the animals carefully. It had soft eyes that glowed with a golden light, and a pretty sprinkling of green dots down the center of its face. "They ben't bad little beasts, when 'ee—you look at 'em," he observed.

"Oh, they're charming." Crumer laughed. "Or at least they would be if they weren't so dashed uncomfortable." Things had indeed grown uncomfortable again. All the tiny toads that inhabited this section of the Elg had become aware of the presence of humans and were coming to greet them. Some of the creatures had followed the travelers from their last resting place, a mile back; with their light bodies that did not sink into the mud, they were able to cover ground very quickly. The earth and water seethed with bodies; the air was filled with their cries. The ones which managed to reach the young men clung to their legs in an ecstasy.

"We must move on," Crumer said. "If we stay here much longer, we won't be able to move."

"Yes," Zargal agreed. "But I wish I could remember what it is I once learned about these toads. What was it?" He frowned. "Never mind. It will come to me."

The band spent the entire day slogging through the mud. Having breakfasted on nothing more than swampfrets, which were not filling, the men were all intolerably hungry. Soon they had to deal with the torments of thirst as well, even in so watery a place as the Elg. For most of the day, every pool that they approached proved to be overflowing with the little toads. It was not possible to drink without swallowing the living creatures, which they were all unwilling to do.

After many hours of walking, they finally left the troubled region behind them. The toad-legions dwindled, their cries died away, and later there were none—the pools and puddles were quite free of animal life. Unfortunately, they were not equally free of vegetable life. Floating plants, alage, and brown scum thickened every drop of standing water to the consistency of sludge.

By late afternoon the young men grew so thirsty that they were forced to drink, but they could not swallow without gagging. The heavy, dirty liquid, almost as much mud as water, had a most evil flavor. Each of the travelers gulped down a mouthful or two, all that could be endured, and walked on with a foul taste burning on his tongue.

It was a dry-mouthed, exhausted, and dejected band that finally lay down to sleep that evening. Rothadd alone stayed up, poring over Hincmar's parchment as long as the light held out. His persistent whispers kept Zargal awake long after the others had sunk into slumber. And then, when the light had faded away completely, and Rothadd had finally ceased his efforts for the night, Zargal remembered what it was that had been taught to him so many years before.

"I've got it!" he cried, sitting up with great suddenness. "Now I remember!"

"What?" Rothadd asked sleepily. "What do 'ee remember?"

The sound of their voices wakened the others. There were irritable mutterings in the dark, and an angry voice snarled, "Shut up!"

"No, this is important," Zargal said. "It's about those toads—"

"I'm not interested in toads, you confounded colossus! Hold your tongue and let me sleep!" the Count requested.

"You will not address me in that manner, my lord!" snapped Zargal, who still possessed a temper of his own.

"If you object, you know the remedy, my lord!" Emce-Slatermul challenged. "I am at your lordship's service!"

"You'll have to be at his service tomorrow morning, Emce," the tired voice of Count sa Wenilow said out of the blackness. "There's not enough light to duel by until then."

"I'll lay twenty Szarish grinlings on Lord Zargal!" Crumer Paskha offered joyously. "Are there any takers?"

"You'll lose your grinlings, Paskha," the Count promised.

"Is it to be swords or daggers?" sa Wenilow inquired.

"Honor demands that Lord Zargal receive first choice of weapons."

"No, Emce gets it."

"He does not!"

"Hang on, now!" the voice of Rothadd broke in. "Hang on! Zargal," he asked, "first off, what do 'ee remember about those toads?"

"Oh, yes," Zargal said, grateful for the chance to speak. "I recognize them. They're Yili toads, I've seen pictures of them."

"Is that what you woke us up for?" Crumer groaned.

"Wait a moment. There are a couple of things you should know about Yilis," Zargal said. "One is that they are not native to the Elg. They shouldn't be here. They belong in the forests of Glam, hundreds of miles away."

"And what's the other thing we should know?" sa Wenilow asked.

"The other thing," Zargal explained, "is that those toads are poisonous. Did you notice the little spines they have? The spines are used to inject venom. Of course, the Yilis are so small that a few stings couldn't harm a man. But take thousands of them, and they are certainly deadly."

" 'Ee be a-sayin' those toads could have killed us, then?" Rothadd asked.

"Easily. Very easily."

"And us smashin' 'em, and squashin' 'em, and throwin' 'em around all that time. Oh, 'tis a lucky chance they be such friendly creatures!"

"Yes, we've certainly had a fortunate escape," Crumer said. "And it's very clever of you to have recognized it. Very learned and all that. But right now it's rather late, we're all tired, and—"

"Wait," Zargal told them again. "Doesn't all this suggest anything to you?"

"My lord?"

"His Majesty Laza warned us that the Godescalc woman would place obstacles in our path," Zargal said. "Surely this must be one of them. How could we find a multitude of poisonous Yilis in the Elg, so far from where they belong, unless Godescalc brought them here to guard the swamp against intruders? What other explanation could there possibly be?"

"But if that be the way of it," Rothadd immediately inquired, "then it isn't like they'd be so friendly, is it? What manner of guard is that?"

"That's exactly what I've been wondering," Zargal answered. "Perhaps the Yilis have lived here peacefully for so long that they've forgotten their original purpose."

"But would Queen Godescalc permit them to forget?" sa

Wenilow asked. "Could she have grown so self-confident that she believes no one will ever come in search of her again?"

"I don't know," Zargal said. "It doesn't really make sense, does it? If Godescalc really is responsible for the toads—if she brought them here to protect the Elg—then she certainly hasn't been paying attention to them lately. Has she relaxed her vigilance, then? I wonder—"

"Maybe you're wrong," Count sa Wenilow guessed. "Maybe all this means nothing."

"Probably they're not Yilis at all," Emce-Slatermul muttered.

"Yes, they are. Now I wonder—" Zargal's mind was working furiously.

" 'Tis like we'll find out for sure soon enough."

"I hope so. But I wonder what on earth—"

Long after the others were again asleep and snoring, Zargal lay awake thinking, his eyes wide open and staring into the dark.

CHAPTER XXII

There was a brief shower of rain during the night. Early morning brought a glooming peace. The five wanderers awoke drenched, chilled, famished, and frustrated. The rain had come and gone while they slept, and they had missed an opportunity to moisten their parched throats with the pure water. There was no more talk of a duel between Zargal and Emce-Slatermul. All of them were too conscious of personal discomfort to think of fighting. There was nothing at hand to eat for breakfast—not so much as a solitary mabkin. With weary sighs they arose to continue the journey.

The thirst grew worse that day, for they were soon deprived of even the questionable comfort of the stinking pools from which they had been taking reluctant refreshment. As they proceeded ever deeper into the swamp, the water that lay in all the holes and hollows started to take on a yellow glow of so obviously poisonous a character that they no longer dared to drink at all. The scene was an eerie one. In the gray dimness of the Elg, murky even at midday, the glow on the water was one of the strongest sources of illumination. It cast a sickly yellow light on the ground, the reeds and bushes, the bare branches, the algae, and the faces of the travelers.

Zargal looked at the haggard, filthy figures of his companions and silently wondered if the trip would ever end. It was only the thought of saving Princess Bellora that kept him going, and he wondered if the same thought sustained the others. Rothadd, he knew, sought knowledge. The others loved the Princess, but loved gold and glory as well. The young noblemen who had begun the journey now resembled the raggedest, dirtiest of beggars. Count sa Wenilow, a little frailer than the others, looked particularly bedraggled and miserable. Zargal found it difficult to believe that a few short months ago he himself had lived in a palace, as the son of a great ruler. His father's palace and all its luxury seemed as unreal as a mirage. It never occurred to him to miss it, although he sometimes thought of Flimm.

Crumer Paskha was more thirsty than all his fellows. As the hours passed, his eyes grew feverish and he began casting speculative glances upon the phosphorescent pools. A couple of times he paused, staring into the lurid depths until the others had to drag him away.

" 'Ee mustn't drink there," Rothadd admonished. "Don't think it!"

It was impossible to tell if this warning had any effect on Crumer.

The group ventured upon another patch of swampfrets around midday, stopped, and lunched in silence. They were too tired to quarrel, and hence had not a word to say to one another. The only sound to be heard was the occasional sharp splat as one or another slapped at the swarming gnats. Despite their discomfort, the travelers stayed to rest for a time, for none of them had the will to resume the trip immediately. Sprawled out on the soggy earth, they stared up through the branches at the ashen skies, and each man thought his private and rueful thoughts. For the first time, Rothadd did not trouble to withdraw Hincmar's parchment from his pocket. The boy simply lay on his back, looking at his long fingers and frowning a little. Zargal began to worry about him.

A sense of duty finally prompted them to get up and continue on their way. But the march through the swamp was turning into a stumble. Another long trek brought them to a place where the earth smelled of rot and the water was positively glaring with its sulfurous light. In the middle of a clearing stood a quiet pool, perfectly circular in shape. A band of polished blocks encircled the water. The blocks were all of gray stone, but for one of black marble. No plants of any description grew within several feet of the pool, and the earth was bare and smooth.

"Well—who's game to drink out of *that* one, lads?" Roth-add croaked, with a brave attempt at humor.

But it seemed that Crumer Paskha took the remark seriously. With an expression of mad determination burning in his feverish eyes, he stalked forward, knelt on the black stone, and bent over the water.

"Paskha, don't touch that!" Zargal cried, and sprang forward to restrain his companion.

His concern was unnecessary, for Crumer made no move to drink. The young man remained where he was, motionless, staring into the luminous depths. The others hurried forward and clustered around to see what had so fixed his attention. Peering over Crumer's shoulder, they beheld a strange sight.

None of their faces were reflected in the pool. What they saw, apparently pictured a few inches beneath the motionless surface, was a human infant. The baby was sitting on the ground. It laughed and gurgled soundlessly, a look of delight upon its face. What was even more remarkable was that the baby was surrounded by a group of scaly silver lizards that Zargal instantly recognized as slatkus, similar in every point to King Laza's companion Bibka. The baby was playing with the reptiles, clutching the dreadful fangs in its chubby fists and snatching at the forked, flickering tongues. Far from resenting this treatment, the slatkus seemed to be enjoying it. They were coiling their long tails into complicated knots and figures for the human child's amusement. One of them nudged the baby gently with her snout, a slatku mark of affection which Bibka frequently bestowed upon King Laza.

"What is *that?*" Emce-Slatermul asked.

"And *who* is it?" sa Wenilow asked.

"This might sound silly to you," Zargal said, staring into

the pool, "but there's somehing about that baby down there that reminds me a little of Paskha."

"What nonsense!" Crumer said, without removing his eyes from the water.

"No, no, he's got something, Paskha," Count sa Wenilow remarked. "That child really does look very much like you."

"What is that supposed to mean?" Crumer asked.

"Does it have to mean anything? Perhaps it's coincidence."

"What's the matter with this pool, anyway?" Crumer demanded nervously. Beneath the still surface, the slatkus rolled the baby in the dust. The infant tumbled over and over, laughing silently. "What's the significance of these images? What's the cause?"

"Magic," Rothadd said. " 'Tis magic." The word did not arouse the lad to the same heights of excitement as it had formerly done, but he still spoke with immense satisfaction. "This be an enchanted pool, for sure. I've heard tell of such things."

"Do you think that Godescalc put it here?" Zargal asked.

"I couldn't say. But 'tis magic right enough. Oh, there's no tellin' what we might see in it! A rare sight it be!"

"Get hold of yourself, boy!" Emce-Slatermul commanded. "You claim this pool is enchanted. Well, what use can we make of it? What will it do for us?"

"It will tell us things," Rothadd replied. "It will tell us things of the past and present and future. A pool of prophecy it be."

"Then how do we get it to tell us where Godescalc is hiding?" Emce-Slatermul asked. "And how do we make it tell who among us will triumph? Who will get the Princess?"

"We can't make it do aught it doesn't want to," the Outcottager answered, somewhat disgusted by the Count's crudeness. "We be—aren't its masters. 'Twill show us what it chooses, and we must wait upon its pleasure."

"That's ridiculous!" Emce-Slatermul fumed.

"Fret till your proud heart breaks," Rothadd said, "but that be the way of it." The Count turned away with an angry sneer.

Under the water, the baby romped with the lizards.

There could be no mistaking its resemblance to Crumer Paskha.

"Could that be you? Did you ever play with slatkus when you were a child?" Zargal asked curiously.

"No," Crumer said. "There were none at Olbiord. Such creatures do not inhabit our mountains."

"Perhaps this shows us the future," sa Wenilow suggested. "Maybe that child is a son whom Paskha will have one day."

"A son," Crumer repeated, enchanted with the idea. "A son. A son born to me and Bellora . . ."

"That son's a little premature," Zargal said sarcastically.

"A child of the Paskha line," Crumer went on dreamily, "and heir to the throne of Obran."

"The heir presumptuous, you mean!" Emce-Slatermul snarled. "I've had enough of this foolery! Stand aside, Paskha. I want to look into the pool."

Crumer had seen all that the pool had to show him. Now, without protest, he got up and allowed Emce-Slatermul to take his place upon the black marble slab. As soon as Crumer moved, the surface of the water swirled and clouded, and the pictures vanished. When Emce-Slatermul knelt and looked in, he saw nothing.

"Show something!" the Count demanded. The water remained hazy. "Show me, I command you!" No results. "In the name of the spirits who created you, in the name of the forces that rule you—in the name of the power that gives man mastery of magic—I charge you to show me what I want to see!" This time the pool obeyed.

The glowing water now reflected the great hall of the castle of Obran. The hall was thronged with people, which was in itself unusual, for King Laza rarely invited guests. Although Zargal and Rothadd, as foreigners, did not recognize them, the others knew that the faces in the pool belonged to the members of the highest Obranese nobility. The guests were evidently assembled for some kind of festivity, for they were clothed in their finest and armored in jewelry. A party atmosphere prevailed. The guests laughed, drank wine, and chattered silently. In the center of the crowd, King Laza sat in the wheeled chair, his twisted form hidden beneath a splendid purple cloak, and his visage hidden beneath his hat. Bibka sat beside him, a jeweled collar fastened about her neck. At one end of the hall stood a table piled high with hundreds of gifts. At the other, a group of musicians plucked at the strings of their soundless kleveens.

"That's odd," Count sa Wenilow said. "His Majesty does not entertain."

At that moment two figures appeared under the archway at the head of the stairs leading down into the hall. One of them was Count Emce-Slatermul.

"It be the Count!" Rothadd whispered excitedly. "Clear as life!"

"Quiet!" Emce-Slatermul demanded, watching his own image raptly.

The Count blazed beneath the water in an overwhelming court suit of cloth-of-gold, encrusted with diamonds. His fingers were stiff with rings, and the Order of Cramarius glittered upon his breast. His periwig was the tallest, the fullest, the most massive that had ever been seen. His face was wreathed in a smile of ineffable complacence. At the Count's side stood Princess Bellora, as fresh and beautiful as she had been in the days before her illness. Bellora wore the trailing rose-colored gown, the transparent veil, and the fresh flowers that were the traditional costume of an Obranese bride. Her only adornments other than the flowers were the unbound curls that streamed down her back and one gold ring upon her left hand.

At the sight of Emce-Slatermul and the Princess, the guests raised their glasses on high and cheered. Amidst much applause, the bride and groom descended the steps together to receive the congratulations of their admirers.

The images dimmed and faded away.

Emce-Slatermul rose to his feet. He was trying hard to maintain an expression of well-bred indifference, but a smirk was pulling uncontrollably at the corners of his mouth. "That's all I needed to see," he said. "I thought as much, and now I know."

Crumer Paskha and Count sa Wenilow were completely speechless. Rothadd was staring down regretfully at the black marble. Only Zargal spoke, as much to himself as to the others. "She will recover," he said. "She will be well."

"Well, gentlemen," Emce-Slatermul said very graciously, "I am satisfied, and ready to go. But do any of you wish to take a look into the pool before we leave?" He spoke with an air of indulgent kindness that the others found hard to endure.

"Aye," Rothadd said. "That I do. I'll have a look." He plumped himself down spiritlessly upon the black marble and glanced into the water. Clearly, all the fun had gone out of it for him. But then his attention was arrested, and he watched with breathless interest as new pictures started to take shape before his eyes.

Rothadd beheld the familiar shape of a certain thatched house that stood on the Eastling Wolds.

"The Wolds!" he marveled. " 'Tis the Wolds of home! And that be the cottage of Hincmar, or I be smetch-happy."

A human figure was approaching the cottage. It was Rothadd himself. As he neared the cottage, Hincmar's huge dogs bounded forward with ears laid back, contorted muzzles, and raised hackles. Upon the dogs' recognizing Rothadd, the canine faces cleared, the shaggy heads came up, and the great creatures gamboled around the lad with soundless barks of joy.

The cottage door opened and the figure of Hincmar appeared upon the threshold. He was as erect as ever, a touch grayer perhaps, the bitter lines of his face a little more noticeable. As he caught sight of Rothadd, however, the sorcerer sprang forward and greeted the boy like a father welcoming a long-lost son—a demonstration that brought tears to the eyes of the real, watching Rothadd.

Under the water, the image of Rothadd stepped back from Hincmar, reached into a pocket, and brought forth a worn and tattered scrap of parchment. Rothadd read off the parchment and performed a quick series of effortless gestures. As the last, unheard words of the incantation passed his lips, Rothadd stood motionless, his arms outstretched. Obedient stalks of wheat began to thrust themselves out of the stony soil of the Eastling Wolds. Higher and higher they grew, springing up on all sides with uncanny speed, until the sorcerer and the triumphant Outcottager were surrounded by a great ring of tall plants; whereupon a turbulence ruffled the water, and the pictures disappeared.

"Did you see that?" Rothadd stuttered, half silly with excitement. " 'Twas the spell that Hincmar did give me,

and I did it perfect! Oh, this gives me new hope, it does. I
won't give up now, no matter what!"

"Why, you'd never thought of giving up, had you?"
Zargal asked, smiling a little at his friend's enthusiasm.

"Truth to tell, sometimes the thought do settle upon my
mind when I try and try and naught comes of it. But I
won't be downhearted now, for 'tis plain that I be marked
out to be a magician. Happen 'twill take twenty year, but
I'll do it, I will. Oh, I'll make Hincmar proud of me yet!"
Rothadd was hugging himself with joy. "Aye, and King
Laza, too."

"King Laza," Zargal repeated slowly, his thoughts recalled to the mission at hand. "To be sure. There's always
King Laza."

"Oh, aye. I wonder how things be back in Obran? Maybe the pool will tell us, if we do ask her nice." Rothadd
tried asking nicely but the water remained persistently
opaque. "Why don't 'ee give it a try, then, Zargal?"

"All right." Zargal, impelled by his own curiosity as
much as by Rothadd's advice, took his place upon the black
stone. "I ask leave to see her ladyship, Princess Bellora of
Obran," he formally entreated the magic pool. "I ask you
to show her to me."

But the pool showed him nothing of the sort. When the
water cleared, Zargal beheld the reflected image of an
august chamber that was not to be found in the castle of
Obran. With a start of amazement, the Duke's son recognized a guest suite in Archduke Jalonzal's palace. It was
the suite normally reserved for the most important of visit-
ing dignitaries. A young girl was standing there, but it was
not Princess Bellora. Her face looked vaguely familiar. A
tiny black star-shaped tattoo at the corner of the lady's
pretty lips marked her as a member of the Strellian royal
house. Zargal realized then that it was Jeria of Strell, whom
he had met briefly once many years before. At Jeria's side
loomed a tall, portly man, his full face marked with authority and arrogance—Jeria's father the Talgh.

The girl carried a beautiful ivory casket, holding it with
the extreme tips of her fingers, as if to avoid contamination.
The Talgh issued a soundless command. With great reluctance Jeria lifted the casket lid, exposing to view a superb
necklace of emeralds, blood-spattered with small rubies.

The necklace was an heirloom of Zargal's family, which he identified readily enough. It was a customary gift of the Dukes of Szar to their brides. At sight of the ornament, tears began to run down Jeria's cheeks.

The Talgh was yelling at her in a terrible, noiseless fury, and she stood before him, her head bowed, tears streaming, offering no defense. The Talgh reached into the box, withdrew the necklace, and fastened it about his daughter's throat like a hangman adjusting a noose. There was a final spate of silent indignation from the outraged father, and then he swept out of the room, leaving Jeria alone.

The girl stood by herself in the middle of the splendid, sterile chamber, weeping bitterly. At last she tore the necklace off and flung it away. Jeria sank to the floor and lay at full length, sobbing hysterically. And then her image vanished, literally dissolved in tears.

"Do 'ee know her?" Rothadd asked curiously.

"My prospective stepmother, I believe," Zargal said. "And a most unwilling one, it seems."

"Poor lass. What ails her?"

"I'd hazard a guess that marriage to the Archduke does not appeal to her," Zargal said. "A very understandable attitude."

"As I see it," Emce-Slatermul put in, "the silly wench has nothing to cry about—not when she's just been given a necklace like that. And she'll be Archduchess, won't she? She should thank her lucky stars!"

"There's more to be considered than jewels and titles, Emce," Count sa Wenilow observed.

"Certainly," Emce-Slatermul agreed, with unwonted affability. "There's also gold, land, and palaces."

"And love," the poet said. "Don't forget love."

"Are you going to start spouting poetry?" Emce-Slatermul demanded.

"No, I am not. I merely point out that no marriage can hope to prosper if it is not blessed with a deep and genuine love."

"Utter nonsense!" Emce-Slatermul scoffed. "What romantic drivel! Love is all very well, of course, but there are practical considerations to be taken into account—"

"And what of you, Count?" sa Wenilow inquired gravely. "You hope to wed the Princess. Do you not love her?"

"Oh, naturally, naturally—"

"Do you think she loves you, my lord?" Zargal inquired.

"Well—if she doesn't now, then she'll learn to after we're married," the Count decided, after a moment's thought. "What's not to love, after all?"

Nobody chose to answer the question.

"For me," sa Wenilow declared, "the hope of love is all that makes life worth living. It imparts a meaning to my existence and breathes life into my art."

Emce-Slatermul threw up his hands in disgust at such folly, but Crumer Paskha clapped the young Count kindly on the shoulder. "Take a look in the pool, my lord," he counseled. "Perhaps you'll find encouragement there."

"I'm not sure I want to know the future," sa Wenilow said, his eyes darkening. "Perhaps it's best to go on dreaming."

"Oh, go ahead, sa Wenilow! Take just one look. It will probably do you good!"

Sa Wenilow's companions were all urging him on, and at last the young Count obeyed them. Kneeling down upon the marble, he gazed half unwillingly into the pool, and the images shaped themselves at once.

Count sa Wenilow could see himself wandering through the murky depths of the Elg. At his side walked two figures, one of them of gigantic stature, easily recognizable as Zargal, the other of normal size, but too blurred and uncertain to identify. A stream ran along beside the trail, its water brown and sluggish. Phosphorescent slime blanketed the reedy verge.

The three travelers proceeded down a gentle incline until they found their way blocked by a great expanse of quiet water. Far off, in the middle of the lake, an island was visible. The travelers paused, evidently at a loss. After a brief conference, they went hunting up and down along the shore. Presently sa Wenilow watched himself discover a hole in the ground, an opening somewhat camouflaged with dead branches. The sa Wenilow in the pool was wearing an expression of such intense dread that it called an answering flash of uneasiness to the face of his watching counterpart. The little group descended into the hole.

Sa Wenilow and the others were making their way along a tunnel cut through solid stone. Dim light reflected off the puddles on the floor and the moisture on the walls and tunnel roof. Suddenly the light vanished, and the tunnel was plunged into utter darkness.

The water swirled, the pictures changed, and a horrible sight was revealed to the watching travelers. Count sa Wenilow beheld himself lying dead upon the stones. His body was unspeakably mutilated—limbs had been lopped off, the throat was cut, and there were other, equally ghastly lacerations. The corpse was still streaming blood. The blood spread out until all the pool was tinged with scarlet; then the image vanished and the water regained its natural yellow hue.

There was a collective sharp intake of breath among the travelers. Count sa Wenilow sprang to his feet. His face was livid, his eyes wild. Placing a hand to his throat, he took several steps back from the edge of the pool. His staring eyes cast about in all directions, as if their owner were contemplating a sudden, solitary flight into the swamp.

"Easy, now!" Rothadd tried to soothe him. "Easy, now. 'Tis not that bad!"

"Calm yourself, my lord!" Zargal advised. "Courage!"

"That's right," Crumer Paskha agreed. "Courage! Nothing's happened to you yet."

"But it will." Sa Wenilow was shaking. His voice was hoarse. "You've seen for yourselves what's going to happen to me." He lifted his agonized eyes to their faces. "Why did you persuade me to look in the water? How much better off I'd have been not looking and never knowing!"

"Well, you *did* look," Emce-Slatermul pointed out, "so there's no use going on about it now. Try to be a man, Count!"

Rothadd shot Emce-Slatermul a glance of loathing. "Take heart, lad," he urged sa Wenilow. "We won't let it happen to 'ee, I take my oath."

Sa Wenilow shook his head. He looked like a desperate animal in a trap. "There's nothing you can do! There's no way to change the future, none at all! None!"

"How do you know?" Zargal asked calmly.

"Oh, it's obvious. Only too obvious!" the Count cried.

"Not to me it isn't," Zargal said. "Quite the contrary, in fact. Whenever an accident or misfortune befalls you, Count, doesn't it cross your mind that you had only to alter one of any number of tiny, insignificant past actions, and the chain of events leading up to the accident would have been broken?"

"Sometimes," sa Wenilow replied.

"Exactly. That's one of the things that makes misfortune so hard to bear—the knowledge that it could, in most cases, have very easily been avoided, up to the last moment."

"If misfortune befalls you, then there's no use torturing yourself with the thought that you might have dodged it," sa Wenilow said. "That's a waste of time."

"True. But you possess foreknowledge of what may befall, and therefore you have every chance in the world of doing something to change it. Doesn't that seem reasonable?"

"Perhaps," sa Wenilow admitted.

"Aye, for certain!" Rothadd agreed, delighted that Zargal's arguments seemed to exert a calming influence on the horrified Count. " 'Tis simple! 'Ee must look sharp, and all's well!"

"It can't be that easy," sa Wenilow said gloomily. "Nothing's ever that easy."

"It is, though," Crumer assured him. "If you should find yourself near the lake and the hole and the tunnel, then you'll know you're in danger. In which case, don't go in!"

"The most sensible thing for sa Wenilow to do," Emce-Slatermul said, "would be simply to turn around and go home."

"Go home, my lord?" Sa Wenilow was startled.

"Certainly. Why not?"

"Why not? Because I'm not at all convinced that's a course I may follow with honor. In any case, the plight of the Princess—"

"You've no need to worry about the plight of the Princess," Emce-Slatermul interrupted confidently, "because the pool has shown us clearly that she'll be saved. As for honor—well, where's the honor in pursuing a pointless mission? Why should you continue, when the pool shows us that I'm the one to wed Bellora? That must mean that I'm the one who will cure her, so there's no reason for *you* to come along."

"Here, now," Rothadd objected. "That doesn't have to

be true. King Laza never did promise that his girl will be a-marryin' with any of you."

"Such things do not have to be put into words—they are understood," Emce-Slatermul replied. "At least, among persons of quality."

"Happen she doesn't want to marry?"

"Gentlewomen don't always know their own minds. In any case, it's not the place of yokels to question them," Emce-Slatermul reproved.

Rothadd set his jaw resentfully. "Well, for all of that," he flung at the Count, " 'ee don't even know if all of those pretty wedding-pictures of yours be aught but mully-twaddle, do 'ee?"

"What are you jabbering about?" The Count glared.

"He may be right, you know," Crumer Paskha suggested mischievously. "Perhaps these pictures *are* meant to mislead us. This must be Godescalc's pool, and isn't the black sorceress also called the mistress of lies?" He smiled in amusement at the expression on Emce-Slatermul's face.

CHAPTER XXIII

Crumer's amusement did not last long. The five travelers had been completely absorbed in the wonder of the magic pool, oblivious to all save the shifting images. But when they resumed their march through the Elg, the thirst they had momentarily forgotten reasserted itself more powerfully than ever before. The pools they passed still glowed with their yellow light. There was water everywhere, but none of it was drinkable. A cool, damp wind blew out of the west, the earth was sodden, and the air was filled with watery mists, yet the travelers were perishing of thirst. Their mouths grew cottony, their tongues turned to leather, and all conversation ceased. Their pace slackened as their strength slowly waned.

Rothadd placed his faith in magic. As long as his power of speech would serve him, he muttered spells and incantations to the uncaring stones, trees, and skies. His hoarse voice was angry, then pleading, then desperate by turns. His enunciation was as perfect as King Laza might have wished; when he practiced magic Rothadd could no longer be identified as an Outcottager. Yet not a drop of pure water appeared at his command. At last his voice cracked, and he stopped trying.

It occurred to Zargal that streams of fresh water might be running underground. A couple of times he paused long enough to dig holes in the moist ground. But at each attempt, the hope that lighted his pale face died away as the water that came seeping into the excavations shone yellow.

Sa Wenilow tried chewing on the grasses and stalks, hoping to extract some moisture. But there was none to be had—the vegetation was dead and desiccated. The Count's delicate features were drawn, his eyes haunted.

Emce-Slatermul disdained the futile activities of his companions. He was evidently determined to prevail by force of will alone. He strode through the swamp, jaw outthrust, features set in the purposeful expression of one who has fixed his vision on a bright, particular star. Emce-Slatermul was as parched as the others, but his every movement proclaimed his confidence. As far as he was concerned, the vision of the pool had settled all questions.

Crumer Paskha was in a sorry state. For some reason, he seemed to suffer more from thirst than any of the other wanderers. Either he had less fortitude, or else he truly required more water than they. Observing Crumer's tortured face, Zargal was inclined to believe it was the latter. Crumer was certainly running a fever. The young man did not complain, but his cheeks were unnaturally flushed. Occasionally he passed a hand across his face, as if to clear his vision. More and more often, he fell behind the others, and they had to wait for him to catch up. His movements grew uncertain; at last he sat down involuntarily in the middle of the narrow trail. The others walked back and sat down beside their comrade. Crumer made ineffectual gestures of apology. The flush on his face at that moment was as much due to humiliation as to fever. The five travelers stayed where they were, resting at the foot of a twisted oak. While Crumer drooped, Emce-Slatermul smoldered with impatience, and the other three merely waited. At the end of half an hour, Crumer manfully hoisted himself to his feet and set off down the trail with his companions at his side. He could not, however, maintain a steady pace. He lagged behind, then caught up again in a sort of rapid stagger. He refused to accept Rothadd's proffered aid.

Late in the day, there came a moment when Zargal realized that Crumer had not been walking with the rest of the group for a long time. With a pang of very real apprehension, Zargal spun around in his tracks. His alarm was not misplaced. Yards behind them, Crumer Paskha knelt beside one of the shallow little ponds. His head was bent, and his cupped hands were brimful of glowing water.

"Paskha!" Zargal managed to yell, his voice a painful rasp. "Don't do it!" At great expense of his own failing strength, the Duke's son sped back along the trail, his long legs covering the distance in huge strides.

At the sound of Zargal's voice, Crumer Paskha raised his head. His fevered eyes were flaming, his lips were curved in a reckles smile. For a moment he watched as Zargal, with the others close upon his heels, approached him. Then, very deliberately and without removing his eyes from his companions, he lifted his hands and drank.

Crumer sat still, and his countenance reflected vast relief as the water soothed his parched mouth and throat. But then his expression shifted, his face crumpled, and a high, thin wailing sound escaped him. The others arrived at his side, but they could do nothing.

Crumer was changing. He was shrinking in size, plumping out, and all his proportions were altering. His brown hair fell out in handfuls, until his skull was as bald as an old man's. His features grew short and round. The skin waxed smooth and fine. His voice was changing in pitch; it rose octave by octave until the wailing cry was higher and shriller than any man's should be. To the accompaniment of thin shrieks, Crumer continued to shrink until the garments slipped loosely from his body.

The four spectators stood by in gaping silence. They were helpless to intervene. The Crumer Paskha they knew had vanished. In his place, naked amidst a pile of clothing, lay the tiny figure of a human infant, vital, beet-faced, and squalling its head off.

They made an early camp that evening. There was a small fire to keep them warm, but no dinner, no water, and no conversation. All of them were feeling weak and ill, to varying degrees. There was hardly a sound to be heard throughout the swamp other than the occasional hoot of a night bird and the ceaseless screaming of little Crumer.

It was not that Crumer was a particularly bad baby, but

the Elg was simply no place for children. His companions
bundled him up in his own linen shirt and took turns carrying him, but it was not enough. Crumer was tired and
hungry and he needed to be changed—and he made sure
that everyone was aware of it.

For some reason, the infant had taken a special fancy to
Zargal and would scarcely tolerate being carried by anyone
else, which was flattering, but sometimes proved hard on
Zargal. In view of the child's size, the volume of noise he
was able to produce was astounding. His strength and
energy seemed inexhaustible; he stormed and cried for
hours on end, hardly pausing for breath.

Zargal strove in vain to lull Crumer to sleep. From time
to time he was strongly tempted to take a handkerchief and
gag the infant, but resisted the impulse. Such a course, he
realized, would be as unjust as it was inhumane, for Crumer Paskha undoubtedly had plenty to cry about.

The five of them remained wakeful all through the night.

The gray dawn found the wanderers huddled upon the
ground in various postures expressive of hopelessness and
exhaustion. As soon as it was light enough to travel, they
were on their way again. Four of them knew that if they
did not find water very shortly, they would be in serious
trouble. Only the infant was spared these worrisome
thoughts. Borne along in Zargal's arms, Crumer was happily unconscious of any danger. After crying all night long,
he had finally tired himself out and fallen into a deep slumber.

By midmorning it had become apparent to the young
men that the swampland through which they struggled was
beginning to change. It was noisier—the birds called, and
the bushes were filled with rustling sounds. The vegetation
was different—there was more of it, and the plants, although for the most part dormant, somehow lacked the
dry and lifeless appearance that had characterized them for
so long.

Best of all, the sulfurous glow was beginning to fade out
of the water. The still pools around them were losing their
yellow color and their opacity. As the travelers proceeded
south, deeper into the heart of the Elg, the air freshened
and a breeze blew most of the oppressive odors away. Another hour of slow walking brought them to the bank of a

stream filled with the clearest and brightest of running water.

It was more welcome than a discovery of lost treasure. With one accord the young men rushed forward, threw themselves down upon the bank, and began swallowing the water in huge gulps. Zargal had set Crumer safely aside. Now the baby awoke and began to cry again. The Duke's son soaked a handkerchief in the stream, handed it to the baby to suck, and returned to his own interrupted drink. The water was delicious—icy, fresh, and as pure as any he'd ever tasted. As Zargal drank, he could feel himself starting to revive. His throat stopped aching, his vision sharpened, and the sense of growing weakness left him. It wasn't until he was able to relieve his thirst that he realized just how bad it had been.

As the water soothed their mouths and throats and lifted their spirits, the travelers found themselves able to talk once again. They had not much to say to one another, but there were certain questions that had to be settled.

"What do we do with the baby, then?" Rothadd asked as soon as he could speak. "What's to be done with Crumer?"

"We'd better find something to feed him," Zargal said. Now that his thirst had been satisfied, he was suffering from his usual ferocious hunger and was therefore in a position to appreciate the baby's situation. "But what on earth can we find in this place to give him?" He regarded the baby, which lay upon its back, gurgling and sucking happily upon the wet handkerchief.

"That's not much trouble," Rothadd said. "At home upon the Wolds, in time of famine we gather together a mort of roots, stew 'em up, mash 'em, and feed 'em to the babes. Prallo, it be called, and 'tis naught so bad. We can make some for Crumer here. But, lads, 'tis a danger to the child to bring him with us to Godescalc's, it is!"

"But what else can we do?" sa Wenilow asked.

"We can leave him here, that's what we can do," Emce-Slatermul said. The others stared at him, stunned. "Well, you can all stop gaping at me. It's the only sensible thing to do, and the sooner you realize that, the better off we'll be."

"Be so good as to explain yourself, my lord," Zargal requested frostily.

"I should think it's obvious." Emce-Slatermul spoke forcefully, as if to disguise a measure of discomfort. "We have a mission, and a baby would be a grave hindrance. Moreover, as your friend has very rightly pointed out, we would be exposing the child to considerable danger by bringing him along with us."

"But I didn't mean to say we should just leave him!" Rothadd broke in.

"Why not? We can leave him here next to the water, with a supply of food beside him. Perhaps someone will come along, find him, and care for him."

"I hardly think that likely," Zargal said, regarding the Count with extreme distaste.

Emce-Slatermul shrugged. "Well, then, we might pick him up again on our way back to Obran. Does that suit you?"

"It isn't sure we'll be a-comin' back this way! And 'ee do know there'll be no travelers to follow us!" Rothadd exclaimed indignantly. "If we leave Crumer here, 'tis certain death for him, and 'ee do know it!"

"There's no way of being sure of that, you malapert bumpkin! Govern your tongue!" Emce-Slatermul flared. "Now listen to me, all of you. When Paskha joined this expedition, he knew perfectly well that he was running a risk. He knew it and he accepted it. Therefore, whatever might befall him is entirely his own responsibility—especially when you consider that this happened only because he didn't have the courage to wait for a drink for a few more hours, as the rest of us did. Paskha would not, I am sure, wish to encumber us or endanger our mission. But that's exactly what will happen if we are forced to march for mile after mile through this swamp, dragging along a heavy, noisy, troublesome baby. Best we leave him here, with food and water; he'll be well enough. Paskha would probably want it that way."

As if he understood the Count's words, the baby started to wail in a lost, forlorn manner. He needed to be changed again.

" 'Ee always did hate Crumer," Rothadd accused, "for that he did laugh at 'ee and win your gold at play."

"I ordered you to keep quiet!" Emce-Slatermul bounded to his feet, his fist clenched, his energy restored. Rothadd, too, started to rise.

"Really, Emce, you go too far," sa Wenilow broke in, with a hint of dislike. "This isn't the place to quarrel. We must come to some decision about poor Paskha."

"As far as I'm concerned, the decision has been made. I refuse to carry him, and that's final. I wash my hands of the entire affair. The rest of you may do as you please." Emce-Slatermul leaned against a tree trunk, his arms folded. "If you're wise, you'll simply leave him here and hope for the best."

"There's no possibility of that," Zargal said, privately thinking how much he had grown to detest Emce-Slatermul. The object of his dislike made a gesture of indifference.

"How can 'ee think it?" Rothadd asked. "An inhuman notion it be."

"Particularly in view of the fact," sa Wenilow put in, "that Paskha would very likely be devoured by wild animals if we left him here."

"What makes you think so?" Emce-Slatermul asked.

"Didn't you notice the footprints on the bank? Look, they're all around us. This isn't a safe place."

The others looked. Sure enough, the muddy bank bore the imprint of many large, clawed feet. Zargal examined them closely. "Did you see that there are two kinds of prints here?" he asked. "Most of them look as if they might belong to large reptiles of some kind. But the others, the big ones—I've never seen anything like them before. They could almost be human, but they're not."

"This isn't a safe place," sa Wenilow said for the second time. "It must be the watering place of a group of these beasts. And whatever they are, it's quite likely they'll be angry that we make free use of their stream. I think we should leave. Let's take Paskha and go."

"I won't carry him," Emce-Slatermul said.

"You won't have to," Zargal told him shortly. "Let's all have one more good, long drink and then be on our way. We can't have much farther to go." His statement contained more of hope than of confidence.

Zargal's well-meant suggestion proved to be an unfortunate one. As the men knelt and drank, there was a rustling from the bushes on the opposite bank and a shine of silver. The branches crackled, and half a dozen full-grown slatkus came thudding forth. They were formidable creatures, each one fully as large as Bibka, whom they resembled closely. As they caught sight of the humans, the lizards halted and stared, unblinking. Without moving, they began to exchange soft, inscrutable hisses among themselves; then the serpentine tails started to coil and writhe.

The young men stared back, as motionless as the beasts. Seconds passed. Then Zargal gathered up Crumer Paskha in his arms and softly started to edge away. The lizards watched fixedly, but made no move. They remained immobile as sa Wenilow, too, backed off along the trail. It was not until Rothadd started to move away that one of the slatkus took a step forward, her snout extended in suspicion, muscles bunched beneath the silver scales. As she advanced, Emce-Slatermul instinctively drew his sword. It was the worst mistake he had ever made.

Seeing themselves thus threatened, the slatkus hesitated no longer. Uttering dreadful roars, the six of them bared their fangs and charged. Together they plunged into the shallow water, then came rushing up the near bank, claws scrabbling for a foothold in the soft mud. The young men were only too aware of the hopelessness of trying to fight the slatkus. Instantly they turned tail and ran for their lives down a winding trail.

But Emce-Slatermul wasn't quite fast enough. Before he had fairly started, the slatkus were upon him. They dragged him to the ground like wolves pulling down a deer. Emce-Slatermul, prostrate and helpless, caught a whirling glimpse of dagger fangs above and around him and of many eyes peering redly into his own. He lifted his voice in a wild scream that died abruptly away into a bloody rattle.

Zargal, Rothadd, and sa Wenilow looked back over their shoulders as they fled, to behold the lizards tearing the body of Emce-Slatermul to pieces. They quickly averted their eyes from the horrid sight, but not before seeing the slatkus abandon the victim's corpse and start off after them again.

The fugitives soon left the trail and struck off through the bushes in hopes of foiling the hunters. Bare branches lashed them as they ran, and the muddy earth clutched at their heels. Weed-choked ponds spread out before them, and exposed tree roots twisted unexpectedly across their path. Yet within a few minutes, the roar of the pursuing slatkus could no longer be heard. Silence reigned, and they paused in a clearing, gasping for breath.

"Do 'ee think we lost 'em, then?" Rothadd asked in a low voice.

"Perhaps, but I wouldn't depend on it," Zargal answered, breathing heavily. "They know this land, and we can't afford to take chances with a baby." They both looked down at Crumer, who had remained miraculously silent during the entire episode. He reposed in Zargal's arms, smiling his unknowing smile and cooing softly. "If those slatkus catch up with us, they'll tear us to shreds. The baby's much safer if he's not with us."

" 'Ee do believe they be like to catch up?"

"Well—I believe it would be wise to leave Crumer hidden here for now."

Rothadd nodded, looking unwontedly grave. Count sa Wenilow paid no attention to this exchange. He was leaning against a rock, doubled up and still gasping. Zargal placed the baby out of sight beneath a bush.

No sooner had he done so than the flat head of a slatku thrust its way into the clearing. The lizard uttered a hissing call and was immediately joined by the other members of her group. Zargal, Rothadd, and sa Wenilow had already leaped to their feet and fled. With purposeful hisses, the slatkus followed. They were not able to move as swiftly as the humans, but they knew the land, and their stamina was boundless. Little by little, they closed in on their quarry.

The three fugitives listened to the heavy footfalls that were drawing near behind them and silently gave themselves up for dead men. Zargal was more furious with himself than frightened—for what would become of Bellora now? So intent were he and the others on the sound of the crashing footfalls behind them that they entirely missed the ominous noises arising from the bushes beside and ahead of them. It came as a complete surprise when those bushes parted and a host of strange figures leaped forth to surround them.

Zargal was at once aware of the nature of the large footprints which had mingled with those of the slatkus in the mud beside the stream. It was very difficult to decide whether the newcomers should be regarded as manlike

lizards or reptilian humans. The creatures walked on two
legs and carried in their hands the crude weapons of humanity—sharpened wooden stakes, chipped stone knives,
and truncheons cut from the branches of trees. But they
were naked, and their skins were covered with scales. Their
foreheads were oddly flat and receding; small red eyes
peered out from beneath heavy juts of bone. Their jaws
were far longer, more prominent, than the jaws of true
men and were filled with the fangs of carnivores. Each
finger and toe ended in a heavy, curved claw.

One of the largest of the creatures spoke, in a sibilant
but perfectly understandable manner. "Men," it said.
"Spies. Enemies."

"No!" Zargal denied, relieved to find that the lizard-
people had not killed them out of hand. "We are neither
spies nor enemies."

"Men do not belong here. Men must not come here.
Trespassers die."

"We didn't intend to trespass," Zargal said.

"Upon my honor," sa Wenilow assured them, "we didn't
realize this was your land."

"Not our land," the creature replied. "The land of the
Black One. We serve Her. Our mothers serve, and our
daughters serve. For all time."

This series of remarks was totally incomprehensible, and
Zargal ignored it. "We were driven here against our will,
he explained. "Six great beasts—vicious slatkus—have
killed one of our number and are hunting the rest of us
through the swamp. You know the slatkus—"

"Yes. The slatkus—our sisters. They also serve. Krenka,
Timla, and the others drive you here to us."

At that moment the band of slatkus came pounding into
view. As they caught sight of their quarry, surrounded and
captive, the lizards slackened their pace and approached
unhurriedly. The lizard-people greeted the animals with
every evidence of good-fellowship. A hissing conversation
ensued, at the close of which the large creature who had
first addressed them turned back to the prisoners and said,
"We go now. You come with us."

"We've already explained that we meant no harm," Zargal protested. "What do you want of us?"

"You are biggest—you are their Lady, then," the creature said to him. "Tell your people it is best not to fight. You come now."

"Wait—who are you?" Zargal asked.

"I am Hadka, the Lady of the Eslatkum. Here, too, are others of the Eslatkum. We and our sisters, the slatkus, are Her choice for guardians of the swamp. Now come." Hadka jabbed a wooden stake commandingly into Zargal's midriff, and the slatkus snarled. The prisoners began walking.

Count sa Wenilow's eyes were roaming everywhere, but there was no immediate possibility of escape. Rothadd was watching the Eslatkum guards in wonder. Zargal was studying their leader thoughtfully. "Where are you taking us?" he asked.

"Eslatkum place," she responded.

"Where is that?"

"Near."

"You say your people are chosen guardians of all the swamp—" She darted her forked tongue out of her mouth in a gesture of assent. "Who chose you?"

"We are choice of the Black One. Do not doubt it." Hadka seemed to have no objections to answering questions in her laconic manner as long as the prisoners were obedient. It was only when any of them showed signs of balking that her lips curled back over her fangs.

"The Black One?" Zargal probed. It seemed to him that he might as well gather as much information as possible. There was no telling when it might prove useful.

"The Black One, blessings upon Her name." Each Eslatkum touched a claw to her lips at the sound of it. "The Queen of Wind and Water, the Mother of Trees, the Lady of all the Sev."

"The Sev?"

"This world around us is the Sev."

"Does the Black One live with you?" Zargal asked. "Shall we meet her?"

"She does not live with us. But you meet Her."

Zargal didn't like the sound of it. "If she doesn't live with you, then how can you be certain you know what her wishes are?"

"We know." Hadka's teeth gleamed. "The Black One comes in the time my mother's mother's mothers do not

yet hatch. The forces of Cramar, the Evil One, drive Her
forth, and She comes here to lick Her wounds and await the
time of vengeance."

"Cramar—Cramarius?" Zargal guessed adroitly.

"The Evil One," Hadka returned. "And the great Black
Lady calls to Her the tribe of my mothers, and the tribe of
the slatkus, and chooses them to be Her guardians. And
thus we are the sisters of the slatkus. She commands us to
seek out strangers and slay them, for they are the servants
of Cramar, come to destroy Her. The Evil One sends many
of his men, and many do we slay, as we are bid. I tell you
this so that you may know we see you for what you are—
the enemies of our Lady of the Sev—and know how we
must deal with you."

A long silence followed this explanation, until at last
Rothadd said, "We be done for."

Sa Wenilow simply stared at the ground as he trudged
along. But Zargal, throughout his life, had never been one
to admit defeat easily. "You never spare any man?" he
asked.

"Never."

"No visitor escapes death?"

"One only do we spare, many years ago," Hadka admitted. "And that one is not a man, he tells us, but a
Turo."

"You're determined to kill us, then," Zargal asked directly, "when we have never harmed you?"

"You and all men are enemies of the Black Lady," the
Eslatkum leader replied. "We know Her will. When the
light finishes today, Her command we obey, and our males
and our young gnaw on your bones."

"Here, now!" Rothadd cried out in great distress. "Here,
now—"

Zargal's analytical expression did not alter. With the air
of a scholar seeking the solution to a mathematical problem, he inquired, "But what if I were to tell you that we've
come here, not as the Lady's enemies, but rather, as her
friends?"

"I do not hear you," Hadka said, which Zargal correctly
interpreted to mean that she did not understand, and desired an explanation.

"We have come, my companions and I, from the House

of the sons of Cramar," he said. This admission produced a great effect on slatkus and Eslatkum alike. A tremendous sound of hissing sizzled the air, tails twitched, fangs slid into view, and eyes gleamed red beneath scaly lids.

"Do 'ee be a-tryin' to move 'em to slaughter us here and now?" Rothadd demanded in a shaky undertone.

Hadka alone received the news without any visible sign of emotion. "No others admit it," she returned stolidly. "Among others of the race of men, you are a Lady."

Zargal inclined his head in acknowledgment of the compliment. His hand strayed to the official document, carefully wrapped in oiled cloth, that rested in a pocket of his livery, but he did not withdraw it. "The son of the sons of Cramar," he explained, "will bend to the power of the Black Lady and acknowledge her as Queen." There was no reply to this announcement. The Eslatkum guards and the slatkus stared at him expressionlessly. Their faces, never very animated at the best of times, were now totally blank.

"That be a-tellin' 'em!" Rothadd encouraged, now perceiving Zargal's aim. Sa Wenilow was paying no attention.

"Your Lady's time of trouble is ended," Zargal said. "Her hour of triumph is nigh."

"This is Her future," Hadka said. "One day She leaves the Sev and returns to Her own world to reign forever. Upon that day begins the Golden Age of the Eslatkum. This is the promise of the Black One."

"Yes, and now it comes to pass. You shall not harm us, for we are messengers bearing news of her victory."

Zargal waited hopefully for the outburst of enthusiasm that should have greeted his revelation, but there was none. The slatkus growled and hissed to one another, and the Eslatkum looked to their leader. Hadka marched along in silence for a time, her face empty, her eyes fixed on Zargal, who endeavored to keep his own countenance as unrevealing as the big Eslatkum's.

"You are clever, man," she said at last. "Cramar is full of guile, and so are his men. But we Eslatkum have not the simple minds of the new-from-the-egg, nor the faint hearts of males. It is not so easy to deceive us."

"I do not seek to deceive you," Zargal argued. "I speak the truth. Does it not fulfill your own prophecy?"

"Fulfill it, yes," Hadka said. Whatever feelings she might

have been concealing were causing her hiss to grow stronger. She was sounding less human all the time. "Why does Cramar give up without a struggle? This water is muddy."

"Much time has passed. The Black One dealt him a wound at her parting, and throughout the years it has festered. He would make his peace," Zargal explained. Rothadd nodded vigorously. Even sa Wenilow had forgotten his despair and his poetry and was listening.

"Peace?" Hadka asked. "Or trap? Trap of Cramar, to catch the Black One. We know the cunning of the Evil One and his servants." The listening slatkus snarled hideously.

Zargal suspected that he was losing ground. "I speak no falsehood," he insisted, throwing all the sincerity in the world into his voice and eyes.

"Isss it ssssso?" Hadka inquired, her words almost lost in the hiss. "Then you mussst prove it to ussss." She darted her tongue out at him. "Yesssss."

"Prove it? How?"

"If you ssssspeak the truth, there mussst be a sssssign. A sssssssign from the Black One that Ssshe hearssss and issss content."

"What kind of a sign? What do you mean?" Zargal asked. For a moment he stopped on the trail and remained so until a prod from the stone knife of one of his captors started him moving again.

Hadka's doubts had abandoned her, and her voice grew considerably clearer. "A sign from the Black One," she said. "We know it when it comes. If it comes not, then you are liars and brothers of the toads, and you die when today's light finishes."

"But you must tell us what kind of sign you expect!" Zargal cried.

"No more words." Hadka calmly cut Zargal's protests short. "Say nothing more, or we do not wait for the dark." Nobody breathed a word. "Good." She extended a crescent talon and pointed ahead. "Now, here is Eslatkum place. We are home."

CHAPTER XXIV

It could scarcely be called a village. The Eslatkum home consisted of a collection of burrows dug into the moist earth, each opening screened with a covering of sticks and grasses. In the center of the clearing stood a kind of hut of woven branches daubed with mud. Three or four small fires threw off yellowish smoke. The area was swarming with Eslatkum and slatkus, who apparently lived together in perfect harmony. Baby lizards and young Eslatkum rolled in the dust, locked together in mock combat. Several Eslatkum, whose short statures and light builds marked them as males, squatted near the fires, stripping the bark off a pile of tree branches.

Now a mob of assorted creatures crowded around to inspect the prisoners and to hiss their congratulations to the successful huntresses. The volume of sibilation was intolerable. Claws and fangs were flashing on every side, and a multitude of scaly tails writhed in the dust.

Hadka stood beside Zargal, and presently she was approached by one of the males, who addressed her quietly. "Lady Merla still grieves. She takes no food. She does not come out of the House. Tonight her teeth are blunt. Another must be found to take her place."

Hadka nodded. The news must have reminded her that the three human prisoners were special, or claimed to be; and she uttered a whistling call that commanded her people's attention. The clamor died away. Eslatkum and slatkus alike paused to listen to her words.

"My sisters," Hadka said, "we of the Eslatkum and you of the slatkus, whose great duty it is to guard the Sev and protect the Black One—Cramar the Evil sends many men to destroy Her, and many men do we kill. Thus do we serve, and so do our mothers serve, and our mothers' mothers before us. Always it is the same, for we are loyal for all time." Most of the listening Eslatkum ran their tongues out of their mouths in agreement.

"But one day comes," Hadka continued, "that our Lady is triumphant, and returns to reign forever in Her own place." She paused, and the slatkus and Eslatkum waited in silence. "Today we take three men prisoner and bring them here to fulfill the command of the Black One. They come from the House of Cramar; this they admit." There was a murmuring among the Eslatkum, and a ripple of snarls.

"Hear me, sisters," Hadka requested. "One of these men claims to bear a message from Cramar to the Black One, word that he bends him to Her power. If this man speaks truly, then he and his brothers must pass freely through the Sev to the dwelling of our Lady, and there kiss the dirt at Her foot. Thus the prophecy comes true. But, sisters, if these men lie, as the servants of Cramar are wont to lie— then we drink their blood tonight."

A confused and uncertain whispering ran through the ranks of Eslatkum. A great female, standing in the forefront of the crowd, called out, "How can we know if these men ssspeak the truth? We ssstand upon quicksssand here."

"That is so," Hadka agreed. "We lack the power to judge these matters, and therefore, sisters, we trust in the power of the Black One Herself." She touched a reverent claw to her lips. "The Black One is with us always. If it is Her will that these men come unto Her, then She sends us a sign before today's light finishes. If She remains silent, we know well our course. Sisters, are you content?"

They were, and let their leader know it. Pandemonium broke loose, and there arose on all sides, from innumerable tongues, a dismal universal hiss. In the midst of a whirl-wind of cries and snarls, the three prisoners were borne through the camp to the edge of a deep, slanting burrow. Dozens of prodding stone knives and wooden sticks guided them toward the opening.

Realizing that argument and resistance were equally use-less for the moment, Zargal lowered himself into the hole and slid feet first down a damp tunnel into a good-sized underground chamber whose walls were shored up with wooden posts. Rothadd came crawling in right behind him.

Count sa Wenilow, however, was not so docile. As soon as he realized the intentions of his captors, the Count began to struggle, hanging back and dragging his feet in a pathetic effort to withstand the reptilian hordes. Relentlessly they drove him onward, forcing him ever nearer to the black opening that he so obviously dreaded. And when at last he stood upon the very brink, with the hole yawning wide at his feet, sa Wenilow seemed to go mad.

"I won't go into that hole!" He flung himself backward, away from the entrance, flailing, kicking, twisting, and bit-ing desperately, while his maniacal shrieks continued to shred the chilly air.

Inside the burrow, Zargal and Rothadd looked at each other in astonishment, then crowded close to the opening to see what was going on. So furious were sa Wenilow's strug-gles that the Eslatkum were momentarily baffled. The Count rolled upon the ground as if racked with convul-sions. His dagger was drawn, his teeth clenched.

"That hole is Death!" sa Wenilow screamed. "Death!" A few of the Eslatkum edged away from the poet's writhing figure, evidently deeming him mad and therefore untouch-able. The majority of them, however, converged around him. Dodging sa Wenilow's ill-aimed blows, the huntresses picked him up bodily, bore him back to the hole, and thrust him into the tunnel.

With one last, choking cry, sa Wenilow came tumbling down into the burrow. He lay where he had fallen, his face buried in the crook of his arm, his entire body trembling. Outside, a couple of Eslatkum, aided by the slatkus, pushed a great rock in front of the hole and then went away.

It was dark in the burrow. Only a few rays of grayish light struggled in through the cracks where the rock did not meet the edges of the tunnel opening. At first Zargal and Rothadd sat listening to the lizards hissing outside. When the lizards left, they sat listening to sa Wenilow's heavy, uneven breathing, but eventually that sound died away, too, and there was silence.

After a time, sa Wenilow spoke. "I'm sorry," he said. "I'm sorry."

"Think naught of it," Rothadd said.

"What came over you?" Zargal asked, not without sympathy.

"It was the sight of that hole," sa Wenilow explained. "You know what the pool showed me would happen if I went into a hole—those mutilations, that blood. When I saw they meant to put me in, it drove me frantic. I made a fool of myself."

"I'm sure this isn't the hole you saw," Zargal said. "That one's to be found on the shore of a lake. You've nothing to fear in this burrow—except what's going to happen when they take us out of it," he added in a much lower voice.

"Aye," Rothadd said, " 'tisn't like 'ee do have aught to fear of any hole, for 'twas a pack of lies that pool did tell us!"

"Lies?" sa Wenilow asked.

"For certain. The pool did show us how Emce-Slatermul would be a-marryin' with Princess Bellora by and by. But that can't be true, for dead as last year's leaves he be!"

They sat in silence underground, thinking of Emce-Slatermul's horrible death and, by natural association, of the horrible death which probably awaited each of them.

"Well, perhaps you have something happy to look forward to," sa Wenilow told Rothadd, in an effort to divert his own thoughts from unpleasant topics. "You saw a triumphant homecoming for yourself, did you not?"

"Naught but a pack of lies, most like," Rothadd muttered.

"Perhaps not," Zargal said. "After all, what I saw in the water agreed with the news from Szar related by the Turos."

"Oh, aye! The pool be as honest as a Turo. I won't quarrel with that!"

"Even if the water lied some of the time, we can't afford to dismiss what it told us," Zargal mused. "After all, didn't

It show us the baby that Paskha would become?" He stopped dead. "Crumer!" he exclaimed.

"Oh, no!"

"He be out there still, a-lyin' under a bush!"

"He'll starve to death!"

"The animals will get him!"

"What are we going to do?"

The three of them regarded each other in the feeble light. "We can't tell the Eslatkum about the baby," sa Wenilow said. "They consider it their duty to destroy human trespassers. They plan to kill us tonight, and if they find Paskha, they'll kill him, too."

"Happen they won't," Rothadd offered. "He be so wee, they have naught to fear from him."

"If Crumer's just left alone out there in the swamp," Zargal said, "then he'll most certainly die, and quickly, too. Unless we can escape from this place and go see to him ourselves—which hardly seems likely—then we'll have to tell the Eslatkum where the baby is and hope that they'll be merciful."

"If they show no mercy to us," sa Wenilow asked morbidly, "then how can we expect them to show any to Paskha? We can't betray him to his enemies."

"And we can't leave him out there in the swamp to starve," Zargal returned. "That's just what Emce-Slatermul wanted us to do."

Nobody had any satisfactory answer to this. "Very well," sa Wenilow at last consented reluctantly. "I suppose we must risk telling them."

Rothadd nodded.

Zargal crawled across the room—he could not stand upright—to the burrow entrance and pounded upon the stone. But nobody responded to the summons. The Duke's son placed his shoulder against the barrier and gave an experimental push. Nothing happened, and he pushed harder; but it was no use—he couldn't budge the stone. Zargal next tried lifting his voice in a loud, clear call, but none of the Eslatkum outside heard the noise, or else they ignored it.

" 'Tis best this way," Rothadd said. "Happen something will turn up."

"And if it doesn't," Zargal decided, "we can tell the

lizards about the baby this evening. We're sure to meet them again then, aren't we?"

It was unbelievable how slowly the hours passed. At first the prisoners spent their time trying to think of ways to escape. They soon found that their combined strength was insufficient to move the great stone that blocked the exit, so Rothadd began to try magic on it. It was his conviction that the right spell, properly applied, would cause the rock to crumble away to dust; and there could be no doubt that the young Outcottager was on the right track.

Unfortunately, his sorcerous technique was far from perfect as yet. Each time he recited the incantation with the appropriate gestures, a fine, almost invisible layer of dust appeared on the rock's surface. Rothadd estimated that about four hundred thousand repetitions of the entire spell might wear the rock away to the point that they could move it, and was forced to conclude that there was not enough time left before dark to accomplish the task.

Zargal made a desultory effort to dig his way out the back of the burrow, but had to give up very early on when he struck bedrock. He hadn't ever really expected the effort to work. Following that failed attempt, he sat still, his dirt-caked hands clasped around bent knees, his mind spinning busily but uselessly. Try as he would, he could come up with no practical way of overcoming the combined forces of the slatkus and Eslatkum. The creatures' numbers and strength were not to be opposed, and their sense of holy purpose armored them against all rational argument. It was true that Hadka had promised that a sign from the Black One would save them. But Zargal seriously doubted that such a sign would be vouchsafed by Queen Godescalc before the darkness fell, and he could think of no way of manufacturing one. In the meantime, as he continued to plot, his mind grew weary and his spirits sank.

Count sa Wenilow, still ashamed of his recent outbreak of hysteria, was making every effort to steel his nerves so that there could be no repetition of the fit when the moment of execution came. He now sat huddled up near the tunnel entrance in order to get the benefit of whatever pallid light was able to squeeze past the rock into the burrow.

In the early afternoon, the prisoners were startled when

an Eslatkum huntress, aided by a group of the slatkus, rolled the stone aside.

"Have 'ee thought better of it, then?" Rothadd inquired hopefully.

Without replying, the creature tossed in a skin of water and several gobbets of raw meat. "Eat," she directed briefly. "Drink. We are not cruel."

"I must speak to your leader," Zargal said.

"Eat. Drink." She signaled to her slatku sisters, who began shoving the stone back into place, pushing it with their flat skulls, guiding it with their front claws.

"Wait!" Zargal cried.

The stone fell into place.

" 'Ee didn't even have a chance to tell her about Crumer," Rothadd said. "I hope he be well yet."

Zargal nodded without answering. Together, he and Rothadd attacked their primitive meal. It was the first meat they had tasted since the night the Turos had made off with King Laza's sleigh, and they were both starving. Sa Wenilow had no appetite and turned his eyes away from the bleeding chunks of flesh. He took deep draughts, however, of the cold water, which had been flavored with some kind of berry juice.

The minutes crept by, and Zargal tried to avoid thinking of what the evening would bring. His capture had been so sudden, the train of events so swift and unexpected, as to leave him a little dazed. He could hardly believe that the Eslatkum really meant to kill him and had to keep reminding himself that the outlandish creatures were actually in earnest. Such thoughts caused Zargal to renew his struggles to devise some means of escape, but he could think of nothing, and the strain was beginning to exhaust him mentally. He simply could not keep his mind fixed on the problem any longer. His thoughts drifted off into a troubled slumber.

Zargal slept the rest of the afternoon away and thus spared himself the agonies of anticipation. He was finally awakened by the sound of the stone being rolled away from the burrow entrance. He opened his eyes and found that the room had become completely black. As the stone moved, a red glare of torchlight dazzled him. A group of slatkus and Eslatkum guards stood outside, and the Eslatkum carried flaming brands. Darkness had fallen over the Elg.

"Come," one of the guards directed the three prisoners. "The Three Ladies await you."

"Three Ladies—what do you mean?" sa Wenilow asked, his face set.

"What do 'ee be a-plannin'?" Rothadd demanded.

"Let me speak to your leader," Zargal requested urgently. "Where is she?"

"Come. Now."

Argument was hopeless. The prisoners reluctantly crawled out of the burrow into a circle of leaping flames and distorted shadows. As each emerged, he was seized by the waiting Eslatkum and his wrists swiftly pinioned behind his back.

Zargal cast despairing eyes around him. The sight that greeted him was a daunting one. He and the others were completely surrounded by an undulating mob. The firelight was striking red sparks off hundreds of thousands of shining scales, fangs, and claws. The night was full of eyes that burned as bright as the torches. The saurian crowd was animated by ceaseless movement; bodies swayed to and fro, tails slithered over the ground like an independent gathering of snakes, and forked tongues stabbed the night air. No words were addressed to the prisoners or guards, but a low hissing arose on every side.

"Come. This way," a guard commanded, moving them off toward the hut that stood in the center of the clearing.

"Where are you taking us?" sa Wenilow demanded, with an outward appearance of calmness.

"House. The Three Ladies await you. This way." She jabbed a claw into sa Wenilow's back. "This way."

"Why?" Rothadd asked. "We have done no harm to 'ee!"

"Come. The Ladies await."

"He's right—this is madness!" Zargal exclaimed. "It's irresponsible—unreasonable! Let me speak to Hadka! Only let me speak to her. What harm can that do?"

"You speak to her if you wish. The Three Ladies await."

"The Three Ladies? Hadka is one of them?" Zargal paused. A couple of Eslatkum promptly took him by the arms and propelled him forcibly toward the hut. Zargal did not fight them. "Who are the Three Ladies?" he asked.

"Hadka, Lady of the Eslatkum," one of the guards informed him. "Merla, Lady of the slatkus. And Lady of Ladies—the Black One of the Sev."

"What? You mean to say that Godescalc—that the Black One—is actually here tonight, in that hut?" Zargal asked with some excitement.

"She is here. She awaits you in Her House."

"And we'll have a chance to speak to her?" Zargal exchanged glances with his fellow captives.

"You may speak to Her."

"The Black One doesn't wish you to harm us," Zargal ventured.

There was a muttering among the guards, and one of them replied at last, "She does not tell us so."

Having been assured that the Black One, whom he guessed to be Godescalc, was awaiting him, Zargal moved toward the hut with much less reluctance. Renewed hope sustained him now, and deliverance seemed close at hand. How could Queen Godescalc order their execution once she learned that they came as the emissaries of King Laza, who was willing to restore her to her throne? When she knew that, she was certain to accept and spare them all. Regarding his companions, Zargal could see that they shared his hopes.

Zargal was pondering how he might persuade the Eslatkum to unbind his arms so that he might present King Laza's document with all due flourish, when he became aware that the nearest guard was speaking. "Lady Merla is brave," the creature remarked, as much to her fellow Eslatkum as to the humans. "She grieves for her egg, yet she does her duty tonight."

"Her egg?" Zargal asked, startled out of his reverie.

"Yes. She grieves for it."

"What do you mean by—"

Zargal's question was cut off short. The prisoners and their escort had advanced through the hissing assemblage to the very door of the hut. One of the Eslatkum huntresses now flung wide the portal. Without any further ceremony, the prisoners were thrust inside, and the door banged shut again. A tremendous roar arose from the watching crowd.

Zargal, Rothadd, and sa Wenilow went hurtling into the rush-lit hut and came to rest full-length, face down upon the dirt floor. It was hardly a suitable entrance for the ambassador of a King, but Zargal carried it off as best he could. Slowly, and with great dignity, he raised his head, breathless with anticipation of his first sight of Godescalc.

But once again he was doomed to disappointment.

Zargal gazed upon the faces of the Three Ladies. There was Hadka, whom he knew, naked and terrible. The Eslatkum leader had adorned herself for the evening's ritual with a long necklace, fashioned of the teeth and dry finger-bones of scores of human beings. The necklace was wound several times about her throat, with the loops hanging low upon her scaly bosom. Each of Hadka's claws was painted red, and her eyes were ringed in red. The effect was horrifying.

Lady Merla was a giant among slatkus, larger by far than Bibka and twice as dangerous-looking. Unlike her companion, she wore no jewelry. But her eyes were rimmed in red, and every fang in her dreadful jaws had been painted the same color, as if she had drunk hot blood. Despite the crimson teeth, Lady Merla's aspect was not one of genuine ferocity. The creature could hardly have appeared more grief-stricken if she'd begun sobbing aloud. Every line of her long body sagged, the tail dragged in the dirt, and the plated head drooped. Merla regarded the prostrate prisoners for an instant, then turned her head away.

And the Third Lady—the Black One? Zargal looked for her eagerly. But the only other occupant of the hut was not a living one. A huge wooden statue towered up to the very ceiling. The statue was crudely carved in the image of a gigantic Eslatkum huntress, complete with ripping talons and eyes circled with daubs of red paint. The only feature other than size that really set the figure apart from the other Eslatkum was a mane of long hair, falling in graceless ripples and painted dead black. The true Eslatkum huntresses were entirely hairless.

"She isn't here!" Rothadd said. "It be the end."

Hadka ran her tongue out of her mouth. "It is time,"

she agreed, and flexed her scarlet talons. She took a step forward. The prisoners struggled to their knees.

"Where is the Black One?" Zargal demanded. By some strange alchemy, his apprehension transmuted itself to indignation. "We were promised that we could speak to her —to Godescalc."

"She is here," Hadka said. "If you will speak to Her— well, do it and be brief. I walk by. I would not kill your unready spirits."

"What are you talking about?" Zargal had lost all fear for the moment. "She's not here. You've lied to us. There's nothing here but a statue."

"Statue is the image of the Black One, Lady of the Sev." Hadka touched a claw to her lips. Without turning around, Merla did the same. "When we call upon Her, Her spirit fills the statue, and She listens to our words. She is here with us now, watching, waiting. She waits to see that we obey Her command that trespassers die. Her handmaidens do not fail Her." At these words, Lady Merla turned to face the captives, her red fangs showing.

"Then do what you must," sa Wenilow urged, his head held high, his jaw set. "We are not afraid."

"You are Ladies." Hadka approved. "We are swift, you feel nothing. Tooth of slatku, claw of Eslatkum, are swift." Again she moved forward, with Merla at her side.

"A moment!" Zargal said. "I tell you the Black One would not desire our deaths. We bear a message of the utmost importance. She must hear it!"

"Then speak it!" Hadka answered. "She hears, She hears all. But do not think we spare you. No sign comes from Her to stop us, so we must do our duty. We are not cruel, but we obey the command of the Lady. Look, you—in the midst of her grief, the Lady Merla does her duty. And so it must be. Prepare yourselves."

"I tell you," Zargal insisted, vainly struggling to free his hands, "that you must not do this!"

"There's no use in talkin'," Rothadd said in a low voice. "I wouldn't give 'em the joy of watching us squirm!"

"Are we not men?" sa Wenilow asked. "Show them that men know how to die."

"I'd rather show you all that men know how to live!"

Zargal returned in a rage. "This must not happen! Roth-add—Count—think of the Princess! You can't accept this!"

"Accept what cannot change," Hadka told him. "As Lady Merla must accept the loss of her egg." At the mention of the word "egg," the Lady of the slatkus hissed in agony and sank to the earth, her head bowed. Hadka laid a sisterly claw upon her shoulder.

"What do ail her?" Rothadd asked, his curiosity intact unto death.

"She grieves for her new egg. Two days ago, the young one vanishes into the Sev." The slatku's red eyes filled. "Since that time, Merla speaks not and eats no meat. She stays here in the House, seeking the comfort of the Black One. And yet," Hadka informed them, "she does not bite at the wind, but takes what comes. So too must the three of you. Do not fear. Death comes with terror only to those who resist her might."

Zargal was forced to admit the logic of Hadka's arguments, but his feelings remained unchanged. The mention of Lady Merla's missing egg, however, reminded him of another lost youngster whose existence he had forgotten until now. Rothadd and sa Wenilow remembered at the same time.

"Crumer," Rothadd whispered. "Still out there."

"We'd better tell them," sa Wenilow said.

The slatku and her sister Eslatkum stood at the foot of the huge statue, looked at the prisoners, and resumed their slow advance. Outside, the saurians stirred and hissed, waiting for the three corpses to be flung to their eager teeth and claws. And inside, Zargal's mind was illumined by the lightning flash of true inspiration.

"Ladies," sa Wenilow was saying, "do what you must— I see there is no help for it. But before we die, there is one thing we must tell you."

"Speak," Hadka said. "But quickly. What is it?"

"It is the sign, madam!" Zargal broke in piously. "It is the sign from the Black One that you yourself have requested. She speaks to us at last," he announced with a suavity worthy of the Ambassador of Strell. His two fellow victims regarded him in amazement.

Hadka's face remained completely expressionless. "I do not hear you," she said.

"The Black One has listened to the prayers of Her hand-maiden the Lady Merla," Zargal explained imaginatively. "And now She at once rewards Her faithful servant, and shows Her favor to us three men by using me and my companions as Her instruments in the replacement of Lady Merla's lost egg."

Lady Merla's head shot up. A volcanic hiss escaped her. The red-rimmed eyes ignited, and her tail lashed.

"Yes," Zargal said, pleased at the effect of his disclosure. "Lady Merla's newly hatched egg has vanished, but she will suffer no longer. The Black One sends another infant to take the place of that which is lost."

Lady Merla's eyes were fastened upon his face.

Hadka studied him a moment, then bared her teeth. "These are lies for fools, man," she said. "Here is no egg."

"Of course not," Zargal replied calmly. "The infant lies hidden beneath a bush at the edge of the clearing through which Krenka, Timla, and the other slatkus drove us this morning. The Lady Merla's egg has vanished into the Sev. Therefore, it is into the Sev that you must go to find another." This statement possessed an appearance of rationality, depite its basic lack of logic, that Zargal found pleasing.

Lady Hadka was not impressed. "The man ssseeksss to buy time," she hissed, unconsciously rattling the dried bones of her necklace with one red claw. "He ssspeaksss what isss not."

"You are wrong!" Zargal insisted. "I swear by my life, by my honor, by myself, that there is a human infant out there, lying under a bush!"

"By my word as a gentleman," sa Wenilow said, "the child is there."

"Will you not believe that the Black One rewards her faithful Lady Merla? Will you not believe that she wishes to preserve us?" Both Hadka and Merla glanced up at the great statue, touching their claws to their lips. But apparently the carved face and painted eyes told them nothing. The creatures hesitated in doubt. "If you refuse to believe us, then go and see for yourselves," Zargal urged them. "Search and you will find the infant in the place I have described. The Lady Merla will grieve no more."

Hadka hissed and shook her head negatively, while Lady Merla watched her.

"Why not?" Zargal asked. "What have you to lose by looking?"

"Time," Hadka replied.

She would undoubtedly have dispatched the bound and helpless captives then and there with three well-directed strokes of her awful claws, had not Lady Merla objected. As Hadka advanced, the slatku uttered a bubbling snarl and bounded forward across the other's path. A hissing, snarling, incomprehensible conversation ensued, during the course of which Merla gestured frequently at the impassive statue. As Zargal, Rothadd, and sa Wenilow watched in suspense, the slatku's voice rose, her breathing quickened, and her tail writhed in a frenzy. From time to time her fangs flashed as red as open wounds. Tears began to spill out of her eyes.

Whatever Merla was saying to the Eslatkum eventually proved effective. At the conclusion of the argument, Hadka hissed and darted her tongue out of her mouth in consent. Merla sprang to the door of the hut, pulled it open, and issued orders to those outside. A low, wondering murmur arose from the waiting crowd. After a moment, the hum of conversation grew louder. Merla stepped back into the room, shut the door, and then, without another glance at the prisoners, prostrated herself upon the discolored flat stones at the foot of the Black One's statue and lay without moving.

"Well?" Zargal inquired.

"What do 'ee do, then?" Rothadd asked.

"We wait," Hadka replied, a little sourly. "Lady Merla sends sisters to test the truth of your story. If you lie to us, then you prove you are not Ladies, and it goes hard with you—very hard." She bared her teeth. "But for now, we wait."

They waited. The endless minutes dragged on. Outside, the slatkus and Eslatkum chattered curiously among themselves. Within, the silence was broken by the incessant, softly voiced entreaties that Lady Merla addressed to the Black One. Sa Wenilow recited poetry to himself. Rothadd had evidently made up his mind that everything was going to turn out for the best, for he now appeared hopeful and content.

Zargal was paying little attention to the others. He was sitting on the floor, examining the statue as if he imagined the wooden image endowed with the spark of life. With narrowed eyes, he stared at the statue's face, seeking to visualize the face that had inspired it; but all he could see was the crude handiwork of the Eslatkum huntresses. Twenty minutes passed, and he was beginning to wonder. Hadka was rattling her necklace. Merla prayed passionately to the Black One.

At the end of half an hour, there was a change in the quality of the noise outside the hut. The crowd's murmur was growing louder, more excited. Hundreds of forked tongues flickered, and the inhuman voices merged into a mutter, then a rumble. There was an outbreak of hissing. Then a great cry and commotion arose outside.

At first sound of the shouting, Lady Merla leaped to her feet and spun around to face the door. Hadka let fall her necklace and listened intently—but not more so than the three captives. There was a sound of quick footfalls at the door.

The door burst open and a band of slatkus spilled into the room. In her jaws, one of them bore a lumpy, squirming bundle of white cloth. The lizard set the bundle down gently. The folds of white linen fell away, and Crumer Paskha lay exposed to view. The baby blinked in the light of the rush-candles and then began to scream.

Very slowly, Lady Merla walked toward Crumer, and the other slatkus made way to let her pass. Very gingerly, she extended her snout toward the child and nudged him. The forked tongue appeared and flicked lightly over his face. Crumer found this diverting. His howls died away. He giggled and made ineffectual grabs at the darting tongue. Merla expelled her breath in the long sigh of relief following a painful ordeal. The scaly lids descended for a moment over the brimming eyes, then lifted again as she looked up into the face of the statue. The great lizard took up the baby and, in a gesture of dedication, laid him at the very feet of the Black One. Then Merla, Lady of the slatkus, coiled her long body protectively around Crumer Paskha, building up a wall of iron muscles and silver scales to shield him forever from any ill the world might offer. Crumer gave a contented chuckle and began to nurse, much to Zargal's surprise. He hadn't suspected that the Eslatkum could lactate.

Lady Hadka had been looking on in silence, but now she addressed the prisoners. "The Black One sends a new egg to console the grief of Lady Merla. You speak the truth to us, and we are wrong to doubt." After a moment she added, "Tomorrow morning, you march on through the Sev to carry your message to our Lady."

Hadka's words were overheard by all her sister slatkus and Eslatkum, who stood outside watching the entire scene through the hut's open door. Now, one by one, the creatures dropped down, humble bellies to the earth, in recognition of the power and glory of their Black Lady.

CHAPTER XXV

The next evening found the three men well beyond the domain of the Eslatkum.

Following the discovery of the infant Crumer, the hunttresses had been kindness itself. Zargal, Rothadd, and sa Wenilow spent the night in the hut under the benevolent eye of the Black One's statue. At sunrise, they continued on their way. The Eslatkum provided the travelers with food, water, and vague directions. The Black One was said to dwell on an island called Trone in the middle of the Sev, somewhere to the south. Trone was a blessed place, filled with streams of pure water and overrun with game. The Black Lady was supposed to live there in great splendor, in a huge burrow lined with blocks of stone to keep the water out, and shored up with posts of carven oak. She was attended by a band of all the mightiest of the slatku and Eslatkum huntresses who had died in battle or during the chase. Every night they feasted in the enormous burrow, and there was music, a never-ending supply of fresh meat, and the handsomest of males to serve them.

An escort of slatkus and Eslatkum accompanied the humans for the first few miles of their journey. Hadka was there, and so were Krenka, Timla, and many others. Merla was unwilling to leave Crumer for the space of half an hour and couldn't be persuaded to come. At the edge of the Eslatkum territory, Hadka and her people halted and uttered a hissing salute. After that, the humans went on alone.

The day's march was not too bad. The travelers were rested and well-fed for a change, and the ground over which they walked was comparatively solid. By evening they had covered a satisfying distance. There were plenty of dry twigs available with which to build a fire, and the earth beneath them was soft with old grasses. As soon as the fire was fairly started, they ate quantities of the dried meat the Eslatkum had given them. After dinner sa Wenilow wrote his poetry, Rothadd doggedly practiced his magic, and Zargal stared into the fire, thinking his own uneasy thoughts.

Despite the relative comfort of their surroundings, Count sa Wenilow was in a dreary mood, and his poem reflected it. After a time, the young man paused to read his verse aloud:

> "I saw eternity the other night
> Like a great tree infected with the blight,
>   A spirit-killing sight.
> And down beneath it, Sin and Death hold sway,
>   To make Mankind their prey.
> Now, to this hungry swamp which is the world
>   Our tired hearts are hurled—"

Zargal and Rothadd exchanged blank looks.

"What do you think of it?" sa Wenilow asked anxiously. "There's more to come, of course, but how do you like it so far?"

"Handsome, I do call it," Rothadd said diplomatically. "But for the first line, which do need changin'." Sa Wenilow nodded and returned to his work.

Rothadd took up Hincmar's spell again and went back to his mumblings and gesticulations. After another twenty minutes or so of useless effort, he suddenly jammed the parchment back into his pocket, rose and walked around to Zargal's side of the fire, and flopped down beside him. " 'Tis never going to work," he complained in a low voice which did not reach sa Wenilow's ears.

"What, you mean the magic?" Zargal asked, startled out of his gloomy torpor. Rothadd nodded. "Why, Rothadd, you look discouraged—that's not like you."

"Oh, aye, but the thickest skull will give way if 'ee do bash it against a rock for long enough." Rothadd's freckled face looked tired, and older than ever before. "I be weary of bashin' mine."

"We're all weary," Zargal said. "But you mustn't think of giving up. Remember what the pool of prophecy showed you?"

"Oh—that pool. Full of lies it was." Rothadd wouldn't lift his eyes from the ground.

"Some lies and some truth, with no way of knowing which is which. Just enough of a mixture to confuse us completely. At least we'll never be bored."

Rothadd smiled faintly, then drooped again. "Nay, 'twas all folly. I be but a poor Outcottager's son. Magic's not for the likes of me. I could keep on a-tryin' till the mountains of Obran be worn as flat as the plains of Shorble, but 'twould do no good. I haven't got the power, and never will have."

"Rothadd," Zargal said, seriously dismayed by his friend's unhappiness, "I believe you have the gift. Even if you haven't learned to use it properly yet, the talent is there, I'm sure of it. Hincmar thinks so, too, and doesn't that mean something?"

"Happen that Hincmar be wrong."

"And King Laza—is he wrong as well? *He* thinks it's worth his time to teach you, and he should know."

"Well, now—" Rothadd finally looked up. "That be something to think about."

"Of course. You might also try thinking about your hands. What would you be doing with hands like that if you weren't born for magic?"

The Outcottager examined his elongated fingers, his long, skinny thumbs. "The true shape they be," he agreed, his usual optimism beginning to assert itself.

"Yes, indeed. There's hope for you yet. Just keep trying —you'll win in the end, if only you don't give up. I'm sure of it." Zargal might almost have been talking to himself rather than to Rothadd.

"Aye, I do be downhearted of late, like all of us. 'Ee don't be a-lookin' so lively yourself, if truth be told."

"No," Zargal admitted.

" 'Ee be afeared of meetin' up with Godescalc, then? 'Twould only be natural."

"No, it isn't that. I'm much more worried about what will happen after we've concluded our business with her. Assuming that we can find Godescalc, and that she is willing to cure the Princess, then how shall we all get back to Obran?"

"Why, we must go back the way we did come. 'Twill take time, but—"

"How much time? How many days have we been wandering through this swamp? How many days will it take us to get back to the Gluis Appli? And once we're there, what can we do? King Laza's sleigh is gone. How many weeks—or months—will it take us to make our way on foot back to the palace? Can you tell me that?"

"Nay, Zargal. All I can tell 'ee is, we must take what do come and make the best of it."

"And what of her ladyship—the Princess? What will be happening to her as the weeks pass and we do not return, because we were so unbelievably stupid as to lose our sleigh to a pack of petty, thieving swindlers?"

"That wasn't something that could be helped—"

"It could certainly have been helped if we'd only had our wits about us. But it is Bellora who must suffer for our idiocy. Where's the justice in that?" Zargal spat out the question with a mixture of self-accusation and rage.

"The sleigh be gone—'tis over and done with. And brooding over it will do the Princess no good neither."

"If she doesn't recover, it will be our fault."

"Nay, it wasn't we that caused her sickness. 'Twould be a sad thing, it would, if aught befalls the lass, but it wouldn't be our doing. 'Ee must use your sense."

"I'm not feeling sensible."

"Aye, I can see it. But King Laza won't blame 'ee if we do fail—'ee must know that."

"I'm not interested in King Laza."

"Oh—the Princess herself, is it?" Rothadd looked at Zargal in surprised comprehension. "Why, 'ee do be set upon the lass like I be set on magic!"

Zargal shrugged and his dark brows arched slightly. "I hardly think that her ladyship concerns herself with the aspirations of her father's kitchen servants," he said, his face frozen.

"Oh, nay? I would have thought 'ee do know her better nor that."

"The question is hardly apt to arise. Whatever the private feelings of her ladyship, her father hates me."

"Well," Rothadd said consideringly, "I won't deny the King didn't feel too kindly toward 'ee, but happen 'twould be different now."

"Why should it be?"

"Because 'ee be different yourself. 'Ee ben't the same lad that did come to King Laza's castle. Lots of changes there be in 'ee."

Zargal reddened and changed the subject. "It's getting very late," he said. Count sa Wenilow had already fallen asleep, and lay with his head resting on his unfinished poem. "Don't you think we'd better get some rest?"

"Aye. But I be a-plannin' to practice my spell a bit first," Rothadd said, demonstrating the success of Zargal's words of encouragement.

The Duke's son soon had cause to regret those words. He had hardly settled down for the night when Rothadd's efforts bore startling results. A muffled booming sound arose, and tremors shook the earth in their vicinity. A couple of shallow chasms opened up, and Zargal rolled into one. The fire was scattered and extinguished. In utter darkness, the three travelers groped and waded their way to a safer neighborhood where, after sa Wenilow's bewildered queries were answered, they again lay down to sleep.

The morning breathed no hint of disaster, and the three young men pressed on to the south in search of the Black One's blessed isle of Trone. None of them possessed much confidence that such a place existed. It was even beginning to occur to them that Godescalc herself might not exist. They did not, however, have any better information to guide them. The travelers walked all day long and discovered nothing but trees and rocks and mud. The next day's march seemed to promise nothing better; but, in fact, a change lay in store.

Zargal, Rothadd, and sa Wenilow were passing through

a murky region filled with life and motion. A stream ran along beside the trail, its water brown and sluggish. Phosphorescent slime blanketed the reedy verge.

The three travelers proceeded down a gentle incline until they found their way blocked by a great expanse of quiet water. Far off, in the middle of the lake, an island was visible. The travelers paused.

"There it be—an island!" Rothadd exclaimed. "Do it be the one we want, though?"

"How are we going to get out there?" Zargal wondered. "Too far to swim, wouldn't you say?"

"I can't swim a stroke."

"I can. But not that far."

"What's to do, then?"

"I don't know," Zargal said, folding his arms and staring out over the rippling barrier. "Blast the woman!" he added.

"Do 'ee think it truly be Queen Godescalc a-livin' out there?"

"We won't find out until we have a chance to see for ourselves. Rothadd, I don't suppose you could part the waters, or conjure up a boat or a bridge, or anything equally useful, could you?"

" 'Ee do know better."

"Sorry. Well, we'll have to think of something. Perhaps we might build a boat."

"Mullytwaddle! A lot the likes of 'ee do know of buildin'! 'Twould take days!"

"Hmmm—we must do better than that. But I can't say how, unless sa Wenilow can swim that distance. Can you, Count?" Zargal asked. "Sa Wenilow? Count?"

There was no answer. Count sa Wenilow had not been listening to the conversation. He was gazing off toward the island, rigid, white, his eyes enormous. His jaw was clenched to control his chattering teeth.

"What's wrong, sa Wenilow? What's the matter?"

"Do 'ee be sick, lad?"

"This place," sa Wenilow replied, so low that they had to strain to hear him. "The lake, the island—don't you recognize them?"

"Do 'ee be a-thinkin'—" Rothadd asked, after a pause. "Do 'ee be a-thinkin' that this here be—"

"This is the place I beheld in the pool of prophecy," sa

Wenilow said. "I see you do recognize it. Here I shall meet my death."

"Ah, nay! Hale and sound 'ee be yet! And so 'ee will stay!"

Sa Wenilow shook his head. His gray eyes were glazed. "Here I shall meet my death," he repeated.

"Look here—" Zargal said hesitantly. "If I'm not mistaken, the pool showed you a vision of yourself descending into a hole, a tunnel of some kind. I see no such hole here. Perhaps this isn't the place after all."

"It is the place." Sa Wenilow was so certain that he did not even bother to stress his words. But his figure periodically quivered. "The hole is somewhere near."

Zargal and Rothadd were somewhat at a loss for words, for they both thought it quite possible that sa Wenilow was right. The best that Rothadd could think to say was, "That pool was a-brimmin' over with lies, it was. I wouldn't place no faith in aught it had to show us!"

"That's right," Zargal agreed, though he had previously refuted that very argument. "The pool wasn't to be trusted. Take heart, Count."

Sa Wenilow didn't answer. He withdrew the half-completed poem from a pocket, scanned it idly, his lips moving, then put it back again.

"Well, 'ee don't see no holes around here now, do 'ee?" Rothadd asked in a tone of false heartiness.

"Let's stop worrying about imaginary holes," Zargal suggested, "and get back to the problem at hand. How are we going to get across to explore that island? It certainly fits the Eslatkum's description."

"Maybe someone's left a boat moored nearby," sa Wenilow said dully.

"That's a thought. We might make a search along the shore." It was Zargal's hope that action of some kind might divert sa Wenilow's thoughts from gloomy topics. Moreover, it was always possible that they might actually find a boat. Accordingly, the three of them went hunting up and down along the pebbled shore.

Not much time had elapsed before sa Wenilow discovered what he had known perfectly well he would find—a hole in the ground, an opening somewhat camouflaged with dead branches. It was undoubtedly the entrance to a tunnel of some kind. The passage slanted sharply down and was soon lost in blackness. Count sa Wenilow stood frozen and silent, staring into the waiting pit.

Presently Zargal and Rothadd took note of their companion's attitude, drew near, and beheld the hole.

"That's it," sa Wenilow said. His fits of trembling were getting the better of him. He took a step backward without shifting his gaze. His face might have been stamped in yellowish wax.

"Sa Wenilow!" Zargal cried. "Calm yourself. No one has asked you to go anywhere near that hole. There's no cause for alarm. Do you hear me, my lord?"

The Count did not. "It's the same," he choked in a dying voice. "It's waiting for me." His eyes showed a rim of white around each iris, but the black hole filled his entire vision. His hands clenched involuntarily.

"Here, now, lad," Rothadd said, stretching forth a hand.

"Get hold of yourself, Count," Zargal urged. "Remember who you are!"

" 'Tis naught so bad, friend."

"Control yourself, sir—you are a nobleman of Obran!"

"Why don't 'ee sit and rest for a time?"

The Count heard none of these appeals. For a while he remained motionless, his blind gaze fixed on the hole. Then, with a strangled cry, he turned and tore off at top speed, plunging back into the darkest reaches of the Elg.

"Come back!" his two companions implored, and set off in pursuit, but their task was a hopeless one. Sa Wenilow ignored the cries and fled with the desperate speed of a hunted forest creature. The mists converged around him as he ran, the trees held out their branching arms, and the dark pools promised protection. The young Count raced on to seek the shelter of the thickest shadows. The human voices were far away and faint; and finally, sa Wenilow heard them no more.

Many hours elapsed before Zargal and Rothadd found themselves back at the lake shore, standing beside the fatal hole. They were both tired, filthy, and covered with scratches and bruises. But half a day's searching had proved useless. Their voices were hoarse with calling, their throats were raw, and it had all been for nothing. Count sa

Wenilow had vanished, swallowed up in one gulp by the hungry Elg.

The Duke's son and the Outcottager seated themselves despondently. "Do 'ee think he'll come back, then?" Rothadd asked.

"I don't think so. Perhaps I'm wrong. But I don't think we'll see him any more."

"Nay."

"We might wait here for a while, to make sure."

"Aye. We'll stay, then."

After about an hour of sitting and listening to the wind harassing the trees, Rothadd spoke again. "He be never a-comin' back here. Ought we to search some more?"

"In all this?" Zargal's hopeless gesture took in all the surrounding tract of swampland.

"Well, what do we do, then?"

"Exactly my thought. What do we do, then?" Zargal was staring off at the distant island. "She's probably out there, you know," he said.

"Aye. She be out there, and we be here. With a whole lake in between."

"I've been thinking about that," Zargal said. "The hole that poor sa Wenilow discovered—it seems to be a tunnel of some kind. It could be that the tunnel runs under the lake, all the way out to the island."

"I was afraid 'ee be a-thinkin' that."

"The thing that troubles me," Zargal went on, unheeding, "is—why should it be here? If Queen Godescalc has chosen to live on an island in the middle of the swamp, out of the reach of all her enemies, then why should this tunnel be waiting for us here?"

"Waiting for us—there 'ee do hit upon it! A trap it be."

"That's very probably true. On the other hand, trap or no trap, this tunnel may be the only way for us to get out to that island."

Rothadd gave a smothered groan. "I knew it! I knew it! 'Ee want to go into that hole! But I do say 'tis madness to think it!"

"But how else are we to get out there? We haven't any boat. Be reasonable, Rothadd."

"Reasonable, 'ee do say!" Rothadd exploded. "Reasonable! Why, 'ee wouldn't know reason if 'ee did stumble over it at noon of a sunny day! 'Ee do know 'tis most like that this here be a trap, but 'ee'll be a-goin' in all the same? Don't talk to me of *reason,* lad!"

"Very well, I won't speak to you of reason. I'll speak to you of honor, obligation, and duty."

"Nay. 'Ee won't talk of them neither. 'Tis not our duty to get ourselves chopped up into hash!"

"Chopped up into hash?"

"Aye, and 'ee needn't stand there a-lookin' blank as paper. 'Ee do mind what the pool showed would become of sa Wenilow if he did set foot in this very hole."

"That was sa Wenilow's vision. What does it have to do with us?"

"Happen the same thing would befall anyone who goes down there."

"How likely is that?" Zargal argued. "You don't believe anything that pool had to show us, do you? Or so you've said upon several occasions."

"Oh, there's no talkin' to 'ee! But one thing I do know," Rothadd's brow furrowed. " 'Tis lunacy to think of goin' down there. I won't go. And if 'ee must, then 'ee be crack-braineder nor Count sa Wenilow ever dreamed of bein'!"

"That may be, but I don't feel I have any choice. The Princess—"

"The Princess won't get much good of 'ee if 'ee be a-lyin' dead under a lake in the Elg! 'Twould be of much more use to her if 'ee would only go about all this cautious!"

"Really? And what would you suggest?" Zargal was growing a little angry. Rothadd's common sense often annoyed him.

"I say we find some other way of getting out there."

"We don't have time! With each passing day, her lady-ship's condition worsens. We can afford no delay!"

"That lass has addled your wits, she has! I tell 'ee, it won't do her no good if the both of us are killed!"

"You are afraid?" Zargal asked scornfully.

"Aye! And so too would 'ee be if 'ee did have the sense of a Yili."

"Be that as it may, I'm going in."

"And I won't!" Rothadd turned away, scowling.

This seemed to finish the argument, which had grown unpleasantly heated. Zargal climbed to his feet. "If you won't go into the tunnel," he said more calmly, "then what will you do?"

Rothadd shrugged. "Set about a-buildin' a boat, maybe," he replied. "Or hike around t'other side of the lake, to see if there be any way out to the island from there. 'Twould be a long hike around, though—it be a big lake. What concern do that be of yours?"

"Well, let's not part on bad terms. You have convinced me of one thing."

"What do that be?"

"That it's up to me to go through the tunnel alone. I've no right to ask you to take such risks."

"Aye. And 'ee shouldn't take 'em yourself."

"Well. Good-bye, Rothadd." Zargal held out a large hand, which the Outcottager clasped in both of his, all rancor forgotten. "Don't give up trying to find a way out to that island. If anything happens to me in this tunnel, the Princess will be depending on you."

"Aye, I know. Will 'ee look sharp down there? Promise that, at least. Must 'ee go, truly?"

"I'll be as careful as I can. Wish me luck, Rothadd. Good-bye." Unwilling to risk the possibility of further arguments that might weaken his resolve, Zargal quickly lowered himself down into the hole.

The tunnel was just as it had appeared in the pool to Count sa Wenilow—a long, dim corrdor cut through solid stone, with damp walls and ceiling and a floor blotched with slimy puddles. The air was still and close. Zargal had not advanced ten paces before he heard the quick splash of footsteps behind him. The Duke's son spun around, dagger drawn, only to confront Rothadd, who must have entered only a moment or two behind him.

"You've changed your mind?"

"Aye," the lad admitted. "I didn't want to. But if 'ee *will* go, no matter what, then it wouldn't seem right to let 'ee go alone."

"I'm very glad. But are you sure?"

"Oh, aye. I did long to see Queen Godescalc afore I'm through, and so I will. That is, if she do be out there, and still alive."

"I have a feeling that she is. Call it foolery if you like," Zargal said, "but I'm almost sure. Of course, that makes this tunnel all the more dangerous, and you're very young. I'm beginning to wonder if you should be here at all."

"A little late to wonder that, after we did come all this way. But a few short years younger nor yourself I be, and King Laza didn't think me unfit to come with 'ee," Rothadd replied with spirit. "Told me to keep an eye on 'ee, he did."

"Did he?"

"Oh, aye. If things get too hard for me down here, why, then, what's to keep me from a-turnin' and comin' back out in a hurry, the same way I did come in?"

Rothadd's query was answered instantly. There was a dull clang, and the tunnel went black. "What happened?" Rothadd cried.

"I don't know, but I think we'd better get out of this tunnel if we can."

Zargal's doubts were well-founded. When he and Rothadd managed to grope their way back to the entrance, they found their way out hopelessly blocked. A pair of heavy steel panels, whose presence they had unluckily overlooked, had come snapping out from under a concealing blanket of dirt and weeds to seal off the near end of the tunnel, trapping Zargal and Rothadd inside.

"Well. Now I'm sure she's out there," Zargal said.

"Much good that may do us!" Rothadd cried. "Starve to death in the dark we will! Oh, I knew we shouldn't come in here!"

Zargal was silent, for he realized it was quite possible that Rothadd was right, and he was responsible for his friend's plight. "We've been in worse spots than this," he said at last.

"When?"

"When the krorks were hunting us across the borderlands."

"The krorks were naught but half-spirits. They couldn't touch us."

"Then there was the night the Eslatkum were going to kill us—"

" 'Twould have been quick, at least."

"You weren't too pleased about it at the time," Zargal's voice crackled out of the dark. "We entered this tunnel because we wanted to find out what lies at the other end of it. Well, let's go see."

"We won't see much in here, I can tell 'ee."

"We'll have to feel our way along."

"Aye. We'll be a-feelin' it, all right, when we do go tumblin' down into some great hole has likely been dug here as a trap."

"You haven't been in good spirits lately, Rothadd. I've noticed."

"I wonder why that be."

Zargal and Rothadd spent the next few hours picking their way through the tunnel like blind men navigating a maze. Their course was straight, and the distance they had to cover was not great. But, as they both suspected a trap, each step forward was accompanied by elaborate preliminary groping. With outstretched arms they explored the floor, the walls, and the air before them—all to no avail. No beasts came leaping out of the dark to assault them, and no pits opened up at their feet. The worst that happened was that once Zargal set his foot squarely in the middle of one of the coldest and slimiest of puddles. He withdrew it, cursing.

" 'Twas stupid of us that we didn't bring candles," Rothadd said. "Or lanterns."

"We had plenty of lights," Zargal reminded him. "The Turos got them."

"We should have brought some from the Eslatkum."

"We were lucky to bring our lives from the Eslatkum. And how were we to know that we'd find ourselves here in a black tunnel under the lake? Though, all things considered," Zargal added, "we might have guessed."

The two of them inched on through the dark. Zargal was finally beginning to hope that their fears had been groundless when his straining ears caught a faint whirring noise. "Do you hear that?" he asked.

"Aye—I do! What do it be?"

"I think it's close ahead of us, whatever it is."

"Stop right here we will, then," Rothadd stated, and did so.

For a little while they stood listening. The noise was low and constant, a whirring sound punctuated by a repetitive creak. It had a mechanical quality about it.

"It sounds like a machine," Zargal said wonderingly.

"What sort of machine would we find down here?"

"A noisy one."

"Aye. If only we did have a light and could see for ourselves what it be! I'm heartsick of bein' blind!"

"I'm sorry I brought you in here. I shouldn't have done it. It's my fault."

"Came in of my own free will, I did," Rothadd told him. "My own master I be. If only we did have a light!"

"A light," Zargal repeated. "We ought to be able to manage that. We're fools if we can't manage that."

"What do 'ee be a-thinkin'? 'Ee do have a headful of thoughts."

"We might try burning some of our clothes. The light wouldn't last long, but at least we could find out what that noise is."

"Aye! Haven't 'ee got a head, though!"

Their outer garments were wet and muddy. But both Zargal and Rothadd were wearing woolen coats beneath their cloaks, waistcoats beneath the coats, and linen shirts beneath the waistcoats. Of these garments, the waistcoats were dispensable and dry. Within seconds, the wearers had removed them and torn them to shreds, which formed a little pile on the stone floor. Rothadd regretfully added his Outcottager's square of oiled cloth to the heap. When Zargal took flint and steel to strike sparks, the square ignited in a flash. An orange glow lightened the tunnel, and Zargal and Rothadd were immediately able to identify the source of the noise that had alarmed them.

It was well that they had paused, for the tunnel was guarded, not by man or beast, but by machinery. A few yards ahead, a mechanical device had been suspended halfway between the ceiling and the floor. The contraption boasted four long arms radiating from a central point; each arm consisted of a broad, double-edged cutting blade. The blades revolved at a fairly swift, steady rate, just barely clearing the floor, ceiling, and walls in their circular sweep. The firelight revealed a number of ominous brown stains upon the metal—rust, and something darker. The floor was hideously littered with split bones. The ancient mechanism was still in working order, but it creaked and vibrated and rattled as it turned. Zargal and Rothadd stood and stared.

Neither of them could think of anything to say for some time, until at last Rothadd remarked, "One thing I do know. 'Tis well that Count sa Wenilow didn't come here."

Zargal nodded and watched, doing his best to ignore the bloodstains and the bones. "It's not really spinning very fast," he observed.

"Fast enough, I doubt not."

"No, look at it—I'm quite sure there's time enough to slip under those blades as they turn."

"Ah, nay! We try that, 'tis like there won't be enough of us left to fill up a pasty. There must be some other way!"

"Not that I can think of. We're lucky to have any chance at all. This machine is old, rusted, and neglected. Otherwise, the blades would surely be spinning faster and we'd never get by them alive. Furthermore, it's only due to neglect that the device is making any noise. If it had been properly oiled, it would be silent. We would have heard nothing—"

"And we'd have walked right into 'er and ended up like sa Wenilow did see himself in the pool. Aye, I see all that. But it doesn't make me want to try a-nippin' in under those knives."

"We have to. You know we can't go back."

"Happen we can bust up this machine and stop 'er flat."

Zargal didn't think it likely, but was willing to give it a fair try. The fire was starting to die down. He replenished it with his livery coat, and Rothadd sacrificed his muffler. The smell of scorching wool started to blend unpleasantly with the odors of dampness and mold already present in the tunnel. In the dim orange light, the two of them stood inches from the great revolving blades, prying and hacking at the central connecting point with their knives. It was no use. Whatever mechanism caused the blades to turn was safely housed behind layers of steel. There followed several attempts to jam the works by thrusting heavy bones between the revolving arms, but the blades swept on, as inexorable as the Grim Reaper's scythe.

"This won't work," Rothadd admitted. " 'Ee be right, then—we must scoot under the knives. But I mislike it."

"I'm not particularly pleased either. When we come face to face with Queen Godescalc, we can tell her so. Who'll go first?"

"That I will," Rothadd said. "I don't want to stand here a-thinkin' about it." Despite his words, the Outcottager did stand there thinking about it. For a few seconds he regarded the spinning blades with a disapproving eye. Then, taking a deep breath, he shot under the knives as nimbly as a mouse dodging a housewife's broomstick. His timing was impeccable, and he passed unscathed.

"Come on!" Rothadd called happily from the other side of the barrier. " 'Tis naught so hard!"

Zargal was tempted to tell his companion to hold his tongue, but felt that such a reply would make a most unbecoming final speech if he should by any chance be killed. "Promise you'll carry on alone if I don't make it?" he asked.

"Don't be a-talkin' ribble-rabble!"

Zargal shook his head in exasperation. He was uncomfortably conscious of his size, which very much increased his danger, and he felt absolutely no inclination to move. But the fire was already starting to sink again. If he tarried much longer, he would be forced to burn his shirt.

"Come on—what's a-holdin' 'ee?" Rothadd demanded.

Zargal took a flat, flying dive under the blades. For a moment, he thought he'd got through untouched; if he'd been a man of normal size, he would have done so. As it was, one of the rusty knives just grazed the heel of his left foot, shearing neatly through the shoe leather and taking the thinnest slice of skin along with it.

The Duke's son sat on the wet floor in the tunnel, inspecting his mutilated shoe and bleeding foot.

"Well, now—got off easy, 'ee did," Rothadd observed with his customary optimism.

Zargal's only reply was a heartfelt curse.

"It could have been much worse. Can't 'ee look on the bright side of things?" Rothadd asked.

At this moment the fire sank down and died, leaving them stranded in the dark, sightless, with no sounds to be heard but dripping water and creaking machinery. Rothadd uttered a faint exclamation of dismay. "This'll do for us yet," he said.

Zargal resisted a strong temptation to advise his companion to look on the bright side of things. Without further conversation, he rose and advanced through the black tunnel, limping slightly, with Rothadd at his side. For a time they progressed slowly, with great caution, ever on the alert for a new trap. But as they went, it began to seem to them that the surrounding darkness was growing less intense. At first they thought it might be their imagination playing them tricks, but eventually there could no longer be any doubt. Zargal could discern Rothadd's moving form beside him. The darkness continued to pale as they progressed, until finally they beheld the tunnel opening, lit with a red glow.

"What do that be—a fire?" Rothadd whispered. "Blocking our way out of here?"

Zargal's heart sank, for it seemed a hideously likely suggestion. But as they approached their journey's end, no blasts of heat assailed them. The light steadily grew brighter. And when at last they reached the opening and climbed out above ground once more, the lake was at their back. An extravagant sunset had dyed the sky deep crimson. Before them, shadowing the shore, rose the black form of a castle whose towers clutched like skinny fingers at the fiery clouds.

CHAPTER XXVI

~~~

Zargal and Rothadd studied the castle and observed no sign of life. No lights flickered behind the deep windows; no sentries paced the ramparts.

"Deserted, it do look," Rothadd said.

"It better not be," Zargal replied.

Together they approached the silent building, and Zargal could hardly fail to admit the truth of Rothadd's words. It did look deserted—very deserted indeed. The grounds around the castle were wild and overgrown. Brambles choked the walk, and weeds thrust themselves up through the cracks in the paving stones. When they reached the broad stone steps leading up to the arched entranceway, they noted that the black marble was velvety with moss, which looked as if it had not been trodden on in a lifetime.

Slowly, they ascended to the door. Zargal's knife was drawn, for he half expected an ambush of some kind—a sudden onslaught of armed guards, or an attack of slatkus or their sister Eslatkum. But no one appeared. Zargal and Rothadd paused at the door, lifted the rusted iron knocker, and let it fall with a clang that must have reverberated for miles across the lake. No one answered.

"Let's go in," Zargal suggested quietly. His voice was

calm and his face impassive, but inside he was prey to sickening uneasiness. Where could they go next, and what could they do? There wasn't any way to get off the island and back to shore, for the far end of the tunnel was closed to them. Zargal didn't want to think about it.

"Help me with the door," he requested brusquely. Despite his size and strength, he needed help, for the hinges were rusted solid. It took the two of them, pulling and straining with all their might, to pry the portal open. The hinges shrieked like lost souls, clouds of rust drifted to the ground, and the ancient timbers groaned. Had there been any guards within earshot, the noise would have attracted them. But still nobody appeared.

Zargal and Rothadd stepped over the threshold, into the dimness beyond. The great stone hall in which they found themselves was unfurnished. There were no torches burning in the brackets on the walls, but enough red light filtered in from outside to illuminate the dust that lay everywhere and the cobwebs that masked the ceiling and clustered in corners. There were no footprints in the dust, no fingerprints on the door frame. It was dank and cold, and the thick castle wall muted the noises from outside.

"There can't be anyone a-livin' here," Rothadd said, his voice echoing sadly in the great empty hall. "All alone we be."

"Perhaps not. There are other rooms we haven't seen yet," Zargal said without much hope, for he was nearly certain that Rothadd was right. The place looked as if no human being had set foot in it for centuries. "Let's go look."

Rothadd nodded glumly, and the two of them commenced a dreary exploration. There wasn't much to see. The cold rooms were devoid of furniture, animal life, or human beings. Not so much as a solitary cockroach scuttled across the dusty flagstones. Damp moss grew in the unused fireplaces. The iron hinges on every door were misshapen with rust. Zargal and Rothadd did not speak to each other. In hopeless silence they searched the building, making their way through one after another tomblike chamber. The silence remained unbroken as they descended a spiral stair that took them down to the very bowels of the castle, to subterranean regions as dark as the tunnel they had lately traversed. And then, in the midst of all that silence and blackness, there came to their ears the faintest of noises.

Zargal and Rothadd both heard it at the same time, and they simultaneously stopped dead to listen. As faint as the sigh of a ghost, it came floating out of the darkness from somewhere ahead of them. After a moment they began to move again. As they went, the sound grew closer and stronger, though it remained elusive yet. Sometimes it sounded like a muted chorus of human voices and sometimes like the wind over the Eastling Wolds. It varied from moment to moment and still remained essentially unchanging.

Zargal and Rothadd followed the sound along the dark passage to a door under which shone a glimmer of light, so weak that Zargal feared he might simply be seeing what he so much wished to believe was there. He knocked upon the door, and when he received no reply, boldly threw it wide. The room beyond was occupied. Both the Duke's son and his companion caught their breath at the first glimpse of the object of their quest.

It was a small chamber. Furnishings were sparse, but all four walls were crowded with score upon score of paintings in ornate, tarnished frames. The air was full of murmurous, rustling noises, whose source Zargal could not as yet identify. His attention was fixed exclusively on the black-clad woman who sat in an armchair near the cold fireplace.

She did not turn her head as the door crashed open, nor did she react in any way as Zargal and Rothadd stepped over the threshold. Zargal beheld a white, sagging profile with a proud eagle nose curving down over a slack, drooping jaw; a mass of unbound hair, marbled with white, yet retaining most of its original raven hue, that went swirling wildly down her back, over the arms of the chair to lie in tangles on the granite floor; thin, stooped shoulders; and pale hands, long of finger and stiff of joint, that lay limply in her lap like the useless talons of a disabled bird of prey. The eyes he could not see.

There could be no doubt that this was the woman they sought. Abandoned and alone in a cellar fit for a slave, she owned all the stark dignity of the ruin of an ancient fortress. For a brief moment Zargal paused, staring and wondering. Rothadd stood beside him, breathing fast. Then the Duke's son recollected himself and his mission and felt quickly beneath his grimy shirt for King Laza's parchment. He withdrew it swiftly, composed his features as best he could, and took a couple of steps toward the silent, seated figure.

"Madam," he said, "allow me the privilege of addressing you. I am Lord Zargal of Szar. My companion is Rothadd, Rotha's son, of the Eastling Wolds. We are here to speak on behalf of his Majesty King Laza of Obran."

Keeping in mind his knowledge of Queen Godescalc's history, Zargal half expected a storm of outrage to greet the mention of Cramarius' descendant. None was forthcoming. The woman in the chair did not speak or stir. She did not so much as lift her head. It was difficult to believe that she could have heard him. Possibly she was a bit deaf. "Your ladyship," he said loudly and clearly, "I bear a message of the utmost importance from his Majesty of Obran."

There was no answer. Godescalc was as silent as stone. The air was a-dance with whispers and tiny rustlings. Zargal still could not tell where they came from. He and Rothadd regarded each other in perplexity.

"Do she be *alive,* then?" the Outcottager inquired.

"She'll hear that! Do you want to get her angry?" Zargal whispered. In a much louder, gently reasonable tone, he said, "Her ladyship is perhaps preoccupied at present. We regret to trouble her at an inconvenient moment." Tact availed him nothing, for she spoke not a word.

"Happen we bashed her door open, and her heart just up and stopped at the fearsome sound of it," Rothadd suggested.

"That's enough, Rothadd! I don't want to hear it."

"*She* doesn't want to hear neither. Leastways, if she be still alive."

The rules of diplomatic decorum prohibited Zargal from approaching any nearer to Godescalc without having first received her permission. Desperation now impelled him to break those rules. Three of his huge strides brought him around the chair and face to face with her. Zargal gazed into the eyes of Godescalc, and it was like looking down twin tunnels leading into black eternity. The great, deepset orbs might once have been handsome; now they were filmed as if with the dust of centuries, shot with a thousand red veins, and expressive of nothing—no thought, no emotion, no knowledge, no memory—nothing at all. Could this empty husk really be the sorceress whose magic King Laza himself could not defeat? Godescalc's sunken chest rose and fell slowly. She was not dead, but she did not know that strangers stood at her side.

Zargal understood suddenly the words King Laza had spoken: "There are ways of prolonging life almost indefinitely. Most magicians eventually conclude that it is unwise to do so." This, then, was the result of life too greatly lengthened—this mindless wreck who could not even guard herself against outsiders.

"Be she alive, then?" Rothadd whispered.

"Yes," Zargal answered, out of the depths of his defeat and despair. "After a fashion. Come and see for yourself. It's all right. Come here."

Rothadd drew near, and he, too, stared into the eyes of the ruined sorceress. "Oh," he said dolefully, "this be a sorry sight."

"Rothadd, you have some magic. Is there any way of restoring her wits by magic?"

"Oh, aye. But I can't do it to save my life!"

"She doesn't even know we're here. Godescalc! Godescalc!" Zargal screamed in her ear, so loudly that the air in the chamber stirred, and the whispering noises were stilled for an instant. Rothadd turned away, his hands pressed to his ears, a look of pain upon his face. The woman in the chair did not move, but something that might have been the faintest shadow of perturbation passed briefly over her features and was gone in an instant. The dust settled and the whispering resumed.

"I saw something," Zargal said.

"What?"

"She heard me shout. Her face changed for a moment."

"Nay." Rothadd inspected the blank, remote countenance. " 'Ee be a-dreamin'."

"No. Watch." Zargal repeated his terrific shout, and it happened again; the air was still and silent for a short span of time, and a split-second flicker of uneasiness or distress animated the face of Godescalc.

"Did you see that?"

"Aye, but—"

Zargal yelled again, and this time it was unmistakable. In the moment of utter silence that followed the noise, a slight tremor shook the sorceress, and the clouded eyes wandered over the walls with a lost and searching expression. Then the whispers recommenced, and she was motionless and lifeless, as before.

"She do come back to life for a bit," Rothadd observed in fascination, "and then she be gone again. 'Tis too quick to catch 'er."

"We *must* catch her, though. But how? It's plain she doesn't like loud noises—"

"Ah, nay, look closer. 'Tis silence she doesn't like."

"Silence?"

"For certain. When 'ee do roar and bellow, she doesn't twitch an eyelid. 'Tis afterward, when all the blangclather dies off and it be quiet, that she do fret."

"You're right," Zargal said thoughtfully, without taking his eyes off the stone-faced woman. "It's true. Perhaps that's the way to reach her. She must be in a quiet place, with no distractions."

"Happen we pick 'er up and cart 'er out of here, then?"

"Cart her out of here, did you say?" Zargal repeated, inexpressibly shocked. "Cart her out? Have you never heard of lese majesty?"

"Nay. What do that mean?"

"It means that we don't do that to a Queen, not even a deposed one. Why, if we did succeed in rousing her, she'd never forgive the outrage!"

"This be no time to think of that," Rothadd replied a little sullenly. "What else can we do? All that wraith-hissin' a-goin' on in here cuts off flat when 'ee do yell, but 'ee can't keep it up. Where do it all come from, anyways?"

"I don't know, unless this woman is a ventriloquist." Zargal examined Godescalc closely, but she was certainly making no sound. Her jaw hung slack, and the yellowing tongue within her mouth was visible and motionless. Her unseeing stare was aimed at the wall above the fireplace.

Following her gaze, Zargal found himself regarding the dark old portrait of a king clad in the robes of a former age. Something about the painting made Zargal curious, for he almost thought that he had glimpsed movement there.

He looked more closely. It was a wonderful piece of work. The portrait depicted a gray-haired man of middle years. The face was lean and bony, the nose long, and the eyes large, dark, and heavy-lidded. These features reflected intelligence and a kind of amused cynicism. The unknown artist had caught the subtle expression perfectly in the arch of the brow and the set of the lips. The King must have been a lover of colorful dress, for his costume was a splendid affair of maroon brocade, embroidered in elaborate designs. His fingers were adorned with many rings curiously wrought. The face was uncannily lifelike.

Zargal and Godescalc studied it with equal fixedness. Once again Zargal glimpsed motion, and this time knew it was not his imagination. Almost invisible in the dim light, obscured by a layer of cracked, darkened varnish, the lips of the painted King were moving ever so slightly, and a muted whisper issued forth.

"The painting!" Zargal breathed. "The painting speaks!"

"Following the successful war with the Wonials," the King was saying, "peace reigned for the space of two years. Then, in the autumn of the great wind, the Varingians under the leadership of Furni of Gluis rebelled. It thus behooved me, Marnssil of Obran, to gather my men-at-arms, subdue the rebels, and chastise their most traitorous lord. Our forces met upon the field of Lan and fought for three days. Toward sunset of the third day, when the ground underfoot and all about was red with the blood of the slain, I ventured upon my chiefest enemy and engaged him in single combat with sword—"

"Marnssil—a great King of the House of Lodi," Zargal said, recalling his history lessons. "And an ancestor of Godescalc. A talking portrait! So that's where the noise comes from."

"Not all of it," Rothadd said. "Look, here be another!"

He pointed to the painting of a fair young woman with soft eyes and a hard jaw. Her whispering voice was small, and as plaintive as a lost kitten's mew. "I was resolved he should rule me no longer," she was saying. "No more would I endure his insults and excesses. My spirit disdained servitude, and I was determined to be rid of him at any cost. To this end, upon the night of the dark of the moon, did I, Princess Keel of Lodi, place the poison in his cup—"

Rothadd pointed.

"And another—"

"I did not credit the truth of his tale," the very ancient portrait of a plump and shrewd-looking monarch was saying, "but fain would I know if such a thing could be. I bade him show me the contents of his oaken casket, and if it were not as he had promised, then he should die. Before my assembled court, he willingly displayed his discovery—"

"Look—that one be naught but a babe!" Rothadd exclaimed, pointing to the painting of a blond little boy that hung on the opposite wall.

"They locked me in a dark closet," the child whispered, "and told me that if my father the King did not bow to their demands, then he should see me no more—"

From all corners of the room, from the mouths of all the portraits of the royal Lodiae, ancestors of Godescalc, the whispers came. Each had a tale to tell, a fascinating story of the history of the land of Obran and of its formerly great ruling family.

"The armies of Gwiveen had advanced to the very foothills of our mountains. Only the icy weather held them—"

"I, Medgard, ruler of all Obran, swore vengeance upon him and all his kin—"

"He was my master in swordsmanship, yet honor demanded that I challenge him—"

The quiet voices went on and on without pausing. Although they all spoke at once, Zargal soon found that by staring hard at any particular painting, he could hear the voice of that one and no other. The temptation to do so was almost irresistible. Zargal turned his head away with difficulty. Godescalc was still staring at Marnssil.

Rothadd, on the other hand, seemed unable to tear his eyes away from the face of Princess Keel. Zargal placed a large hand on the Outcottager's shoulder, and Rothadd started as if awakening from a dream, then smiled ruefully. "Spellbinding, they do be," he said.

"And Godescalc is spellbound," Zargal replied. "We must silence these pictures, or she'll never listen to us."

"They quiet down for a bit when 'ee do roar," Rothadd observed. "Trouble be, 'ee can't do it for long. Happen they be like woldcocks? 'Ee do fling a clout over their cage, and they drop off to sleep in a wink."

Putting his theory to the test, Rothadd stripped off his cloak and draped it a little reluctantly over the dimpled face of Princess Keel. Her voice was immediately smothered. Godescalc took no notice. "It works!" he exulted, then realized, "But we don't have enough clothes to muffle up the lot of 'em."

"Perhaps if we turn them to the wall—?" Zargal suggested.

As soon as Medgard's face was turned to the wall, he grew quiet. Seeing this, Zargal and Rothadd swiftly circled the room, turning portrait after portrait, and the voices were silenced one by one.

At first Godescalc seemed unaware of what was happening. Then, as more and more of the familiar voices faded away, she grew uneasy and shifted restlessly in her great chair, while her clouded eyes roamed vaguely over the walls. As the room grew quieter, her gaunt white face assumed a confused and troubled expression. Her fingers began to drum on the arms of the chair.

At last only King Marnssil remained visible. The King had reached a most interesting point in his narrative and was describing his own death at the hands of an offended courtesan. The vengeful woman, who possessed some art, had created his image in a distorted mirror, then shattered the glass with dire results. Without pausing to listen, Zargal and Rothadd together turned the painting in its great gilt frame to the wall. The room became silent and remained so.

The effect upon Godescalc was alarming. Her entire frame stiffened spasmodically, her back arched, and she clawed at the arms of her chair. Her head thrashed from side to side, and a high, thin, lost wailing escaped her. Her heels beat a violent tattoo upon the floor.

For a moment Zargal and Rothadd stared, aghast at their handiwork. Then they ran to the side of the stricken sorceress. While Rothadd patted her hand in a feeble attempt to calm her, Zargal stood near, wondering miserably if his meddling had destroyed whatever remnants of reason she had left. But as he watched, Godescalc's convulsions ended, the film seemed to lift from her eyes, and she became conscious of her surroundings.

"Where are they?" she croaked in a voice hoarse with long disuse. "My forefathers, my friends, my people, where are they?" She shuddered once. "Where are they? I demand an answer!" Her voice rose to a shout.

"Peace, madam," Zargal soothed. "All is well. The portraits have been turned to the wall."

Godescalc glanced around the chamber to assure herself that Zargal's words were true. Having thus satisfied herself, she looked briefly at Rothadd, and then her gaze traveled more slowly up Zargal's unnaturally large figure. The great black eyes were growing brighter and keener by the minute. "Did you do it?" she asked.

"We did."

"How dare you? Those portraits are mine. How dare you lay hands upon the royal Lodiae? Answer!"

"We had no choice, your ladyship. There was no other way of catching your attention."

"Out upon you! I want no strangers here to disturb my solitude."

"Like Hincmar, she do sound," Rothadd observed in a low voice.

"My crown, my realm, my glory—all are gone," Godescalc ground out hoarsely, her face contorted, her fingers digging into the arms of her chair. "All has been stripped from me. All! Shall I lose my dignity as well? No one must see me here like this. Leave me!"

"Nay, your Majesty—" Rothadd began. "We did come here—"

"To mock me in my shame?" the woman interrupted half frantically. "To feast your eyes upon the sight of an exiled Queen? Well, look your fill! And may you be accursed for it!" The film had cleared away from the midnight eyes, and they gleamed wildly through the tangled dark locks of her hair.

"Moonstruck, she do be!" Rothadd whispered, very low; but Godescalc heard him.

"Moonstruck?" she repeated with a harsh laugh. "You think me mad? Far better that I were. But no. I see clearly yet—too clearly! The past is with me always."

"It is not of the past that we come to speak with your

ladyship, but rather, of the future—" Zargal commenced artfully, but he did not get far.

"I have no future. My life ended an age ago, upon the night I left my native land. All else is a black void. Godescalc is no more! Only her shadow remains. Look at me! Look at what I have, and think of what I had! Look at what I am, and think of what I was! All is lost. My foes have triumphed and left me in ruins. But Godescalc still has a voice, and though it is not like the voice of Cramarius, she prays that it may yet be heard." She slowly rose from her chair and lifted her clenched hands above her head. "Let not the power of mine enemies protect them from my curses," she entreated whatever dark spirits might serve her, and Zargal felt a chill come over him as he listened. "Give way, dull clouds, to my quick curses! Corruption rot the blood of Cramarius! Decay mar his flesh, twist his bones, make thick his blood! May the power he has usurped utterly destroy him! Horror, rage, and pain haunt his life, attend him at his death, and disturb his rest throughout eternity! In blood is he risen to greatness, and even thus may his poisoned blood torment him! Blood be the instrument of my curse, and let the terror fall on blood of his blood, on flesh of his flesh, until his despair is as mine! May he suffer as I have suffered and know that I am the cause! May he hear my voice mock his greatness!"

Blood was running on her clenched hand. Her fingernails had sunk deep into the palm. The raven voice faltered. Her burst of unnatural energy exhausted, Godescalc tottered forward a few steps, gave a choking cry, and collapsed, apparently unconscious.

For a moment Zargal and Rothadd looked down upon the fallen sorceress. "Gave me gooseflesh to hear her, it did!" Rothadd whispered.

"She's mad, completely mad," Zargal said bitterly. "She can't help us—we have come too late."

The two of them lifted Godescalc back onto her chair, where she reclined without moving. But when at last her eyes opened again, the frenzied gleam had left them. "How did you win past the safeguards that surround me?" she asked dully. "And why have you come?"

"Your safeguards want attention, madam," Zargal informed her. "And luck held with us. As for our reason in coming—it should interest you. We bear a message from King Laza of Obran."

Godescalc's eyes narrowed. "I will hear no word from the Pretender," she snapped, and her nostrils flared slightly as she pronounced the word. "He has usurped my place."

"I hope your Majesty won't bear a grudge," Rothadd began. "The past be dead and gone—"

Godescalc's withered face assumed a ghastly expression, and Zargal quickly cut his friend off short.

"King Laza has not usurped your place, madam. That was the deed of his distant ancestor. On the contrary, King Laza desires to right the wrong that was done you." He spoke quickly and did not waste time in dramatic flourish, for he had no idea how long the sorceress' spell of sanity would last.

"The wrong that was inflicted on me can never be righted! How can your Laza atone for my ruined life, my lost throne, my vanished greatness? Or for all the years— the eternity—of suffering I have endured? Tell me, giant —how can the past be altered, the deed undone?"

"Madam, the King will make full amends—"

"He cannot! Why should he wish to do so?" Godescalc asked with a hint of craftiness. "Am I to believe it is conscience alone that prompts this generosity?" A slight sneer accompanied the question.

"Your ladyship, although your life has been filled with misery, never forget that by your action the existence of Cramarius was equally blighted. So too have been the lives of his sons and a host of his descendants, including that of the present King, and now—of his daughter." The quality of Zargal's voice altered almost imperceptibly, and the sorceress darted a sharp look at him. "The suffering on both sides has continued throughout the centuries," Zargal continued. "You have worn the weary years away, hidden in this swamp. The Varingians upon their throne of gold have watched their sons and daughters sicken and decay. It has all been hopeless and without purpose! But now King Laza seeks to end this useless torment. He wishes to make peace."

Of this entire speech, Godescalc had grasped the one essential point. "He is beaten!" Her exultant cry stabbed the air. "I have prevailed. He is beaten at last!" She lifted her head, smiling. Age and weakness seemed to retreat, leaving her vital and strong and triumphant. "My power has struck at him across time and space, and he is beaten and broken!"

Godescalc sprang from the chair, her movements full of vigor, her bony figure erect. The black eyes were wide and blazing, the lips set in a thin line, the jaw grim. Zargal and Rothadd began to see what the sorceress must have been in the days of her glory. The transformation unsettled them. "The world shall know me once more!"

"Madam," Zargal asked carefully, "will it be possible for you to cure King Laza?"

"Is he past his youth?"

"Yes."

"Then he must remain as he is." Godescalc's teeth showed.

"And his daughter? The illness has come upon her but recently."

"That may be different, if I choose to make it so." She paused, perhaps enjoying the moment, then demanded, "What is the Varingian's offer? There is only one I will accept."

"King Laza awaits your ladyship's decision." Zargal presented the sorceress with the parchment he had carried from Obran.

Godescalc broke the seal, tore the missive open, and scanned the contents. When she came to the end of the document, she whispered feverishly, "My throne! My throne!" She threw her head back and burst into a high-pitched shriek of hysterical laughter. For minute upon minute the shrill sound continued, until the woman was bent over double and clutching her sore sides, but still she did not stop. Her face grew wet with tears. Her breath was coming in gasps. But the mirthless peals went on and on.

It was Rothadd who finally put an end to Godescalc's hilarity. Laying an uncertain hand upon the sorceress' arm, he observed, "Your Majesty, if 'ee be a-comin' back to Obran with us, best we start plannin' out the trip. A weary way back it do be, over the lake, across the Elg, and mile after mile of the Gluis Appli afore we do venture upon the mountains. And *then* 'twill take a mort of time to climb up 'em. Truth is, we'd best make an early start of it in the morning."

At the Outcottager's first words, Godescalc's weird laughter had died away. Now she straightened herself. The marbled hair was streaming over her face, and she flung it back with an impatient hand. "Bah—Godescalc has no need to toil over the face of the earth like a peasant," she declared. "There are other means at her disposal."

"What means, madam?" Zargal asked.

"Ha! I shall tell you. It can do no harm now." A sly smile split her face like a razor slash. "Picture the scene in your mind, giant. The armies of the traitor Cramarius have overcome my forces and driven me back within the very confines of my own castle. It is the dead of night. Within the castle I keep vigil, awaiting the setting of the moon. Without the walls, the troops are thickly clustered, and they, too, are waiting. At the coming of dawn they will storm my stronghold, drag me forth, drive a stake through my heart, and fling my body upon a pyre. They are like nothing so much as a pack of hounds whipped to a rage by the urgings of their master Cramarius. They thirst for my blood, as the guilty must always persecute the innocent whose very existence accuses them. There are thousands out there in the dark, yet they fear my power."

A triumphant expression lighted her eyes. "They are right to fear. Defeated, deserted, and faced with a shameful death at the hands of the traitors, I am Queen Godescalc still. My followers have abandoned me, but I possess servants worth more than men! The moon sets at last, and the night grows dark. Then, mark you, I climb by winding stair up to the roof of the castle. There my chariot awaits —the chariot Vla that I have fashioned with my own hands, whose like the world has never seen. Vla walks the air, and serves Godescalc alone! I enter and make my will known to Vla. She carries me out into the darkness, over the heads of the heavy soldiers of Cramarius. I look down and behold their campfires like a pox upon the mountainside far below me. But the fools never think to look up into the night sky, and I pass unseen beyond their ranks.

"I speak the word, and Vla descends to earth. My escape is certain now, but I have sworn that my enemy's triumph will not be complete. By art, I change my form. I appear as an ancient hag, far older and feebler than you see me now. In such a guise, I approach the soldiers on foot, and I walk among them unrecognized by all. They take me for a harmless almswoman, and I am permitted to draw nigh Cramarius himself.

"He sleeps. Aye, he sleeps!" she whispered, intense as a banked fire. "He alone of all his cohorts sleeps, so confident is he of success! I stand looking down at him as he slumbers, his helm laid by at his side. The false voice that has deceived thousands is stilled, its owner at my mercy. How I long to take dagger and strike him to the heart! But another way is better. Softly I speak the words, and the spell is complete. Soon he will begin to change, but now he sleeps undisturbed.

"I leave him to his victorious dreams and come away. Vla bears me safely to this island, and here I remain, having sown that night a seed of vengeance which never came to full flower—until now."

"So that's how you did it," Zargal said shortly.

" 'Ee did have the power right enough," Rothadd marveled.

"Yes, boy, and I have it still, as you will see. As the Varingian, and all the world besides, will see soon enough," Godescalc responded in a tone of suppressed ferocity. She drew herself up and spoke with authority. "Vla carried me safely upon that night. Upon this one, she carries me back. The two of you will attend me."

"Can your magic wagon still do it, your Majesty?"

"Vla is old, but she will serve. It is for this moment that I have preserved her throughout the centuries—as I have preserved myself. Tonight we return in triumph. Queen Godescalc reclaims her realm!"

Zargal felt a moment's pity for the citizens of Obran. For the first time it occurred to him to wonder if King Laza's decision to abdicate had been the right one. For Bellora, he reminded himself. And yet, what fate would befall the folk of a land governed by a crazed witch?

"We leave at once," Godescalc decreed. "I wish to confront the Varingian. I wish to sit upon my throne."

"Your ladyship is prepared to fulfill your part of the bargain?" Zargal inquired gravely. "You will cure King Laza's daughter and end the curse forever?"

"His daughter? Cramarius' children deserve to suffer—I have! But if the Varingian returns what is mine, then I will cure the girl. Two things will be needed." Godescalc bent her head and thought for a moment. "One is a handful of shernivus leaves—"

Zargal had never heard of shernivus, but Rothadd had. "Shernivus!" the Outcottager cried in distress. "Your Majesty, that can't be! Rarer nor ghroulstones those leaves do be. 'Twould take a year to hunt 'em down, for they grow on the far side of the Sea of Ice."

Zargal said nothing, but simply watched the sorceress. Godescalc listened to Rothadd's outburst with unwonted patience. When he had done, she smiled her razor smile and told him, "Silence, boy. Am I Godescalc for nothing? At the foot of the south tower, my herbs and aromatics flourish. A shernivus bush grows there. You will run and fetch me the leaves."

"Aye?" Rothadd's face cleared. "But 'ee do say 'ee have need of two things to cure the Princess. Shernivus be one. What's t'other, then?"

"The leaves! Fetch them!" She turned on him, and her voice climbed to a hoarse shriek. Rothadd fled the room without another word. "Not you!" Godescalc snapped as Zargal started to follow his friend. "Stay where you are. I will let you know what more is needed to save the Pretender's daughter." She stared into his eyes with a disquieting air of mockery. "I believe you should be told."

CHAPTER XXVII

The moon was high in the sky when Zargal finally emerged from the castle and made his way to the herb garden at the foot of the south tower. The frigid white light bleached and deadened the landscape and lent Zargal's face an extraordinarily pallid, grim look—grimmer by far than it had worn when he had toiled in the kitchens of King Laza. He found Rothadd huddled in a heap on the ground, his face buried in his hands. Zargal advanced to the Out-cottager's side. "What's wrong?" he asked tonelessly.

Rothadd looked up. His eyes were swimming in tears. "Useless, it all be!" he cried. "Everything we've done, all of us that didn't make it here to this place—all of that comes to naught at last! 'Twas useless!"

"What do you mean?"

"That Godescalc—that moonstruck Black One—she has need of the shernivus leaves, but none be here. Happen a bush grew here once, but now 'tis dead and gone, with no way to call it back! Look there—finished it do be, and us along with it!" The tears spilled out of his eyes and slid down his freckled cheeks.

Zargal examined the lifeless garden. No spring growth had appeared as yet. The ground was littered with dead stalks and broken twigs. Even the abundant weeds were colorless and dry. Close beside Rothadd a number of forlorn, broken stumps poked themselves out of the earth. This was all that remained of a bush that had died many years ago. "Would that have been the bush?" he asked, pointing.

"So I think," Rothadd replied, choking back sobs. "What's the difference? It doesn't matter now."

"There's nothing that we might give Godescalc in place of the shernivus? No acceptable substitute?"

"Nay, Zargal, 'ee don't understand. That's not the way it works; it isn't the same as cooking up supper! If she do call for shernivus, then shernivus it must be, or nothin'. And there be none to be had!"

Zargal's face, gray in the moonlight, showed little expression. If anything, he wore the abstracted, analytical look that sometimes came over him at particularly bad moments. "All right," he agreed at last. "Then shernivus it will be. The bush lived and grew here once. Could that spell bring it back?"

"Hincmar's spell, 'ee mean?"

"Yes."

"Happen it might."

"Rothadd, you must use that spell."

"Ah, Zargal, do 'ee think I haven't thought of that myself? Thought of nothin' else since I come out here. All that time 'ee tarried inside—what kept 'ee?"

"The woman had something to say to me. It's not important right now," Zargal answered flatly. "Then you've tried the spell already and failed?"

"Nay." Rothadd shook his head vigorously. "Nay!"

"Why not?"

Rothadd seemed to find it difficult to answer. He stared at the ground for a few seconds before he spoke. "Because it do seem like if I can't do it now, then I never will. Something inside me do cry out that this be the time, if ever. And so—what's to say if I do try, and fail like always? If I leave it alone, at least I can go on a-hopin'."

"I don't know what to say to that," Zargal replied. "What do you think Hincmar would tell you? And King Laza—what would he think of you?"

" 'Ee needn't remind me! But 'tis hard. Magic is all in all

to me! I never did try out Hincmar's spell without a-seein'
myself in my head as a true magician like him! 'Tis like I
watch myself from the outside, a-lookin' to get everythin'
just so, and yet 'tis never right. I couldn't say why."

"Perhaps you should forget about yourself, and keep
your mind fixed on what you're trying to do," Zargal suggested. "Don't watch yourself, don't think of how much
you want to be a magician, don't think of anything in the
world but forcing those plants out of the earth."

"Happen there be something in that," Rothadd admitted.
"But I mislike this business. All afeared I be."

"It's now or never, Rothadd. You must at least try. You
know that. Stand up and try it once more."

Rothadd nodded. He wiped his swollen eyes with his
sleeve and slowly rose to his feet. For a few seconds he
stood in silence, staring down at the broken stumps with a
fanatically determined expression.

Slowly, distinctly, and with every evidence of intense
effort, he repeated the words of Hincmar's incantation,
which he knew by heart. When he had done, he paused,
staring anxiously at the ground. But nothing happened. The
garden remained lifeless, and Rothadd gave a cry of passionate sorrow and vexation. "I knew it!" he exclaimed.
"'Tis always thus, and always will be! Hopeless, 'tis just
hopeless!"

"Try it again."

"Nay! I've done with tryin'! Mule-headed I've been, but
no more! I be finished with it!"

"Try it once more."

"For your Princess Bellora, 'ee mean to say? I can't help
her! I can see in my mind's eye Hincmar and King Laza,
both of 'em a-knowin'—"

"Rothadd, forget about Princess Bellora. Don't give her
another thought. She doesn't really concern you." Rothadd
stared, openmouthed at Zargal's words. "Forget Hincmar
and forget King Laza as well," Zargal went on intently.
"Neither of them matters here and now."

"*What* do 'ee be a-sayin' to me?"

"Forget about yourself, your hopes and dreams and am-
bitions. Forget the pretty idea of being a sorcerer. Think
of the words, Rothadd. Think of nothing but the words.
Fix all your thoughts upon them, and let nothing on earth

distract you! Forget the world and everyone in it. Nothing, *nothing* exists but those words, and the plant life that your will must reawaken."

"King Laza did talk like that, often."

"I do not believe that Hincmar gave you a simple spell, as he claimed. But try it again. Try it one more time."

Once more Rothadd directed his gaze at the ground, which he regarded with all his former determination, and even greater concentration. He did not speak as yet. There was a long pause, and during that pause, Zargal watched Rothadd's face undergo a change. His expression of intense resolution faded. A kind of blankness settled over his features. His wide eyes were fixed unwinkingly upon the bare ground, and it seemed as if he didn't see what was truly there, but something quite different. So obviously was Roth- add watching something that Zargal automatically followed his gaze; but to Zargal's vision, the earth remained barren.

A passing cloud partly obscured the brightness of the moon, and a cold breeze started up. Rothadd didn't notice. The wind ruffled his reddish hair and flung a handful of dust in his face, but he did not feel it. He began to speak in a voice he had never used before—a voice that came from some unexplored region inside him, a voice that King Laza sometimes used. Rothadd repeated the incantation, speaking rather rapidly, but without any obvious strain.

As soon as he had done, a sweet odor filled the sleeping garden—the fragrance of hundreds of different herbs and medicinals. The next moment, the plants began to rise. All around, on every side, feathery gray-green stalks appeared. Emerald shoots sprang out of the ground and burst into bloom. The skeletons of bushes were fleshed out with leaves. And everywhere there was the scent—the scent of herbs that had no business showing their heads above ground for weeks or months to come.

But it was the stump of the shernivus bush that com- manded Zargal's and Rothadd's attention. The dried frag- ments of wood were lengthening and dividing into branches. The branches bore twigs. And from each twig exploded clusters of the rare, arrow-shaped leaves they sought.

"Look!" Zargal cried. "The leaves—as many as we need!"

"Of course," Rothadd answered absently. "Here all the

time, they were, if we'd only been a-lookin'." He seemed slightly dazed.

"Don't you understand what this means? The spell, Rothadd—you've done it! You've finally done it!"

Rothadd began to come to himself. "I can't believe it," he said. "Like I was off in a dream somewhere, it was, with somebody else a-speakin' the words— not me!"

"It was you, all right. I can vouch for that."

"Oh, I can't think I did all of this my own self!" Despite his words, he was obviously starting to believe it, for he radiated joy, and his eyes were as bright as lanterns. " 'Tis true magic right enough. But truth to tell, I scarce minded how I was a-doin' it!"

"Could you do it again?"

"Aye. I think—I think so. I think I be getting the hang of it, at long last. I can't wait to show Hincmar! Be pleased, he will. Aye, and King Laza, too." The mention of King Laza reminded him of the task at hand. "But what be I a-thinkin' of? We can't stand here jawin' all night. Here be the leaves her Majesty asked for. Let's gather 'em in, then pack up the Queen and be on our way. How glad I be that this whole muddle's over at last!"

"Not quite over," Zargal said, almost to himself. Rothadd was triumphantly stripping handfuls of leaves off the shernivus bush and paid him no heed.

Zargal and Rothadd returned to Godescalc's cellar chamber. While they still stood outside in the corridor, they heard the sound of whispering, and both knew what it meant.

"Gemini!" Rothadd breathed. "They be at it again!"

Zargal opened the door and the two of them went in. During their absence, Godescalc had turned several portraits away from the wall. The faces of Keel, Marnssil, and a number of others were again visible, their voices audible. Having related the tale of his own death, Marnssil had gone back to the beginning of his life and was now describing a hunting expedition of his youth. Godescalc was as they had first seen her, remote, unaware, with glassy, staring eyes fixed upon the painted features of her ancestor. King Laza's parchment lay forgotten on the floor beside her.

Zargal looked at her. "The future Queen of Obran," he remarked.

"Well, let's wake 'er up again and be on our way, then," Rothadd advised.

"Rothadd, doesn't this disturb you in the least?"

"Don't what disturb me?"

"This woman here. Look at the thing she has become. Then stop a moment and think—she is to be the ruler of all Obran. The absolute monarch! This poisonous wreck of a human being."

Rothadd's expression was doubtful for a moment, then he brightened. "It won't happen," he said airily.

"What are you talking about? We are making it happen ourselves."

"I know. But 'ee needn't worry. Happen something will turn up. Wait and see."

Zargal regarded his friend in complete amazement. "You don't seem to understand—" he began.

"Oh, Zargal, always a-lookin' on the black side of things 'ee be! 'Twill all sort itself out in the end. 'Ee'll see. Now, oughtn't we be a-wakin' up this Queen?" Rothadd spoke with a cheerfully businesslike air.

Zargal decided that it was pointless to argue with him. He nodded briefly, and the two of them went to work. Within seconds they had once more silenced the paintings. The effect upon Godescalc was not as violent as it had been the first time. She trembled, uttered two or three low moans, and returned to her senses.

Zargal stooped and handed her back the neglected parchment with a curt bow. "Yours, madam," he reminded her. She fingered the creases, and a tight-lipped smile curved her mouth.

"Well, your Majesty," Rothadd urged as soon as the sorceress had recovered herself, "we've got the shernivus right enough, so we'd best be a-leavin', then. Where be your flying chariot 'ee did speak of?"

Godescalc rose from her chair and drew herself up to her full height. "Vla awaits," she told them, the archaic flavor of her speech more pronounced than ever. "She has waited for centuries to bear me forth from this house of degradation, to bring me back to what is mine. But I will not go alone."

"Nay, your Majesty, 'ee needn't fear, we be a-comin' with 'ee—"

"I shall be accompanied," Godescalc continued as if he had not spoken, "by my friends, the companions of my solitude."

Rothadd looked blank, but Zargal inquired, "The portraits, madam?"

"That is my will, giant."

"I urge you to reconsider. In my opinion—"

"Enough!" Her enraged shriek cut him off in mid-sentence. "The faces and voices are mine! I desire them, and I will have them!"

Zargal inclined his head. "We are at your ladyship's service," he said coldly.

Godescalc meant to have them all. It was with some difficulty that Zargal and Rothadd managed to convince her that this would not be practical. In the end, after a long argument, it was agreed that the portraits of Marnssil, Medgard, Keel, and three others should return to Obran. The rest would be left behind, and Godescalc would send for them later. "As they have shared in my misery, so shall they share in my glory," she decreed. As if drawn by a force she could not resist, she turned Marnssil's face to the light.

"The four of us pursued the wounded tebel along the passages of the cavern," Marnssil whispered, "but it eluded us. By means of its secret knowledge, it hid itself away in crevices where no man could follow, and there it died."

Godescalc was starting to slip away into a trance. Zargal lifted the painting off its hook and set it face down on the floor. The sorceress was alert again at once. "The others," she rasped. "They must not be left behind."

Zargal and Rothadd obediently gathered together the other five designated portraits. "It is well," the sorceress approved. "We will leave immediately."

Rothadd nodded cheerily, but Zargal was stunned at the suddenness of it all. "Has your ladyship no further preparations to make?" he inquired carefully.

"I have been prepared for a dozen lifetimes!"

"The journey is likely to be a long one, and—"

"The journey will be brief. We shall be there this very night."

"Perhaps you should rest before we——"

"Silence!" The sorceress looked as if she might be about to relapse into another crazy rage. "I am leaving at once. The faces come with me. If you would come as well, you have my leave. But I will not stay to argue with you." Without another word, she snatched up an ancient lantern from the corner, lit it, and stalked out of the room, leaving Zargal and Rothadd to stare after her in consternation.

"Well, now. A hot-headed one she be," Rothadd observed at last. "She didn't even think to ask us if we'd like somewhat to eat after we did come all this way!"

Zargal didn't reply. It pained him to realize to what extent the subject of food occupied his thoughts. Even in the midst of all his troubles and worries, he remained as indecently hungry as ever.

Rothadd was already moving toward the door. "Wait a moment," Zargal told him. "We'd better bring these paintings along."

"Oh, aye! She won't stir a step without 'em."

The two of them quickly gathered up the portraits and hurried out of the room in the wake of the retreating sorceress.

CHAPTER XXVIII

⌒

Godescalc was not far ahead. They could easily see the lantern swinging in her hand as she advanced along the pitchy corridor. Zargal and Rothadd stumbled and faltered beneath the burden of the portraits in their ornate frames. Godescalc never hesitated, but led them up out of the cellar, through the silent chambers, up more stairs, through a dangerously narrow passage, and then up still more stairs —ancient wooden ones that groaned and protested beneath their feet.

At last she reached the top and threw open a small door. Moonlight came rushing down the stairs in a white flood. Zargal looked up to behold Godescalc's bony figure poised above him, a black silhouette against the sky. Her head was thrown back, her gaunt arms outstretched to embrace the night. Then she was gone through the open door, leaving them to follow as best they could. Zargal and Rothadd struggled up the remaining stairs and out onto the tower roof. There, dark in the moonlight, was Godescalc, and next to her was Vla.

Vla was massive, venerable, and crumbling. Her great body, hollowed out to accommodate five or six passengers, sagged with age, for the timbers were split and rotted. The gilding had peeled from her carved scales, and the tip of one broad wing was completely broken off. The heavy legs were worm-eaten. The tail was chipped and marred. But Vla's magnificent head was still intact. The snarling jaws and wrinkled lips, the silver fangs, were untouched by time. The eyes, red jewels set in spheres of milky glass, still shone as fiercely as ever beneath their jutting brows.

Godescalc was crooning to the chariot, murmuring love words in a voice softer and more gentle than anyone could have dreamed she possessed. She ran a caressing hand over the arched neck and pressed her cheek against the scarred surface. Zargal and Rothadd stood watching in silence. As soon as Godescalc remembered their presence, she straightened up and glared.

Rothadd was inspecting the chariot with great interest. "A beauty she do be," he remarked. "And an old one."

"But still good!" the sorceress snapped.

"Happen she can't take the mountains?"

"She can."

" 'Tis like she doesn't have the power she once had."

"No more!" the sorceress commanded. "Vla bears Godescalc in triumph to the throne. If you are fearful, then stay behind. If you come, then have done with complaints and trouble me no more." The Outcottager subsided. "Attend to the faces," Godescalc ordered.

Rothadd obediently placed three of the portraits on the floor inside the chariot. Zargal had already packed the other three. "Now," Godescalc said. Without waiting for assistance, she took an amazingly agile step up onto Vla's drooping wing, made her way expertly along it to the shoulder, and from there allowed herself to drop down into the body of the chariot. She assumed a position near the front and remained standing. "Enter. I will brook no further delay," she warned irritably.

Zargal and Rothadd followed the sorceress, one at a time. Zargal heard an alarming creak as he stepped up onto Vla's wing. The sound grew louder with each step he took, and he wondered what Godescalc's reaction would be if the brittle old wood should break beneath his great weight. No such mishap occurred, however. The chariot withstood the strain, and Zargal descended into the body cavity as lightly as he could.

Rothadd came next. As he stepped down from the wing to enter, he laid his hand upon Vla's peeling scales, then snatched it away again. His palm was riddled with splinters. At the sight, Godescalc gave a dry chuckle. "Vla loves not strangers," she said.

Rothadd shrugged. "What now?" he asked.

Godescalc didn't reply. Instead, she leaned far forward and whispered in Vla's ear. In the deceptive moonlight, Zargal thought he saw the wooden creature's ears twitch slightly at the sound. Godescalc spoke again. Her voice was too low for the words to be overheard, but the tone was loving, almost maternal.

Old as she was, Vla responded to it, and a slight vibration rocked her. Then she began to shake. Her joints screamed and her timbers groaned. The loose paint flaked off her sides and drifted down in clouds as the violence of her movements increased. Zargal was finding it hard to keep his balance. He lowered himself to a sitting position, braced himself firmly, and watched. Rothadd remained standing, clutching for support at the side of the chariot.

Godescalc paid no attention to either of them. Her arms were wrapped tightly around Vla's neck as she leaned forward and whispered into the pointed ears. With her gaunt, bent figure and long black garments, the sorceress resembled some vampire attached to the throat of its victim. But no vampire ever wore such a loving aspect.

Zargal had thought he was prepared, but was nonetheless amazed as the shuddering, creaking chariot slowly lifted itself from the castle roof. It did not move with the swift power of King Laza's sleigh. Vla hauled herself painfully into the air like a cripple attempting to run uphill. Her entire frame was vibrating, and the rattle and clatter she produced as she went was truly unnerving. Rothadd lost his footing and sat down suddenly. Godescalc straightened up. A thin shriek of triumph escaped her, and then one of her nerve-ripping laughs.

The rooftop receded slowly, and then more rapidly as the chariot picked up speed. Zargal could see the entire island and the lake below, gleaming coldly in the moonlight. On the far shore, the black, dense mass of the Elg began. And somewhere off beyond that, lost in the darkness, the long

Gluis Appli sloped up to the first foothills of the mountains of Obran. But could they ever reach Obran?

Vla was traveling more swiftly with each passing moment. She could never come close to matching the speed of King Laza's sleigh, but she possessed an immense advantage. Because she flew through the air and did not cling to the mountains and valleys of the earth, the distance Vla had to cover was much less, and no obstacles hindered her progress.

The chariot, however, had grown feeble with age, and the effort of flying for the first time in centuries was almost beyond her strength. The unaccustomed weight of three passengers, one of them enormous, was nearly too much for her, and Zargal found himself waiting for them all to fall out of the sky. From time to time Vla took a steep downward plunge, and Zargal imagined that the end had come. But each time Vla recovered herself and labored on through the night.

They soared unsteadily over the dark Elg. Overhead, the stars burned, and the air was cold and dry. The only sounds to be heard were the whistle of the wind and the agonized creak of wooden joints.

Godescalc stood up front, behind Vla's head. Her own head was held high, her eyes fixed on the dark horizon, her lips parted in a smile of pure exhilaration. The loose black garments that she wore had caught the wind and spread like vast raven's wings. Her long hair streamed out wildly behind her. For no apparent reason, she lifted her face to the moon, and the heavens resounded with her lunatic laughter.

Zargal and Rothadd were both seated on the bare floor of the chariot. For the first hour or so of the flight Rothadd kept up a steady flow of conversation. Zargal sat with his arms folded over his bent knees, trying to move as little as possible, for each time he stirred, Vla faltered and lost altitude. He said nothing, and his eyes, which remained fixed on Godescalc, were unreadable. Rothadd finally gave up talking and turned his attention to the earth and sky.

Hours passed, and the scenery beneath them changed with amazing speed. The Elg was gone, and they were skimming over the Gluis Appli. It was impossible to mistake that endless, featureless, slanting terrain. Rothadd soon sank into slumber. Godescalc alone remained on her feet, hands clenched at her sides, hair whipping in the wind, as Vla groaned on toward the north.

Vla managed to clear the low foothills successfully. It was when she came upon the mountains of Obran that her troubles really began. Zargal opened his eyes and forgot about trying to sleep when the chariot started to wobble like a drunken aerialist. He looked down and beheld the snow-covered slopes only a few feet below. The air had grown much colder. In Obran, winter still held sway.

Rothadd was on his feet again, clutching the side of the chariot and peering down at the snowy rocks and chasms. The Outcottager was shivering, as much with excitement and tension as with the cold. "I do fear she can't make it!" he cried. Godescalc shot him a venomous glare.

As if she heard and understood, Vla gave a kind of a hitch, which all three passengers could feel. With a great moan of tortured old timber, she dragged herself a bit higher into the air, and her speed picked up slightly. Pitching and heaving violently, she struggled on her way.

"What will happen to the three of us if she do go down?" Rothadd asked.

"Quiet, you fool!" Godescalc snarled in reply. "I tell you she still has power!"

"Aye, but do she have enough?"

It was a sensible question. There could be no doubting Vla's gallantry, but the ancient chariot should never have been called upon for a journey so taxing. Now she was sinking again, just barely clearing the peaks over which she had soared without effort in the days of her youth. As she jerked and strained, there came a crackling noise, and part of her left wing broke off and fell.

A short time later, when Vla lumbered over a group of trees and the bare branches loudly raked her belly, Zargal could not help flinching at the sound. His slight movement was enough to set the chariot to shuddering, and Godescalc turned on him in a fury.

"You are the cause of our troubles!" she screeched. "You hulking prodigy, your weight must be twice that of a normal man! How can my Vla be expected to bear such a monster? But that can be remedied." Her eyes narrowed.

"I have but to speak the word, and you are flung from this chariot, leaving us free to fly."

Rothadd was alarmed. "Here, now," he appealed to her nervously. "Here, now—there be no need for that. If the load be too heavy, 'twould be a good thing to take these old pictures and heave 'em overboard—"

"Plague take you!" Godescalc screamed, her face distorted. Then, with a great effort, she managed to control herself. "If it should ever come to a choice between your death by slow torture and the loss of a single fleck of color from one image, your life would not be worth a fistful of cold ashes."

"I do hear 'ee," Rothadd replied, setting his chin. "But there be no cause for 'ee to talk so—"

"Perhaps your discussion might best be postponed," Zargal suggested politely. "I think this chariot is about to crash into the rocks."

Godescalc and Rothadd stopped quarreling. Vla was swooping low over the frozen ground. Only a few hundred yards ahead, a cliff rose straight and sheer. If Vla maintained her present course, she would inevitably smash herself and her cargo upon the stone. The chariot wavered up and down, as if attempting to rise, but the strength wasn't in her. A broad fissure opened up in one wing, running from tip to shoulder.

"She can't do it," Zargal said. "You must bring her to earth."

"She can do it," Godescalc insisted. "She *will* do it. She will take these mountains, else we'll all perish here together!"

Vla grazed an outcropping of stone, and the collision cost her a couple of claws from her left forefoot. She rattled pathetically, sank nearer the ground, but continued her rush at the looming cliff.

" 'Ee must stop this!" Rothadd cried.

"Silence, you craven!" the sorceress commanded. "If Vla dies, so do we all!"

Zargal eyed the fast-approaching stone wall. "We'll have to jump for it," he decided. He glanced briefly at Godescalc. "We'll take her with us, whether she likes it or not. We still need her for Bellora."

"Aye." Rothadd took a step toward Godescalc. Zargal gathered himself for a spring.

"When I give the word—" Zargal said. Vla blundered helplessly on toward the rocks.

"Keep away from me!" Godescalc shrank back as far from Zargal and Rothadd as she could. "Stay back! Dare to lay hands upon me, stir an inch, and I will call down lightning from the heavens to blast us in midair!"

"What would you have, madam?" Zargal cried. "We'll all be dashed to pieces against the cliff!"

"Not so, for Vla will prevail! Watch her—watch!" Once more the woman leaned forward and whispered urgently into Vla's ear. Her hair lay like a cloak over the wooden neck, her cheek was pressed hard to the sculptured scales, and her words were inaudible to her human companions. But Vla heard, and was inspired to one final effort. With a last burst of desperate energy, she took a giant leap up into the air, struggled higher, sank a trifle, and then just barely managed to reach the top of the cliff, where she alighted for a moment, exhausted. "You see," Godescalc whispered. "You see."

The stars had faded, and the sky in the east was starting to pale. It would soon be dawn. Far away, at the top of one of the highest mountains, the three voyagers could see a group of tiny orange lights, perhaps six or eight of them.

"What do that be?" Rothadd asked.

"It must be close to King Laza's castle," Zargal said. "Perhaps he's lit bonfires to guide us back."

"We need no fires—Vla knows the way. She can never forget," Godescalc said. Now that the immediate danger was over, she looked calmer, but her breath was ragged, and the black eyes still burned feverishly.

No spoken command was needed to set the chariot in motion once again. For a few seconds Vla rumbled along over the surface of the ground and then, as the mountain sloped sharply away beneath her, bravely flung herself into space and headed out toward the cluster of orange lights. Her brief rest had served her well, and there were no more obstacles rearing themselves between Vla and the beckoning lights. There was nothing to cross but miles of empty air, but it took her a long time, for Vla's speed and altitude were steadily decreasing as she went.

Hours passed, and the blackness of night gave way to the iron-gray dawn of a cloudy day. As the light grew stronger, Vla's three passengers were able to discern King Laza's castle ahead, with fires burning atop all eight towers of the Crown. Godescalc's intense gaze shifted from the castle to the ground below. Zargal's eyes were fixed upon the castle. And Rothadd was staring worriedly at the cracks and new fissures that had opened up in Vla's great wings.

Vla's power was all but spent. As she sailed in low over the castle, she suddenly plunged into a steep, sharp dive. Her speed increased tremendously, and the passengers realized that Vla was falling rather than flying.

"On, my beauty!" Godescalc shrieked to her chariot in mad exultation. "Courage, my lovely!"

The ground came leaping up to meet them. The speed of their descent was not even slightly abated as Vla's tail scraped over the castle wall. A split second later she struck the earth with a violent shock. The passengers were badly jarred, but unharmed. But Vla's condition was far different. All four of her legs and one wing had broken off short. There was a gaping hole torn in her belly. One of the glass-and-jeweled eyes had popped out of its socket and shattered on the ground beside her, and the long neck had been knocked out of alignment with the body. Brave Vla had finished her last journey.

CHAPTER XXIX

Godescalc was out of the chariot in a flash. There were tears in her eyes as she regarded the ruined chariot. "So you have come home only to die," she mused aloud. "But rest assured, my Vla, you will be avenged. This is yet another item added to the account. He will pay."

"Your Majesty," Rothadd ventured, " 'tisn't like she were a real livin' creature—"

Godescalc's midnight eyes lifted to his. "You know nothing," she told him, and turned away. "The two of you bring the faces. A place of honor awaits them in my house." She stalked toward the door of the castle. Zargal and Rothadd alighted from the chariot and followed, bearing the portraits.

The three of them walked into the great entrance hall of King Laza's silent castle, and the first person they encountered was Master Guggard. The major-domo, attired in his handsome livery, looked much the same as ever. At the sight of Zargal he stopped dead, and his sallow face reddened. "*You!*" Guggard exclaimed accusingly. "What are *you* doing here?"

"We've come back—" Zargal began.

"I can see perfectly well that you've come back! Let me

ask you one thing, boy. Just what makes you think you can leave this place whenever you please and then come wandering back in when you feel like it? Just what makes you think that?"

"Here, now," Rothadd protested. " 'Ee don't know what we've been doin'—"

"Oh, I can guess what you've been doing! Gadding about the countryside, like as not. Why, *look* at the two of you, the condition you're in—unkempt, bedraggled, and filthy, absolutely filthy! That was a brand-new set of livery, boy," he told Zargal, "and just look at it now! Ruined, completely ruined, and half of it missing! I suppose you gambled away your clothes?"

"Did no one ever tell you," Zargal inquired, "where we were going and why?"

"I did not trouble to inquire," Guggard returned disdainfully. He cracked his knuckles at them.

"And Vaxil, he didn't tell 'ee?" Rothadd asked.

"Oh, don't talk to me of Vaxil, that slacker! The day you left, he finally put the finishing touches on his precious veal stock. But that evening, his Majesty Laza refused to dine. Vaxil took to his bed, claiming illness, and he's remained there ever since." Guggard returned to the subject at hand. "You have not yet explained your behavior to my satisfaction. How dare you run away? And how dare you bring your disreputable cohorts here to his Majesty's palace? *Who* is this woman? Some Turo fortune-teller?"

"The lady has come at the invitation of King Laza," Zargal said. "Please be so good as to inform his Majesty of her arrival."

"His Majesty is in the northern tower and does not wish to be disturbed. In any case, do you imagine that I'd trouble him with news of every beggar or vagabond arriving at his gates? If this woman wants a meal, you have my permission to take her down to the kitchen."

For the first time since she had entered the castle, Godescalc's black gaze came to rest on Master Guggard, and before it the major-domo shrank back in sudden fear. "Who are you, woman?" he asked shakily.

"Fetch the Varingian here to me," the sorceress rasped.

Guggard's face paled to light yellow. "This is your

doing," he accused Zargal in a faint voice. "I hope his Majesty will follow my advice and never take you back!"

"The Varingian—summon him!" Godescalc commanded.

"There's no need, Guggard." King Laza spoke from his wheeled chair, which had appeared in one of the doorways, unnoticed by all. Bibka stood at his side. "I am here."

Guggard turned gratefully to the King. "Oh, your Majesty," he babbled, "thank goodness you've come! These people here—this—this *woman* here—"

"It's all right, Guggard," King Laza broke in gently. Bibka drew him forward. "You may go now."

With one last, frightened glance at the sorceress, Master Guggard scurried out of the hall.

For a moment King Laza and Queen Godescalc studied each other in intent silence. Finally Laza spoke. "Madam, I bid you welcome to Obran."

"Laza, you are the true descendant of Cramarius," Godescalc said. "I see it in your face." Zargal was certain that she was about to start laughing again, but she restrained herself. "You speak as falsely as ever he did. Varingian, you do not welcome me."

"Madam, you mistake me," the King assured her with formal courtesy. "I have long awaited your coming."

"You beg my aid now because you have been left with no other recourse. Beyond that, you would gladly see me dead."

"I have invited you back to your home and your throne."

"Because the power of my curse has prevailed. Because you need me to undo the work that has destroyed you and all your line." Her hatred was poisoning her hoarse voice. "You cannot deny it. And now I have come and I will be Queen again."

"So you shall, if you will only make my daughter well," King Laza conceded. "Can you do so?"

"If I choose."

"Then madam, let there be peace between our two Houses."

"There will be peace," Godescalc consented, smiling strangely. "And there will be justice. At last there will be justice."

King Laza regarded her consideringly from beneath the shadow of his hat. Bibka hissed quietly beside him. Zargal and Rothadd watched raptly. Godescalc was staring off beyond them all, lost in visions of the future. Her spine was straight, her carriage regal. All at once she turned back to King Laza and exclaimed unexpectedly, "My chariot, my Vla, has been destroyed. I hold you responsible, Cramarius, for I know you hated her as you hated me!"

Zargal stiffened, and Rothadd jumped visibly, but a quick gesture from King Laza silenced them. "May we speak of the chariot another time?" he suggested. "It is my daughter who requires immediate attention. Will you go to her?"

"Softly, Varingian." Godescalc spoke with a touch of hateful amusement. "Tarry a little. What provisions have been made for my restoration to the throne? When shall I be crowned?"

"As soon as my daughter is cured, madam, I shall affix my seal to a formal declaration of abdication. The news will be carried by messenger to all corners of Obran."

"And my coronation? The robes, the crown, the royal orb and scepter? The cheering crowds, the triumphant hymns? When will they be mine?"

"That will be as your ladyship pleases. Will you come to the Princess now?" A note of strain crept into King Laza's hitherto expressionless voice.

"Tarry, you. Your girl can wait. I have waited, and I will not be hurried now. Will you set me to work in such haste, without offer of rest and refreshment, when I have come so far? Is this the hospitality afforded a Queen in her own house? Know, Laza, that I am royal, and I will be treated in royal state!"

"I entreat you, madam, the Princess' condition is desperate—" The King's misshapen hands were twisted upon the arms of his chair.

"Aye, you may entreat how you can, and yet she will wait! She will wait while I rest me in my own chamber, as of old. She will wait until I have enjoyed the banquet that you will prepare in my honor this evening. She will wait until I have supped off my golden plates, sampled the finest wines, and listened to the music. She will wait through all this, and then—then we shall see. For that is what I desire, and I am ruler here. I will have it!"

Zargal had never felt so strong an urge to strike a woman, but he did not give way to it. King Laza similarly controlled himself and inclined his head. "As you wish," he conceded in an ominously mild voice.

Godescalc subsided from full rant to relative quiet. "What a glorious thing is sovereignty," she reflected, and moved toward the wide staircase. "I retire to my own chamber. You will summon me when the banquet is prepared." Godescalc paused, one foot on the first step, and turned back to regard her portraits. "The faces must come with me. Order your giant and your clown to bring them." She ascended, leaving Zargal, Rothadd, and King Laza behind.

"Zargal, Rothadd, I'm pleased at your safe return." King Laza spoke hurriedly. "But the others?"

"Sa Relmer was kidnapped. Emce-Slatermul is dead. Sa Wenilow's vanished. Paskha is well, but could not come back with us," Zargal told him, and then burst out, "Sire, that woman is not fit to rule!"

"I have made the offer and I cannot retract," Laza said.

"It's not fair to your people!" Zargal argued. "You cannot place such a woman on the throne! What of your subjects?"

"And what of my daughter?"

Zargal was silent.

"Through all of this," Rothadd said, " 'twas sort of spinnin' 'round at the back of my mind that when we did get back here, 'ee'd do somewhat, King, and 'twould all end well. Will 'ee not?"

"What would you counsel, gentlemen? I'm curious," the King said, with a touch of his old sarcasm.

"Force her to cure the Princess," Zargal suggested at once. "She's here in your power, isn't she?"

"And I have promised to do her no violence. If I break my oaths, am I much more fit to rule than she?"

"But there must be some way——"

"We'll speak of this later." Laza cut the discussion off short. "The Lady Godescalc desires her property at once, and I think it would be best to humor her. What has she brought?" Bibka was nosing curiously at the portraits.

"Talking pictures they do be," Rothadd explained. "Kings and Queens and other royal folk a-tellin' tales of their lives of long ago." To illustrate, he reversed the portraits of Medgard and Keel.

King Laza listened for a time, then turned his head away. "Very interesting," he said, "but it would be unwise to listen to them too long. They are the finest of their kind I've ever seen, and therefore the most dangerous. Cover them up and take them to Godescalc. You'll find her upstairs. I shall see you again when we dine. In the meantime, I must think." Without awaiting a reply, Laza made a sign to Bibka, and the chair rolled swiftly away.

Zargal and Rothadd gathered up the paintings and trudged wearily up the stairs in search of Godescalc.

Dinner that evening was elaborate, but hardly festive. Godescalc had demanded a banquet, and Vaxil rose magnificently to the challenge. The chef abandoned his sickbed and labored throughout the day to produce a meal of nine splendid courses. During the meal, King Laza's four lackeys stood apart, playing softly upon their kleveens. Master Guggard attended to the serving, a task he performed with great style.

The ancient and massive set of golden plates, cutlery, and serving dishes had been taken from the castle treasure vaults and put to use for the first time in decades. Godescalc was seated at the head of the table. King Laza sat far off at the other end, with Bibka coiled beneath his chair. Zargal and Rothadd were on either side of the long table, near the middle, with an immense centerpiece placed squarely between them.

The air in the banqueting hall was cold and somewhat musty, for the room had been shut up for years. The old tapestries and hangings were threadbare and torn. A number of brocaded chairs showed signs of mildew. Godescalc did not seem to note the deficiencies. Her tangled hair fell all the way down to the floor, her black robes were rusty and shapeless, but she glittered with a fortune in jewels—the spoils of the royal treasury, which she had insisted must ornament her triumph. A dreaming smile softened her face as she sipped her pale wine.

There was not much conversation at first, for no one knew quite what to say. The four of them sat in the great banqueting hall, separated by the length and breadth of the huge mahogany table, and listened to the music play. Zargal, Rothadd, and Godescalc did full justice to Vaxil's creations. Zargal in particular devoured everything in sight as if it were to be his last meal. King Laza sat toying with a cup of bouillon.

But when at last the hors d'oeuvres had been disposed of, the King asked to hear the tale of the journey to God-escalc's island. Zargal and Rothadd described it all, from the meeting with the Turos and the theft of the sleigh to Rothadd's summoning of the plants. In return, King Laza told of the return of the sleigh, bearing the Marquis sa Relmer and the larcenous Turos, the sentencing of the Turos to sixty days imprisonment, and the subsequent escape of the entire band. He did not speak of Bellora.

Hours passed. The candles burned low, the musicians tired, and, one by one, the various dishes were consumed. During this time, Godescalc remained silent, ate her dinner, drank much wine, and listened closely. When she heard the tale of Crumer Paskha and the pool of prophecy, she smiled. When she learned of Emce-Slatermul's encounter with the slatkus, her laughter crackled, but she offered no comment. At last, however, when the tales were all told, Godescalc finally spoke. Her manner was calm, but the rigid set of her neck and shoulders boded ill.

"You have spoken of your journey from the mountains to my island," she said to Zargal, "but you have not told of the return."

"Madam?"

"No," Godescalc continued, "you have not seen fit to speak of the death of Vla, my beautiful Vla. Is it, then, a matter of such small importance?"

Her voice was still steady, but her fingers were starting to twitch a little. Zargal noted the signs and braced himself. "We deeply regret the loss of your chariot—" he began.

"You regret? My Vla is dead—*dead*, mark you—and you merely regret, giant?"

"Perhaps the chariot may be repaired, madam," King Laza suggested.

"Repaired? Never. What's finished is finished," Godescalc said. She turned suddenly on the King. "No doubt that pleases you, Varingian."

"On the contrary, I admired your chariot. I could not rejoice in the destruction of so fine a piece of work."

"You lie!" Godescalc slammed two fists down upon the

table so hard that the dishes in her vicinity jumped. "You lie, Cramarius! Do you think I don't know how you hated my Vla? Now you have watched her die, and you are glad. I see it in your eyes!" King Laza regarded her, completely unmoved. Beneath his chair, Bibka stirred and hissed. "You hated Vla and you hated me," Godescalc continued, "but your malice has availed you nothing. I have returned, and I am here to stay."

"No one disputes that, madam," the King assured her with icy courtesy.

"Yes, now that I am once again Queen, there will be no more revolts, no unrest, no plotting against me. I shall see to that. Oh, believe me, I shall see to that." She took a stranglehold on the stem of her wine goblet. "There shall be no conspiracies, I say. Never again."

Zargal and Rothadd were regarding her in fascinated disbelief. "I hope that your ladyship will have no cause to doubt the loyalty of your subjects," King Laza said.

"Do you, Varingian? Do you truly?" She laughed jarringly, her eyes wild.

"I pray that your reign will be such that your people will have every reason to love their Queen."

"To love me? Oh, you hypocrite!" she exclaimed. "You wish me naught but ill—I know it well!" She shut her eyes and pressed her fingers to her brow as if distracted. "My people love me? Love me? Well, and why not? Why should not subjects love their rightful Queen? Aye, and so they may, if their minds be not poisoned against me." She opened her eyes again and glared at the impassive King. "I know you. I can divine your hopes and your schemes. You think to rouse my subjects to revolt, as your forefathers did before you—I see it all! Well, look not for it! I am not such a fool as that. I know well how to deal with you and yours."

"I do not understand you, madam," the King said.

"Do you not? Then know, Varingian, that I do not cherish weeds in my garden. You will not remain in Obran to spread unrest and discontent. You will not win my people to your cause! I shall cure your daughter and lift the curse—but after that, you and all of your line will be banished forever from my mountains!"

A gasp of dismay escaped Rothadd at this announcement, but King Laza showed no sign of emotion. Bibka

slithered forth from beneath the chair. Her eyes, glowing
like molten steel, were fixed on Godescalc. Laza ordered
the slatku back again. "I expected as much," he said.

"But this here be King Laza's home—" Rothadd began.

"It is *my* home! Mine! Long before Cramarius ever
came, it was mine! And now the Varingians in their
treachery will pollute my House and my kingdom no
longer!"

Rothadd was looking horrified. King Laza's face was, as
usual, nearly lost in the shadow of his hat brim. "We shall
leave willingly," he promised.

"Once the weed has been cut, its roots must be torn
from the earth," Godescalc declared, her face sinister in
the candlelight. "I shall hunt down and deal with all sup-
porters of the House of Varingia. The evil must be purged
from the land. I will make my realm clean again."

"What does your ladyship intend?" the King inquired
expressionlessly.

"That need not concern you," Godescalc replied. "You
will not be here."

"As you wish. When my daughter is well, I will take her
and go."

"Not so fast," the sorceress said. "I must think about
that."

"Madam?" King Laza prompted, a slight hesitation be-
traying his surprise.

"It would not do to allow you to take refuge on foreign
soil and there gather mine enemies about you to kindle
revolution. I'll prevent that, Varingian. Therefore, it may
be my will that you go, while the girl remains here with
me as my perpetual guest. I must think on it."

Zargal blanched horribly. Rothadd's jaw dropped. King
Laza appeared to be studying the minced herbs in his cup
of bouillon with concentrated attention. For a while there
was complete silence in the room, until at last King Laza
spoke in a mild and thoughtful manner. "Your ladyship
will have time to ponder that question at leisure once my
daughter has been cured," he remarked. "Perhaps we
might begin assembling the materials that your ladyship
will require."

Godescalc leaned back in her chair. "I'll need but two
things," she said. "One is a boiled poultice of the shernivus

leaves which this farmer's boy has brought from my garden. As for the other—as for the other—" Her eyes lit and she smiled slyly. "The giant will speak of it. I think it best that he tell you."

All eyes turned to Zargal, who had been sitting silently.

Zargal directed a level gaze at King Laza and disclosed the secret he had carried from the island. "The Lady Godescalc has informed me," he said, "that the blood of Cramarius' descendants has been poisoned. In order to cure Princess Bellora, her diseased blood must be drained away and entirely replaced with the blood of a healthy human being. It may come from a man or woman, but it must all come from a single person."

"One person," Godescalc emphasized as she watched King Laza's face. King Laza stared back at her with equal intensity.

"I have offered to supply the Princess with the necessary blood," Zargal said. "Since time is of the essence, I'm certain no one will question the decision. Therefore, there's no more to be said, and we may begin the operation immediately." He finished hurriedly, obviously hoping to forestall an argument.

Rothadd shook his head. "Nay," he said. "If the Queen here do take your blood to fill up the Princess with, then there won't be none left for *you*. Don't 'ee see that?" Zargal didn't answer, and Rothadd looked at him, stricken. "'Ee can't mean it," he breathed. "'Twill kill 'ee, it will! Zargal!"

"Can't be helped," Zargal said.

"Moonstruck, 'ee do be! 'Twill never do! There must be some other way!"

"There is not," Godescalc informed him, without regret. "If the curse is to be broken, then the Varingian woman's blood must be replaced—all her blood. You know the consequences of that. But it is *your* choice, Laza. Will you watch your daughter sicken and change? Or will you slay this brave young man who has already chanced his life in your service? I offer you free choice. But choose quickly." She had something of the look of a bird of prey as she regarded King Laza. She seemed stronger and saner than she had ever been since they first encountered her.

"King, 'ee can't let this happen! 'Ee must *do* somewhat!" Rothadd cried. "King!"

"Your Majesty has very little choice," Zargal said steadily. "The curse must be ended, else the members of your family will go on suffering forever, and you cannot allow that. Moreover, I'm eager to do this thing for the Princess, for reasons that you already know. I make the offer gladly, and you are bound by loyalty to your House to accept."

"What is your decision?" Godescalc demanded of King Laza.

" 'Ee can't mean to kill Zargal!" Rothadd cried out in a panic. "King, how can 'ee think it?"

"Sire, you are in a difficult position," Zargal observed, pale yet quite calm. "But there is only one way to save your daughter, and you must take it."

"Ah, nay—"

"What is your answer?" asked Godescalc, who was watching King Laza with merciless enjoyment. "Come, is it so difficult a question? At least you have a choice. *I* had none when I was driven from my home!"

King Laza was silent and motionless for a time. He sat with his head bent, his bloodshot eyes fixed upon the floor. No one could guess what thoughts were passing through his mind, but the grip of his misshapen hands upon the arms of the chair indicated they were not tranquil ones.

"Your answer?" Godescalc's question snapped like the lash of a whip.

King Laza's head jerked up. "I accept Lord Zargal's offer with deepest gratitude," he said. "I will never forget his generosity."

"And he will never forget yours!" Godescalc replied with a harsh laugh.

Rothadd's loud and anguished protests fell on deaf ears. Godescalc was now inspecting Zargal with a professional eye. And King Laza watched the sorceress with a redly baleful expression that was observed by none save Bibka.

They repaired to the northern tower. There was no need of any lackey to bear Godescalc's equipment, for all that the sorceress demanded were the shernivus poultice, a pallet, certain small cutting instruments, and a great length of King Laza's special transparent tubing. These items were carried by Rothadd, who never ceased to plead that they all stop and think it over.

The Outcottager lad was weeping, and his face was streaked with bitter tears. King Laza and Zargal were both silent and self-contained. Zargal stood up straight, his pallid face calm and expressionless, but sweat beaded his forehead despite the chilliness of the air. Laza's expression, whatever it was, was lost in the shadows; only the occasional red flash of his eye could be discerned. Godescalc, too, was quiet and purposeful. She made her way along the corridors with the quickness born of complete familiarity. Only when she beheld King Laza's device that carried them all straight up a tower of the Crown did a low chuckle escape her.

The Princess' sickroom was just as Zargal remembered, but Bellora herself was not. Her motionless figure lay twisted strangely beneath a heavy coverlet. Her face was veiled with a few thicknesses of gauze, but the horrible changes in it glared through the light fabric.

Godescalc surveyed the unconscious figure briefly, gave a nod, then set to work. She hurried restlessly about the chamber, looping the length of tubing around hooks affixed to the walls, while the others stood waiting. When Godescalc had hung up all the tubing, she began laying out the silvery blades and instruments upon a square of white linen. Occasionally she tested the sharpness of a cutting edge. Once the razor smile gashed her face.

It was at this point that Rothadd began to tremble so noticeably that King Laza suggested he leave. Rothadd shook his head and turned to Zargal. " 'Ee can't go through with it," he said.

Zargal was evidently undergoing a mental struggle and took a long time to answer. "I've made the offer," he replied at last.

King Laza looked at him for a time. "I will not hold you to it. You owe us no such sacrifice as that."

Zargal drew near Bellora and lifted the gauze that shrouded her face. What he saw there decided him once and forever. "Let's get on with it," he said.

Godescalc nodded with something like approval. "Lie down," she commanded indicating the pallet. "Your young friend has a brave heart," she tormented Laza. "It must grieve you to lead him thus to his death."

Rothadd choked miserably. "I'll not forget 'ee!" he told Zargal. "Not ever!"

"I will not forget either," King Laza promised, with darker significance. "My debt to you shall be rapid. Fairwell, Lord Zargal."

"Good-bye, your Majesty," Zargal responded in a clear voice. "Don't cry, Rothadd. I know you'll be a fine magician one day. Good-bye."

Zargal reclined upon the pallet, which was not long enough to accommodate his enormous figure; his legs and feet extended far beyond the lower end. At first he watched the sorceress as she applied the shernivus poultice to the diseased body of Princess Bellora and recited the appropriate incantations. He continued to watch as Godescalc labored with knives and tubes over the girl's still form. Then the sorceress crossed over to Zargal and made an incision near his heart, ignoring his gasp of pain, inserted the tube, and secured it in place. She spoke again, in an ancient tongue, and the tube filled with the blood that sprang from his arteries.

The Duke's son looked on in disbelief as the eccentric loops that coiled around the room turned dark crimson. The blood sped from his heart and he felt himself weakening by the second, but his mind remained clear. He looked across to the Princess and beheld her discolored blood draining into a great porcelain basin on the floor.

He glanced up to find Godescalc bending over him, staring closely into his face, her glowing eyes inches from his own. Zargal quickly turned away from her and sought out King Laza, who was whispering urgently into the ear of Rothadd. Zargal wondered vaguely what the two of them were planning, but he was too exhausted to care.

His thoughts drifted away from the tower room, and he found himself remembering Bellora as he had first known her, kneeling in a green gown beside the kitchen fire.

Overhead the crimson loops twirled in fantastic designs, but his vision was dimming and he could no longer discern their color.

It was with a sense of wonder rather than fear that he lay and watched the world turn black around him.

CHAPTER XXX

Rothadd fled the tower room before Godescalc's work was done. Not staying to learn the outcome of the operation, he raced out of the hexagonal chamber, down hundreds upon hundreds of stone steps. Tears burned like acid in his eyes, and the echo of King Laza's whispers still hissed in his ears. He did not stop for breath until he had descended to the second level of the palace.

The Outcottager ran down the hallway until he reached the door he sought. For a moment he paused, still panting, outside Godescalc's apartment. Then, his face set in an expression of anguished determination, he entered and slammed the door behind him.

It was a large, richly furnished suite of rooms that no one in King Laza's family had ever used. There were only two signs present to mark the arrival of Queen Godescalc. One was an old black cloak flung over the back of a chair. The other was the assortment of portraits, their faces carefully turned to the wall, just as Zargal and Rothadd had hung them that very morning. As the recollection struck him, Rothadd sobbed aloud.

"Knew all the time, he did!" the Outcottager muttered to himself. "Knew from the time we were back on the

333

island what the old she-devil was aiming for, and went
ahead anyways, without speaking aught to nobody about
it until the time did come. Just like him—aye, just like him
it do be! But she won't have it all her own way neither!"

Rothadd deliberately turned all six portraits to the light,
and at once the air was alive with their soft voices. The lad
listened for a moment only, then forced himself to leave
the room.

Hours later, Godescalc returned. The smile on her face
was a clear sign that the result of her labors satisfied her
enormously. Her bearing was that of an empress, and she
seemed to wear an invisible crown. Still smiling, she entered her apartment. Rothadd sprang from the place of concealment wherein he had crouched, watching and waiting
for half the night. In an instant he was at the door, sliding
the bolt home to lock it from the outside. The Outcottager
stood motionless and listening, his forehead pressed to the
locked door.

At first there was silence within. Then Godescalc spoke.
"Treason," she said. "I know you are there. I can hear your
breathing, Cramarius. I can sense your hatred and your
fear."

Rothadd did not lift his forehead from the door. "It isn't
Cramarius," he said.

When Godescalc spoke again, her voice had taken on a
more intense quality of malevolence than ever before. "He
sends servants against me. He sends children. Does he use
me thus with such contempt and shall he live?"

"I be no servant," Rothadd replied. "Nor yet a child."

"No?" She sounded almost amused. "I shall not argue
the point with you. Unlock the door."

"Nay. That I won't."

"You are afraid. Your mind is filled with visions of what
your Varingian master will do to you if you fail to aid his
treachery. No need for that, for I intend to deal with him
as he deserves. Unlock the door."

"Nay," Rothadd said again. "I'm a-doin' this for my own
self and for my friends."

"Are you, boy? Then listen to me, and listen carefully.
By choice I would not wage my battles against such as you.
But if you attempt to hinder my great designs, you leave

me no alternative. Have you any idea what I can do to you if you refuse to obey me? And do you imagine that a paltry locked door will stop me?"

"Happen it will. Do your worst, then," Rothadd defied her.

"Obey me!" Her voice shot up in pitch, and she rattled the door so viciously that the entire frame vibrated. "Open the door, or I'll tear it open myself. And when I do—when I do, boy—" The hoarse voice dropped unsteadily, she was obviously making extraordinary efforts to control herself. "—your doom is upon you. I'll have you hung in chains from the highest tower of the Crown. There you will hang, beyond the reach of friend or help, crying upon death for deliverance. But I have magic at my command, fool—and you shall not die."

Rothadd did not reply. His eyes were shut, and the sweat stood out upon his forehead. Godescalc allowed him time to consider the prospect carefully before adding, "But if you release me now, I may yet extend a merciful hand."

The Outcottager was silent, and Godescalc uttered an involuntary shriek of rage. "You think to aid your friends!" she exclaimed. "You but seal their fate as well as your own! The Varingian and his daughter—yes, his daughter— I thought to spare them, but they will suffer with you. The girl—she will not long enjoy her cure! As for your master, the false King—he's a dream of beauty now, compared with what he will become. His heart, his lungs, his brain, I'll consume with liquid fire—but he, like you, will live! All this will I do, unless you unlock this door at once. Open it!"

"For me, I don't care overmuch," Rothadd said in a faint but determined voice. "And the King, he can look after himself."

Godescalc screamed, and then there was silence for a time as she strove once again to collect herself. When next the sorceress addressed him, her manner was calmer, but her low-voiced words were edged with repressed hysteria. "'I should not have tried to frighten you. You are no coward, and you deserve better—much better. Have you ever thought what a thing it would be to return to your homeland in a gold carriage, dressed like a prince, with enough wealth to set yourself up as a lord? With my help, you can do it."

"I wouldn't care about it much," Rothadd returned promptly.

"What *do* you care about, then?" Her voice sharpened, and she deliberately waited a moment to calm herself before continuing. "Magic? You are King Laza's apprentice, and you watch him with a worshipful eye. Would you gain his knowledge?"

"He be a-learnin' me the art," Rothadd admitted.

"But the Varingian can teach you nothing, nothing at all compared with what you could learn from me as my apprentice, if you will unlock this door. Think on it—you, Rotha's son, a great necromancer, renowned and feared throughout the world. Greater than King Laza ever could be!"

For a moment it almost seemed as if Rothadd were tempted. He was silent for a minute or two and rested with his forehead pressed to the locked portal. A dreamy look misted his eyes, but soon vanished. "Fine words," he said. "But 'ee couldn't teach me even if 'ee would. 'Ee hasn't got the power, lady. Gone from 'ee it do be. Else why could 'ee not open the locked door yourself?"

"I can. I will! It's only the words, and I have them somewhere. The words—" She sounded distracted. "Where are they now—now that I need them? Oh, fool, I shall go mad!"

"Your power be gone from 'ee," Rothadd told her. " 'Tis only right."

The restraint that Godescalc had so striven to impose upon herself now began to fail. "Who speaks of right?" she cried out. "Is it right that I should be thus betrayed and imprisoned here? The Varingian is a traitor, like his ancestor before him. He gave his word—I was promised safety!"

"Nobody will hurt 'ee," Rothadd said.

"You have thrown in your lot with a liar and a cheat, you feeble waif! He will betray you as he has betrayed me!"

"He had the right. 'Ee didn't deal fairly with 'im."

"Fairly! Hypocrite! Cramarius promised me my throne again if I would cure his daughter. I am to be a Queen. A

Queen!" She beat her fists against the door, rage over-coming her. "I will have what's mine! Open this door, I command you!"

"Nay! 'Ee be unfit to be a Queen!" Rothadd shouted in return, all his own feelings finding an outlet at last. "Your wits be a-slippin' away all the time, they are! 'Tisn't Cramarius! Cramarius be dead and gone these centuries past, like you should be! 'Tis Laza here—King Laza of Obran, who never did 'ee any harm, but 'ee must destroy all his kin, himself included. Half mad 'ee be all of the time, and all mad sometimes! A wicked, bad woman 'ee be, as well as loony! Not an ounce of kindness in 'ee! 'Ee must have vengeance on King Laza and his daughter, and on others who never lifted a hand against 'ee! And finally 'ee must kill off poor Zargal, just when he might have started to lead a better life! A cruel thing that was, and a cruel old ugly witch 'ee be, and moonstruck!" Rothadd paused be-fore delivering his deadliest blow. "Your magic powers be a-dwindlin', and one day soon they'll all be gone, a-leavin' 'ee naught but a helpless old crone that folk will be sorry for! A Queen—a right fine joke that be!" His voice failed him, and he could say no more.

Godescalc's self-control broke down completely, and the last vestiges of reason deserted her. She screamed at the top of her lungs, pounded furiously on the door, and kicked it with all her might. Rothadd stood amazed. So violent were the woman's struggles to escape that he feared the door might actually give way, particularly when she started battering it with pieces of furniture. The door held, how-ever, and Godescalc began flinging her body against it again and again, so hard that it seemed her bones must break. She still raged aloud, shrieking out mad accusations, invectives, and curses upon the entire House of Varingia.

The night wore on, and she continued to scream and curse, beat the door, and smash the furniture. Only once did she summon enough sanity to call magic to her aid, and Rothadd watched in horror as the door slowly began to un-bar itself. Into his mind sprang the image of a page in one of Hincmar's journals, and he spoke the words of a spell he had studied long ago. The lock held, quivering, and Godescalc's howls waxed wolfish in their grief and sav-agery.

It was not until the first break of dawn that her voice subsided, the sounds of struggle died away, and the castle was silent at last.

Something was puzzling Zargal. As he fought his way out of the deepest of slumbers, he became gradually aware that something was wrong. For a time this troubled him only vaguely, but as he drew near to full consciousness, his uneasiness grew. It was not until he was quite awake, lying with his eyes still closed, that full memory returned to him. He should not be awake at all. He was supposed to be dead, his life's blood drained from him to restore life and health to Princess Bellora.

Zargal's eyes snapped open and he tried to sit up, but found himself too weak to do so. The first sight he beheld relieved his fears but heightened his confusion. King Laza and Bibka, Rothadd and Princess Bellora, were all grouped at his bedside.

The Princess appeared to be in radiantly good health and spirits. She was, if possible, more vital and beautiful than ever. Her green eyes, already shining with health and hope, took on a brighter sparkle as Zargal awoke. "He's better!" Bellora cried. "He's going to be all right!"

"Aye!" Rothadd chimed in. " 'Tis a wonder!"

"Bellora?" Zargal spoke weakly and with some difficulty.

"She's well," King Laza assured him. "She's entirely cured. Neither she nor any children she might have will ever again be so afflicted."

"Because of what you and Rothadd did," Bellora said softly. "You've saved me and all my family."

"It worked?" Zargal asked. He was very faint, and could speak only in short sentences.

"Aye, for sure!" Rothadd exclaimed. "Why, just look at the lass now! Pretty and full of life as a woldhen she be!"

"Yes." Zargal's eyes were fixed on the Princess' face, and he smiled at her.

"Godescalc's curse upon our House has been broken forever," King Laza said, his bloodshot eyes emptied of all former bitterness. "The blood you gave, Lord Zargal, has cleansed the veins of Bellora and all the Varingians who follow her."

Zargal frowned, obviously confused. "If she took the

blood," he said, with an effort of concentration, "then why am I not—"

"Not dead?" King Laza finished for him. "Ordinarily you would have been, for all my daughter's blood was replaced with blood of yours. But you were not ordinary—you were half again as large as other men, and therefore bore a greater quantity of blood. Bellora is not a large woman. When her veins had been replenished, enough blood remained in your body to sustain your life—though just barely enough. We didn't know for a time if you would live or die."

"Near killed 'ee off, it did," Rothadd said.

"You've been unconscious for four days," Bellora told him. "It seemed like forever."

"But all's well at last," Rothadd said gleefully. "Didn't I tell 'ee something would turn up? But did 'ee believe me? Nay!"

"It's true that all's well," Bellora agreed, "now that we know you're all right. You'll be your old self in no time. Oh, Zargal, but I was frightened for you!"

"So too did I be," Rothadd said, "when I did watch your blood go a-whirlin' through those tubes the old lady had strung up. But mark 'ee, 'twas only because 'ee was so great and huge that 'ee lived through it at all!"

"Was?" Zargal repeated questioningly. "Was?" He forced himself to look away from the Princess, to glance around the room and down at himself. He was no longer stretched out on a pallet in the northern tower. While he slept, he had been carried to an airy room in the main body of the castle, and he was now lying in a four-poster bed with a velvet tester above him. He noted that the bed was of normal size, and yet he fitted it perfectly. His feet and legs did not dangle over the edge, and the ropes that supported the mattress did not sag beneath his weight. Amazingly, for the first time in many months, he was not at all hungry. Zargal's eyes sought out King's Laza's.

"Yes," Laza said in response to the unspoken question, "in view of the circumstances, I could hardly let you remain as you were. Therefore, Lord Zargal, I was willing to overlook your five-year debt and undo my work. Now my charms are all overthrown."

"Well, then," Rothadd said, "now that Bellora's sound

and Zargal be on the mend, we've got naught to trouble us more! I can scarce believe it!"

"One thing," Zargal contradicted with a weak shake of his head. "The woman—Godescalc. She'll be Queen."

"No," King Laza said.

"Why not?"

"The Lady Godescalc," King Laza explained suavely, "does not choose to pursue her claim to the throne. Her mind is set on other things. She has lost all interest in affairs of state."

"She won't plague us no more," Rothadd said.

Zargal looked thoroughly bewildered.

"The lad speaks truly," Laza continued. "The lady is alive and well, but no longer desires the crown. She prefers a quiet life, spent in contemplation of works of art."

"And history," Rothadd added. "Mighty fond of history she be."

Zargal was beginning to understand. "You mean," he whispered, "the pictures—"

"Aye!" Rothadd replied eagerly. " 'Ee do hit upon it! 'Twould have been wicked to let 'er be Queen, and yet the King here couldn't raise a hand against 'er. But that wasn't to say she couldn't be her own ruination. So King Laza bespoke a word in my ear while your blood was draining away, and we both did think 'ee was a-dyin'. And I ran on down to Godescalc's room and switched the pictures around, and they all started a-jabberin' away the way they do. I left 'em that way and went across the hall to hide until Queen Godescalc came along. When she did, up I jumped and locked 'er in for the rest of the night. 'Ee should have heard 'er scream and curse—give 'ee the shivers to hear her, it would. Finally she quieted down, though. Then, in the morning, 'ee should have seen—"

"I think Lord Zargal understands well enough what happened," King Laza interrupted. He had noted that Zargal's lids were drooping, his head starting to nod. "You can tell him the details later," he consoled the crestfallen Outcottager. "But right now he needs to rest. Bellora, we'll leave Lord Zargal here with you. Can you look after him?"

"Oh, yes, Father. I'm sure I can."

"Excellent. Bibka, we'd like to leave now, if you please. Come, Rothadd."

Rothadd, following in King Laza's wake, looked back once more. Zargal was nearly asleep, but still watched Bellora, who was standing close beside him. The Outcottager smiled cheerfully and left the two of them together.

"Well, lad," King Laza inquired, "now that Lord Zargal is himself again, or nearly so, what are your plans?" His chair was wheeling steadily down the sunlit corridor. Rothadd walked buoyantly alongside. "What are you going to do with yourself?"

"Why, I mean to keep on a-studyin', for sure, King. I think I be gettin' the hang of the magic art at last, but I still do have a lot to learn, wouldn't 'ee say?"

"Undoubtedly. You are only just beginning."

"'Twill take a mort of sweaty work for me to master it. But now I be sure that the power's in me. 'Tis there inside, a-waitin' to be let out."

"I always thought so."

"But I can't understand," Rothadd brooded, "why it did take me so long afore I started to learn the way of it. And when I did, back in the Elg, 'twas partly on account of needin' it so bad and partly for what Zargal told me about keeping my mind on business. If it hadn't been for him, we might be back there yet. But why do it be that I could never manage a spell before then?"

"Perhaps," King Laza suggested, "you just weren't old enough. It takes some people longer than others. But when the moment came, you were ready, which is what really counts."

"Hincmar did tell me back then that he was a-givin' me a simple spell, but I couldn't do it no matter how I tried. Zargal thought that maybe it wasn't so simple after all. Was Hincmar a-mullyin' me?"

"No," Laza replied. "Hincmar told you the truth. It was a simple spell he gave. But no one ever told you, lad, that simple means easy."

"Happen you be right," Rothadd said thoughtfully.

"But all this still doesn't answer my original question. Where do you expect to go? You're more than welcome to stay here with me as my assistant if you like, and I'll teach you whatever I can."

"Oh, your Majesty, 'tis good of 'ee! A mighty handsome

offer it do be, but—" A perplexed frown creased Roth-add's forehead.

"You don't have to stay if you don't want to, lad. I won't be offended."

"Oh, it isn't that, your Majesty! 'Twould be my pride and pleasure to stay here, only—well, now, Hincmar be a-waitin' for me back upon the Wolds, and I think 'twould grieve his heart if I didn't come back. And me, I wouldn't feel right if I didn't see him again, nor yet my homeland, so—"

"I understand," Laza reassured him.

"Well, I do wish I could split me in two. But I can't, so the next best thing would be for me to spend half my time with Hincmar upon the Wolds and half here with 'ee. Would that suit?"

"Excellent," Laza said.

"Aye, 'tis just the thing. Only—do it be safe for me to leave 'ee, King?"

"Why should it not?"

"Well, what if—how do we know that she'll stay like she be right now? What's to happen if she do wake up again? How can we be sure she isn't awake *now*?"

"She isn't. The curse she brought on herself still binds her."

"But how do we *know*? 'Tis like it could happen any hour of the day or night, and then where would we be?"

"I don't really think you have much to worry about," the King said, his ruined face quite tranquil. "As long as she's left undisturbed, she'll remain as she is indefinitely. But come see for yourself if you doubt—maybe it will set your mind at rest."

They were approaching Godescalc's chamber, the door of which was now unbarred. At a word from her master Bibka paused, and Laza knocked politely. There was no reply, and he pushed the door open.

The room was a shambles. The floor was strewn with broken glass and sticks of broken furniture. The curtains had been torn down from the windows, and the door frame was marked with deep gouges and scratches.

Godescalc sat on the edge of the bed, her legs crossed beneath her, her disheveled black hair falling in disorder. Her hands lay folded slackly in her lap, and her face was devoid of all expression. All six portraits on the wall were whispering at the sorceress, but Godescalc's blank stare was fixed upon the face of her ancestor Marnssil, who was now describing some of the experiences of his boyhood in the court of Obran.

"The sorcerer Zinkori was famed throughout the land," Marnssil whispered, "and when he came to the palace, I begged to be made his apprentice."

Godescalc's face was empty, and it was impossible to tell whether she could understand Marnssil's words or not. She sat as still as a discarded puppet, while the whispers went on and on. Rothadd's eyes were taking on a dangerous glaze as he listened. King Laza drew him gently from the room and shut the door once again.

"You see," Laza said. "She has forgotten her purpose, forgotten the crown—forgotten everything."

"Aye." Rothadd drew a deep breath, and his eyes cleared. He was at last becoming fully aware of the peril of watching King Marnssil too closely or too long.

"There's every reason to believe she'll remain as she is as long as the portraits keep talking," the King continued smoothly. "However, just to be on the safe side, I plan to assemble in that room a group of my own family portraits, upon which I will bestow the power of speech. The Lady Godescalc shall not lack for entertainment as long as she remains my guest."

"Aye. Will 'ee lock up that door, then?"

"By no means. The lady is not a prisoner. She may leave, or renew her claim to the throne at any time the fancy strikes her."

"Good!" Rothadd exclaimed. "Good! Then that be the end of it. She won't trouble us more, and all's like it should be. Your daughter's well, Zargal's a-mendin' fast, and 'ee be King still."

"So you see it's quite safe for you to go and visit your old teacher Hincmar," the King said. "But I hope, lad, that you won't neglect your friends in Obran. I'll miss you while you're away, and so, I'm sure, will Bellora and Lord Zargal."

"Zargal! Will he still be here, then?" Rothadd asked.

"I'm certain that he'll be here often."

"What, your Majesty! After all he done, 'ee can't mean to

have him stay on as your kitchen boy! 'Twould chafe him worse nor he could stand, I doubt not."

"Kitchen boy?" the King repeated in amusement. "Certainly not. That's all over and done with. You don't imagine I'd let my daughter's husband-to-be work as a scullion?"

"Zargal and your daughter to wed, King?"

"I assume so. They obviously love one another, and I don't intend to stand in their way. Besides," the King added, "I'm beginning to develop a sneaking fondness for that boy."

Rothadd was silent, mulling this over for a while, until at last he asked, "Happen he won't have 'er?"

For once, King Laza was taken completely by surprise. "Not have her? Not have *Bellora?*" he asked in tones of total disbelief. Bibka stopped dead and crouched in the middle of the corridor, hissing. "What do you mean, sir?"

"Now, don't 'ee take it the wrong way! 'Tis plain the Princess be the only lass in the world for Zargal, and he'd do anything for her, and all of that. 'Tis also plain that Zargal isn't the same as he once was. But no matter how he's changed, he be Zargal still, with mighty high ways and a devilish proud temper. Even if he be your scullion no more, he be in sorry straits, for he don't got nothin' to call his own, ever since his dad the Duke kicked 'im out. Truth to tell, between you and me, he isn't much better off nor a beggar. Do 'ee think truly that he'd wed your daughter, even if 'ee'd allow it, and live here on his wife's father's charity? For that's the way he'd see it, I do take my oath!"

King Laza relaxed. "Oh, is that all?" he asked. "But that's no problem. That's nothing."

"Oh, aye? 'Ee don't know Zargal, then."

"You haven't heard the news from Szar, I see. I have not yet informed Lord Zargal, as he's in a weakened condition, and what I have to say may prove upsetting to him. But he'll learn soon enough."

"Learn what?"

"Five days ago, on the very eve of his marriage to Talghya Jeria of Strell, Zargal's father Archduke Jalonzal was out on a tour of inspection of his realm. He was accompanied only by some two dozen hand-picked guards. As evening approached, the Archduke realized that his party was too far distant from the gates of Szar to return

THE CURSE OF THE WITCH-QUEEN

to the palace before dark. Accordingly, he made plans to spend the night at an inn. The men knew that the Peacock Inn was not far off, but were unsure of the exact route.

"Their difficulties seemed to be resolved when they stumbled upon an encampment of Turos. In exchange for a sizable consideration, the Turos provided directions to the inn. The directions, however, appear to have been faulty, for when the darkness fell, Jalonzal and his guards had not located the Peacock.

"They found themselves before an abandoned house, surrounded by huge vegetable gardens, and there the Archduke decided they would spend the night. Several of the guards complained. The house, which once belonged to Professor Horm of the University, was supposed to be haunted. Jalonzal would not listen. He dispatched one of the guards back to Szar with several messages, while he and the rest of his men prepared to cut through the gardens to the house. The guard galloped back to Szar with the dispatches, and early the next morning returned to the Professor's house to rejoin his ruler.

"There he found a scene of carnage awaiting him. Twenty-three of his fellow guards lay dead upon the soil. At the center of the group he discovered the corpse of Jalonzal. Of course the guard was horrified, but his horror gave way to superstitious dread when he noted that not one of those twenty-four dead bodies bore a sign of any wound. The damp garden earth showed no trace of human or animal footprints. Thus he was forced to conclude, and many people agree, that the place *is* haunted and that Jalonzal died at the hand of Professor Horm's avenging ghost.

"Personally, I am not sure what has happened, and am not yet prepared to make a judgment. But one thing is certain, Rothadd," King Laza told the young Outcottager, who had been listening to the story with wondering eyes and parted lips. "Zargal is now Archduke of Szar."

About the Author

Paula Volsky has always wanted to be a writer and has been amazed at the difficulty of fulfilling that seemingly modest ambition. *The Curse of the Witch-Queen* is her first published work. She was born and brought up in Fanwood, New Jersey, and throughout her childhood she loved reading, particularly fairy tales and adventure stories. When she grew older, went to Vassar, and worked on a B.A. in English literature, her interest in fantasy changed, and she was caught up in the gruesome pleasures of the occult. She developed a deep affection for haunted mansions, werewolves, and vampires—especially the handsome ones. After completing her undergraduate work, Ms. Volsky sold real estate for a time in New Jersey, then traveled to England to complete an M.A. in Shakespeare Studies at the University of Birmingham. Upon her return to the United States she found herself nearly unemployable, and used her unlimited free time to begin work on what was intended to be a fairy tale for children. She quickly realized that she didn't have the slightest notion of how to write for children, at which point it dawned on her that adults love fantasy, too. She kept writing, and the result is *The Curse of the Witch-Queen*. Prior to the completion of the novel, Ms. Volsky landed a job at the U.S. Department of Housing and Urban Development in Washington, D.C. and remains with HUD today. She now lives in a Virginia apartment with her growing collection of Victoriana and looks forward to the day when she will be able to devote her full time to the writing of fantasy.

Enchanting fantasies from

DEL REY BOOKS

Available at your bookstore or use this coupon.

___**THE DOOMFARERS OF CORAMONDE**   29180 **$2.25**
In Brian Daley's first novel Gil MacDonald and his platoon are magically transported
from the fields of Viet Nam to save a kingdom in Fantasy Land.

___**THE STARFOLLOWERS OF CORAMONDE**   30142 **$2.75**
More Brian Daley excitement as brave adventurers become tangled in time.

___**THE DRAGON AND THE GEORGE**   29514 **$2.25**
Gordon R. Dickson's magical novel in which a love-sick knight is mysteriously
transformed into a dragon.

___**THE DRAWING OF THE DARK**   27604 **$1.95**
Written by Tim Powers, a powerful fantasy about a soldier of fortune in time-twisted
Vienna, when Merlin had to call Arthur back from the dead.

BB   **BALLANTINE MAIL SALES**
           Dept. AL, 201 E. 50th St., New York, N.Y. 10022

Please send me the BALLANTINE or DEL REY BOOKS I have
checked above. I am enclosing $. . . . . (add 50¢ per copy to
cover postage and handling). Send check or money order — no
cash or C.O.D.'s please. Prices and numbers are subject to change
without notice.

Name_____

Address_____

City_____State_____Zip Code_____

09   Allow at least 4 weeks for delivery.   AL-2